Labyrinth Arcanist

Astra Academy Book V

Shami Stovall

Published by
CS BOOKS, LLC

This is a work of fiction. Names, characters, places, and incidents either are the product of author imagination or are used fictitiously, and any resemblance to actual persons, living or dead, business establishments, events, or locales, is entirely fictional.

Cover Design: Darko Paganus

Editors: Nia Quinn, Celestian Rince

IF YOU WANT TO BE NOTIFIED WHEN SHAMI STOVALL'S NEXT BOOK RELEASES, PLEASE VISIT HER WEBSITE OR CONTACT HER DIRECTLY AT

s.adelle.s@gmail.com

Contents

To John, my soulmate.
To Justin Barnett, who is way too good to me and helped so much.
To Gail and Big John, my surrogate parents.
To Drew, my agent.
To Henry Copeland, for the beautiful leather map and book covers.
To Mary, Emily, Scott, James, Ryan & Dana, for all the jokes and input.
To my patrons over on Patreon, for naming the Academy.
To my Facebook group, for all the memes.
And finally, to everyone unnamed, thank you for everything.

A Recap Of Events

L ast time in the Astra Academy series, Gray Lexly,
along with Ashlyn, Knovak, and Nini, was pulled into
the abyssal hells by Death Lord Naiad. Naiad had
intended to kill Deimos, but instead, Gray and his friends
stopped her.

Trapped in the abyssal hells, Gray and the others had to
find a way out. They journeyed through the *Wraithborne
Orchard*, befriending Death Lord Deimos along the way.
They also encountered Everett, a mutated man fused with his
eldrin. Everett asked them to deliver a necklace to his husband,
who is still alive, and Gray agreed.

While in the hells, Gray learned about Death Lord
Kallikore and his army of elder creatures. Any mystical
creature that consumes souls becomes twisted and hungry for
human flesh. Kallikore, having half-fused himself with his
eldrin, had turned into a monstrosity.

Lastly, Gray discovered Death Lord Umbriel's plan to
open the Oblivion Gate at the bottom of the abyssal hells.
While its purpose remains uncertain—either to grant her

unparalleled power or to destroy everything—it is clear the gate must never be opened.

Death Lord Kallikore confronted Deimos and the others, bringing with him Xuandi, an elder phoenix dragon. Furious at humanity, Xuandi wanted to unleash the abyssal hells on the world, allowing elder creatures to consume everyone.

Deimos, Everett, and Nini fought Kallikore and Xuandi to give Gray, Knovak, and Ashlyn a chance to escape. Before returning to the realm of the living, Knovak's unicorn eldrin consumed a fruit filled with human souls. Tragically, Nini, who should have escaped with them, was left behind.

Much to everyone's surprise, Gray and the others emerged in Lord Oto's compound. They materialized from magical fruit, as souls from the abyssal hells reincarnate into all magical entities, including rocks, plants, and mystical creatures. Deimos's brother, Zahn, was there—the one who had pulled them through.

Zahn explained that Lord Oto, the cruel ruler of the area, had been funding his research in exchange for future abyssal dragon parts. Meanwhile, Knovak awakened, and his eldrin had transformed into an elder unicorn. No one knew what to make of this new development.

In the ruined and suffering city, Gray was worshipped by cultists who believed he was a vessel for Death Lord Deimos. He also encountered his classmate, Raaza, who was being blackmailed by Lord Oto to work for him. If Raaza refused, Lord Oto threatened to kill his sister and mother.

Gray helped Raaza save his family, but in the process, he encountered Lucian, an old god-arcanist sent by Headmaster Venrover to retrieve missing students. Gray attempted to bluff his way past Lucian, but the situation escalated into a fight. Lord Oto and the cultists clashed with Lucian, who proved to be overwhelmingly powerful.

Gray managed to escape and agreed to return to the

Academy with Lucian. Zahn decided to join them, seizing the opportunity to leave Lord Oto. However, before they could reach Headmaster Venrover, Lucian took Gray and the others to the Dodger family compound to report the dangers lurking in the abyssal hells.

Along the way, Gray faced Ashlyn's father and brother in combat to win the right to marry her. Using clever tactics, Gray emerged victorious, much to Ashlyn's delight.

At the Dodger family compound, Gray warned the assembled powerful arcanists about the Death Lords' threats. Lynus Dodger, Everett's husband, pledged the Dodger family's support to Astra Academy.

Meanwhile, Nini remained missing in the abyssal hells.

And now, the story continues in *Labyrinth Arcanist*.

CHAPTER 1

RETURN TO THE ISLE OF HAYLIN

This would be an exciting week—not only was it my birthday, but I was also getting married and starting a new year at Astra Academy. Oh, and I'd also be searching for a way back into the abyssal hells.

Perhaps a little *too* exciting for some people, but I wasn't *some people*.

I rode on a sailing vessel, *the Distant Dream*, heading for my home island of Haylin. The waves were kind for the journey, which I appreciated because it let me focus on the task at hand. I leaned on the railing of the ship, keeping my eyes on the far horizon. The sun set behind me, and the orange hue blanketing the sky was breathtaking.

Sometimes I missed my home island, but I'd never admit that to anyone.

"Gray?"

I glanced down. My mimic eldrin, Twain, was curled up on top of a coil of rope. He was an orange kitten—halfway to a cat, really—and he had two differently colored eyes, one pink and one a grayish blue. His ears were much larger than normal, practically those of a lynx, and he had nothing but a bobtail at the back.

When he stared up at me, he twitched his whiskers in suspicion.

"Are you talking to Death Lord Deimos again?" Twain asked, his tone bordering on *accusing*.

I shook my head. "Not yet."

"You talk to him way too often." Twain stood, arched his back as he stretched, and then leapt up onto the ship's railing. He was rather nimble and didn't slip at all. "You're *my* arcanist, and I'm your eldrin—we're destined to do everything together. I shouldn't be jealous of a Death Lord! You should talk to *me* more."

After I slicked back my black hair, I smirked. "Well, what do you want to talk about? Fish? Why do dogs smell so bad when they get wet?"

Twain narrowed his eyes and laid his ears back. "First off— it is really unreasonable how much dogs smell when they're wet, but I don't think you meant any of those conversation suggestions seriously. I think you're playing with me."

"Me? Never."

Twain patted my arm with his paw. "We should talk about your twin brother, Sorin."

I caught my breath when he made that suggestion, only because I hadn't seen him in a few weeks. A normal person wouldn't think that was very long, but Sorin and I did everything together.

The only reason we were separated was because I was pulled into the abyssal hells—the realm of the dead.

Supposedly, after the Twilight Gate was sealed, no living being could enter the hells. Since I had a piece of Death Lord Deimos's soul in my body, I was yanked into the abyssal hells by Death Lord Naiad—a wicked abyssal dragon arcanist intent on ending Deimos's life.

Well, technically all the other Death Lords wanted to end his life. He wasn't the most popular man, to put it mildly.

I shook the thought away. "Why do you want to talk about Sorin?"

The ship shook as a heavy wave hit the hull at an odd angle. Twain clung to the railing, his claws digging into the wood. He managed to hold on, despite the turbulence. Once our ship settled, he huffed.

"I just wanted to know what you were going to tell Sorin." Twain smoothed his orange fur. "The love of his life is still in the abyssal hells. You don't think he'll be upset?"

Nini Wanderlin...

Nini, Ashlyn, Knovak, and their eldrin had all gone with me into the abyssal hells, but only Nini and her reaper eldrin, Waste, had gotten stuck there. Everyone else had made it out.

Sorin wouldn't like this—and I didn't know how I was going to break the news.

A small part of me felt responsible for what happened. The only reason Nini was in danger was because of me. I should've been more proactive in making sure she escaped.

Then again, Nini was a reaper arcanist. Reapers were creatures of death themselves, and her magic allowed her to wander the hells without suffering some of the effects. Ashlyn and Knovak, on the other hand, had been slowly dying the entire time they were there. If I hadn't gotten them to safety as quickly as possible, they would've become corpses.

"I think Sorin will understand," I finally said after mulling everything over. "Plus, Headmaster Venrover said we're going to start a new division of study at Astra Academy. He's going to train *abyssal sentinels* to one day delve into the hells. Or, ya know, fight whatever comes *out* of the hells. If Sorin and I join that, we'll have all the training and resources we need to help Nini."

The ship shuddered a second time. Twain leapt off the

railing and landed on my shoulder, clinging for dear life. I moved away from the side of the ship, even as it rocked. Normally, I would've stumbled and staggered, but ever since Deimos became a part of me, I had his skills.

The movement of the ship didn't bother me. I kept my balance, and made my way over to the mast without issue.

"So, we're just going to *leave* Nini?" Twain asked straight into my ear. "She could be in danger right now, but we're going to head to Astra Academy instead? And you think Sorin will be okay with that?"

I held onto the mast, my eyes drifting to the cloud-filled sky. Apparently, the weather wanted to wear black to my birthday.

That was a bad omen.

"We still don't have a way to get into the abyssal hells," I whispered, my gaze stuck on the gathering storm. "So, no matter what I want to do personally, we can't go searching for Nini. The only real option is to prepare for when we *can* get there."

Twain shivered. When he glanced upward, it was only to frown. "Okay. I trust you. But I worry—I think Sorin will take the news poorly."

"Yeah, me, too."

"Your twin brother will understand," I said—well, *I* didn't say that, Death Lord Deimos did.

Our connection was so thorough, and so bizarre, that his soul fragment could speak through me, using my mouth and voice. He spoke differently, but it was still *me* speaking. To anyone who didn't know my situation, I probably seemed insane. I spoke to "myself" all the time.

"Why do you think Sorin will understand, Dee?" I asked.

Deimos's emotions filtered into my thoughts, and I knew he hated the nickname of *Dee*. Actually, I knew whenever he was tired, angry, irritated or...

Well, Deimos really only felt those three emotions, if I were being honest. Sometimes he felt worried, and when I had spoken to Deimos's twin, Zahn, he had seemed happy, but that was rare.

Deimos was a Death Lord through and through, and his demeanor was closer to ice than it was to a normal mortal or arcanist.

When Deimos spoke again his words were somber. "You and your brother shared your time in the womb—your souls were forged side by side—no matter your explanation, your brother will eventually come to see that you had little choice. And then he will forgive you."

Twain twitched his whiskers and sighed. "See? *This* is what I'm talking about. You and Deimos have all these side conversations. But I was the one who started this one! Not Deimos. You should ask *me* for advice."

I waved a hand and half bowed my head. "You're right, my loyal eldrin. Please, do advise me. How should I go about speaking to my brother, o' exalted one?"

Twain pressed a paw to my cheek. "You should... break it to him gently. And reassure him everything is going to work out, and that we'll get Nini back eventually."

"Should I tell him that before or after I announce I'm going to get married?" I sarcastically rubbed my chin. "Or how I made sure Ashlyn made it out of the abyssal hells, but not Nini? I feel like there's going to be some follow-up questions."

Twain moved his paw from my face and huffed. "Obviously you shouldn't have both those conversations at once! You, uh, gotta tell him about Nini first. Then once he calms down, you tell him about how you *have* to marry Ashlyn because the Kross family demands it. I think Sorin will take it over then."

"Your brother is a knightmare arcanist," Deimos said through me. His interjections sometimes took me by surprise, and this was no different. "Knightmare arcanists are known for their honor and steadfast—often stubborn—adherence to duty. He won't calm down. He will be anxious until his lover has returned."

"I wouldn't call Nini his *lover*," I muttered. "At least, I don't think it's at that point yet. She's just his honeysuckle."

"That's kinda the same," Twain said.

Several sailors on the *Distant Dream* ran across the deck and started securing everything. We were getting close to Haylin—it was the only island around—and once we reached port, they'd have to buckle down for the storm.

I held up a hand. "The plan is to speak with Sorin, get him to understand the situation, and then speak to my father and stepmother to invite them to my wedding. After that, I actually get married, and then I head back to Astra Academy to prepare for my inevitable return to the abyssal hells. Sound good?"

My eldrin nodded along with my words. "An excellent plan, Gray."

"Let us pray that everyone conducts themselves with sound judgment," Deimos ominously stated as our ship drew ever closer to the docks.

Bad omen or not, I refused to let darkness into my thoughts. We'd get Nini back, or we'd die trying.

CHAPTER 2

LOST IN THE LABYRINTH

--Nini's Perspective--

I was blind and lost in the second abyss, a gigantic labyrinth of wandering souls.

Apparently, whenever someone traveled deeper into the abyssal hells, descending the many layers, they lost their senses. Venturing from the first abyss to the second abyss meant the loss of eyesight...

I rubbed my face, trying not to cry. Now wasn't the time for that. Weakness would kill me, and I couldn't die here.

"Never fear, my arcanist," my eldrin, Waste, said. He floated around me, his chains clicking, his cloak swishing. He was a reaper, a mystical creature born of death. To some people, these noises would be ominous, but I loved them. They made me feel safe.

"I can't remember the way to the fountain," I whispered.

If I drank from the labyrinth fountain, I would regain my eyesight. Death Lord Deimos had given me directions to the nearest one, but I had been too dazed to remember. Everything had happened so fast...

"I remember the route," Waste stated, cold and confident. "We must press forward. We must take a right coming up in this next portion of the labyrinth."

"All right..." I whispered.

That sounded correct. Waste knew the way. I was so thankful to have him as an eldrin—his quiet strength was everything I wished I was. Why did I always second guess myself and worry? Why wouldn't my doubt ever go away?

Although I couldn't see him, I pictured Waste in my mind's eye.

He was a floating cloak with a hood, a face mask, four gold chains, and four lanterns filled with flames—that was it. He had no body, just a hollow inside, as though an invisible person wore him. The chains acted of their own free will, moving through the air, the lanterns at the end, swaying with the movements.

A scythe glided through the air around him, circling. It was somehow part of his body, but I didn't understand how. When he was young, the scythe looked rusted and worn, but now that Waste was true form, it was a golden scythe, wicked and deadly.

"Come," Waste beckoned.

I nodded and walked forward, shuffling my feet so I didn't trip. "O-Okay."

The darkness was absolute, a weight pressing against my senses. My imagination was my greatest enemy because it painted pictures of the labyrinth that disturbed me. Walls made of bones, weeping blood while souls twisted throughout.

Each step I took forward, I assumed I was just narrowly missing a blatant trap or a torture device meant to kill individuals who wandered into the abyssal hells.

Was my imagination correct?

"W-Waste?" I whispered.

"Yes, my arcanist?"

"What does the labyrinth look like?"

"I am also blind."

Right... Right. We both were.

"What do you *think* it looks like?" I asked, hoping his imagination was kinder than my own.

My reaper eldrin floated around me. The slight heat from the lantern flames radiated enough that I felt them.

"I imagine it is beautiful," Waste said. "The labyrinth is made of alabaster stone that shines white, and the floor is polished to mirror-like perfection. It reflects everything, even the sky. The land of the living doesn't know such beauty."

My heart quieted, and the tension in my shoulders faded a bit. Now I almost wished I could see everything.

"Really?" I rubbed my arms. "You think that's what it looks like?"

Then, fueled by a sudden burst of bravery, I placed my hand on the wall. It was smooth. Then I knelt and touched the floor. Even smoother.

Perhaps Waste was correct.

"No lost souls?" I asked.

"Oh, many lost souls," Waste muttered.

I almost gasped. "*Really*?"

"They float through the walls, and drift off into the sky. They are not tangible, my arcanist. You need not fear them. But I can sense them. If you concentrate, you can sense them, too."

I disliked the fact that I was wandering through souls. That didn't sit right with me at all, and I felt no urge to concentrate. After a deep breath, I forced myself to continue. Once I reached a turn, I went right, following Waste's instructions.

"We'll take another right," he said.

It wasn't long before I had to make that turn as well. I kept my hand on the wall, thankful that I had something to support me.

"Another right," Waste said.

So many rights... Wouldn't I be going in a circle? I trusted Waste, though. And I trusted Death Lord Deimos. It was difficult to describe, but I knew Deimos wasn't out to get my soul. It seemed he respected me whenever we spoke, probably because I was bonded to a reaper.

"Do you think Death Lord Deimos knows I killed my brother?" I whispered.

"I do," Waste replied, casual and unconcerned.

"D-Do you think he thinks I'm insane? Or evil?"

That was what my family had said. I was sick in the head. I had no heart. Everyone on my island hated me. *Everyone.* No one ever trusted me again. My mother disowned me; my father said I had been a mistake.

Deimos must think that as well.

"Deimos can speak to souls, my arcanist. He would know the truth of your struggles."

The truth...

No one ever believed me when I told the *real* truth. Not my mother, not my father...

Well, Sorin believed me. And Waste. They were the only ones who ever truly listened. They were the only people I loved.

My hand on the wall brushed against cold, rough stone slick with some unidentifiable moisture. The texture felt alive, pulsing faintly beneath my fingertips. I shuddered, a chill running down my spine.

Was that my imagination? Or had the walls changed?

Probably my imagination.

"We need to travel down three intersections and then take another right," Waste said.

Another right...

We *were* going in circles. We had to be.

My footfalls echoed slightly, but the sounds swirled around me, creating an eerie effect that made it seem like I was heading toward someone. But that was impossible. It was just me. Waste could sense people—living souls—and he would know if someone else was nearby.

The labyrinth was just playing tricks with my ears.

Then the air began to smell of decay and dampness, tinged with something acrid, like ashes.

Ashes...

I stopped walking, my heart pounding all over again. "Waste," I whispered. "Is there a fire nearby?"

"Only the fire in my lanterns, my arcanist."

I hated fire. It haunted all my nightmares. That was how I had killed my brother—the lanterns in our house. I had knocked one over, and the fire spread across the floor, up the walls, and crawled across the ceiling.

Everywhere.

My shoulders and back still had burn marks from the event.

I kept my hand against the wall as I moved, shuffling forward step by step. The smell of smoke became more prominent. The ground beneath my feet turned uneven, shifting from jagged stone to a strange, sticky surface that made every step a small act of courage. My breathing was loud in my ears, I heard nothing else, not even my strange footfalls.

What did the labyrinth look like now? It wasn't just my imagination anymore—it *was* different. Twisted. Disgusting. Terrifying.

After a few more steps, the crackle of flames reached my ears.

"We're walking toward a fire," I said, coming to a complete halt.

"There is no fire, my arcanist."

"No." I shook my head. "There is. I can smell it. I hear it. There's a fire somewhere here in the labyrinth."

Flashes of that terrible night went through my mind. My brother had been hurting me—he always hurt me, touched me, made me feel unclean—and I was trying to get away. I hadn't meant to knock over the lantern. I hadn't wanted him to *die*.

Or maybe I had.

A tiny part of me—the disgusting part of me my parents hated—wanted my brother to go away forever. Maybe that had been the part of me that pushed over that lantern. I had wanted my brother to leave me alone.

Instead, the fire had consumed him like a pig consumes slop.

He was gone forever.

"You need to take even breaths," Waste said.

I couldn't control my breathing. There was a fire nearby, and I was going to die the same way as my brother. I knew it. *I knew it.*

Then, Waste's cloak wrapped around me. His magic, his power, his presence—they all fused with me, merging our beings together. The threads of his cloak sewed their way into my skin, fusing on my shoulders, down my arms. His white mask fitted itself over my face, and I touched it, grateful I had Waste's calming demeanor now part of my own.

We were now one being—we'd live and die together.

"*I'm here,*" Waste telepathically whispered. "*Fear not.*"

"I'm a bad person," I said aloud, my voice a perfect blend of my Waste's and my own.

"*It's a test, my arcanist. There is no fire. We have to keep going forward.*"

"It smells like fire," I said, my throat becoming dry. The air even tasted of ash.

Waste's scythe slipped into my hands. The cold metal of his weapon gave me a little more courage.

"*I am a true form reaper,*" Waste said. "*And when reapers gain their true form... they take on aspects of their arcanist's deepest fears.*"

The four lanterns...

Waste had only gained those four lanterns when he achieved his true form. It was because I was afraid of fire? That was why they lingered around me, forever? Was this some sort of divine punishment for what I had done?

"*My magic doesn't punish you,*" Waste telepathically said. "*It's reminding you. This labyrinth... its magic is similar to mine. Whatever smoke you smell, or fire you hear—it isn't real. You must push through it. Deimos said there was only one way.*"

"I miss Sorin," I said, my double-voice echoing.

"*We will see him again—but only if you're brave enough to continue.*"

CHAPTER 3

LANTERN LIGHT

--Nini's Perspective--

The fire...

I didn't know if I could brave the fire.

"What if the fire is real?" I asked, my voice a blend of mine and Waste's.

His cold power coursed through me. My anxieties lessened. I held his scythe in one hand, and placed my other hand back on the wall.

"*And if the fire is real?*" Waste telepathically asked. "*What will you do then? Give up? Die here in this labyrinth without ever seeing Sorin again?*"

That was a fate worse than dying in a fire. I couldn't give up. I couldn't.

"We push forward," I said, our double voice echoing throughout the labyrinth.

Waste's approval washed through me. This was what he wanted, too. Did he also miss Sorin? Or perhaps he missed

Thurin, Sorin's knightmare... Either way, I wanted to get back to him. I wanted it more than anything.

And that would only happen if I took a step forward. And then another. And another.

I continued, my hand on the rough, yet moist, wall. With each inch I moved, the smell of smoke worsened, and my stomach twisted into knots. Soon, the crackle of fire became too overwhelming to ignore.

There *was* a fire. The labyrinth knew what I was afraid of, and it was using that against me.

Waste's memory—and the directions Death Lord Deimos had given us—were now etched into my own. I walked forward, and turned when needed, regardless of how logical the turn was.

The fire...

The wall became hot, and I ripped away my hand. The pain quickly faded, but it had been real.

"Waste, this isn't an illusion," we said together.

"*Then you must hurry.*"

I hurried forward, practically running.

The heat was suffocating, wrapping itself around me like a living thing, pressing against my skin and filling my lungs with each gasping breath. But the floor was uneven. I tripped, and on instinct, I touched the wall. The blistering heat caused me to cry out. I leapt away, my teeth gritted, my shoulders shaking.

"*Don't stop.*"

Waste was right...

So I ran.

Again, my imagination played tricks on me. The floor felt like it was shuddering or moving, and I pictured the whole labyrinth crumbling around me, nothing but ash and cinders.

The flames worsened.

Then the fire roared around me, an angry beast that

gnawed at the walls. The air was thick with smoke, choking and acrid, burning my throat with every breath. My steps were hurried and clumsy, driven more by instinct than reason, as though sheer speed could outrun the pyre.

My brother...

He had been trapped in his room. The people of my island said I had locked the door to keep him there.

I hadn't. I told them all I hadn't. But no one had believed me. They said his hands were found with the charred door handle clutched in them—he had been trying to open the door and couldn't.

But it hadn't been me.

Well...

That was what I had thought, but occasionally, in my darkest dreams, I imagined that I *had* locked him in that room. That I had wanted him dead so badly, that everything had been intentional.

What if I died in this labyrinth? Was that my punishment?

"Pay attention, my arcanist. You must take the second left."

Each footfall was treacherous. The floor beneath me shifted unpredictably, the stone cracking and giving way in places. When my balance faltered, Waste's chains reached out like additional limbs. He kept me steady, and away from the blistering walls.

Waste...

I grabbed his cloak and held it close, sweat soaking every inch of my clothing as I ran.

His chains also helped me feel for the turns. The clattering of the metal whenever it touched one of the walls alerted me when they gave way to another path.

Left...

I turned left this time.

A piece of the ceiling fell nearby, crashing to the floor with a sound like a thunderclap, showering me in a rain of molten debris. I forced myself forward, each step a battle against the urge to freeze, to give in to panic.

The air shifted, carrying a faint, blessedly cool breeze—a whisper of freedom amidst the suffocating inferno. I turned toward it, though my legs felt like lead and my lungs burned with every ragged breath.

"*No*," Waste telepathically said. "*That's the wrong way, my arcanist!*"

I fought with my baser instincts. Every fiber of my being wanted to flee the flames, but Waste wouldn't lie to me. I had to turn around.

After gulping down some of the fresh air, I went back, trying to picture the layout of the maze in my mind's eyes. I had to focus on something other than that terrible night—something *other* than my brother.

"*Think of Sorin.*"

Yes.

Sorin would've helped me out of here. He would've fought the flames for me—chased away the heat. He would've given his life if it meant I would never suffer another blister again.

Sorin...

"*You must follow the curved walls,*" Waste telepathically said.

The fire seemed to sense my presence, its fury redoubling. A new roar erupted behind me, and the ground trembled beneath my feet. I tripped, but Waste's chains managed to keep me upright. I stumbled and hurried forward, never giving up.

I'd crawl my way out of this inferno if I had to.

The fountain was close. *It had to be.* I just had to keep going!

The curved walls... The chains struck them, and I had to turn with them, away from the heat and the pain. Sorin's knightmare magic would be useless against fire—all shadow magic broke apart whenever it was struck with fire—but he would've fought it anyway.

I wanted to be brave and selfless like Sorin.

But...

Was I too evil for that? Too monstrous and terrible? I had killed my brother, after all...

Could I ever hope to be as noble and wonderful as Sorin? I was tainted with blood and ash.

"*You spoke to him about this.*"

Sorin had said I hadn't healed from my brother's death, because the pain still hurt—still controlled all my actions. And then, in poetic fashion, he had said, "*Healing does not undo the pain, but softens the grip of its heavy chain.*"

He told me...

That I was the only one there. If I remembered the lantern flames as an accident, then it *was* an accident, and that my family had lashed out because they were hurting, too. If I couldn't accept my own truth, who else would? I had to be confident. I had to heal. I had to move on.

Dwelling on this didn't help anyone.

And if I really felt guilt over my brother's death, I had to live a life so glorious, it would make up for his absence—and atone for my actions.

Sorin...

I ran forward, following the curve, pushing past all my insecurities.

Then I heard it—something other than fire and destruction. The splash of water, cutting through the chaos like a lifeline. Driven by a surge of desperate hope, and I stumbled toward the sound, every step a defiance of the inferno that sought to claim me.

The floor beneath me gave way, collapsing with a deafening crash, and I hurled myself forward, my arms outstretched into the unknown. Waste's chains reached outward as well, and then my foot caught on the edge of something solid. I fell hard, skidding on a smooth surface.

Cool air rushed past me, and I realized I had made it.

The splash of water in a fountain lifted all my spirits. I stood and ran toward it.

This was it. The fountain that would restore my sight! I would be free of this place soon!

Still merged with Waste, I hurried to the edge of the fountain. Even though I couldn't see, I felt the cold stones, and the angle of their curve. It was a large fountain—perhaps bigger than a small house.

I plunged my hands into the cold water and cupped them enough to grab a mouthful of water. Then I brought my palms to my lips and drank deep.

The chill sensation of the water washed over my whole body. My throat felt better, my stomach unknotted, and everything seemed bright.

My eyes...

The blackness died away, colors invading my perception.

I blinked several times until my sight was fully restored. I stood in the middle of a large space, deep in the labyrinth, the fountain before me a work of art. It was *gigantic*, and in the center was a statue of an abyssal dragon. Water gushed from its wings and spine, splashing in the pool around it.

Bluish motes of light wafted around the waters, dancing over the smooth surface.

They were lost souls...

And Waste had been correct. The floor was polished alabaster, so smooth and beautiful it reflected everything like a mirror. The walls were at least fifteen feet high, and they stretched toward the black sky, somehow glowing and keeping the labyrinth illuminated.

"We made it," Waste and I said as one.

This wasn't the exit, however...

I turned around, my heart hammering. I expected to see a charred hallway—evidence of the inferno that had tormented my entire trek here.

But I saw nothing.

It was just... a long corridor. Like all the other corridors around us. No burn marks. No ashes. No embers floating through the air.

Had it all just been an illusion? All in my head?

The screech of something drew my attention to the sky. The midnight black was too thick to see beyond, and it honestly made me nervous.

I had heard this shriek before. It belonged to the elder phoenix dragon, Xuandi...

CHAPTER 4

HOME SWEET HOME

As *the Distant Dream* pulled into port, it began to rain. I held Twain close to my body, his shivering little feline form both cute and sad. I wore a white cloak, made from some of the finest leather and silk, and pulled it tight around the both of us. The hood shielded my eyes from the worst of the weather, but the wind picked up, blowing some of the rain into the side of my face.

The storm cloud blocked out the setting sun and the first hints of the moon, casting the world around us into darkness.

"The weather at sea changes so dramatically," came a singsong voice.

Phila Hon walked across the deck of the ship, her large eyes on the sky. Her long strawberry-blonde hair fluttered behind her as the wind picked up once more. There was no taming it—she didn't even try to wrangle her long locks—and instead Phila waved her hand, using her slender fingers as a conduit for her magic.

She evoked wind to swirl around the ship, stopping it from assaulting us with the droplets of rain. It was like an invisible barrier flew up on all sides, shielding us from the weather.

Only then did Phila comb her long hair with her fingers, straightening everything until it was beautiful again. She smiled, her happiness infectious. Of all the people in my class, Phila was the only one who had an artist's expression—wide-eyed and dreamy, as though she weren't even in the same world as me.

The evening was dreary and cold, yet she smiled anyway.

Who did that?

But then Phila bounded over to me, wearing a pair of long pants, and a long black coat tied at her thin waist to create a sort of makeshift dress.

"I'm so excited to see your home isle," Phila stated. "You will give me the grandest of tours, won't you?"

I sarcastically glanced up at the sky, as though I hadn't noticed the weather until right now. "Wow, those clouds snuck up on us, didn't they? Maybe I'll show you around in the morning." Then I gave her a sideways glance. "Why are you really here, huh? Everyone else went to Astra Academy or to their homes to prepare for the next academic year."

When I left the Dodger family's summer home to go fetch my brother, all my other friends went about getting everything in order. Ashlyn had to return to the Kross family home to prepare for the wedding. Nasbit went straight to the Academy. Knovak went to the Gentz home to gather supplies and see his kin before departing.

And Raaza stayed with the Dodger family so he could make arrangements for his mother and sister. His family no longer had a home, but the kind arcanists of the Dodger estate said they would help. I assumed Raaza would join us at the Academy when he was done, but I hadn't asked for specifics.

Phila was the only person in my class who demanded to go

with me to the Isle of Haylin, and I didn't have a reason to deny her request, so here she was.

But I still didn't understand *why* she wanted to go with me.

Phila did a little hop-step over to me, until we were only half a foot apart. "I was hoping to speak with you on a more one-on-one basis."

"You know I'm getting married in a week, right?" I asked, deadpan. "You lost your chance at *this* a while back." I motioned to myself.

She sincerely laughed and waved away the comment. "Don't be silly, Gray! I was being serious. I wanted to speak with you as a friend, on many subjects." Then Phila tilted her head to the side. "As long as that's okay with you?"

"I suppose," I muttered.

Twain poked his head up out of my cloak. He purred as he said, "Gray just likes to joke around. He's a jester at heart."

"Ashlyn has told me many times that she really appreciates your ability to make her laugh," Phila stated. "But that's not what I wanted to talk to you about."

The sailors on *the Distant Dream* finished tying down the ship to the dock and then they let down the gangplank. We were finally here, and several of the men immediately began unloading supplies meant for Haylin.

"How about we get to my house, and then we'll talk?" I asked.

Phila nodded, her smile brightening her heart-shaped face.

Just then, a coatl came up from the hold. It was Tenoch, Phila's eldrin. He was a five-foot-long corn snake with bright orange scales, glittering red eyes, and wings so colorful they looked as though they had once belonged to a parrot. Tenoch dragged a satchel along behind him, his wiggling body rather cute as he made his way over.

"Oh, my arcanist, I gathered all your things." Tenoch

bowed once he was close, his wings stretched out to the side as he did so. "I believe we're set to disembark."

I turned on my heel and headed for the gangplank, but Phila held out a hand and hesitated. "Shouldn't we wait for your escort?" she asked.

I stopped and sighed. I had forgotten about Lucian. He was a powerful arcanist—bonded to the Source of the Storm, a unique creature—but he was also abrasive in his personality. I hadn't spoken with him much, because I doubted that we had much in common, but Headmaster Venrover had insisted that Lucian stay with me until I returned to Astra Academy.

As if waiting for a dramatic cue, Lucian strode up from the hold of the ship and walked onto the deck with confidence. His skin was darkly tanned, his clothing nothing more than leather armor with half-plate metal over vital parts. His arcanist mark, a nine-pointed star, was wrapped in clouds.

Phila and I both had seven-pointed stars. From what I learned in class, the nine-points symbolized that an arcanist was bonded to something *unique*. There was only one Source of the Storm—once it died, there would be no others.

Lucian kept his black hair short, and quickly wiped it back once it was soaked with rain.

His eldrin fluttered up from the hold. While it had an intimidating name, and its magics were fearsome, the Source of the Storm was nothing more than a white hummingbird. It darted around, its tiny wings fluttering, and then landed on Lucian's shoulder.

Despite being so tiny, it held itself straight, its head high, like a miniature knight guarding its post.

The tips of its minuscule feathers sparked with bits of lightning.

I wondered if it had the power to alter the weather around us.

Lucian walked over. His armor was covered in sheaths that

held a dozen or so daggers, and he tightened everything in place before motioning to the gangplank. "We're here to see your family, aren't we? Let's hurry through this task so that we can head to the Academy."

"My family's home isn't large," I said as I headed down the plank of wood. Once on the dock, I shrugged. "We have three rooms—one for me, one for Sorin, and one for my father and stepmother. I'm not sure where the two of you are going to sleep."

"Doesn't your isle have a plethora of inns?" Phila hurried down the gangplank, excitement in her voice. "Little villas on the beach for relaxing?"

Villas? On the beach?

I slowly shook my head. "No. None of that. I think there are spare rooms in the tavern. That's kind of like an inn."

Phila's smile waned for just a moment. Her eldrin slithered his way over to her feet, dragging her satchel behind him. Lucky for her, the pack seemed waterproof, so at least her belongings weren't getting soaked.

"I thought all these islands had places to vacation," Phila murmured as she glanced around. "Isn't that the appeal of living on an island?"

"I'm pretty sure this isle was settled because there were hippogriffs living here." As we walked down the dock, I continued with, "Most of the islands in these parts were explored, and only the ones with mystical creatures on them were really developed."

Phila clapped her hands together once. "Oh, how fun! Is the tour beginning? Do you know all the history of this place?"

"I know a lot about it, yeah."

Lucian and his tiny eldrin walked along behind us. His footfalls were heavy, and it was difficult to forget he was here. He didn't bring any belongings with him, however, and I wondered why. I had told him we would likely spend the night, but I supposed I didn't care much.

At night, the Isle of Haylin wasn't impressive or interesting.

Actually, even during the day it wasn't particularly impressive, but at least everyone was awake. I wondered if anyone here would be happy to see me return. That thought was fleeting, though. My mind kept circling back to Sorin.

There was one main road in my hometown, which made it rather easy to navigate. Rain hammered on the rooftops and created pools on the edges of the walkways. I enjoyed the sound of it all, though. Phila's ability to evoke the wind meant there wasn't a constant *howling* from the storm—it was just the gentle rhythm of the water splashing all around us.

"Thank you for this," I said to her. With a wave of my hand, I gestured to the tranquil area. "It's really impressive you've mastered your magic enough to do this."

Phila held a hand over her mouth as she playfully giggled. "Gray, you're getting married in a week. You lost your chance at all *this*." She twirled in place, allowing her long coat and hair to flare out as she did so.

That honestly made me laugh. "It's just one compliment. Don't let it go to your head."

"Actually..." Phila stopped smiling altogether and then jogged to keep up with my pace. "One of the things I wanted to speak to you about was *how men think*."

"Oh no," I muttered.

Phila held up a finger. "I don't think I understand men sometimes."

I glanced over my shoulder. Lucian trailed behind us, his attention more on our surroundings than us. The city was covered in shadows, with only a few lanterns lit to keep the walkways safe. Did he think someone was lurking nearby?

I'd let him worry.

I returned my attention to Phila.

"What about men is so confusing?" I asked. "Is it the way we breathe? Because not all women know this, but we actually have gills on the side of our neck."

Phila giggled again. Then she shook her head. "You're never fully serious, are you?"

"It's rude to treat my arcanist that way," Tenoch said, slithering faster to keep up. "She has honest questions and needs advice. Why would you mock her?"

I shook my head. "I'm not mocking her."

From inside my cloak, in a muffled voice, Twain said, "*Hey*! Gray is awesome and he'll give Phila real advice." After a few seconds of silent pause, he added, "When he feels like it, of course."

But before we could cross that awkward hurdle, I turned and headed straight for my childhood home. It was easy to find it, because there were several signs that pointed people to the candlemaker's residence. Despite the fact that most people used lanterns or glowstones for illumination, my father still kept up the *candle chandler* business. He made tallow and wax candles, and even occasionally made soap using the honeysuckles that grew on the island.

I supposed, the more I thought about it, my father was a good man. He had always taken care of Sorin and me, though he hated taking any risks.

"Here it is," I said, motioning to the house at the end of the narrow road.

A candle was lit and perched on the interior sill of the front window, illuminating some of the front. It was calm and inviting, and I knew immediately that my father was still awake.

He wouldn't know I was arriving—I hadn't had the time to send him a message—so this would be a surprise.

"*This* is your whole home?" Phila asked. She glanced

around, as if looking for more. "Do all islanders live in such cozy environments?"

"It's okay—you can just call it small." I patted her on her wet shoulder. "And yes, this is my old abode. Lucky for all of us, my father is still awake."

I walked over and knocked on the wooden door. It was a solid piece of the house, practically carved from one giant tree. I had missed so much about this place, and I hadn't realized it until I started reexamining all the details.

Before I could comment, the door flew open. I tensed, not expecting someone to answer so quickly. My father stood before me, a giant of a man. Well, not *all* of him was giant. It was just his gut.

He was as tall as Sorin, though, a few inches taller than me, and his tunic and pants were stained with wax. He had a beard, which wasn't always the case, but he always wore it when it got cold. It was speckled with white hairs, just like the top of his head.

"Gray?" my father asked, shock in his tone. "You... You're back!" He took a deep breath and then waved me to come inside. "Hurry, hurry! Before you catch a cold."

I chuckled as I stepped inside. Our dining room was quaint. A single table, a stove—there wasn't much here. Still, the nostalgia of this place warmed me to my bones.

"You have guests," my father said, his eyes widening.

Phila hopped into the house. Then she gave my father a deep bow. "It's a pleasure to meet you. My name is Phila Hon, and I'm a coatl arcanist."

Her eldrin slithered inside, shook himself like a dog to rid his scales of the water, and then *also* bowed. "I am Tenoch. Thank you for allowing us into your home."

When Lucian stepped into my house, my father frowned. He looked the man up and down, and then eyed the Source of the Storm with suspicion. The little hummingbird puffed out its feathers and glared.

Then my father shut the door.

With only four people, the dining room was already crowded.

"Gray," my father muttered. "I... I'm surprised you're here. I was told you went missing. We were all at the banquet but then you just *weren't*. The headmaster had no explanation. Sorin was so upset."

Just hearing my brother's name made me happy.

"Where is he?" I started heading for the hallway. "Is Sorin asleep in his room?"

"Oh, no. Sorin left a few days ago."

"*What?*"

My heart sank into my gut. Why would he leave?

"Everyone was so worried about you." My father walked over to the table. He grabbed the back of a chair and leaned his considerable weight onto it. "Sorin had no idea where you went, but all his classmates, and most of the arcanists at your Academy, claimed you eloped."

I scoffed. "I didn't do that."

"Sorin told me all about it, but then one of his classmates came to get him."

Phila tapped her bottom lip with a finger. "Who?"

My father shrugged. "A beautiful girl by the name of *Exie Lolian*. She came here and asked Sorin to stay at her family's home while they investigated your disappearance."

CHAPTER 5

HONEYSUCKLE

"Exie came here to get my brother?" I asked, half flabbergasted, half enraged.

"That's what I said," my father replied.

I tried to calm myself. Exie couldn't have known the truth of the matter. She, like everyone else, probably thought Ashlyn and I eloped, and Knovak and Nini went missing shortly afterward. Sorin had just lost his love and his twin brother, and from Exie's perspective, now was the time to swoop in and console him.

After all, if Nini stayed gone forever, this was Exie's ideal situation—she had openly admitted to me she wanted Sorin for herself, and now that Nini wasn't in the picture, what was stopping her?

So, I took a breath, and then groaned.

My father stood straight. With nervous energy, he tapped the back of the chair with his knuckles. "Gray—where did you go? Why didn't you tell anyone? If you *didn't* elope, why the secrecy?"

Twain poked his head out of my cloak, his orange fur

frizzy. "Hey! Gray didn't leave without saying a word. He was taken by a Death Lord and spirited away to the abyssal hells."

The blood drained from my father's face as he stared at my eldrin. Slowly, he turned his gaze to me, peering into my eyes and wringing his hands like he was afraid there would be a monster in the depths of my pupils. He started to speak, stopped, then swallowed and tried again.

"I see," he muttered. "Headmaster Venrover explained most of this to me, but he always assured me you would be safe at Astra Academy. This is a bad omen if I've ever heard one."

"I escaped the clutches of Death Lord Naiad *and* made my way out of the abyssal hells," I said as I placed Twain on the table. "You don't need to worry."

"You're so young." My father was speaking more to himself than anyone else. "But I suppose you were always talented beyond your years. I just... I can't believe this would happen. To anyone."

I stepped around the table so we were a little closer. My father seemed older than I remembered, with deep lines in his face, most of which were curved downward with worry. It worried me in turn.

"I have good news," I said in a pleasant tone.

He lifted an eyebrow and stared at me. "You do?"

"I'm getting married."

My father lifted his other eyebrow as well, until he was just *staring* at me with wide eyes. "Wait, you didn't elope, but you are to wed someone?"

I nodded. "That's right."

My father's gaze immediately drifted over to Phila. "Oh, pardon my manners. I didn't realize I was meeting the future wife of my son." He hurried around me to offer Phila a bow of his head. "You're as beautiful as you are graceful."

Phila smiled as she shook her head. "I'm not Gray's honeysuckle. I'm just his classmate."

"O-Oh," my father muttered. "Well, I apologize. I jumped to conclusions..." Then my father turned his gaze to Lucian. "It's a pleasure to meet you. You're as handsome as you are stoic."

Lucian rolled his eyes. "I'm here as the boy's bodyguard— as a favor to the headmaster. I'm to escort him back to Astra Academy."

"My esteemed and honorable arcanist is already wed, thank you very much," the Source of the Storm stated. Its voice was electric and loud, despite its tiny hummingbird size. When it puffed its white feathers, it more closely resembled a snow grape than a fearsome mystical creature.

My father awkwardly rubbed the palms of his hands across the front of his clothing. When he turned to face me, his confusion was evident. "I don't understand."

"I'm marrying Ashlyn Kross," I stated. "She's a typhoon dragon arcanist, and she's in my class. However, she went to arrange the wedding with her family. I wanted to invite you, Sorin, and—" I hesitated. I was about to say *stepmother*, but in this personal and family moment, I didn't want to alienate her. "—and I also wanted to invite Mother to the ceremony."

I had never called my stepmother my *mother* before, and the significance wasn't lost on my father. He brightened up, his confusion and worry vanishing instantly.

"Of course we'll be there," he said, practically breathless. "It would be an honor. A privilege, even. Are you, uh, marrying into the Kross family?"

I nodded. "Yeah. I'll be Gray *Kross* after the ceremony. Which is a huge change. You won't even be able to recognize me."

My father and Phila both chuckled.

It was tradition for arcanists of smaller families to marry

into the bigger ones. Since I didn't really own anything—no land, magical items, ships, or real businesses—there was little for Ashlyn to gain by adopting the *Lexly* name. However, once I became a *Kross*, I would be part of their family for all intents and purposes, including legal.

It was a shame, because I liked the last name *Lexly*. However, I didn't really care. My last name was more a signifier of my allegiance to my family—my sacrifice to them, my show of dedication, my willingness to put them first.

My father held out a hand. "Are you going to gather honeysuckles to present to your bride? They're flowering this time of year."

"I'll get some before I leave tomorrow," I said. "That was another reason I wanted to come here in person."

Gathering a bouquet of honeysuckles and presenting them to your lover was a tradition unique to the Isle of Haylin. And while I thought it silly, I wasn't going to break it. I'd gather some of the flowers and bring them to Ashlyn, as a way to showcase my admiration and dedication.

Hopefully she'd like them.

"Then I think you should go take your old room and get a good night's sleep," my father stated. "Your friends can take Sorin's room, and tomorrow we'll go over all the details." He clasped my shoulder and then pulled me into a tight embrace. "I'm so proud of you, Gray. So very, very proud."

I returned the gesture, my face heating, only because Phila and Lucian were watching the entire time.

"But you're growing up too damn fast." My father ended the hug and wiped the corners of his eyes. "It was just yesterday you were a little thing. Your mother would be proud, too."

My real mother.

The one who died in childbirth.

I held my breath as I nodded.

Twain yawned. "Okay, well, I think we really do need a catnap. Let's go, Gray! To your old bedroom." He leapt onto my shoulder and I petted him.

"Goodnight," I said to the others, my chest tight.

I couldn't sleep.

Lying on my old bed—which smelled of dust—in the room I used to experience nightmares, only fueled my thoughts and imagination. Twain slept at the foot of my mattress, curled up tight, his body in the shape of a bread loaf.

Instead of just staring up at the ceiling, I waited until the rain stopped and then quietly got out of bed. Twain took even breaths as I headed to the door, never waking, even when the hinges squeaked as I made my escape.

I crept through my old family home, taking note of how dark it was outside, and then went for the front door. This whole house smelled of wax and perfumes, and it made me nostalgic. Never in my life would I have thought I would miss this island...

Once I was outside, I turned my gaze to the sky. The clouds had parted, allowing the moonlight to spill across the town, illuminating the walkways and covering the windows in glittering light.

Despite the bitter chill, I headed down the main road.

"You're restless," I said—Deimos said, actually.

I shook my head. "It happens when I worry."

"You said you wished to help me set things right in the abyssal hells. This isn't a problem that you can ignore in favor of petty dramas. You need to prioritize it."

I chuckled as I headed into town. The road was clean, but there was horse manure in the gutters dug alongside the stone. Since it had rained, it only smelled of fresh earth, but I remembered how badly the city would smell on the hot summer days. Funny what the mind remembers from simple visual cues.

"I am prioritizing the abyssal hells," I muttered. "Once I'm at Astra Academy, we're going to be learning and focusing all our efforts into helping you."

"I meant your mind, boy." Deimos's tone took on a hint of frustration. "We don't have time for you to be woebegone. You must steel yourself—improve your magic, your body, your willpower."

I took a deep breath as I walked.

How would I become stronger? What could I do to improve? What was something I could do *right now* that would have a significant impact?

One of my classes had talked about how creatures gain a *true form* once a certain requirement was met. Every mystical creature had a true form, and they gained them through a geas or a virtue.

I had read about the atlas turtle once... In order for an atlas turtle arcanist to achieve a true form with their eldrin, they had to embody the virtue of defense. They had to become a true *defender*, protecting what they held dear, no matter the cost.

I wished the mimic's true form requirement had been that easy.

No, instead, in order for a mimic arcanist to achieve a true form with its eldrin, they had a geas—they had to defeat *fear itself*.

Who had ever done that? No one I knew. Well, to be fair, I didn't know many mimic arcanists. I knew Zahn, and that was it. He didn't have a true form mimic.

And what would Twain look like once he was a true form mimic? Would he change completely?

A normal atlas turtle was the size of a small ship, but a true form atlas turtle was the size of a small island. That was a huge difference. Would Twain get bigger? Would he become a lion? Or something else?

A true form creature was much stronger than a normal version... If I could somehow defeat fear, Twain would become stronger than ever, and so would I.

Perhaps we'd have enough power to defeat any of the Death Lords. With Deimos's help, of course.

Lost in my musings, I almost didn't realize I had walked through town and was now standing by the fence that surrounded Honeysuckle Meadow. It was a quiet and beautiful place, where the fields were covered in hundreds of honeysuckle bushes.

Most people didn't know that honeysuckles were the most fragrant at night. They barely had an aroma during the day, but once the moon was out, honeysuckles erupted in a sweet-smelling scent that carried for miles.

"I've never seen this flower before," Deimos muttered.

"They're pretty amazing," I said as I hopped the fence into the field.

The flowers were mostly white, and trumpet shaped, but there were occasional golden ones that sparkled whenever any sort of light touched them. According to Isle of Haylin legend, a person was supposed to pick white flowers to show their deepest and most romantic of love.

The golden flowers didn't symbolize that, though...

I carefully waded through the bush-like plants, my eyes seeking out the golden flowers. With delicate movements, I plucked them from the bush, careful not to disturb the white ones.

Most people also didn't know that honeysuckles were the favorite of moths and evening hummingbirds. I spotted a few in the field, half a dozen of them flitting about. All the creatures fled from me as I made my way deeper and deeper into the honeysuckles, however.

"This is what I'm talking about," Deimos said. "Why aren't you taking this time to hone your skills?"

"I just have a few things to do." Once I had a dozen of the golden trumpet-shaped flowers, I held them close. "And once these things are done, I'll dedicate myself to becoming stronger. I think... I know of a way to achieve Twain's true form."

Deimos's curiosity was clearly piqued. "How so?"

"My brother."

"What about your brother? He hardly seems like the type of person who can help you overcome *fear itself*."

I held up a finger and waggled it, as though Deimos were here and could actually see me. "Ah, you've underestimated Sorin, I see. That's fine. Most people do. But I have an ace up my sleeve."

"Please, elaborate."

I smirked. "My brother is a knightmare arcanist. They evoke terrors, right? And make you hallucinate your worst fears?" I remembered learning all about that in class as well. My smirk faded as I imagined what would happen if my brother turned his evocation on me.

"You're going to suffer through his terrors to strengthen your own willpower?" Deimos asked.

I nodded. "That's right. Maybe—just maybe—if I get Sorin's help on this, I really can defeat fear itself, and gain an edge for the battles to come."

CHAPTER 6

HELL'S BELLS

--Nini's Perspective--

Now that my sight was back, I needed to get out of here. Unfortunately, I didn't have my glasses, which meant my vision would be blurry whenever I unmerged from Waste.

With Waste, however, my sight was perfect. A random, and appreciated, gift from my eldrin. We were just stronger as a single unit.

I needed to escape the labyrinth before the elder creatures could reach me. Death Lord Deimos said I would be safe with him in the Requiem Throne—some sort of building in the third abyss—but until then, I was in danger.

"We should leave this place," Waste and I said as one.

I ran toward the nearest wall. My reflection beneath me was perfect, and the light from Waste's four lanterns glittered across the surface as I ran. The golden chains represented people I had killed, most of which came from the undead monsters I had slain here in the abyssal hells. Only a few chain links were from people in the land of the living.

My red hair fluttered behind me, as dark as blood. It matched Waste's cloak, and we truly seemed like one perfect being. My new face mask, white and seemingly made of porcelain, had a face that was neutral.

In all ways, I appeared... spooky.

I liked that, because it felt like a shield. If someone was intimidated just by looking at me, they probably wouldn't bother me.

I used the golden chains of Waste's body like tentacles. With them, I jumped into the air and attempted to grab the top of the wall. Why travel through a labyrinth when I could just escape out the top?

The instant I lifted myself beyond the height of the wall, my sight failed me a second time. Instantly, everything became a void of darkness, and I couldn't see.

I gasped, and the chains faltered. Then, I fell. Fortunately, Waste was with me, and he was never caught by surprise. With his focus, I managed to use the chains to buffer my fall. They hit the ground and eased me down onto my feet, no damage to my body.

Frantic and blind, I stumbled my way back to the fountain, the sound of the splashing water guiding me. I took a drink of the cool and clear liquid, and within seconds, my sight returned.

"We can't leave the labyrinth through the top," we said together.

The roar of the elder phoenix dragon reverberated through the labyrinth. Xuandi was coming—heading my way.

"What're we going to do?" I asked in my double voice.

"*We must navigate the labyrinth,*" Waste telepathically replied. "*Fear not, my arcanist. You are stronger than you realize.*"

46

I shook my head. "I'm only strong because of you."

"*You made it through the fire on your own. You can make it through this maze. But we'll never know for certain unless you begin right now.*"

I half smiled under my mask. Waste thought I overcame the fire on my own? No. It was because I had *his* strength. I wouldn't have made it on my own.

But I didn't want to dwell on that. With my sight restored, I turned on my heel and glanced around. There were five pathways that led from this fountain space. One of them was the way I had entered. That probably wasn't the correct path.

Wait...

Didn't Death Lord Deimos say the way to navigate the labyrinth was through the use of bells?

"*Yes,*" Waste replied. "*He said that. Do you see any nearby?*"

I glanced around, hoping to spot any sign of bells. The glassy floor and walls were immaculate; there was no chance a random bell was just left around. Where would I even find one?

The only thing here... was the fountain.

With my breath held, I stared at the statue of the abyssal dragon. It was curled in a semicircle, its tail long, its six eyes closed. But then I noticed something—where the scales were rotted, tucked deep into its body, were glints of silver. The bells were part of the statue, hidden away.

My heart pounded as I stepped into the pristine fountain and trudged forward. Using my chains, I hoisted myself up. The statue was as large as the abyssal dragons themselves, and the bells were a foot within, so I had to stretch to reach the nearest one.

The bell...

It was small enough to fit in the palm of my hand. Inside, it was empty. There was no clapper, just a hollow bell.

Was this really how I would escape the labyrinth?

But at some level, I was too late! The heat in the area intensified, and I fell off the statue and splashed into the fountain, my breaths shaky. The flaps of dragon wings were unmistakable.

Xuandi swooped down from the darkness of the void sky and landed atop one of the fifteen-foot-tall walls.

He was monstrous, and just as large as the abyssal dragon statue. My stomach twisted as Xuandi lowered his head into the labyrinth, his gigantic mouth riddled with dark gold fangs. Rows and rows of them—double set like a shark's maw.

The beast's wings unfurled, a grotesque patchwork of red feathers and yellow, leathery skin that stretched unnaturally in the heated air. I hated fire so much, and this dragon reminded me of the worst flames.

Xuandi's body was no better—a monstrous mix of scales and feathers, each a burning scarlet hue that seemed alive, radiating heat and malice with every subtle shift.

"Reaper arcanist," Xuandi said, his deep voice shaking the foundation of the labyrinth. "Here you are."

Xuandi's claws were sharpened talons, far too long and hooked, and buried into the wall.

He stared at me with sickly eyes. They were the shade of diseased yellow, his pupils broken like a shattered mirror.

Wisps of blue, ghostly forms that twisted and flickered like dying embers, flowed around his head and neck—a mane of souls. *Human* souls. He was the most elder of creatures I had yet to see.

Waste's scythe floated into my hands and I held it firm.

"W-What do you want?" I asked, my voice and Waste's merged.

The dragon let out a low, guttural chuckle. The souls in his mane seemed to cry and moan, adding to the haunting noise. Was Xuandi amused?

"*We're not afraid to fight you,*" Waste and I shouted. "We

saw how you avoided striking us before. Reaper arcanists are guarded by the King's Revenge—and you know it."

If anyone killed a reaper, they would immediately be struck dead in return—that was the nature of the King's Revenge. And Xuandi had hesitated to breathe fire on me during our last fight. He didn't want to die in turn.

Despite that, Xuandi continued his chortling.

Then other creatures rushed through the labyrinth and emerged from two of the corridors. They were reptiles the size of horses, with dark gray scales, six legs, and giant round eyes. The scales on their back were curved and sharp, flaring almost like spines. Each of them had a small soul mane around their neck, the humans attempting to flee them, with little outstretched arms and twisted faces of misery.

At least ten of these horrible creatures raced into the open area of the fountain. They turned their round eyes on me, their faces twisting into smiles.

"We fight for Death Lord Kallikore," Xuandi said, smiling wide. "And he has a whole *army* of elder creatures. I might not strike you down, but there are plenty who would give their life to the cause."

I tensed, my knuckles turning white as I tightened my grip on my scythe.

"*Those are elder basilisks,*" Waste telepathically said. "*A bite from them can cause instant death. But we—*"

Xuandi exhaled, cutting off Waste, and heat washed over the whole area, followed by a trickle of embers. His smile never faded. "But I didn't chase you down just to kill you. I came to offer you another option."

"Leave me alone," I snapped. "I don't want anything you're offering."

"Listen, child. Listen with your heart. Humans are disgusting, but you are different. You bonded with a reaper—a creature who merges with their human. In my eyes, you have become a mystical creature yourself. Even now, you wear your eldrin like a second skin. Together, you are made whole. So, you aren't *just* human... You're one of my kind."

The basilisks scurried forward, but never attacked. They fanned out, surrounding me in a semicircle. They flashed their own teeth, each smiling, some even echoing Xuandi's sentiments.

"Yeah, you're a creature just like us," one said.

After a hissing laugh, another added, "And look at your chains... Each a soul fragment. Reapers are the *original* elder creature. They gain power by harvesting humans."

Xuandi nodded along with the elder basilisk's words. "That's right. You're different. Special. You're *meant* to join Death Lord Kallikore and usher in an age of new rule. You're one of us."

My heart hammered and I didn't know what to say. Elder creatures were mystical creatures who had consumed far too many human souls, and were distorted in ways I didn't understand. Was Waste the same? He was more powerful now... And he had changed shape...

"Even if they speak the truth, would you turn on humanity?" Waste asked.

"No," I whispered in my double voice.

"Then your answer is obvious."

"I'll never join you," I shouted.

Xuandi's smile slowly faded. His nostrils flared, but he didn't move from his perch on the labyrinth wall. With a powerful flap of his wings, more heat flooded the area.

"Fool," he hissed. "Don't you see? Humanity is malicious. Humanity is disgusting. Haven't you been mistreated? Haven't you known suffering at their hands?"

He waited, obviously wanting an answer.

But I couldn't. My throat was tight, and my hands shook. Humanity *was* all those things. For all my life, I had been hated and mocked. Even my mother and father—and especially my brother. They were my *family* and yet they were the worst of all.

"Human souls could empower us," Xuandi said, his voice growing louder with each word. "Their blood can water our lands. All your suffering could come to an end—so I have but one last question. What're you waiting for? *Join us.*"

But not *all* humanity was like that.

Sorin never hurt me. He was never cruel. Even if it was silly, and everyone made fun of him, Sorin only filled the world with poetry, never agony.

I held my scythe at the ready. "You're suffering made flesh and bone. If the abyssal hells aren't enough to end you, I'll have to send you into the oblivion myself."

"*Feh,*" the phoenix dragon huffed. "You're as stupid as every other human who has come before you. *Kill her.*"

All ten elder basilisks hunched and then lunged.

I leapt backward, my strength and speed enhanced by having Waste merged with me. I released the scythe with one hand and evoked terrors, the invisible force washing over five of the basilisks and filling their minds with haunting images.

The souls in their manes screamed, and those five were halted in their tracks.

The other five went for me, their fangs long and needle-sharp at the points. One snapped its jaw close to my arm. I swung with my scythe and buried the golden blade straight into its temple.

Blood gushed from the injury and the basilisk twitched as I yanked the scythe out.

Another one went for me, biting at my face. I leaned away, backing up with each step, fighting on the defensive. With another wave of my hand, I manipulated the blood from the dead basilisk, forming the crimson liquid into physical objects —like knives.

The crystalized blood shot up and pierced straight through the second basilisk, the knives cutting through scale and bone and then shooting out the other side.

Oh, my...

My blood manipulation had never been so powerful before.

Now that Waste was a true form reaper, he was so much *stronger*.

I was stronger.

The other three basilisks leapt for me at the same time, threatening to pin me under their large bodies. I managed to sidestep two of them, but the third bit down on my left shoulder, his fangs piercing Waste's cloak, my clothes, and then through my flesh.

No!

In frantic desperation, I evoked more terrors. The remaining three basilisks cried out, even the one who had bitten me. I was free, but my heart was pounding so loudly, I almost couldn't hear anything else.

Didn't Waste say the basilisks had deadly bites?

And then, the basilisk who had bit me locked up. Its body went so stiff, it was practically a statue, and then it fell over, its last breath leaving it.

Blood wept from my shoulder as I took several steps away. The first five basilisks were free from my terrors, and they joined the other two who were still alive—but they all stopped to stare at the basilisk who just died.

"What happened?" one asked.

I didn't know.

"*I'm true form now,*" Waste telepathically said. "*All true form creatures gain a phenomenal power. Reapers gain the* Duke of Demise, *an ability that makes both you and I immune to instant death effects. Additionally, if such magic is used against us, it gets reflected back on the attacker. These basilisks never stood a chance."*

Xuandi roared, shaking the labyrinth with his frustration. "*Kill her!* I don't care how. Rip her limb from limb! Choke her with her own chains. Just end her!"

The seven elder basilisks lunged for me. I backed away swinging, striking one in the throat. Blood exploded from its injury, painting the once white labyrinth a sickly red.

Another basilisk crunched its fangs around my leg. It died from its own magic, but my leg...

I hobbled as another attacked. I used my terrors and then manipulated the blood around us into the form of a blade and decapitated the beast.

Two more came at me from the side. One bit my left arm. Dead. The other rushed in, but I managed to stab it through the heart with a lance of hardened crimson blood.

The next elder basilisk aimed for my throat. I manipulated the blood upward into a dozen spikes. I skewered the beast before it reached me, killing it without much thought.

The last one...

It was the smartest of the bunch. It turned tail and ran.

Xuandi growled, his fangs flashing. When he roared, my ears felt like they might burst. The sounds of more creatures—many, many more—came echoing down the labyrinth corridors. He *had* brought an army.

"*We should flee,*" Waste said to me. "*We're injured, and we can't keep taking small amounts of damage like this. Eventually, we'll be the ones who have bled out.*"

I nodded as I whirled around and ran. With my bell, I figured I could find my way out of the maze eventually.

I hoped.

Xuandi didn't follow me.

The other elder creatures roamed the labyrinth, but after a few turns, I didn't see them again. So I kept going.

The labyrinth stretched on endlessly, its white walls gleaming with an eerie, unnatural light that cast no shadows. The floors beneath my feet were mirrors, cold and slick, reflecting not just the environment and my own wavering form, but also distorted shapes that seemed to move just out of sight. The reflections taunted me, showing twists and turns that didn't exist.

My blood dappled the walkway where I went.

The injuries from the elder creatures stung more than any injury I had ever sustained.

Something was wrong...

"I'm scared," I said, my voice a mix of Waste's and my own.

I refused to unmerge with him. Together, I had the cold comfort of his power, but if we split apart, I'd have nothing.

"*You must stay strong,*" Waste telepathically said.

"You keep saying I shouldn't worry, and I can't give up—but how long, Waste? How long?"

My words echoed through the empty corridors, and my agitation was weakening our magic. If I kept up my panic, I would inadvertently unmerge with my reaper. I couldn't do that. I had to keep it together.

"*As long as it takes,*" Waste eventually answered me. "*That's the essence of bravery. You hold on until it's done—whatever the task.*"

I placed a hand on the facemask over my own face. Could I hold on? I had to.

That was when I reached into my cloak and pulled out the bell. With no clapper, how I was supposed to use it? I wasn't entirely certain.

"Show me the way," I commanded in my double voice.

The bell did nothing.

"Please," I whispered.

The silver bell remained motionless in my palm, and my heart sank. What was I supposed to do with this? I didn't understand.

"*We should keep moving,*" Waste said.

I nodded once. What other choice did I have?

CHAPTER 7

MY MOTHER

Once I had gathered enough golden honeysuckles, I bundled them together, using the stem of one as a tie. As I stood, and admired my work, I heard a rustling near the fence around the meadow. I turned on my heel, my hand reaching up to the collar of my shirt.

Technically, I had my weapon close at hand at all times. Vivigöl, Silencer of the Damned, was crafted from abyssal coral, and it was dangerous to the touch. Thankfully, Death Lords were immune to the soul-damaging properties of the coral, which meant I was as well. And since Vivigöl had absorbed some of my mimic magic, it could change its shape. Normally, it was a trident, but right now, it was a set of jewelry around my neck and shoulders, away from anyone who might accidentally graze their fingers over Vivigöl's deadly surface.

I glanced around, searching the evening darkness.

Then I spotted someone.

Phila.

She stood off from the road, by the fence of Honeysuckle Meadow, her long hair flowing. Once our eyes met, she offered me a wave. Her eldrin, Tenoch, did the same, waggling his little tail. His little coatl body practically glowed in the moonlight. He seemed more magical than usual.

"Gray," Phila quietly called out. "What are you doing?"

I trudged through the honeysuckle bushes until I made my way to her location. She wore a simple dress of pink and white, with tall boots made for hiking. She also wore gloves that went to her elbows, giving her a lady-like demeanor that was almost unheard of for the Isle of Haylin.

"I'm just burying a dead body before the villagers figure out who the murderer is," I quipped.

Phila giggled at my poor attempt at a joke. Probably just to be nice to me—Phila seemed to do a lot of things just to be nice. She eyed the flowers in my hand. "Are those for Ashlyn?"

"No." I gestured to the white honeysuckles. "I'll get some for her in a bit. These ones are for someone else."

Tenoch poked his snake head up above the fence. "Your father? Or maybe your brother?"

"My mother, actually," I said, keeping all emotion from my voice.

Phila nodded once. "Oh. I see." Then she tilted her head. "Nini said Sorin's mother died in childbirth. Since you're twins..."

She didn't actually finish the sentiment. I hopped over the fence and offered her a smile. "You got it."

"Can I join you?"

"I guess."

Moonlight washed over the island like a comforting blanket, but I hadn't realized how lonely my trek was until I had Phila and her eldrin with me. She grinned as she pointed out every little tiny thing along the route.

"What beautiful craftsmanship on this post," she said, pointing to a perfectly ordinary wood post that held up a portion of a fence for Farmer Li-jon's sheep. "Do you see this?"

"It's a post," I sardonically replied.

"But look." She knelt and grazed her fingers over the grains until her fingertips reached the base, where the wood was firmly planted in the ground. At the bottom, I spied little sheep designs I had never noticed before. "Someone took a lot of time and care for this post."

Tenoch nodded and pointed with his snake tail. "I suspect this is an enclosure for sheep, my arcanist. A thoughtful gesture."

"I've only seen things like this in journals and letters." Phila stood straight. "I never got to leave my house often. I really appreciate you taking me on this trip, Gray. It's so special."

She had always been kind—even now, it seemed as though she were trying to help me.

"The graveyard is over here." I motioned to the small path that led away from the town. "We keep it far from the animals, and the farms, and tucked behind a cluster of trees so you can't see it most days."

Phila hopped to my side and we walked the smaller path together. "I'm so excited to see a real island graveyard."

"Are you afraid of dying?" I asked, my thoughts still on fear.

"Hm? No, I don't believe so."

"What *are* you afraid of?"

A sharp pain lanced through my shin. I yelped and leapt up, surprised to see Tenoch had bitten me through my pants! I rubbed my injury, small droplets of blood staining my clothing from where his fangs had left holes in my flesh.

"You better not be venomous," I said through clenched teeth.

Tenoch flapped his colorful wings. "Hmpf! I won't allow anyone to scare my arcanist."

"Tenoch..." Phila knelt and patted her coatl eldrin. His

snake body shuddered as she stroked the part between his wings. "He wasn't scaring me. You don't have to worry." Then she hugged him.

Tenoch let out a contented hiss. Then he narrowed his red eyes at me.

"I wasn't scaring her." I stood straight and held my honeysuckles close. "I was just curious. Is that a crime now?"

"You weren't about to tell ghost stories?" Tenoch tilted his head.

"No."

My injury had been small, and thanks to my arcanist magic, had basically healed shut. I itched at my new skin, irritated but not angry. Phila did seem gentle; I didn't blame the little snake for wanting to protect her.

"Are *you* scared of dying, Gray?" Phila asked. She stood, and together, we continued down the winding path to the graveyard. Tenoch slithered close to my ankles, which I didn't care for.

"I'm not afraid of dying," I said.

"What are you afraid of then?" Phila eyed me.

"Heights," I muttered.

"But why are you afraid of heights?" Tenoch asked. "Is it because you'll fall to your death *and die?* If it is, I submit to you that you're actually afraid of dying."

I shook my head. "It's not that. It's..." It was hard to put in words, but I had already given it a lot of thought. "I don't like... being out of control." The thought of tumbling through the air, unable to do anything about my situation until I finally hit the ground...

It didn't sit well with me. My hands started to sweat just thinking about it.

I wanted to be in control. I wanted options. I wanted to plan and think and maneuver and *falling* didn't allow for any of that.

"I'm afraid of being alone," Phila whispered, almost too low for me to hear.

I held my breath as we rounded the corner and finally made it to the gates of the graveyard. The twisted iron bars were the shapes of waves to represent the abyssal hells. If they had been more accurate, the gates would've been upside down, but I figured, for practical reasons, they didn't do that.

"You're not alone," I said as I pushed open the gate. It screeched the entire time, grating my ears. "And what does that even mean? I've seen lots of arcanists at the Academy looking your way."

Phila snickered. Then she stepped past me, her smile fading quickly. "I wanted to talk to you about boys. You see, I'm..." She sighed and rubbed her arms through her gloves. "I'm also afraid of boys."

I laughed out loud as I walked into the graveyard. The tombstones and headstones were all the shape of hippogriffs, as was our island's tradition. Names were carved into the stones, along with their profession and how they died. My favorite was probably: *Muir Manning, Baker, Several Accidents.*

Another amusing one read: *Jaime Lingrad, Schoolmaster, Cancer and a Wolf.*

I walked around one of the tombstones and eyed Phila. "If you're afraid of boys, why are you here with me in a dark graveyard, away from everyone else?" I motioned to myself. "I'm as boy as it gets."

Again, Phila laughed. "Oh, I'm sorry. I was trying to be polite. I'm not afraid of you, as a person—I'm afraid of being... uh... well, of being intimate with someone. A man, specifically."

"Oh."

This was the most awkward conversation I could have in a graveyard.

As I mulled over her statement, I made my way over to my mother's grave. She was nestled in one of the far corners, in a cluster of graves dedicated to women who had died in childbirth. While some headstones were dirty and overgrown with plants, my mother's was practically pristine.

I assumed Sorin had been here, and this was his doing. My brother would always clean her grave when he came to visit.

I placed the gold honeysuckles down.

They represented love for the departed. Love undying. Love that lasted beyond someone's last breath.

I sighed.

"Is that your mother's grave?" Phila asked.

"Yeah."

It read: *Aleksandra Lexly, Chandler, Childbirth.*

Phila walked over to stand next to me. The cold evening winds whipped over us, and Phila rubbed her gloved hands across her upper arms.

"There's nothing to be afraid of," I finally said. "Men aren't scary."

"I'm afraid of the act of intimacy," she whispered. "And I don't know how to tell that to people. I'm worried they'll think me weird. Or maybe they'll think I'm childish and weak."

I crossed my arms as I stared at my mother's tombstone. This felt like a bizarre thing to discuss here, but I supposed my mother would understand.

"You've never been intimate with anyone, right?" I shrugged. "Maybe it'll be great."

"The thought disgusts me." Phila glanced over and frowned. "But I feel selfish for thinking that."

I shook my head. "Don't. You're not getting married yet, right? You don't need to worry about this. And if you *do* want to worry about it, maybe you should discuss it with, I dunno, a lady?"

Phila chuckled as her attention slid to her boots. "I just wanted some outside perspective. From someone who wouldn't think poorly of me."

"Talk to Nasbit," I said. "He thinks poorly of no one—and he definitely won't judge you. And he might know a book about this subject that will help you. He's great like that."

Tenoch lifted his serpent head. "You think so?"

"Of course." I petted him. "And don't worry—even if you hate everyone's physical touch, you aren't going to be alone. You'll have lots of friends, and family, and Tenoch. You've got nothing to fear."

I spoke it all so confidently that I was momentarily proud of myself. I almost sounded like I could see the future.

Phila perked up. With a bright smile that chased away the evening darkness, she said, "I'm glad I spoke to you, Gray. I do like Nasbit. He makes me feel safe and happy. I just... I worry I won't like *being with* him, and then he'll hate me." She clasped her hands tightly together as she spoke the last bit.

"That's tomorrow's problem," I said. "Today, we just have to worry about making it back to my house before anyone knows we're missing."

"Right! Everything will work out." Phila turned and headed for the path out of the graveyard. Her eldrin hurried after her.

She was much happier now.

Before I left my mother's grave, I whispered, "What are you afraid of, Deimos?"

"Failure," he replied without missing a beat.

"Truly? That's it?"

"One failure, and everything I've worked for, or hoped to achieve, will crumble. I can't lose. I can't be beaten. I can't give up. But when I sleep, and nightmares fill my restless nights, it's visions of failing that wake me."

Yikes.

His words settled around my heart like a cold vice. I thought of Everett and Nini, and all the people who would suffer if the problems in the abyssal hells couldn't be fixed. Deimos's fear was real. I understood.

Failure scared me as well.

Chapter 8

Out of Control

As soon as the morning sun crested the distant horizon, we left the Isle of Haylin.

My father and my stepmother had been invited to my wedding, but they would travel there separately. They both had promised to wear their finest clothing and arrive with wonderful gifts. It was tradition for the family gaining an arcanist to host the festivities—so since I was marrying *into* House Kross, they would handle everything, and my parents wouldn't have to worry.

My family only needed to give me and Ashlyn a gift to wish us well in our marriage.

We rode on *the Distant Dream*, heading for the mainland where we'd eventually arrive at Exie's family's estate. House Lolian was supposedly wealthy beyond my wildest imaginings, but after seeing the Kross family and the Dodger family, I assumed it would be about the same.

I was more worried about my brother.

Exie had her eyes on him, and she was the type of person that didn't relent.

As I paced around the deck of the ship, I spotted several other vessels in the distance, a few with smoke stacks. They were powered by engines—probably magical artifacts that would cut down on the amount of fuel they needed—but I didn't know for certain.

I held Twain in my arms. He refused to go anywhere else. When I stared at the distant ship for a few moments, he pawed at my arm.

"What're you thinking about?" He glanced up at me, his large ears twitching. "You're boring when you're just in your own head."

"Well, excuuuuuse me," I sardonically stated. "I didn't realize I needed to entertain you."

"You're my arcanist. You definitely need to entertain me when I'm bored."

I glanced down at him, an eyebrow lifted. "Why aren't you entertaining *me*, huh?"

He blinked his eyes and purred a little bit. "Who? Widdle ol' me? But I'm so smoll, and adorable."

After a good chuckle, I rolled my eyes. "All right, how about this... Let's practice that fear thing. We're about to meet my brother. Why don't I climb up the main mast of the ship, and jump off the crow's nest?"

"*Did you just say you're going to jump off the crow's nest?*" someone shouted.

I wheeled around on my heel to see Lucian standing just a few feet from me. When had he come to the deck? I hadn't even heard his footsteps.

His eldrin, the Source of the Storm, sat on his shoulder, the little hummingbird puffing out all its white feathers until it was perfectly spherical. It glared at me like I was a murderer attempting to flee.

Lucian stomped over until we were only a few inches from each other. "You will *not* jump off the crow's nest. It's sixty feet up from the deck, lad. Do you know how high sixty feet is? Do you?"

"A lot." I shrugged. "But I need to overcome my fear of heights one way or another, and this seems like a good place to start." I snapped my fingers and pointed at the main mast. "A fall from *this* height can't kill me."

"It most certainly can," the Source of the Storm stated. It huffed and then shook out its feathers. "Can you imagine what would happen if you broke your back? Or your neck? We don't have any healing arcanists aboard this ship."

The little hummingbird was correct—none of the mystical creatures on the ship could heal people, but that didn't matter for me. *I* was a mimic arcanist and could transform my mimic into any nearby creature to gain their magic, both useable and innate. One such creature was Deimos's abyssal dragon, which granted its arcanist tons of self-healing. Even if I fell, I suspected, as an abyssal dragon arcanist, I would live.

"You should keep in mind that as an arcanist, others will look to your leadership and guidance," Lucian stated. "Your actions will inspire others. Throwing yourself needlessly from the crow's nest to overcome a minor fear is hardly the type of behavior you want others to imitate."

He was lecturing me like I was a small schoolchild.

It took most of my willpower not to roll my eyes.

"Listen, I need to deal with my fears because I'm a mimic arcanist. It has to do with my true form. How about—so you don't flip out—I just *visit* the crow's nest and look around. Happy?"

Lucian inhaled a deep breath, held it for a second, and then exhaled. "Fine."

"Do I have to go?" Twain hesitantly asked.

"Of course." I eyed him. "You're my eldrin. Why wouldn't you go?"

"Sixty feet is a lot of feet," he muttered.

I waved away his comment as I headed for the main mast. "You'll be fine. We'll both be fine. Everything will be fine."

"Now I'm more nervous," he quipped.

I ignored him. While my plan was to have my brother use his terror evocation on me, I figured this wouldn't hurt. What if I managed to get a true form mimic all on my own? That would also be a huge accomplishment.

The main mast was large—wide enough around that I couldn't even wrap my arms around half of it. I placed Twain on my shoulder, grabbed the rigging they had strung up along the side, and then I hoisted myself upward. Climbing wasn't difficult for me. I was wiry, and didn't weigh too much.

Twain clung to me with his claws, piercing my shirt and even my skin. I gritted my teeth, trying to ignore the irritating pain.

"You think this will gain you a true form eldrin?" Deimos asked through me.

I laughed. "Obviously. That's why I'm doing it."

"In the abyssal hells, there is a building located in the fourth abyss. It is known as the *Shelter of Lost Souls*, and it contains wisdom beyond your fathoming. They say every answer to every question is located there. Any question you ask, the Shelter of Lost Souls will provide it."

I continued climbing, wondering what kind of building that was. "Like a library?"

"Much more impressive than a library."

I shrugged. "Okay. If that's true, why haven't you gone there to ask about how to escape the abyssal hells? Huh?"

"Yeah," Twain chimed in. "What Gray said! I bet you never thought about that, did you?"

"*Of course I thought about that, fools,*" Deimos growled, hurting my throat in the process. "But the Shelter of Lost Souls isn't in a location you can mark on a map. It moves. According to Death Lord Umbriel, it only appeared to her when she had lost her way in life—when she no longer had purpose."

I took a deep breath as I pulled myself higher. Out of curiosity, I glanced down to the deck.

Which I definitely shouldn't have done.

I was only twenty feet up, maybe not even that high, and my vision tunneled. My veins filled with ice, and my heart pounded hard against the side of my ribs. My thoughts immediately ground to a halt.

This fear...

It had taken hold of me.

"I once sought the Shelter of Lost Souls so that I might ask it how I could obtain a true form abyssal dragon," Deimos muttered, ignoring my terror. "I thought that, if I had the extra power from a true form, I might be able to create an exit —I might be able to escape the abyssal hells."

Twain nodded along with his words. "Oh. Maybe."

"But I'm uncertain what's required of me," Deimos said. "I don't know whether an abyssal dragon requires a virtue or a geas. Perhaps it will always be a mystery."

Shaken, I decided to move my gaze upward. I glanced up at the blue skies above, trying to imagine what the crow's nest would be like. After gulping down some air, I tried to push away the fear, but my body felt colder and colder.

When I glanced out to sea, I saw those two engine boats much clearer than before. The added height made it easy to count that they each had three smoke stacks, which was a lot.

Once I wasn't thinking about the height, I felt my heart pounding softer than before. Was *this* defeating my fear? Just ignoring it completely? That didn't feel like the correct solution, that was for sure.

"Maybe you'll obtain a true form by grafting a whole *ton* of souls to your dragon," I said, finally able to speak again.

"No," Deimos whispered. "If you had ever grafted a soul, you would know that wasn't the solution."

That seemed cryptic, and vague. But I trusted him. I didn't know anything about abyssal dragons other than their impressive power set.

I reached for the next rope step on the rigging, and my fingers slipped.

The terror of falling crashed through my system all over again. I gasped, clung to the side of the mast, and shook, my vision black around the edges. My heart threatened to leap up my throat and abandon me here.

"*This* height frightens you?" Deimos scoffed. "Pathetic."

"You're not helping!" Twain snapped. Then he pawed me across the face, like he was playfully slapping Deimos. Unfortunately, it was just me he was hitting.

I almost laughed, though. It was amusing.

"Gray?" Phila called out. "What're you doing?"

She was beneath me, probably at the base of the mast, but I dared not look. I needed to calm down and focus on either getting to the nest or getting back to the deck.

"I'm just relaxing," I sarcastically said, shouting loud enough for her to hear.

"You look terrified."

Wow. That wasn't helping.

"He's attempting to overcome his fear," I heard Lucian state.

"Ooooh," Phila replied. "Do you need some help?"

I really didn't want to ask for help. That would defeat the whole purpose of this. How was I supposed to defeat fear if everyone was attempting to make it go away for me? No. I needed to do this on my own.

"I'm fine," I shouted.

My hand shook as I attempted to grab the rope a second

time. With all the chill in my blood, I almost didn't feel anything. When my fingers took hold of the rigging, I wasn't even entirely certain if I had a good grip.

Everything was numb.

"Maybe you should get down," Twain whispered into my ear.

"Y-Yeah," I managed to say. "Maybe you're right."

I fumbled with one of my feet, searching for the rigging below me. Once I had something, I slowly eased myself back down to the deck. When I closed my eyes, everything seemed more manageable.

I didn't even care if I looked like a coward—I just wanted this over with. I *hated* how fear made me feel. It was that loss of control all over again.

With each inch down, I felt calmer and more in control of myself. Once I was only a few feet from the deck. I leapt off the rigging and landed with a loud *thud* on both my feet.

"Ta-da," I said, holding out my arms. "See that? I'm already getting better."

Phila snickered. Then she walked over, the ocean wind whipping through her long hair. She had to work to keep her locks out of her face. "Sailors go up to the crow's nest all the time, you know. If they're okay, I'm sure *you* will be okay."

I held up a finger. "Let's not attempt to beat fear with logic. That never works. What I need is encouragement."

"Oh. I see." Phila clapped her hands together. "Bravo, then. You almost made it halfway up. A splendid showing of bravery!"

"Now you just sound sarcastic," I muttered, narrowing my eyes.

She stopped and then shrugged. "I apologize. I'm not sure how you would conquer this fear. I don't think coddling you is the solution."

"It isn't," Deimos said through me.

After a long exhale, I turned around and faced the bow of the ship. "Listen, let's never speak of this again, all right? I'll just wait until I meet up with Sorin. He'll have all the magic I need to do this properly."

CHAPTER 9

THE LOLIAN HOUSE

It didn't take too long to reach the mainland.

We sailed along the coast until we came to a river mouth with a bustling port and active city. From there, we disembarked from *the Distant Dream*, climbed into carriages, and headed for the hill that overlooked the delta. Apparently, the Lolian family owned this whole town and port—which would explain their vast amounts of wealth.

Phila and her eldrin, Tenoch, rode in the same carriage as Twain and me. The windows of our vehicle were so clear, I sometimes forgot they were glass. Both Phila and I admired the lush green hills, sapphire river waters, and blossoming poppies.

Twain was curled up on the seat next to me, and Tenoch had curled his whole serpent body around Twain twice over. They slept peacefully, even if Tenoch's feathers occasionally bothered Twain's large ears.

"Have you ever been here before?" I asked Phila.

She shook her head. "Oh, no. But Exie has told me quite a bit about it. I'm excited to see the many mystical creatures."

"She owns mystical creatures?" I lifted an eyebrow. "How many?"

Phila shrugged. "Exie told us her aunt is an artificer. They breed their own mystical creatures, and take parts from them —not killing them, mind you. Exie stressed that part. Then they allow the creatures to conduct their Trials of Worth. Most of the Lolian family become arcanists, it seems."

When the carriage went over a patch of bumpy road, everything shook. Twain and Tenoch were jostled awake, both lifting their heads at the same time, their eyes wide.

"What's going on?" Twain leapt onto the seat cushion, his back raised, his fur on end. "*Who wants a piece of this, huh*?"

"Calm down," I said, rolling my eyes.

Tenoch flapped his parrot-like wings. "Are we there yet?"

With a giggle, Phila nodded. "We are. Look here, Tenoch. We just reached the gates."

Twain leapt to my shoulder. He moved like someone who hadn't been sleeping for the last hour, his eyes bright and alert. "Oh, I'm excited. Do you think Exie will have a banquet ready to greet us?"

"I seriously doubt she knows we're coming to visit," I muttered.

"Eh. Boo. I'm hungry."

I glanced out the window and admired the Lolian estate.

The main compound was built atop a hill, with vast fields all around it. Some of those fields had their own buildings, including a greenhouse. Around all that was a wall. The bottom half of the wall was made of white bricks, and the top half was made of black wrought iron.

The gates to the estate were a work of art. All the bars of irons were a different mystical creature, elongated and twisted, but flowing beautifully. Phoenixes, dragons, rare kinds of avians—all sorts of creatures.

Twain pressed his face against the clear glass, purring as he did so. "Do you think there's a mimic in that gate?"

"Probably," I muttered.

Two gate guards bowed at the waist and then pulled open the gates for our carriages. That surprised me. *Did* Exie know we were on our way? Or perhaps the gate guards recognized Lucian and his Source of the Storm. These were *his* carriages, after all, and he was a famous warrior from the God-Arcanist's War.

As our carriages rolled up the hill, along the inclined road toward the massive compound, I admired the compound and all three of its stories. What kind of architecture had been used to craft such a massive building? It was in a style that had tiers, with the roofs flaring out on the sides of the building to mark each floor.

"That's where they keep some of their mystical creatures," Phila said, pointing out the opposite window.

There was a path that wound around the compound, which led to a garden house constructed of fine wood and with large, arched doorways that allowed light to spill onto the smooth stone floors. I spotted several griffin cubs prancing around the outside, their golden fur sparkling in the afternoon light.

A single charberry tree grew near a silo by the side of the garden house, and several red flashes in the branches told me a pair of phoenixes lived there.

As we drew closer to the compound, my attention remained on the dwelling for the mystical creatures. Inside, I noticed different rooms outfitted for all kinds of creatures, including little snake-shaped holes and large bird cages stood on stands.

It reminded me of the Menagerie that was built into Astra Academy. But unlike the Menagerie, which was made to house mystical creatures for students to bond with, this was a personal breeding facility for House Lolian.

I was surprised.

According to Headmaster Venrover, caring for mystical creatures was extremely expensive and troublesome. They all needed their own kinds of food, and sleeping facilities, and care. Did Exie's family really have *that* kind of wealth?

Before we reached the front, we had to pass a glorious fountain, one with a bronze statue of a fairy at the center. The water was so blue—almost unnaturally so—that it reflected the bronze of the statue above, though the ripples prevented it from being a beautiful mirror.

The playful growl of griffin cubs hung on the gentle wind as we made our way to the front door. Once the carriages stopped, I leapt out with Twain in my arms. Phila waited, and I turned to offer my hand. She delicately stepped out, Tenoch slithering alongside her.

Lucian exited his carriage, his white little hummingbird asleep on his shoulder. If I hadn't been paying attention, I might not have seen it at all. The Source of the Storm was tiny.

"Did they know you were coming?" I asked.

Lucian replied with a curt nod. "I sent someone ahead as soon as we reached port."

"Are you good friends with the arcanists of the Lolian family?" Phila asked. Then she tilted her head back to get a better look at the three stories of the compound.

It was just... so much taller than normal.

I had seen normal three-story buildings, and they were impressive, but this was a compound. There had to be hundreds of rooms, and each floor was like two floors in one. Most of the levels had their own balconies.

"I wouldn't say I'm *friends* with any arcanists here," Lucian muttered as he crossed his arms. "But Heena Lolian was the arcanist who brought my eldrin to life, so I do owe them quite a debt."

I lifted both my eyebrows as I turned to face him. "Ya know, I've been meaning to ask. Where do *unique* mystical creatures come from? Huh? If they're unique, that means they're never born or created ever again. That doesn't make much sense to me."

Lucian patted his sleeping eldrin, his expression becoming distant. "When the god-creatures died at the end of the war, their pieces were gathered and used in some great innovations. Some of them were given to the Lolian family for research, and—"

Before he could finish his history lesson, the front door—which was a massive double door—flew open. Half a dozen servants stepped out, held the doors open, and then bowed.

Then Exie strode out into the sunlight.

She had the shiniest chestnut hair I had ever seen on a human being. It hung loose around her face, her skin luscious and smooth. When she fluttered her eyelashes, her green eyes practically sparkled.

"Oh, there you all are," Exie said as she walked down the front couple of stone steps. She smoothed her dark blue dress, somehow showing off that there were diamond cutouts down her sides, showing skin on her ribs and hips.

She also wore tall heels that showed off the tops of her feet.

Her eldrin, an erlking named Rex, fluttered out of the compound and then swirled around her person. He had the wings of a peacock, and whenever he moved, there was a sort of after-image that followed him, like he was trailing little illusions of himself.

Erlkings were humanoid, and Rex appeared to be a tiny man with little clothes. It was sometimes difficult to see everything about him, since he darted around the air so quickly, and everything about him was diminutive.

When her green eyes met mine, Exie stiffened. "Oh. You weren't lying, Lucian. You *did* find Gray. How... wonderful."

Lucian nodded to Exie. "Where's your aunt?"

Exie quickly regained her composure. Then she fluttered her hair and smiled. "She's inside, of course. You'll find her in the library." With a flick of her wrist, she motioned to the front room.

The front doors were just held open by the family's attendants. They made no sign of moving—they were clearly going to hold those doors until we finally went inside. That amused me, but only in a dark way. What if we just stood around outside for an hour or so? Would they be obligated to maintain their position?

Lucian huffed and then strode into the massive compound.

Phila and I exchanged glances. She coyly smiled and then shrugged. I wasn't entirely sure what she was trying to say, so I just responded in the same manner. That made her giggle.

Then I walked over to the stone steps and stopped at the one just below Exie. "Wonderful to see you, too," I darkly quipped.

She narrowed her eyes. "Oh. I see you're finally done eloping. How was it? Are you a member of the Kross family yet?"

"Actually, I was spirited away to the abyssal hells." I lifted an eyebrow. "And my wedding is in a few weeks."

Exie forced a laugh. Then she frowned. "And Nini is with you?"

She didn't even flinch when I said I had been in the abyssal hells. That was impressive in its own way.

"Nini isn't with me," I said.

Exie brightened a bit. "Then *she* ran off, like I suspected?"

"She's trapped in the abyssal hells."

Exie contemplated my statement for a prolonged moment.

Then her eldrin landed on her shoulder, and she offered him a gentle pat. "Oh. How unfortunate. Well, would you look at the time? Why don't you come inside." She smiled at Phila. "You, too, dear! Come in. Come in. We have things to discuss, obviously."

But before we went anywhere, I grabbed her wrist. Exie flashed me an icy glare, as did her eldrin.

Despite that, I held firm.

"Where's Sorin?" I asked. "I want to see him. Right now."

Exie jerked her wrist out of my grasp and then wiped it off as though I were dirty. "Your brother is having the time of his life out in the courtyard, thank you very much. He's practicing his melee techniques. Plus, I think he's already crafted a weapon or some such thing that knightmare arcanists do."

I stared deep into her eyes. Exie glowered back.

She could act like this was all innocent—that she was just helping Sorin—but I knew better.

"He's going to be delighted you're okay," Exie said matter-of-factly, almost in a bored tone.

"Thank you." I walked past her and headed into the Lolian compound. "I can't wait to see him, either."

CHAPTER 10

MY BROTHER

As I strode through the main hall of the Lolian compound, my gaze kept getting dragged up to the ceiling. Someone had painted it with gorgeous depictions of dragons. Within the dragons, inlaid in the ceiling itself, were glowstones. They were positioned as the dragon's eyes, as a halo around their head, or strategically placed as a few scales—it made the ceiling more wondrous.

A typhoon dragon was coiled and leaping through water. It reminded me of Ashlyn and Ecrib. Typhoon dragons had slightly elongated and serpentine bodies, but they were still dragons, complete with front legs and back legs.

And then I spotted something interesting.

A phoenix dragon.

I stopped walking, my eyes wide.

Twain glanced up and followed my gaze until he, too, spotted the phoenix dragon.

Then Phila bumped into me from behind. I stumbled forward and glanced over my shoulder.

"I do apologize," Phila said, placing a hand on her cheek. "I was distracted."

"Me, too," I muttered.

Exie walked over, fluffing her hair. "What's the matter here? The courtyard is all the way down this hall."

Her erlking fluttered around her head, tsking at us and our delay.

I pointed to the phoenix dragon on the ceiling. "Who painted this? Is that Xuandi?"

"Who?" Exie balked.

I glanced back up at the painting. The red and yellow scales were nearly identical to Xuandi's. The wings, a mix of leathery bat and feathered bird, were forever etched into my memories. This painting was of a normal phoenix dragon, though. Xuandi was twisted, with actual human souls grafted to his neck like a mane.

"That's a phoenix dragon," Rex said. He fluttered his erlking wings. "They're extinct."

"I saw one in the abyssal hells," I muttered.

Rex snorted.

"You were *really* in the abyssal hells?" Exie narrowed her eyes. "I thought you were exaggerating. Or maybe using a euphemism."

"What *euphemism* would I be using?" I snapped.

Twain growled while in my arms, his orange fur puffed. "We were definitely in the abyssal hells. The actual, literal hells, mind you. The kind with souls and messed-up plants and *hands* just growing out of the ground."

Phila's eyebrows lifted.

Exie, on the other hand, just crossed her arms over her chest. She had a way of posing herself whenever she thought on a subject for a prolonged period of time, and she did that now—leaning her hip out to the side and tilting her head in the opposite direction.

She clearly didn't believe me.

"And you saw a phoenix dragon?" Phila asked.

I nodded.

Her eldrin, Tenoch, slithered around her feet. "My," he muttered, "that must've been quite the adventure. Was the dragon friendly?"

"Not at all." I turned on my heel, gave the ceiling one final glance, and then continued down the hall.

Where was my brother when I needed him most? I wanted a comforting presence—and someone who would believe me, no matter how outlandish my claims seemed. Sorin would understand. He always did.

I hurried my way down the hall, practically jogging. I glanced over my shoulder, motioning for them to join me.

"Excuse you," Exie called out, but she didn't hurry her steps.

Phila, on the other hand, quickened her pace. Her coatl eldrin slithered alongside her, his concertina movements rapid. When Phila and I became too quick, Tenoch flapped his wings and took to the air.

The hallway was wide and spacious—a coatl of his size could easily glide through it without hitting anything. He soared over me, and headed for the door.

"No fair," Twain shouted.

He leapt out of my arms, rolling forward as he went, his body shifting and bubbling. Scales exploded from his orange fur, wings sprouted from his back—before Twain ever touched the floor, he was a coatl identical to Tenoch.

My forehead burned as my arcanist mark changed. Instead of a seven-pointed star that was empty, I now had a seven-pointed star with a winged snake wrapped throughout.

Twain flapped his newly formed wings and took off after Tenoch. The coatl laughed and stuck out his serpent tongue.

"Foolish mimic," Tenoch shouted. "I'm a master at flight! You're just an amateur."

"We'll see about that!" Twain flapped his wings as hard as he could, gaining on Tenoch.

They both laughed, and I charged ahead into a full run. Phila's giggles filled the hallway as she, too, decided to run. Exie and her erlking were left behind. I assumed running was a bit impossible in her outfit—or perhaps she didn't want to get herself sweaty.

While running, the compound didn't seem *too* large.

Tenoch and Twain reached the massive double doors to the courtyard in under a minute, and they both slammed their way outside before the door attendants could open it for them. With a loud *bang*, they took off into the sky outside, both struggling to get ahead of the other.

I slowed my pace, gave the door attendants an apologetic shrug, and then continued outside.

Phila waved to them and continued after me, smiling the whole way.

Once the sun washed over me, I held an arm up to shield my eyes. The courtyard was magnificent. One half of it was dedicated to a garden—or maybe I should've called it an *orchard*. There were all kinds of fruit trees, including another charberry tree, which were quite rare.

The other half was a raised stone platform. There were fountains and furniture, and even large umbrellas to keep the sun at bay. Most of that was pushed to the side, however, creating a makeshift arena.

Two individuals were sparring—my brother, and Professor Jijo, the combat arts instructor from Astra Academy. They were practicing with wooden spears, with Jijo pointing to my brother's footing and clearly giving instruction.

"*Sorin?*" I yelled.

My brother stopped mid-swing and whirled around on his heel.

He was larger than me in almost every way. He had more

muscle, he was taller—his shoulders were broader—but his eyes were the same gray-blue as mine, and they lit up the moment he spotted me.

"*Gray?*"

Sorin threw down his practice weapon and then lunged forward. To a normal person, it would've looked like he was diving face-first into the stone platform, attempting to break his nose, but I knew he wasn't in danger.

Sure enough, Sorin *disappeared* into his own shadow, plunging into the depths of the darkness like only a knightmare arcanist could. The shadow darted across the platform, down the side, and then across the grass of the courtyard.

The puddle of darkness made it all the way to my side before Sorin *leapt* out of its inky depths. Honestly, it caught me by surprise. My brother was so much larger than me that I almost toppled over. He slammed his arms around me in a tight embrace, and I returned the favor.

"Gray!" he shouted again.

"Sor—*erk*!" All the air in my lungs was crushed out of me by his ever-tightening hug.

"I'm so glad you're back. *I was worried*. I could barely sleep. Why wouldn't you tell me where you were going?" Sorin somehow held me tighter. It was getting impossible to take in breath. "Where have you been? Tell me everything."

I squirmed out of his embrace and pushed him away, keeping him at arm's length. "Sorin—calm down. I'm here now."

He ran a hand over his sweaty forehead, clearing it away. His black hair was slicked back, and his chin covered with stubble. Sorin even appeared older than me now, which was both impressive and irritating.

But I pushed that thought away.

This was a time for celebrating! I had missed Sorin more than any other person.

"Sorin, I'm sorry," I said.

He grabbed my shoulders. "Don't be. We're together again. There's no need to apologize."

"Well..." I cringed as I thought of everything that had happened. "Listen, I was transported to the abyssal hells by Death Lord Naiad. She tried to kill me, and Death Lord Deimos, but we teamed up to defeat her. And then Deimos helped me find a way out of the hells."

"Where is Ashlyn? And Knovak? And Nini?" Sorin didn't let go of my shoulders. "They went with you, didn't they?"

I slowly nodded. "Yes. They did."

"And?" Sorin smiled, but his voice quavered. "Are they here, too?"

Twain and Tenoch circled over the courtyard, now engrossed in their own personal race. They darted through the air, flapping their wings, doing laps around the orchard portion. Phila cheered them on, but kept glancing over at Sorin and me, her expression fretful.

Even she knew this wasn't going to end well.

Thankfully, Professor Jijo stayed out of this. He cleaned up the practice equipment and stayed on the other side of the stone platform, admiring one of the fountains.

"Ashlyn and Knovak made it back with me," I said. "Uh, Nini... She wasn't as lucky."

My brother didn't reply. He stared into my eyes, and it was like gazing into a mirror. Even though I had been mentally preparing myself for this moment, I still didn't know what to say.

"She died?" Sorin finally whispered.

"N-No," I quickly stammered. "She didn't die. Nini is alive. She's just lost. In the abyssal hells."

"All alone?" The pain in Sorin's voice hurt.

All I could do was force myself to nod.

Sorin swallowed hard, and then he stepped away from me. We were only a foot apart, but it felt like a chasm was between us.

"You left her there?" Sorin never glanced away from me. His eyes drilled into me.

"It wasn't *intentional*," was all I managed to say.

We *were* supposed to escape together, but that was when Death Lord Kallikore and Xuandi attacked us. Deimos and Nini went to stop them, to buy us all time, and the rest of us escaped.

"Nini is the only reason I'm here now," I said. "She was beyond brave. Her and her eldrin, Waste—they stood down monsters in the abyssal hells that would cause most men to crumple."

Sorin shook his head. He took another step away. "But why did you leave? If she was fighting a monster, you should've stayed. You should've helped her."

"I—"

I didn't know how to answer that. In reality, Ashlyn and Knovak *needed* to leave the abyssal hells, because if they didn't, they would've eventually perished. But Nini and I had ways to prevent that. As a reaper arcanist, Nini was immune to the death effects of the hells. And because I had a fragment of Deimos with me, I was also immune.

I *could've* stayed.

But then I wouldn't be here. And it was important I warn everyone about the condition of the abyssal hells—and the plans of the other Death Lords.

I had to leave.

But I struggled to convey that to my brother. I already knew what he would say.

Sorin was a noble soul. He did what was right in the moment, no matter what. The long-term needs weren't as important as the immediate in his mind. He would've stayed behind with Nini. He never would've left her side until everyone could escape.

My brother's expression hardened into something pained and angry. He quickly ran his hand through his sweat-soaked hair. With his gaze on the ground between us, he asked, "So what happened after that? How did you make it back?"

I stumbled through a quick explanation of how Zahn had pulled us out of the abyssal hells, the cult that worshipped me, and then Raaza.

"That's everything." I shrugged once I finished my explanation. "Headmaster Venrover sent a man to bring us home. We ended up fighting him, which was awkward, but then he brought us here. Together, we're going to head back to Astra Academy so we can regroup and figure out a way to get back to the abyssal hells."

Sorin didn't reply.

After a few moments of silence, Exie finally joined us in the courtyard. She came striding out of the double doors, her dress immaculate, her hair flowing. She wasn't winded or sweaty—Exie just allowed the sun to wash over her, bathing her in a sparkle.

When she spotted Sorin and me, she immediately headed in our direction.

I wished she'd give us some privacy, but I was hardly in the mood to argue with her.

Exie stopped nearest to Sorin. She glanced between us, before fully turning her attention to my brother. "Gray told you everything?"

My brother nodded and then sighed.

"I told you not to worry about him," Exie said as she placed a comforting hand on Sorin's shoulder. "And I'm certain, once we're finished with the wedding, that we'll get straight to finding Nini."

"Wedding?" Sorin snapped his attention to Exie. "What wedding?"

"Why, Gray's of course." Exie turned to me. "Isn't that what you said at the front door? You're going to marry Ashlyn?"

My brother faced me with an incredulous expression. "When?" he demanded.

"Soon," I muttered. "I wanted to do it before—"

"Nini is *lost* in the abyssal hells, and you want to do something like *have a wedding?*" Sorin huffed an angry laugh. Then he stomped a few paces away from me, the most enraged I had seen him in years. "Do you even *care*, Gray? You left her there, and now you want to hold celebrations and go back to the Academy? *Really?*"

"Sorin, listen—I can explain."

He threw up a hand, dismissively waving me away. "*Don't*, Gray. I've heard enough."

Then Sorin dove into the shadows and darted away.

CHAPTER 11

WOLDRÄM, VOICE OF THE DEPARTED

Twain flew back to me, still in the form of a beautiful coatl. The moment he reached my shoulder, he bubbled and shifted, until his scales and feathers became bright orange fur. As a young cat, he clung to me, purring as he did so, his large lynx-like ears twitching.

"Is, uh, Sorin coming back?" he asked.

I just stood there, staring at the shadows where Sorin had vanished. "I don't think so."

Exie crossed her arms and lifted an eyebrow. "You didn't tell your brother about your marriage?"

"There were a lot of other *important* things to discuss first," I snapped.

"Hmpf. It would've been the first thing that passed my lips if I was talking to one of my siblings. How is getting married not important?"

I rolled my eyes. "It's important, just not as important as all the problems in the abyssal hells, Exie!"

My words—loud, due to my anger—carried across the courtyard. Professor Jijo tensed and half glanced over to us, but he didn't approach. Phila, on the other hand, hurried over immediately, her brow furrowed.

"I think you two should take a deep breath," she said as she hurried over. Once close to us, Phila forced a smile. "Please. Remember that you're friends. We need to work together if we're going to handle all the problems we're facing."

I dismissively waved my hand. "I'm going to find Sorin. We need to talk. *In private.* I'd appreciate it if you two gave us some space."

Phila and Exie exchanged quick glances. I didn't know what they were silently signaling to each other, and I didn't care. I stomped toward the door and then slammed my way inside. The door attendants flinched back, clearly not expecting my sudden departure from all the activities outside.

"Did a shadow come this way?" I asked, my voice closer to a shout.

One of the attendants nodded. Then he pointed down one of the side hallways. I said nothing else as I made my way in the direction he indicated.

A part of me was angry. Why was Sorin so upset with me? I saved Ashlyn and Knovak, didn't I? Nini was the one who willingly put herself in danger. I wasn't her keeper! Why did I have to help her?

But...

I stopped walking and stood in the middle of the hallway.

Sorin didn't deserve my anger. He was just upset—Nini meant the world to him, and now she was in peril.

And there was nothing he could do. It was probably beyond frustrating. Additionally, from his viewpoint, I wasn't doing anything to help. I was just celebrating all my good fortunes. Of course he was upset.

Of course.

"Gray?" Twain asked, tilting his head.

"Maybe I should give Sorin some time," I whispered.

"You should apologize," Deimos said through me.

In blind anger, I just punched the wall—and instantly regretted it. A lance of pain shot from my knuckles all the way up to my elbow. I sucked in air through my teeth and then leaned against the wall while cradling my injured hand.

"I did apologize," I eventually muttered.

Deimos's derision flooded my mind. "It was a pathetic apology at best. If you mean to make things right between you and your brother, you need to sacrifice."

"Why? I didn't do anything wrong."

It was odd sharing a piece of Deimos, because the moment I spoke those words, I felt anger, and then his determination to restrain that kind of emotion, almost like he was a father trying to speak to a child without injecting too much emotion.

"An apology isn't about admitting right or wrong—it's about admitting that your relationship is more important than your ego."

"Is it, though?" I quipped.

Deimos's pensive attitude also seeped into me. "My brother and I had many arguments, but once I knew I valued him over all others, I realized that compassion, forgiveness, and apologies were all tools used to break walls and build bridges."

Twain's eyes widened. "Wow. That was surprisingly *nice* from the Death Lord who once suggested we kill people to make a good impression. Are you sure you're okay, Deimos?"

"I will do a great many things to further my goals," Deimos drawled, "but I will never betray or harm Zahn."

Sorin was my brother—the only one who had had my back my whole life. He was weird, but he was often right. And he always meant well. Sorin would never do anything to upset me, at least not intentionally. Could he say the same about me?

I wasn't so sure.

I stared down at my hand. The pain was already gone, but I flexed my fingers just to make sure.

The darkness in the hallway thickened. I stood a little straighter, my throat tight with raw emotion. When the shadows coalesced in front of me, and formed into a suit of plate armor, I just remained silent.

Sorin and his knightmare, Thurin, were merged into a single entity. The armor was inky and majestic, even if parts of it were missing, a plate over the leg, and one over the arm—it was almost a full suit of armor, and once Thurin was old enough, it would be. But now, he had a cape that looked like it was made from a hundred crow feathers, and a helmet that covered my brother's head.

"Gray," my brother and his eldrin said as one.

But I felt so ashamed, that I didn't know what to say.

Thurin and Sorin unmerged. The suit of armor seemingly melted off my brother's body, becoming a pool of darkness at his feet.

"I gave it some thought," Sorin said. He took a deep breath, his expression devoid of all anger. "I'm sorry for leaving you in the courtyard. It's been really rough since I lost you both, and I don't want to lose you again."

My sight grew foggy with tears.

Sorin...

Deimos was right. Apologizing was just a way of saying that the relationship was more important than ego—and even though *I* had messed up, Sorin was still here, by my side, no matter what.

He was always sure and true.

I stepped forward and wrapped my arms around him just as tightly as he had hugged me in the courtyard. It was obviously a surprise, because his eyes widened as it happened. Sorin returned the embrace just as fully, though, no hesitation.

Twain, who couldn't balance on my shoulder while I was being crushed by my brother, leapt off and landed on the floor without a sound. A dark shadow flitted around him, seemingly saying *hello*.

"I'm so sorry," I said into my brother's chest, even though he was squeezing most of the air out of me.

Sorin loosened his grip, but he still held me in a hug. "I'm glad you're back, Gray."

"If you want, I'll call off the wedding. We'll wait until Nini is back."

"I don't want that," Sorin whispered. "You two should be happy. The world has too much suffering in it already—I don't need to spread mine around to others."

I tightened my grip on Sorin's shirt. He was too nice sometimes. Too forgiving.

After ending our hug, and taking a deep breath to clear away the worst of my raw emotions, I asked, "What can I do to make things right between us?"

Sorin gave it thought for only a moment. Then he said, "You need to promise me that saving Nini will be your top priority. That when we somehow find a way into the abyssal hells, we'll save her *first*."

I nodded. "I promise."

"Really? You mean it, Gray?" His words were hopeful and genuine.

I nodded again. "Definitely. I'll make sure we find her. Above all other things."

Sorin smiled, though it was fleeting. When it seemed that he might slip into depression, he brightened and took a step back. "Oh, Gray—I meant to show you something. I've been working with Professor Jijo, and this morning, I made a weapon out of shadows."

"You did?" I asked.

"You did?" Twain also asked, nearly at the same time.

"He made a fabulous weapon," Thurin said from the depths of the darkness, his voice regal and gruff.

Sorin held his hand out to his side. "Watch. I can summon it to me, and both Thurin and I can fight with it."

The shadows under him darkened. Then a weapon shot upward until it flew into the palm of his hand.

It wasn't a sword or an axe—it was a trident.

Well, it was an odd trident. The middle tine was longer and more intimidating than the other two, but it was still impressive overall. This was a black trident, made of hardened darkness, the points sharp, the shaft as long as Sorin was tall.

"Sorin," I whispered. "You... picked a trident?"

"To match your weapon," Sorin happily replied. "I couldn't decide which weapon I wanted to master, and I kept thinking about you, because you were missing, so I thought this was fitting. It matches yours, right?"

I reached under my shirt and grabbed Vivigöl. The moment my fingers grazed the golden abyssal coral the weapon was made out of, it *click-click-clicked* as it transformed. It had been jewelry around my shoulders, but in a matter of seconds, it transformed into a mighty trident.

This was the weapon Deimos used when atop his dragon eldrin.

It was different from Sorin's, with each tine the same length, but it was damn close.

Sorin held up his weapon to compare it to mine.

"Twins," he playfully said.

I held Vivigöl straight up. "Yeah," I whispered.

"Let's make a promise never to fight again, all right, Gray? We're going to save Nini, and do whatever we need to do in the abyssal hells—together."

This all seemed so formal now that we were holding our tridents aloft. It reminded me of old knights in fairy tales, or how kings and queens would declare arcanists heroes.

"We'll do it together," I said, feeling it from deep inside my chest.

Sorin nodded, his smile genuine, his unhappiness dispelled.

"*Tied by blood, a bond profound,*" Sorin said, his love of dramatic poetry on full display. "*Their souls entwined, forever bound. In battles fought and battles won, they faced the darkness, two as one. No foe too strong, no night too black, with steadfast hearts, they never lack.*"

He was going to end his poem there, but that didn't seem right.

So I continued. "*For when one stumbled, the other stood— their brotherhood, a fortress of good.*"

Obviously, that was the worst of all rhymes, and childishly simplistic, but I wasn't an expert. I just wanted to show my support, like I hadn't before.

The corner of Sorin's lip twitched, as though he was so happy he might cry. When he dropped his trident, it fell into the shadows instead of clattering to the floor. Then he hugged me again, and I had to be careful so that he didn't touch Vivigöl.

"Gray, that was beautiful," he muttered.

I patted his back. "Okay, okay. That's enough."

Sorin released me. Then he rubbed his eyes, still smiling. "All right, well, now comes the hard part. What should I name my weapon? I mean, yours has an amazing name! I can't *not* have a name for mine."

"Well, I didn't name mine." I brought the trident to my neck and it *click-click-clicked* back into place. "Deimos called it Vivigöl, Silencer of the Damned."

"Could Deimos name mine, then?"

"You should call yours *Woldräm, Voice of the Departed*," Deimos said through me. "It's the name of a creature who once dwelled in the abyssal hells. It was the brother of the creature who I named my weapon after."

Sorin lifted both his eyebrows. "Wow."

"You hate it?" Twain asked.

"No. I love it." Sorin summoned his weapon back into his hand. "Woldräm, Voice of the Departed! No name has ever been more fitting. And soon, I'll use it to cut a route straight to Nini."

CHAPTER 12

FEAR TRAINING

Sorin and I stood together in comfortable silence for just a moment. I could've stayed there longer, just content to be reunited, but Twain cleared his throat.

"Are you two done waxing poetic at one another?" He tilted his feline head. "I get it. Hurray. Woo." Twain finished by rolling his eyes.

I chuckled as I knelt and picked him up. Then I rubbed his head, tussling his orange fur. "Aw, is someone *jealous*? Is that it? You want to find your little mimic twin?"

All of Twain's fur stood on end. "I'm not jealous!"

"I think you are. Look at your little face." I poked his whiskers.

Twain hissed with the anger of a hundred cats facing down a dog they hated. "I'm not jealous!" He scratched my arm, and I laughed as I quickly set him down on the floor. Red droplets of blood welled over my tiny injury, and then slid down my arm.

"Gray?" Sorin stepped close to me. "What do you mean *twin*? Does Twain have a twin?" He kept his black trident in one hand, holding it as though it didn't weigh much.

"The Mother of Shapeshifters said he was born with another kitten," I replied. "So, he's kind of a twin."

"I'm a real twin," Twain interjected.

Sorin frowned, his expression one of concern. "So there's a missing mimic? Are you okay, Gray?"

Twain "stomped" his little padded paw. "*I'm* the one being tormented here! You should ask about how badly *my* feelings are hurt."

I stood straight and rubbed the scratches on my arm, always amazed to watch my own flesh knit itself back together. One moment the wound had been bleeding, and the next it was a scab, almost gone.

"Don't worry, Twain," I said. "Once this stuff with the abyssal hells is over, we'll find your twin. It'll be fun. We'll search the world over, seeking out other mimic arcanists until we finally find the right one."

Twain's large lynx-like ears stood straight up. With wide eyes, he whispered, "Really?"

"That's right. We can't leave you out of all our *twin power*." I spoke the last words as playfully as possible because I knew, without a doubt, Twain had been sad watching Sorin and I. He *had* felt jealous.

Twain purred a bit as he said, "Thank you."

"I'd do anything for my favorite eldrin."

"I'm your *only* eldrin!" He pouted again, frowning at me with intensity.

It just made me chuckle.

But things didn't keep me happy for very long lately. My thoughts immediately returned to the situation at hand. I had wanted to find Sorin because he was, specifically, a knightmare arcanist. He could evoke terrors—he could make me live through my worst fears. What better way to achieve a true form with my mimic than grappling with my fears nonstop until I overcame them?

I turned to my brother.

He tensed, as though he sensed an incoming request. "Gray?"

"Sorin, we should go back to the courtyard," I said. "I was hoping you would help me with something." I leaned in close. "And I'd like it if you kept quiet about it."

Sorin blinked. Then he leaned in even closer, until we were almost touching. "Are you going to do something illegal?"

"*What?*" I balked. "No. I want you to use your terrors on me. *But I don't want you to tell anyone what my terrors are,* okay? I mean, it's one thing to be afraid of heights—people get that—but I have a feeling whatever your magic summons is going to be ten times worse, and I don't want anyone to know. Okay?"

Sorin lifted an eyebrow. "Why would you... want me to do that? If Twain turns into a knightmare, *you'll* become immune to terrors, so you don't have to learn how to fight through them."

"My true form," I whispered. "Remember? I told you this. I have to defeat fear. It's insane, I know, but I didn't make the rules."

"And I'll help," Twain proudly proclaimed. He sat on my shoes, staring up at us both, in a much happier mood than before.

"Oh, okay." Sorin grabbed my upper arm and tugged me toward the door to the courtyard. "Professor Jijo is still here, Gray! I bet he could help us."

"We don't need him," Deimos said through me.

Sorin shook his head as he practically dragged me down the hall. "Nonsense. He's really wise and knows a bunch of things. I'm certain he could help."

"He was extremely instrumental in helping Sorin craft his weapon," Thurin muttered from the depths of the darkness.

I just sighed. While I didn't mind Jijo, Deimos was

extremely distrusting of the man. Apparently, Jijo was related to some long-dead group of people that Deimos used to fight? Or something. I didn't fully remember, because Deimos was thousands of years old, and this happened so long ago that every nation Deimos knew no longer existed.

All that meant was that it had nothing to do with me, really.

Sorin brought me to the double doors, and the attendants opened them for us. They smiled and bowed, but I sensed their irritation with the fact several people had slammed in and out of them multiple times already.

Once outside, I spotted Phila and Exie speaking to Professor Jijo.

They were up on the raised stone platform—I supposed it was just a fancy deck or sunning area. I was thankful no one had put the furniture or umbrellas back in place, because it meant we could train.

Sorin brought me to the platform. He stepped up to it and then yanked me upward. Once we were with the others, all conversations ceased.

"Ah," Professor Jijo said. "Arcanist Hon has informed me that you were in the abyssal hells. I'm... shocked. But, since I have no way to disprove your statements, I'll just have to assume you're correct."

Professor Jijo always had the straightest posture. He was confident, even if he wasn't that tall, perhaps a few inches under six feet. He wore a tight shirt and loose pants, as usual, and it complemented his well-balanced, lean-muscle physique.

"Still not wearing any shoes," I muttered as my eyes fell to his feet. "Do you always train like that?"

"I do," Jijo replied matter-of-factly. "The most skilled combatants know how important *balance* is when fighting. By walking around barefoot, I'm improving my natural balance. You would improve yourself if you did the same."

"I'm not doing that," I stated.

Twain lifted a paw and showed me his little toe beans. "I have natural padding. Flesh shoes, if you will."

Exie sneered in disgust at the mere mention of *flesh shoes*. "What is wrong with you?" she silently mouthed at my eldrin.

Professor Jijo ran a hand over his perfectly bald head. His arcanist mark was the most prominent one I had ever seen, really. It was as clear as day—a seven-pointed star with a serpentine dragon and a whole bank of clouds woven through the points.

His eldrin, a nimbus dragon by the name of *Cirrus*, was perched on the roof of Exie's massive compound home. He was small—all nimbus dragons were—but he was rather distinct.

Cirrus was a creature who had six short legs with bird-like talons, a mane of wispy clouds, and sky-blue scales that shimmered whenever he moved. Although he had no wings, Cirrus could fly as effortlessly as the breeze.

"Professor," Sorin said. "Please stand back. Me and my brother are going to practice our magic."

Jijo lifted an eyebrow. "Stand back?"

"I don't want to affect you when I evoke my terrors."

"Hah!" Jijo waggled a finger and offered a disapproving frown. "A knightmare arcanist can *shape* his terrors—like a mist, or an invisible cloud—so that he may affect only his enemies, even when fighting in close quarters with allies."

Sorin nervously chuckled. "Yes. Well. I haven't been able to do that. Yet."

"Then this is the perfect opportunity to practice. Why don't we have your brother stand here." Jijo pointed to a place in the middle of the open stone platform. "And I will stand on his left, while Arcanist Hon will stand on his right."

Phila pointed to herself. "Me, professor? You want *me* to help?"

"Yes." He waved to her. "You have a... trembly demeanor. That isn't becoming."

"Trembly?" she whispered.

"You need more confidence."

Exie crossed her arms and huffed. "What about me?"

"You have enough confidence." Jijo rubbed his chin. "Perhaps *too much* confidence."

It seemed as though Exie were about to launch into a tirade over this comment, but my brother adeptly slid over and placed a confident hand on Exie's shoulder. She silenced herself, glanced at his touch, and then back up to him.

"You've been such an amazing friend to me," Sorin said. "You let me come here to clear my head, when I was worried about my brother and Nini—and I would never do anything to cause you distress. I think it would be best if you *did* take a seat. Perhaps on the plush chair?"

Exie smoothed her beautiful hair. "Well, I suppose, when you put it like that."

"Thank you."

With rosy cheeks, Exie flounced over to the nearest sunning chair and took a seat. Her erlking, who had been flying around with Phila's coatl, immediately flew over and sat next to her. The little fairy king looked like a doll more than a mystical creature, but I wasn't about to risk Exie's anger by mentioning *that* to her face.

I moved over to the spot Jijo had indicated. Phila stood on one side of me, and then Jijo stood on the other. Deimos's irritation with the man's presence spread into my own thoughts. I didn't... like him being close.

Twain hopped over to Sorin's side, observing from a safe distance.

"Now, Arcanist Lexly," Jijo said, "you want to focus your evocation on *only* your brother. If you manage to visualize this properly, you will avoid affecting me or your classmate."

Sorin nodded along with the professor's words. "Right."

"Don't overthink this, though."

"Uh, okay. I'll try."

I cracked my knuckles and attempted to steel myself to the eventual blast of terror. While I wanted my brother to learn to improve his magic, it was *more* important that I learn how to defeat my fears. I needed to focus. Whatever happened, I needed to overcome.

Jijo rolled his hand. "Anytime now."

After a deep breath, Sorin held up one hand. He hardened his gaze, stared straight at me, and then...

I felt it.

His evocation wasn't really visible—it was a mental attack that formed visions in my mind, creating hallucinations.

And, oh boy, did I get some crazy hallucinations.

I stumbled backward, my vision changing until all I saw was the edge of a cliff. I was going to fall, but also, so was Sorin, and my father, and my stepmother. Twain was there—he was already falling—and they were all screaming.

My heart slammed in my chest. I wanted to save them, but I wasn't fast enough, not strong enough.

At first, I thought they were shouting for help, but it was *screaming*, as though the fear of falling had robbed them of the ability to speak.

But this cliff wasn't a normal cliff. It was in the abyssal hells. My hallucinations shifted—I kept stepping backward, trying to escape them, but the bizarre hellscape was warping. There was mist around, so I couldn't see where I was stepping, and an overwhelming sense of dread gripped my heart.

"Stop!" I shouted. "*Stop!*"

The beating of wings. The smell of blood. In the mist, I swore I saw Zahn. He was lying on the ground, dead, and for some reason, that made me feel worse. Sweat soaked my clothes, and I pulled at the collar of my shirt, trying to gulp down air, even though I was perfectly capable of breathing.

Finally, the hallucinations ended.

I was sitting on the stone platform—or maybe I had fallen backward—and my heart refused to calm itself. It beat upward, into my throat, making it even harder for me to breathe.

Over the course of my life, I had experienced thousands of weird dreams and nightmares, and whatever I had just witnessed was like combining all of them. It had been a surreal experience.

"Gray?" My brother dashed over and then knelt next to me. "Are you okay? You're so... pale. And sweaty."

I ran a hand through my hair. It was wet. Weird.

"I think... I'm also experiencing Deimos's fears," I whispered.

I was afraid of the abyssal hells, but the misty area I had briefly witnessed wasn't like the area I had been to—the first abyss. I didn't know where that was. And why would I care if Zahn died? For some reason, that made me both angry *and* frightened.

"But you're okay?" Sorin asked again. He rubbed my shoulder. "You were screaming... I mean, people get afraid, but they don't normally yell as loudly as you did."

I patted my throat. It did feel a little raw. "I'm okay."

Professor Jijo strode over. He, too, had sweat across most of his exposed skin, but he held himself with more regal confidence than I had at the moment. "You reacted rather *poorly* to your brother's evocation."

"Wow, thanks," I sarcastically said. "What a pep talk."

"It's an observation, not a word of wisdom."

I pushed myself to my feet. My knees wobbled, and I laughed at how shaken I was. What was that? The terrors hadn't even been that coherent. I mean, I understood that I didn't want anyone I knew to die, but...

"Let's go again," I said.

Sorin raised both his eyebrows. "Uh... Are you certain, Gray? Maybe you should get some water."

I shook my head. "No. I don't have time. I need to master this. I have to defeat my fears. All of them, apparently— because some new ones snuck into my head when I wasn't paying attention."

My brother chuckled at that joke. Then he nodded. "Well, I need to practice as well. I managed to miss Phila, but I hit the professor, so..."

I glanced over. Phila stood in the same spot as before, smiling wide. "I knew you could do it, Sorin." She gave him a thumbs up. "I'll be rooting for you." Then she glanced over at me. "And you, too, Gray. Know that your friends are here, and we care about you. Maybe that's how you defeat your fears?"

"I seriously doubt it," I whispered.

I needed to focus. Whatever weird visions I had, there had to be a way to overcome them... Perhaps I could learn to do it before we even made it back to the Academy.

CHAPTER 13

SOUL CATCHER HUNTING

The good news was: I understood what I was afraid of.
The bad news was: I didn't understand how to defeat any of them.

For *two hours* my brother evoked his terrors. Phila and Professor Jijo helped for the first hour, but then after that, they took a break because Lucian wanted to speak with them. Apparently, after his talk with Exie's family, he had more business to wrap up before we could leave.

Which left me and Sorin alone in the courtyard. Twain and Thurin watched on the sidelines as I lay on my back, staring at the radiant sky above.

My brother stood over me, his hands on his knees, bracing his upper body with posted arms.

"Do you want to take a break?" Sorin asked.

I slowly blinked my eyes. Most of my face was sore. "No."

"You don't look so well, Gray."

"I'm fine. It's more important that I handle this."

My brother offered his hand. I took it, and he effortlessly pulled me to my feet. After wobbling for a moment, I rubbed my temples. "Okay. So far, whenever you evoke terrors, I seem to be the *most* afraid of losing people and falling—things outside of my control. But also, I sometimes see centipedes, corpses, the abyssal hells, and a weird flamingo I once dreamt about when I was a kid."

Sorin nodded along with my words. "All reasonable fears."

"And then sometimes I see Deimos's fears, which all seem to be centered around *losing*, or *failing*, especially his brother, Zahn. And while those aren't necessarily scary to me, my body still reacts like I'm frightened, so I guess we're going to add those to the ever-growing list."

Sorin lifted both his eyebrows. "Okay. What're we going to do with this list?" He tilted his head to the side.

"Well, I had been hoping that I would only have *one* fear, and it would be easy to deal with, but obviously I have a whole boat's worth, and if I'm going to get through them all, I might as well start a damn list." I was trying not to be sarcastic, but I failed wildly.

"Everyone has lots of fears, Gray. Some minor, some crippling. You can't expect to never be afraid."

I rubbed my hands together, my gaze distant. "No one ever expected us to go to the abyssal hells, either. But I did. So... I have to keep doing the impossible, Sorin."

When I was honest with myself, I knew that being an arcanist was one of the few things I was proud of. Well, I was proud of a lot of things, but some of them weren't all *my* accomplishments. Deimos sometimes helped me in a fight, Sorin had always been there for me as a brother. Professor Helmith had saved me from certain death when I was younger...

But Twain...

I glanced over to my eldrin. He must've known I was thinking about him, because Twain perked up and smiled. His mismatched eyes sparkled in the afternoon light.

I had bonded with Twain, and become a mimic arcanist,

all on my own. It was one of the few things in my life I had been in *full* control over.

"Maybe my fear of being out of control stems from the fact that I was plagued by nightmares for a good portion of my life," I whispered.

Professor Helmith had been there to prevent my death, but I could still feel the intensity of my terror when I thought back to those dreams with the soul catcher creatures. Nothing had been more terrifying.

My brother's eyes widened. Then he pointed at me. "I think you're right, Gray. That makes sense. After years of being afraid of sleep, it probably had an impact on you." Sorin snapped his fingers. "Wait—what if you did something about that?"

"What do you mean?" I asked.

"What if you, uh, defeated the soul catcher arcanist and her eldrin? The people who tormented you for so long? Do you think you would unlock something in your soul? Something that would allow you to stop being so afraid?"

I hadn't thought of that.

A smile crept across my face. "Sorin, you're a genius." I patted his shoulder and laughed. "That's a *great* idea, actually. And I think I know where she is."

That woman had worked for Zahn—and I knew where Zahn was hiding! If I could get to this soul catcher arcanist, confront her, and defeat her, perhaps I *would* overcome some long-dormant strength.

It was at least a concrete plan. That was better than what I had two seconds ago.

Twain trotted over, his head held high. "I heard everything." He leapt up with such feline grace that he made it to my shoulder in a single bound. "And I completely approve! Let's go get this chump!"

I scratched his head and chuckled. "You're the best eldrin ever."

Sorin's stomach grumbled so loudly, a flock of birds took off from the roof and shot into the sky. He nervously laughed as he patted his belly. "We've been going at this for a long while, Gray. Why don't we step inside for some food? Exie's family has three chefs on staff, and they make *amazing* food."

After a pained sigh, I rolled my eyes. "All right. We eat here, and then we convince Lucian to leave."

I wasn't a fan of Exie's home. We needed to get out of here as soon as possible.

As I stepped into the grand dining room, I couldn't help but marvel at the sheer scale of it all.

The room was larger than most people's homes, with ceilings high enough to make a sovereign dragon feel comfortable. The chandeliers were so opulent and diamond-crusted, they had probably once belonged in a palace.

The walls were adorned with portraits of stern-looking ancestors, all of whom seemed to be judging my choice of attire. Fabulous.

The long, polished mahogany table could easily seat twenty, though today it was set for a modest six. Plates gleamed with the kind of sparkle that said, "You can't afford to replace me if you break me," and the silverware looked heavy enough to double as workout equipment.

Twain craned his head as he took in the whole room.

"Do you think I can jump up to one of those chandeliers?" he whispered in my ear.

"I would love it if you did, but you probably shouldn't."

My brother smacked me on the shoulder and guided me

around the table. "I love this spot right here. You can see out the window." He placed me in a beautifully carved chair.

I stared out the massive window and pretended to admire the scenery.

"Exie really helped me when I thought I had lost you and Nini," Sorin whispered as he took a seat next to me. "I was just... so upset. And Exie was there to remind me that things have a way of working out. Storms bring destruction, but they also bring water."

"Sorin, I think—"

But I didn't get to finish my tirade. The door to the gargantuan dining room opened, and in strode Exie and Phila. They were chatting merrily all the way over to their seats across from Sorin and me.

Exie sat directly across from my brother, her eyes all aflutter. Her eldrin, Rex, flew upward and landed on one of the chandeliers, obviously making Twain extremely jealous.

Phila gracefully took a seat opposite me. Her eldrin, Tenoch, pulled out her chair and then tucked it in for her.

"Are you comfortable, my arcanist?" Tenoch asked.

She nodded and smiled. "Very. Thank you."

Then, before any more conversation could be had, in came the chefs—a small army of them. They paraded in with the first course like this were a show. One of them even had a bell.

Ding.

The men and women placed plates down in front of us. And what a first course it was: a dainty little salad that looked like it was arranged by a florist. Three leaves of lettuce, artfully drizzled with something that was probably too fancy to be called "dressing," and a single, strategically placed raspberry.

"This is what I like to call *a deconstructed forest garden*," the chef said with a smile. "With a hint of summer."

"More like a hint of starvation," I quipped.

Exie's glower was so intense, I almost regretted making my joke. Almost.

Sorin leaned over to me. "Please, Gray," he whispered. "Please just be respectful. Exie has been extremely kind."

I picked up my fork and exhaled. "Fine. I will."

Phila beamed a smile down at her tiny offering. "This looks so fabulous."

Exie immediately dropped her anger. "Oh, it's delightful. Trust me. You'll love this."

It only took me a few bites to finish everything. Then *my* stomach started grumbling, and like Twain was following in a song, *his* tummy had a cute little cat grumble.

"You have to share whatever meat you get," he hissed in my ear.

"So, Gray." Exie finished her last bite of salad and then forced a little grin. "Are you nervous about your wedding?"

"No," I said.

"Not even a teeny tiny bit?"

I shook my head.

Phila's eyes widened. She smoothed her strawberry-blonde hair. "Oh, I would be... distraught."

"Are you sure it isn't one of your fears you're trying to overcome?" Exie pointed her fork at me. "You're marrying into a *much* higher class of family, and... well... Let's just say you don't have your brother's wonderful graces."

In all of the terrors I had experienced at the hands of my brother, I never once saw or feared being married to Ashlyn. She was wonderful—a delight in every way—and I always preferred her company to not having her company.

Her family, on the other hand...

I just didn't care for them.

"I don't care what her family thinks of me," I stated.

This seemed *too* scandalous because Exie actually gasped. She turned to Phila, and the two of them mumbled things to each other, which I found surprising. Phila frowned and tilted her head, but Exie just kept going.

Next came the main course, served with all the pomp and circumstance of a royal banquet. The chefs appeared again, and this time they cleared away the two plates that weren't being used. Who had they been waiting for? Perhaps Lucian?

A plate was placed before me, revealing a perfectly seared piece of red meat, garnished with something green that I couldn't identify. The chef regaled us with the tale of the dish's origins, which involved a mountain, a river, and probably a unicorn if I had been paying closer attention. Instead, I was too busy cutting it in half and then into tiny pieces.

One half for me, and all the tiny pieces for Twain.

My eldrin licked his lips the entire time I worked.

The chefs disappeared, and I hand fed Twain some of the bites while he remained on my shoulder.

Once again, Exie disapproved.

"Have you ever considered that you'll be a disappointment to Ashlyn?" Exie asked.

I huffed a laugh. "No. I'll be an amazing husband."

Twain chewed and swallowed his steak. "Yeah!" he finally said after a loud gulp.

Exie fluffed her hair as she gave me a sidelong glance. "Hm. Have you ever actually been with a woman intimately? Because there are lots of ways to be a disappointment."

I bit my steak, but I didn't chew. Nor did I taste anything.

While I was certain Ashlyn was the woman for me, and that I would love every second with her, I *hadn't* thought too much about our wedding night. That wasn't entirely true—I had thought about it—but not in great detail. I had the weight of the world resting on my shoulders, and also a Death Lord lingering around. There was hardly any time for me to relax.

"Is this really an appropriate lunch discussion?" Phila

poked her meat around the plate. It was obvious she hadn't eaten any. "I don't think... it's our business."

Sorin nodded. "I agree. And also—Gray is amazing at everything. I bet Ashlyn and him will have kids in no time."

Oh, Sorin.

Sweet, sweet Sorin.

Bless his heart.

Now I had lost my appetite. I forced myself to swallow my steak, and then I cut up the last of it to feed to Twain.

When did I have time to think about *family building?* What was wrong with everyone? We had the abyssal hells to fix, dammit!

Thankfully, before this conversation could curdle any more than it already had, the dining room door burst open.

Lucian stepped into the room, his tiny eldrin on his shoulder.

"Grab your things," he shouted, his voice echoing off the walls. "We're leaving. *Right now.*"

CHAPTER 14

HEENA LOLIAN

Lucian definitely had a commanding demeanor.

Everyone leapt to their feet—even Exie—the moment Lucian finished shouting his demands. I hurried over to his side, my brother next to me, my eldrin on my shoulder. Exie and Phila followed behind us, but our movements were still *too slow* for Lucian.

He grabbed my shirt and yanked me toward the door.

"*C'mon,*" he growled.

"What terrible fate has befallen us?" my brother's knightmare asked from the depths of the shadows. "Why are you so panicked?"

Lucian slammed the door open, only to find a woman standing there, waiting for us.

Her attire was a curious mix of practicality and sheer madness—wool robes covered pockets bulging with strange tools and vials. She wore thick glasses, the sort you might expect an elderly person to wear, and her chestnut hair was pulled back in a haphazard bun, as if she'd wrestled it into submission.

"*Lucian,*" the woman said, disdain in her tone. She crossed her arms, and I realized she was more slender than her giant robes let on. "Where are you going?"

"I don't have time to stay," Lucian said with a growl.

His Source of the Storm puffed its little white feathers. "We're on a very important mission, thank you very much. We don't have time for your inappropriate and bizarre requests!"

"Have you forgotten that you owe me a few favors?" Heena asked, her voice dripping with the kind of condescension usually reserved for small children and particularly dim-witted dogs.

"Auntie Heena," Exie said as she stepped around Lucian. With a fluff of her hair, and a flash of her smile, Exie continued, "Is this really how an arcanist of the Lolian family conducts themselves in front of guests?"

Heena turned to face me and my brother.

I finally got a good look at her arcanist mark...

It was the seven-pointed star, but there was a fat bull woven through it. Or perhaps a cow? An ox? Whatever was that? It certainly wasn't majestic—it was the type of creature I assumed barely knew how to form words, and probably dwelled alongside normal animals.

Then it struck me.

Professor Helmith had taught us all about this creature very early in our classes.

Heena was a *behemoth arcanist*.

Behemoths were gigantic creatures with legs like elephants, tusks like boars, horns like a ram, and heads so wide and fat, they could've belonged to a hippopotamus. They were known for being sturdy, their skin impenetrable, and their strength legendary.

They most certainly weren't known for their intelligence, and it was clear even from the simple design on Heena's arcanist mark.

"Aren't these your schoolmates?" Heena asked, lifting an

eyebrow. "Why don't you take them to your room and play with some toys."

I had never seen Exie's face grow so brightly red before. She pursed her lips and balled her hands into fists.

"*Auntie*," she snapped. Then Exie lowered her voice to a whisper. "*I'm. An. Adult.* How many times do I have to tell you that?"

Heena dismissively waved away Exie's comment. With a roll of her eyes, she retorted, "I have too many projects to handle to remember your age. I don't care what you do with your classmates—*do it elsewhere.* Children shouldn't witness what I have in store for Lucian and his eldrin."

I slowly glanced over at Lucian.

The man sneered so hard his mouth almost escaped his face.

"I'm not going to do any of your experiments," he stated.

Heena lifted *both* eyebrows this time. "You most certainly *will.* What did I tell you about your mystical creature? It's unique, and I need unique creatures to continue my research. I *allowed you* to bond with him, and I *need you* to cooperate whenever you're here."

Lucian let go of me and then jabbed his own chest with a single finger. "Why do *I* have to do all those weird things as well?"

"You were once a god-arcanist, with the most mighty of magic flowing through your veins. I just want to... test some theories."

Sorin and I exchanged looks. Whatever was happening here, I knew I didn't want to be part of it.

Phila poked her head around Lucian. "Um. I don't understand. What's happening?"

Heena straightened her posture. Glass vials in her pockets *clinked* as she moved. The woman had an intimidating glower

—like she was debating on what kind of curse word would be the most cutting.

But then she took a breath and calmly stated, "You students all know that mystical creatures are born two ways, correct? Some breed and produce offspring—"

"Progeny," Sorin muttered.

"—and some just *appear* when certain conditions are met."

"Fable births," Sorin also added.

Heena lifted a finger. "Us humans haven't yet learned *all* the ways creatures can appear. Some are birthed from blood, some from ritual. What I need now is to see if an old god-arcanist is the trigger for a new mystical creature we've never seen before." She narrowed her eyes into an icy glare, her glasses magnifying her pupils to comical levels. "Which is why Lucian must help me."

Lucian actually shoved Heena to the side and then strode into the hallway. "I'm married," he barked. "And I never said I would do *anything* you asked. What's wrong with you, woman? Some lines should never be crossed!"

The man was practically the living embodiment of a storm as he raged down the hallway. Heena hurried after him, huffing and cursing under her breath.

"Come back here," Heena practically barked. "Don't make me get my eldrin!"

Phila leaned closer to us. "Wait, what's going on?" she whispered.

"I think we need to go," I muttered.

Sorin nodded. "I have a bad feeling that if she can't get Lucian to do... things... she's going to want you, Gray. You're the only other one here with strange magic coursing through your veins."

Her face still red, Exie shook her head. "I'm so sorry my

auntie is this embarrassing. I don't like it when guests interact with her. She's so... *Arg!*"

"Wait," I said, suddenly struck with an idea. "That's your artificer aunt? The one who knows a whole bunch about mystical creatures?"

Exie shrugged. "Yes. What of it?"

"Does she know much about soul catchers? They're, uh, rare creatures that invade dreams."

For a good portion of my life, I had been terrified of them. But Sorin's idea was genius. I needed to defeat one—I needed to feel powerful enough to conquer anything. It would help me overcome all the other minor fears in my life.

And what better way to defeat one than finding out all its weaknesses?

"I'm not really familiar with *soul catchers*," Exie said with a hint of disgust. "But I'm certain that Auntie Heena knows something."

Phila kept her attention on Lucian until he rounded a corner down the hallway. Then she returned her focus to us. "Do you think Lucian will be okay? I'm... a little worried."

"He's fine," I said with a wave of my hand. "How about we go to Heena's study? Or library? Wherever she keeps all her notes or whatnot."

With a powerful sigh, Exie gestured in the opposite direction down the hall. "Heena has been writing her very own Bestiary. Headmaster Venrover actually asked her to write it because apparently the old Bestiary that Astra Academy uses isn't good enough."

Interesting. I completely agreed—our books never mentioned soul catchers, which was a gross oversight.

"Lead the way," I said. "I need that book. I need to know everything that's inside."

CHAPTER 15

GABBRO DRAGON

Exie led us through her massive family home with a smile on her face. Her erlking eldrin fluttered behind her, leaving behind a trail of glittering afterimages of himself. Exie's eldrin was probably the most intriguing creature I had ever seen, since he was so small, but so powerful.

When the little fairy man noticed me, he sneered.

"Didn't anyone ever tell you it's rude to stare?" Rex asked, fluttering his wings.

"You're the only erlking I've ever seen," I stated.

Rex crossed his arms as a smile bloomed across his face. "Yes, well, we're quite unique. Quite valuable. Quite sought after."

"That's quite a lot of *quites*," Twain sarcastically muttered. He trotted by my side, his head high, his ears perked up. "I'm pretty certain that mimics are rarer, actually."

With a forced laugh, Phila stepped forward. She grinned at me, and then Rex. "Why don't we focus on something else? Something fun?"

My brother pointed at her. "Yes. If Gray really *is* getting married, I need to get him a gift. Any ideas?"

"I'm right here, Sorin," I said.

"And you're the perfect person to give me an idea." Sorin smacked my shoulder. "You're not giving me much time to make or get you something, so the least you can do is tell me what you want."

I heard the hurt in my brother's voice. Even though he had forgiven me for marrying while Nini was in danger, he wasn't pleased by the situation. That was reasonable. I couldn't fault him for his anger.

"Your presence is gift enough." I shrugged. "Besides—we should put all our spare resources into preparing for our trek into the abyssal hells. Since Nini is—"

"*Ahem*," Exie said with a cough, interjecting.

She stood in front of an ornate door. Several mystical creatures were etched into the heavy wood, all of them coiled around one another in loving positions. Probably too loving, actually. I squinted at the door, one of my eyebrows rising, but then Exie opened it with a huff.

"Here it is." Exie motioned us in.

As I stepped over the threshold, the air itself seemed to hum with latent power, a symphony of barely contained magic that set my skin tingling. The room was a sprawling labyrinth of cluttered workbenches and towering shelves, each surface covered in an eclectic mix of books and mystical creature parts.

Well, "parts" was too harsh.

Exie's aunt obviously loved to collect hairs, feathers, whiskers, and bits of hide from creatures of all shapes and sizes. There were jars filled with the hairs from a unicorn mane, and another stuffed full of caladrius down, and even more with the scales of a leviathan.

Those scales were *huge*.

The center of the lab was dominated by a massive wooden table, its surface scarred and stained from years of experiments.

At least, I assumed it was from experiments. I hoped it wasn't anything else, because it almost looked like a butcher's block.

"Your auntie doesn't harm mystical creatures, right?" Phila asked, her eyes on the same gouges in the table I was staring at.

Exie shook her head as she entered the lab. "Of course not. She helps mystical creatures. Sometimes, they come to her wounded, or very ill, and she does everything in her power to help them."

"Oh, very good."

Sorin leapt into the room and smiled. "Okay, let's split up and look for that bestiary."

He hurried to the far end of the lab, never even waiting for anyone to reply. His shadow danced around his feet, and Thurin actually emerged from the darkness to help in our quest. The knightmare picked up a pile of books and quickly sifted through the titles before moving on to the next mountain of literature.

Phila and her coatl took the eastern side of the room.

I turned to take the western side, but that was when Exie stepped in front of me and Twain.

"Why are we looking for a bestiary?" she asked. "You said you needed it to find information on soul catchers, but I don't understand why."

"So I can get more powerful," I replied matter-of-factly.

"That's not a proper reason, and you know it." Exie narrowed her eyes and crossed her arms.

I slowly stepped around her, irritated she would slow us down. "We're going to save Nini in the abyssal hells, remember? And fight a bunch of Death Lords. You think I can afford to be weak? Of course not."

"We're gonna make ourselves super strong," Twain said with a smile. "Gray is gonna make me true form by defeating a soul catcher."

I wasn't entirely certain if that would work, but it was currently our plan of action. I had to defeat the creature that had always made me feel powerless.

"So this is for Nini?" Exie spoke each word with a neutral tone, no indication of anger or joy.

I nodded. "That's right. Or at least, partially."

My words seemed to settle onto Exie like dust onto an inanimate object. She didn't like what I had to say, but she didn't voice any protests, either. She motioned me away with a silent gesture of her hand.

I went for the nearest pile of books and started sifting. Something here had to be labeled *bestiary*.

Rex fluttered around overhead, glancing at all the books on the tops of piles.

Scrolls and books lay open, their pages covered in intricate diagrams and handwritten notes in a variety of languages, some of which I could not even begin to identify.

A large chalkboard on the far wall was covered in a chaotic array of sketches, interspersed with hastily scribbled observations. A half-finished drawing of a griffin took centerstage, its wings spread wide as if ready to take flight off the board and into the room.

And then there were the cages, all of which were made of black and blue material.

"Nullstone," Deimos whispered through me.

"I knew that," I muttered back, even though I hadn't been entirely certain. "And where have you been, huh? You haven't said a thing about the soul catcher to me. Do you know anything about it?"

"I do not."

That was all the Death Lord had to say on that matter. His emotional state told me he was busy—or perhaps irritated. This subject matter didn't interest him. He had other things to dwell on.

The sounds of scratching and scraping filled the room. I stood straight and whirled on my heel, wondering who in here was making such an odd noise. Twain's orange fur puffed out as he leapt to my shoulder. He flashed his fangs—which was adorable, but also a little frightening.

He reminded me of a mountain cat, his pupils constricting into tight slits.

"What're you doing?" came a gruff and semi-high-pitched voice.

A creature came walking out from under Heena's experimentation table. It was the size of a large tortoise, but it was in the shape of a dragon. The mystical creature was basically made of black rock that was flecked with gray and white.

The dragon's eyes appeared to be mirror-like diamonds, and its claws shone like polished steel. It walked on all fours, the scratching and scraping coming from its weight pressing against the tiles with each step.

It was obviously a little hatchling dragon, but I had never seen this species before.

"Well?" the dragon asked, eyeing us all. The beast didn't seem to have pupils, which was odd. "What're you doing?"

"We're looking for a bestiary," I said.

"Hm? Have you come to steal it? Because if you have—I won't let you." The dragon lowered its head and narrowed its reflective eyes. "The only path to Heena's treasures is over my grave."

"That's a little dramatic," I quipped.

Sorin leapt over the table with expert athleticism. He jumped to my side and smiled. "Don't worry! We would never steal from Heena. Isn't that right, Exie?"

To my surprise, she was still searching through the books. "Huh?" Exie glanced over with a frown. "Oh. Yes. No stealing. My auntie won't mind if we borrow a bestiary. We're all students at Astra Academy, after all. The book is being made for us."

Then she returned to her search.

I was impressed. Did she want to help us that bad? I had assumed she wouldn't want to help rescue Nini, but perhaps I was thinking too lowly of her.

Sorin placed his hands on his knees and leaned down to speak with the dragon face-to-face.

"What are you?" Sorin asked.

The dragon calmed a bit and lifted its head. The horns on its skull reminded me of a goat's. "I'm a gabbro dragon."

"What is *gabbro?*"

"It's one of the heaviest rocks in the world," Phila answered from the other side of the table. She smiled even brighter as she said, "It's one of the few rocks with metal flakes inside of it, along with peridotite and, uh, a few others." She waved her hand. "I'm sure Nasbit would know. He loved telling me about things like that."

"So, you're a *rock* dragon," Sorin said, returning his attention to the mystical creature.

With a deep frown, the beast snorted. "How dare you. *Gabbro dragons* are indestructible. Our hides can't be penetrated by human weapons. They can barely be harmed by magic. We are *far superior* to common rock."

The dragon slapped its tail on the floor. It hit with a *slam* that was so loud, I almost jumped. The little dragon had cracked the tile with its outburst.

"What's your name?" my brother asked. "I'm Sorin Lexly and this is my brother, Gray."

"I'm Bedrock, Son of Regolith," the dragon replied, flexing his claws. "Heena has taken me in, since so few gabbro dragons live in these parts anymore. She's quite kind."

"I'm sure she is. But, uh, do you mind doing me a favor?"

Bedrock tilted his head. "Favor?"

"Can I test out my new weapon on you?" Sorin stood straight and then held out his hand. His black trident formed from the darkness and lifted up into his grasp. "I haven't been able to really use it on anything interesting yet."

I gave him a sidelong glance. "Seriously?" I whispered. "It's a little baby."

Even Twain gave my brother the stink eye. "This is so unlike you, Sorin."

My brother held his trident in both hands and then shrugged. "The dragon said he was indestructible. You heard him."

"What if he isn't?" I sarcastically asked. "What happens then? Because mystical creatures don't have souls like people—we can't add Bedrock's name to the list of people to save in the abyssal hells."

Bedrock slammed his claws on the floor. "I *am* indestructible. I told you—*I'm the son of Regolith*—the most fearsome dragon who ever bonded to a human of all time! Never defeated in battle, a beacon of fortitude, a pillar of—"

"We get it, we get it," I said with a sigh. "Fine. You want to risk your life? Do it."

I crossed my arms and waited.

My brother held his weapon at the ready, and then turned to the bizarre dragon. Little Bedrock widened his stance and seemingly prepared himself for the blow. Sorin's knightmare watched from the corner of the room, a book in his shadowy gauntlets.

Everyone watched—except for Exie and her erlking. They continued the search regardless of anything else happening around them.

Sorin thrust his trident straight into the dragon's chest. I held my breath, my body tense as the tines of his weapon *clanged* into the scales of the gabbro dragon. Bedrock stumbled back, scraping up the tiles, and my brother's trident was practically bounced back.

Bedrock was unharmed.

The little dragon gave a squeaky roar.

"I told you," he crowed. "*Indestructible.*"

Phila and her coatl both clapped—the coatl slapping his snake tail to his body—like this was an incredible feat. I wasn't as impressed. Would the dragon's scales hold up against Vivigöl? I seriously doubted it.

Out of the corner of my eye, I spotted Exie just *stop* searching. Halfway through a pile, she stopped, turned, and then also clapped.

"Bravo!" she said as she walked over. "I knew you wouldn't be harmed." With a smile, Exie stood next to me. "Gabbro dragons are *very* fearsome. Their Trial of Worth involves picking them up and lifting them above your head. Since they're so heavy, people sometimes die from the effort."

"How heavy are they?" Twain asked, lifting a brow.

"Two or three hundred pounds," Exie said matter-of-factly.

She was entirely too happy. I wondered why.

My brother bowed to the hatchling dragon. "Thank you, Bedrock, Son of Regolith." Then he stood straight and dropped his trident back into the shadows. "I think I'll need to imbue stronger materials into my weapon before it compares to my brother's."

"How many star shards did you use to make it?" I asked.

"Only one," my brother whispered. Then he shrugged. "Professor Jijo was kind enough to let me have it."

"Ah."

It was a shame—my brother deserved nine more star shards so he could turn his trident into an artifact. He would need it if we were both going to the abyssal hells...

Perhaps...

As an arcanist of House Kross...

I could get him those.

"Let's keep searching," Sorin said, breaking me out of my thoughts. "C'mon. Before Lucian or someone else comes to take us away again."

CHAPTER 16

OR ELSE

We searched the lab for at least an hour. No one came to stop us, which was a boon, but we also never found the bestiary, which seemed preposterous.

I did, however, find notes about the Source of the Storm, and I stopped to read them halfway through the search.

Unique creatures have strange and interesting properties. They create nine-pointed arcanist stars whenever they bond with someone, and they're all capable of giving birth to lower-tier creatures. They can also merge with their arcanist's body, similar to other creatures, such as the knightmare and the reaper. However, all unique creatures are born from god-creatures, which is a problem. All god-creatures are currently extinct.

Fortunately, I have the flesh from the corpse of the progenitor behemoth, a god-creature known for birthing more mystical creatures into the world. If I fuse some of its magic to a normal behemoth, I suspect I can artificially create unique creatures.

Testing will be difficult, due to the fact that most unique creatures are gigantic. Normal behemoths might not be able to carry something so large.

Perhaps, tiny creatures can be bred.

Why did Heena want to make unique creatures? I didn't know. None of her notes gave a *why*. It just seemed like she wanted to do it because she *could*.

"What a weird lady," Twain whispered as he read over the notes as well.

"I've known people like that," Deimos whispered through

me. "They're never satisfied. They create, and make, and gather knowledge like it was water, and they were stuck in a desert, on the verge of dehydrating."

"Kinda reminds me of your brother a little bit," I murmured.

"My brother gathers knowledge for a purpose. Everything he does, he does for the betterment of me, a Death Lord, his family."

I was impressed with Deimos's and Zahn's dedication to each other. While I was close with Sorin, I didn't know if we were *that* close. Deimos and Zahn might've been *too* close, whenever I thought about it too hard, actually.

As I tucked away Heena's notes about unique creatures, I wondered...

"Do you ever blame yourself?" I asked.

"For?" Deimos growled.

The others in the lab continued searching, overturning every book. They even got the dragon, Bedrock, to help them.

"For wasting all of Zahn's life," I muttered. "Your brother has apparently been working to free you for, what, hundreds of years?"

"Thousands," Deimos stated.

"You never feel guilty about that? You never think that—if you didn't exist—he would've been happier?"

I was asking Deimos these questions, but I was also talking to myself. Nini was in the abyssal hells—because of me. Sorin's happiness was obviously suffering from this. And now he would have to journey with me to the depths of darkness, to the very core of death itself, just to get her back, and there was no guarantee we would return.

How could I *not* feel guilty?

Sorin didn't deserve this.

Perhaps...

I should just do this alone.

"I sometimes regret my brother's loyalty," Deimos whispered, his emotions a reflection of my own. "But I will make things right once this is behind us. It's a promise I gave him, written in blood, sealed with magic."

I wondered if I could make things up to Sorin...

A crash of books and paperwork interrupted our conversation. I glanced over only to find my brother getting increasingly frustrated. He was normally calm and collected.

"It's not here," Sorin stated. "Let's search somewhere else."

Phila and her eldrin leapt to his side. She beamed a smile to him, like she was trying to be extra happy so she had some cheer to share around. "That's a great idea, Sorin. We should check another room! Or we could even ask Heena. So long as she isn't roping Lucian into something terrible. Don't worry, okay?"

Sorin lifted an eyebrow and motioned to the mess. "Shouldn't we clean this up first?"

"Don't be ridiculous." Exie waved away the suggestion. "We don't have time, and my family pays people to organize things for us. Trust me—we can go right now."

Sorin nodded. "Okay. Let's go."

Exie, as pleased as ever, started to follow the others, but I moved over to her and held up a hand. My brother, Phila, and Bedrock, all wandered out of the lab and into the long hallway, leaving me, Twain, Rex, and Exie alone in the lab.

I closed the door.

For a short moment, Exie just stared straight into my eyes. After another short moment, she raised an eyebrow. When I still refused to speak, Exie finally glared.

"*What?*" she snapped.

"You know where that bestiary is," I stated, no hesitation.

We stared at each other for another long moment, Exie pressing her lips into a fine line. Her eldrin fluttered around and then landed on her shoulder. Rex folded his tiny arms and *also* glowered at me.

Then Exie half smiled, her eyes still icy. "You can't prove anything."

"You're just saying things to be hurtful," Rex chimed in. "My arcanist and I are trying our hardest."

Twain leapt up onto the table in the middle of the room and huffed. He wasn't convinced. Neither was I.

I pointed at her. "Are you seriously this callous and cruel? *What possible advantage could you get by hiding things from us?* Sorin isn't going to suddenly start liking you if Nini is permanently lost in the abyssal hells."

"I'm *way* better than Nini in every way," Exie snapped. She held up her fingers to count them out. "I'm prettier. I'm wealthier. I'm smarter. I didn't murder my own brother." Exie placed her hands on her hips. "But whatever. I'm not going to hinder Nini's rescue efforts. I'm just going to be there for Sorin through all these hard times. He'll see. *You'll see, too.*"

"Then why hide the bestiary?"

"*I didn't hide it.*" Exie stepped around me, sneering.

Before she reached the door, I called out, "Exie—I can have Twain transform into an erlking."

She stopped dead in her tracks.

"I know erlkings and their arcanists can see through illusions," I muttered. "If I become an erlking arcanist, will I find the bestiary in this lab? And if I do, what do you think Sorin will think when I tell him what happened?"

Silence.

Rex hesitantly glanced over at his arcanist. Exie remained still and quiet, never turning around to face me.

I knew. I knew in my gut that Exie found the book before all of us, and then used her erlking magic to create an illusion to hide it. That was the only explanation.

"Gray," she whispered, "maybe you should continue the

search with your brother, and I'll stay here and search everything a second time." Exie whirled around on her heel and faced me with a pleasant grin. "You're so *clever*, after all. You really should be helping Sorin in every way you can."

She sounded both sweet and sarcastic.

I stormed over to her, until we were mere inches apart. Twain even leapt onto my shoulder, and he glared down at Rex, like this were a standoff.

"Don't mess with me, Exie." I spoke all the words calmly, and never raised my voice, but the anger was there in every syllable. "And don't mess with my brother. You better find that bestiary—*and you better do it fast*. Or else."

Technically, my weapon, Vivigöl, was made of abyssal coral. It was capable of scarring arcanists, and I almost wanted to remind her of that fact. Would she really want her beauty marred? But I held back from articulating that threat. That was... dark. Too dark.

It was something Deimos would do, though.

I swallowed hard, trying to calm down—to remind myself that Sorin wouldn't do that. Sorin would never do that. I needed to be more like him.

I was about to apologize to Exie, but when I returned my attention to her, she was blushing so fiercely, she was almost pure red. That wasn't the reaction I was expecting.

"G-Gray." She held a hand up and stepped away from me, her back pressed up against the closed door. "I never knew you were such a scoundrel."

"What?" I asked, genuinely confused.

"I know I'm beautiful—probably the most beautiful woman you've ever met—but you're just not my type. And if you try to force yourself on me, *you'll* be the one regretting all your decisions."

I understood her words, but I didn't really understand what she was saying.

"*What*?" I barked, repeating myself, only louder.

Her eldrin snapped his small fingers and a burst of heated light flashed in front of him. Erlkings could create blinding light that was so hot, it burned flesh. This was a tiny blip of light, and Rex flew over and hissed at me afterward, as though I was about to ravage Exie at any moment.

Yeesh.

I *should've* voiced my threat—at least then she would've known what my intentions were. Not whatever bizarre fantasy she had going on in her head.

"Sorin is beautiful, truly he is. That's the kind of man I want." Exie stepped aside and motioned to the door. "You can go. I'll find the bestiary—no need to take out all your pent-up frustrations on me."

"I..." After a long exhale, I shook my head. "Fine. Whatever. Just get the damn book."

Exie was still pink in the face as I passed her. She gave me a sideways glance, and I sighed. Of all the women in my class, she was probably on the bottom of my list in terms of compatibility. There wasn't a single moment I had even entertained thoughts of being with her.

She was just as weird as her aunt.

Once in the hallway, Twain tensed, his claws digging into my shoulder. I glanced around and spotted Sorin—just leaning on the wall next to the door. Had he been there the whole time? Phila, her eldrin, and the weird rocky dragon were nowhere to be found.

It was just us.

"Hey," I awkwardly said with a jut of my chin. "How long... have you been there?"

"Oh, I just got here," he said.

Which was a lie.

Sorin was terrible at lying.

He pushed away from the wall and offered me a genuine

smile, though. "Thank you, Gray. I really appreciate you helping."

I half shrugged. "Uh. Don't mention it." My guilt about the situation still weighed on me. It was the least I could do to help Sorin. "We should probably head to the ship. I have a feeling Exie is going to find the bestiary pretty quick—and then we can leave."

Sorin nodded. "Good idea."

CHAPTER 17

SOUL CATCHERS

Sorin, Phila, and I stood outside the Lolian family compound while we waited for carriages to take us back to the port. I had wanted to get to the ship before Exie joined us—so we didn't have to ride in a carriage together—but I wasn't lucky, I supposed.

She strolled out of her family's compound with a large black tome in her hands. Her eldrin fluttered around her, his little nose high in the air. When Exie reached us, she smiled brightly and handed the book over to Sorin.

"I found it," she said matter-of-factly. "The bestiary. *And* my aunt doesn't mind if we borrow it. I asked."

"Thank you, Exie." My brother took it and offered her the same smile.

How was he able to be so kind? I would've gagged.

Twain must've felt the same way because he circled around my feet, his eyes narrowed, like an angry tiger caught behind bars. He was too adorable, though. I couldn't take his rage seriously when he was in his mimic form.

Our carriage arrived just a moment later.

Sorin handed me the bestiary. "Here, Gray. I think you should have this. So you can study it."

"Thank you." The book was *heavy*. I took it and had to tighten my grip or else drop it. "I'll read it during our trek."

"We're going to the Kross family house next, right?" Phila giggled as she turned to me. "For a super special wedding."

"I almost forgot," I sarcastically replied.

Servants opened the carriage door for us, and I got in first, followed by Twain. Phila—for some reason—got in and sat next to me afterward, her eldrin slithering in close to her heels. Sorin and Exie sat across from us on their own little bench seat. How awkward. Exie seemed pleased with this arrangement, though. She scooted close to my brother, smiling just the same as before.

As to not cause a scene, I cracked open the book and immediately started flipping the pages.

Where was the *soul catcher*?

Fortunately, everything was in alphabetical order, and unlike the books we had at school, it was much more detailed. Exie's aunt had also filled in a bunch of notes in the margins. This wasn't something she mass-produced... It was her personal notebook.

"Oh, look!" Phila leaned onto my shoulder and stared at the pages as I flipped through. "I love these pictures. Who do you suppose drew them?"

"My aunt," Exie said. "Obviously." She fluffed her curly hair and sat a little straighter, as though this accomplishment was somehow reflective of her skill as well.

As I flipped through, I spotted a picture of a beautiful blue dragon. Curiosity got the better of me. I stopped and stared at the page labeled '*typhoon dragon.*'

Phila leaned onto me even more. "Oh! Ashlyn's eldrin..."

Typhoon Dragon

Typhoon dragons are known as regal guardians of the sea. Their body is elongated, serpent-like, but they still have four legs, horns, and a muscular chest. Their scales are every color of blue, from the mildest, to the deepest of sapphire. Instead of wings, they have fins along their spine, arms, and tail.

Trial of Worth

In order to bond with a typhoon dragon, one must swim down into a dark bay to collect an abyssal pearl.

I remembered Ashlyn saying something like that.

My heart hammered when I remembered her saying she didn't know how to achieve a typhoon dragon's *true form*. Technically, Zahn had told me that typhoon dragons needed to consume a piece of abyssal coral, but I hadn't double checked that. Maybe now was the time.

Aura

Ocean Heart—when a typhoon dragon arcanist creates an aura, the sky darkens and the waters in the nearby area become restless. Anyone at least halfway submerged in water finds their energy and magic being drained away. Arcanists will become tired within a minute, and most mystical creatures will fall asleep from fatigue. The energy and magic are transferred to the typhoon dragon and its arcanist.

True Form Type: Geas

The typhoon dragon arcanist must collect a chunk of abyssal coral and have their eldrin eat it in order for a typhoon dragon to transform.

Twain poked his head up and also glanced at the page.

I grazed my fingers over the portion of the text about the abyssal coral. Zahn had been correct.

Which meant my weapon was the solution.

"So my weapon really is made of abyssal coral, correct?" I whispered.

"Yes," Deimos replied through me, in a darker, gruffer tone. "Vivigöl, Silencer of the Damned was shaped from the abyssal coral I harvested myself."

Phila leaned away from me, her eyes wide. "I, uh, forgot you're sometimes a Death Lord."

I shrugged. "I sometimes forget, too."

Exie cringed back, her lips folded down into a deep frown. She had not experienced Deimos talking, and it was clear she didn't approve.

I leaned back in my seat. Nothing to do about it now. "So, if I let Ashlyn's typhoon dragon eat a *little* bit of my weapon, he'll achieve his true form? Am I reading this right?"

Sorin leaned forward to listen better. Once Exie shook off the thought of Deimos speaking through me, she, too, leaned forward. Everyone was fascinated by this conversation, obviously.

Deimos snorted, his irritation rising. In a curt and disinterested tone, he replied, "Yes. But you will weaken Vivigöl in doing so. The dragon needs a good chunk to absorb."

"And that will... make her eldrin stronger?" I whispered.

"It will."

Deimos's thoughts rattled around my own. Although he didn't speak, I knew what he was thinking. Something about... typhoon dragons visiting the abyssal hells, before the gate was sealed forever. Apparently, true form typhoon dragons were immune to the life-draining effects of the hells. Well, the dragons *and* their arcanists.

I touched the weapon that rested just under my shirt. Guilt clawed at me. I didn't want the weapon to be weaker, but...

Ashlyn was soon to be my wife.

Then again, I told Zahn I wasn't going to do this. He had brought this all up before, when I was discussing true forms with him. Why was I considering damaging my weapon now? Just because we were getting married?

Sorin knew what I was thinking. He always knew.

"You should do it," he said.

"You think so, huh?" I whispered.

"Of course. Ashlyn is the love of your life, remember? You fought so hard to be together. And isn't it the perfect wedding gift?"

I caught my breath and glanced up to meet Sorin's gaze. He had the same gray-blue eyes I did, but he always seemed happier. He smiled more than me. He was smiling now.

"It is a great wedding gift," I said.

Sorin clenched a hand into a victorious fist. "Yes! It *is* perfect. You should do it, Gray. Definitely. For Ashlyn."

"I'll think about it..."

Deimos didn't want this, but he also wasn't voicing any objections. I was thankful for that. We needed to work together to save the abyssal hells, after all. We couldn't be arguing over things like this.

"I can make a new one," Deimos eventually said through

me. "But it won't be as special as Vivigöl. You did something to it with your mimic magic—when I wielded the trident, it never transformed. So, when you weaken it, know that you will never have another like it."

Yeah, I knew that part.

That was why I was hesitating.

"Love requires sacrifice," Sorin said as he sat back on his carriage bench. "You shouldn't second guess yourself, Gray."

As our transportation went over the cobblestone road that ran through the town, it wobbled and rocked. Exie seemed to dwell on Sorin's words, absorbing the little bit about love as much as possible. Phila played with her strawberry blonde hair, her attention on her own eldrin.

"Uh, Gray?" She turned to me. "Would you mind looking up what the requirement was for a coatl's true form?"

"Uh, sure."

I flipped through the book, searching for her eldrin. It was easier to just glance at the pictures as I went, as each was lovingly done with a beautiful color illustration. I stopped once I found the red and white snake with colorful parrot wings.

"Here it is," I muttered.

Coatl

Coatls are creatures with a deep passion for nature and life. They have long serpent bodies, sometimes reaching upward to twenty feet when fully grown, and a pair of wings. Coatls come in three color varieties. The standard coatl has red, white, and orange scales, while having bright rainbow feathers. A rare coatl, known simply as the *blue variant*, has a green snake body, and blue-jay feathers. Lastly, albino coatls have been observed, but infrequently. They have white scales and feathers, and their eyes are bright red.

I glanced down to the most important part... the true form.

Phila slammed back into me, her eyes wide as she quickly read the section.

True Form Type: Geas

The coatl arcanist must eat the heart of an adult xototl in order for their coatl eldrin to transform.

"Oh, no," Phila muttered. She backed away from me, the color draining from her face. "I've never even heard of a *xototl* before. And I don't want to kill something to eat its heart."

Her eldrin slithered up onto the bench next to her and gently patted Phila's shoulder with his tail. "There, there. You don't have to fret. We don't *need* to achieve a true form."

"A *xototl* is a fairly common psychopomp," Deimos said.

I rubbed my cheek afterward. I had never, in my life, said the word *psychopomp* before. I had no idea what that was.

My brother must've felt the same way, because his face twisted in confusion. "What?" he asked.

His shadow stirred, and his knightmare, Thurin, answered this one. "A psychopomp is a mystical creature who guides souls to the abyssal hells. Once the hells were sealed, it was said all the psychopomps vanished."

"They're sealed in the hells with us Death Lords," Deimos muttered.

Mystical creatures who guided people to the afterlife? I didn't know those existed.

Phila's expression never changed. If anything, she seemed *more* worried than she was before. "That sounds like a kind creature. Why would I kill it? It just... doesn't sit well with me."

"Maybe you can find an evil one," Exie said with a shrug.

Her erlking shrugged alongside her, as though it was mimicking all her movements.

I flipped through the bestiary until I came to the erlking.

Erlking

Erlkings are known as the "king of fairies" and are small humanoid creatures with tiny features. When fully grown, they are no taller than a foot, and their wingspan about two-and-a-half feet. Erlkings have peacock wings, delicate features, and an after-image of illusions that trails behind them whenever they fly. They can dress themselves in many types of clothing, though most create illusions to wear instead of actual outfits.

I went straight down to the true form requirements.

True Form Type: Geas

An erlking arcanist must get at least three individuals to fall in love with them in order for their eldrin to transform.

No.

I reread the section three times before slowly glancing up at Exie. She sat with her arms crossed, her full lips pouty, and one eyebrow raised. Did she *know* what her true form requirement was?

"What is it?" she asked. "Staring is rude, in case you weren't aware."

"Nothing," I murmured. I went back to searching the book for the soul catcher. Everything else was irrelevant, and I really didn't want to think Exie was using my brother so she could achieve a true form with her eldrin.

There was no way she was doing that.

Right?

I couldn't shake my doubt. I didn't want to believe it. Besides, if she *wanted* the love of three random individuals, I was certain she could get it much easier than from my brother.

Finally, I found the section on the soul catcher.

The drawing to the side was as creepy as I remembered the actual mystical creatures being. After a long exhale, I read the section.

Soul Catcher

Soul catchers are terrifying creatures who prefer to wander the dreamscape, spying on nightmares. Their bodies are made of several common fears: they're shaped like a spider, made of wood from puppets, and have face masks reminiscent of clowns. They can grow to be ten feet tall, and just as wide. Their spider-limbs have human-shaped hands often adorned with weapons, such as rusty hooks, knives, or serrated edges.

Trial of Worth

In order to bond with a soul catcher, one must survive through a night of the creature's nightmarish manipulation.

I almost laughed at that one. Clearly, I had the right to bond with a soul catcher.

Twain read the same sentence and giggled. "Wow. If I ever die, I know what kind of arcanist you're gonna be next."

"I would *never* bond with a soul catcher," I muttered.

Instead of looking up its true form requirement or any of that, I skimmed through the entry, looking for some sort of weakness, or a list of things the soul catcher was capable of. Fortunately, I found something interesting...

Research Notes

Soul catchers were once quite popular with inquisitors. Since the creature has a unique form of "torture" in the ability to harm people while they dream, some inquisitors used that to pry the truth from supposed criminals. However, once that was deemed inhumane, soul catchers were ousted from most of polite society.

Since the soul catcher is a creature that can capture a human soul, it was said they were also bonded with frequently in ancient times. Unfortunately, soul catchers, outside of dreams, are quite frail. Because of this, people who collected souls were targeted and killed in retaliation frequently. Outside of dreams and nightmares, soul catchers have few magics they can wield offensively. Additionally, the soul catcher's heart is actually located in its head, behind the mask. The rest of the body is merely a puppet, and just for show.

That was what I needed.

I closed the bestiary just as the carriage pulled up to the docks.

"Did you find what you needed?" Sorin asked.

I nodded. "Yeah. But... I think I should still hold on to this. For the time being." Perhaps I could learn more about mystical creatures—especially if I was going to have Twain turn into them all the time.

CHAPTER 18

ELDER MONSTERS

We boarded the *Distant Dream* and waited for Lucian. He arrived not just with himself, but with Exie's aunt as well. Heena carried a large wooden box with a silver lock and only released it once she reached the gangplank—then she handed it to Lucian and boarded.

Her eldrin, a behemoth, also joined us.

The lumbering cow-like mystical creature was *large*. It was scaled, and had large black horns that curled tightly along the side of its head, like a goat. It also had clawed feet, despite its bovine-shaped head.

It was like... a whole jumble of creatures had been chopped up and put back together in order to make Heena's creature. That was odd, but fascinating. Unfortunately, the fat creature almost broke the gangplank getting on the ship, and several sails had to come out to lay down reinforcements to help the hippo board.

Professor Jijo and his nimbus dragon also joined us. The man gave me a curt nod when he boarded, but otherwise didn't say much. That was fine. We didn't need to get along.

To my surprise, however, the gabbro dragon, Bedrock, also sauntered aboard.

From afar, the little dragon definitely looked like a walking mass of rocks. Only his claws gave him away for what he was—they were polished and reflected and glinted in the light so much it sometimes hurt my eyes to look at them.

What a bizarre creature.

Once all settled, the *Distant Dream* set out for the Kross family estate, which had an ocean dock due to all the many typhoon dragon arcanists. Additionally, their whole family was trained in boating at a young age, so they all had their own little vessels, and a place to tie them down.

I stood on the deck of the ship as we sailed away from the mainland. Twain fell asleep nearby atop a coiled rope. He purred with each exhale, completely unbothered by the rocking of the vessel on the ocean waves.

Sorin, Phila, and Exie were all together in the galley down below. I assumed they were eating, but I didn't want to participate.

Now that I had my bestiary, and my brother, all my thoughts fixated on my upcoming wedding.

I wasn't entirely prepared for that.

What if Exie was right? What if I was a disappointment to Ashlyn on our wedding night?

"You already borrow all my combat skills," Deimos said with a chuckle. "You can always borrow all my other skills as well."

I ran a hand down my face as he finished the last words. Nothing—absolutely *nothing*—could have prepared me for that comment. Apparently, Deimos was some sort of *warrior prodigy in the streets, love god in the sheets*, but that didn't mean I wanted pointers from the man. I most definitely didn't want him involved in any way on my wedding night.

I leaned onto the ship's railing, the wood creaking under

my elbows as I groaned. Salt water splashed up high when the waves crashed against the hull, dappling my hands and cheeks.

Something moved under the water.

A dark shadow slithered by, and a shiver went down my spine.

What was that? I stood straight and narrowed my eyes. I had felt this before—a presence. When the boat shuddered, I clenched my hands into fists.

"There is a secret to being a competent lover," Deimos muttered.

I shook my head and jogged down the deck of the ship. "I don't want to hear it. I can figure this out on my own." Then I called out over my shoulder, "*Twain!* Get up!"

My eldrin groggily lifted his head and blinked his eyes. "Huh?"

Deimos didn't seem to care that I was preoccupied. "You won't even take advice, boy? Feh. Fine. Keep in mind you can't hide your most embarrassing moments from me."

"*Will you shut up?*" I gestured to the side of the boat. "Something is here!"

With panic in my movements, I glanced over the side of the ship again, searching the waves for signs of whatever was here. Then I realized how hard my heart was pounding and I stopped moving.

Was I... afraid?

Of what? The unknown?

I took a deep breath and tried to quickly logic out what would be here. What could possibly be under the ship, with a presence I had felt before?

It was one of the elder creatures.

Technically, the shattered Gate of Crossing that allowed Deimos to first enter the land of the living, had allowed creatures from the abyssal hells to spill out. I had fought a couple of them in the past, and while Headmaster Venrover had gone out of his way to collect the fragments, I wasn't entirely certain if he had gotten them all.

And even if he had, there was a chance he missed some of the monsters...

Those elder lunatics wanted Deimos destroyed—which meant they wanted me to die a quick and painful death, since I was carrying his soul fragment.

My fear lessened as I went over the cold facts in my mind.

Was *this* how I was going to obtain my true form?

Twain ran over to my feet, his orange fur puffed. He stared up at me, his breathing heavy. "Well? What is it?"

But he wasn't his true form yet...

So I supposed this wasn't defeating fear *enough*. I still had to face off against that soul catcher arcanist.

"Gray?" Twain tilted his head. "Why did you call me? I was napping pretty hard and having a wonderful dream about—"

The ship rumbled. I grabbed the railing and gritted my teeth. "I think we have company."

As a mimic arcanist, I could sense mystical creatures, the thread of their magic, and tug on them to get Twain to transform. Unfortunately, the magic of elder creatures was warped and twisted. Twain couldn't take their shape.

"What're we going to do?" Twain asked.

Before I even replied, Lucian burst out from a nearby door. He was tense—*prepared*—and his eldrin was fluttering around him at lightning speeds. The small hummingbird creature was practically a white line through the air as it zipped in an orbit around Lucian's head.

The clouds overhead darkened and thickened, all in a matter of seconds.

"*Get below deck*," Lucian commanded.

He had the authority and presence of someone legendary —like a warrior who had seen a million battles.

But the fates clearly didn't want me to avoid this fight. The ship quaked a second time and a monster *burst* out of the water. It wasn't just any water-based mystical creature, either. It was one I knew quite well.

A typhoon dragon.

Only... it didn't look like a normal one.

All normal typhoon dragons had vibrant blue scales. This monster had midnight black scales with only a handful of sapphire scales spotted around. Normal typhoon dragons had fins, but this elder creature not only had fins, but small tentacles as well. Its face had six eyes on either side of its mouth, like it needed more limbs to shove things toward its fangs.

"Just my luck," I muttered as the dragon continued upward into the sky, looming over us so much that water dripped from its body, spilling across the deck and casting a long, dark shadow.

When the elder typhoon dragon lifted a clawed hand, Lucian stepped forward and blasted the beast with lightning. The *crack* and burst of power singed the air.

Unfortunately, typhoon dragons were immune to the brutal effects of lightning. The dragon took the hit of Lucian's magic like a champ, and then chuckled.

"Humans are nothing but food," the dragon said, his voice rumbling from deep inside his body. The tentacles around his mouth wiggled with each word. "Once we've taken the world, we'll harvest your souls to grow our young."

Well, *that* was rather dark.

"Kill this abomination," Deimos said through me.

I grabbed Vivigöl and it *click-click-clicked* into the shape of a trident. Twain leapt to my feet just as a shadow slithered out onto the deck. From the darkness rose my brother wearing his knightmare, Thurin.

Together, they were an intimidating sight. Wrapped in

black shadow armor, Thurin covered most of Sorin's body. The feather cape that fluttered behind Sorin reminded me of raven wings, and when Sorin reached into the darkness, he pulled out his own trident—Woldräm.

His black weapon was practically a mirror of my own.

The elder typhoon dragon slammed one of his clawed hands down onto the deck of the *Distant Dream*. Wood shattered beneath the blow as the elder dragon tore a chunk of our vessel away. Crew members shouted commands, people from within the ship screamed, and I almost fell over due to all the shaking.

The shadows around Sorin's feet stabilized him.

Lucian's Source of the Storm dove into his neck. Yes, the flesh of his neck, just below the jaw. And then, moments later, white feather wings burst from Lucian's back—the type of wings so large and so majestic, they could easily carry a man.

Lucian shuddered, as though this merging transformation was painful, but with the look of a warrior who had seen every injury, and faced down death itself, he gritted his teeth and regained his composure. If I had blinked, I would've missed the agony and the recovery.

Everyone was preparing to fight, so I mentally searched for a thread of magic—something to transform Twain.

In a split second, while the typhoon dragon was pulling his claw from the ship, I took stock of my options.

A knightmare.

A nimbus dragon.

A behemoth.

A gabbro dragon.

An erlking.

A coatl.

And an abyssal dragon.

I couldn't mimic the Source of the Storm or the elder typhoon dragon, which was beyond bad luck. They both wielded lightning. If I could become an arcanist of either, I'd become *immune* to the lightning, but as it stood, I had the ability to shield myself from that type of attack.

And just as I thought that, the elder dragon opened his maw wide. His tentacles moved out of the way as lightning cracked between his fangs. Then the beast exhaled a bolt of sheer power. It sizzled through the air and struck the middle mast of the ship, splintering it down the middle and exploding most of it outward.

Fires broke out as flaming bits of wood rained down all around us.

"Gray!" Twain shouted.

Having Twain transform into an abyssal dragon was my ace, but...

Lucian took to the sky with a single, and powerful, flap of his white wings. He shot upward, and then soared straight for the face of the dragon.

My brother didn't hesitate, either. He slipped into the shadows and then emerged at the edge of the ship, close to the typhoon dragon's claw.

But that was when I sensed something *else* in the waters.

The elder typhoon dragon wasn't the only enemy here...

CHAPTER 19

CLEVER TACTICS

"Overwhelm them with abyssal dragon power," Deimos said through me. "They're monsters who have used the souls of humans to strengthen their own magic. If you underestimate them, you'll regret it."

Sorin waved his hand and manipulated the shadows. Tendrils jutted up and grabbed the claw of the elder typhoon dragon, seizing it as though caught in a gigantic snare. The dragon roared, its fins shuddering, spittle from its gargantuan mouth spraying across the ruined deck.

Lucian dove straight for the dragon's left eye. With one powerful downward kick, he ruptured the jelly of the eyeball. The typhoon dragon screamed and the tentacles surrounding its mouth all struck out at Lucian. But Lucian was too fast, dodging the tentacles in a series of astonishing acrobatics before a powerful beat of his wings carried him away from the dragon.

"You've no idea the power I have," the dragon growled, hate in his voice as his eye wept its inner fluids. "*I've emerged from the abyssal hells itself to end you!*"

The elder typhoon dragon's eyeball closed and began

stitching itself back together with astonishing speed. All mystical creatures and arcanists healed, *but not like this*. Lucian hadn't even returned to the ship, and it was as if the dragon's injury had never happened.

Phila, Exie, Professor Jijo, and Exie's aunt, Heena, all emerged onto the deck. Of the four, it was only Jijo and Heena who sprang into action. Heena ran to join Sorin, seemingly with no weapon.

Jijo's eldrin, the cute nimbus dragon, Cirrus, flashed his fangs and immediately took to the sky. His serpent body had little legs but no wings—and that didn't matter. Nimbus dragons manipulated the wind, and they flew as though swimming through the air at high speeds.

Zipping into action, Cirrus evoked clouds from his mouth. He basically vomited an entire storm front's worth of dark billowing clouds. I thought we would all be blinded, but the little dragon whipped the wind to contain the clouds like a fog around the elder typhoon dragon.

To my surprise, Jijo didn't join the fray. He began touching everyone. He grabbed Phila, Exie, Heena, and then grazed his fingers over the nearby crew members. Jijo would lay his hand on a person for just a second before quickly speeding away and touching the next.

He was using his augmentation.

Professor Jijo was pushing his magic into the others, granting them some of his nimbus dragon magic. What did nimbus dragons grant again?

Flight.

And... cloud-stepping. The ability to move through clouds as though teleporting.

I recalled reading it in our textbooks at Astra Academy. Nimbus dragons and their arcanists could allow others to fly through the sky without the use of wings.

The ship creaked and groaned. The sky had darkened to a

bruised shade of purple, the sun swallowed whole by the churning clouds that now swirled around the head of the typhoon dragon.

And then, as if the sea itself had drawn a breath, the water around the ship swirled. A shadow rose from the depths on the opposite side of the boat as the dragon, and it did so with a speed that defied its monstrous size.

It wasn't another typhoon dragon—it was a *cetus*, a type of ocean-based mystical creature that was regarded as a terrifying man-eater.

The beast had a head the shape of a dog, though it was massive, with a mouth capable of fitting three people. It was like a hound had a baby with a sea serpent. Its body was serpent-like, with only two little arms that ended in claws.

A cetus was nowhere near as powerful as a typhoon dragon, but it was clear this creature had *also* consumed human souls in the abyssal hells.

The cetus's massive head was crowned with jagged fins. It had teeth as long as a man's arm that gleamed in the dim light, and a tongue the length of a small rowboat. Water cascaded off its scaled hide, each drop shimmering like molten silver before it plunged back into the sea. The creature's eyes, dark and devoid of mercy, fixed on the ship.

Its mouth...

Deep in its gullet were visions of ghost-like souls clinging to the creature's throat. This was an elder cetus.

"What have we here?" the cetus asked with a dark chuckle.

It was half the size of the elder typhoon dragon—the size of a full deck of the ship, at least—and since it was on the other side of the ship, there was little hope of escape.

"*Curse the abyssal hells,*" I muttered under my breath.

I didn't want to just be an abyssal dragon arcanist—it was costly, the magic so powerful it could be painful, and the more

I used it, the more I knew I'd become a target for immediate elimination.

But the enemy already knew what I was so...

Why hesitate?

I tugged on the thread of magic that led back to Deimos's abyssal dragon eldrin. The arcanist mark on my forehead burned, and Twain's body bubbled outward until his orange fur became rotting scales, and a pair of translucent blue wings burst from his back. The wings weren't in any way solid—they were made of stretched-out human souls, each one sewn to the next in a nightmarish tapestry.

Twain grew so large, he rocked the ship, straining the already broken deck. Before he was fully transformed, he leapt upward, rocking us further, but thankfully never capsizing our vessel. He became a dragon, with four legs, a long neck, and a mouth filled with razor teeth. His six eyes—three on each side of his head—were disturbing.

Twain flapped his soul wings, flying higher into the sky.

The elder typhoon dragon roared and it practically shattered my eardrums. A *crack* of lightning blasted from his mouth, piercing the cloud cover around his head, and then arcing off into the water, narrowly missing Twain's huge form.

But as Twain was distracted, the cetus reached its two arms up and grabbed one of Twain's back legs.

I lunged forward, Vivigöl in my hand. Abyssal dragons and their arcanists could use the souls grafted onto their dragon's bodies to temporarily empower themselves. I used a soul from Twain to heighten my speed and strength, dark magic filling my body with endless, impossible power even as my skull felt like it was splitting from the strain.

"Don't you dare touch my eldrin," I roared as I leapt onto the railing of the ship. Vivigöl *click-click-clicked* as it transformed into a sword mid-swing.

I slashed right through the arm of the cetus, cutting the limb from the body of the creature.

The beast screamed and released Twain.

My eldrin flapped his grotesque wings again and took to the darkened sky, roaring like only a dragon could. The higher he was, the better an angle he would have to attack.

The cetus twisted and struck at me, its dog-shaped head flashing its fangs. I was fast, but the beast was just as quick. When I attempted to leap away, the cetus caught my arm in a bite. The fangs crunched down on my left arm, shattering bone and causing my vision to flood with white-hot agony.

With force so powerful it almost tore my arm from the socket, the cetus thrashed its head and tossed me overboard. I hit the water and plunged beneath the surface.

It was difficult to see, and I was momentarily confused, but I eventually righted myself and swam up. When I managed to get my head above the waves, I gasped for air.

My arm...

It wasn't responding. It hung limp. On instinct, I reached for abyssal dragon magic to heal my arm, but the soul essence that filled the wound simply flowed outward with the blood.

"Elder creatures scar the soul as well as the body," Deimos growled. "Focus on the battle. I will repair the damage."

Fortunately, I had never released Vivigöl from my grasp. And for some reason, in the water, my weapon seemed stronger than ever—it pulsed with a heartbeat of its own.

"*Get back on the ship,*" Deimos said.

The ocean, once a vast and indifferent expanse, now seemed a living thing, churning in the cetus's wake. Waves rose and fell with the creature's movements, the ship tossed about like a toy in the grip of an angry child.

But the cetus was relentless. Its tail, a muscular column of raw power, slammed into the ship's side, sending men and debris flying. The sails were now tattered and useless, flapping helplessly as the ship listed dangerously to one side. The beast reared back, preparing for another strike, its form a terrible silhouette against the boiling sky.

Vivigöl *click-click-clicked* as it transformed again, its metallic abyssal coral shifting quickly as it transformed from a sword, into a whip-chain. With just one arm, I lashed at the beast, snapping the end of the whip so that it took a huge gouge from the back of the cetus. The monster whirled in the water, its eyes burning with rage.

Like me, it only had the use of one arm.

Then a blinding beam of light cut through the gloom of the clouds. Twain, as an abyssal dragon, evoked raw magic, and it acted like a scorching pillar of light that cut through anything it touched. The blast of raw magic went through the cetus, piercing its body.

The creature roared and then gurgled. The hole through its body was too much.

The cetus began to sink beneath the water, color draining from its eyes.

Struggling to swim, I attempted to get back to the ship, but I wasn't entirely sure how I would. Although my arm was bleeding and broken, I no longer felt it—the adrenaline of the fight was coursing through me so thoroughly, I felt nothing.

Twain turned his magic beams on the typhoon dragon, but they didn't damage the elder monster like I had thought. Twain's evocation cut through the clouds and then pierced some of the dragon's hide, but nowhere near what it should have done.

Human souls swirled around the typhoon dragon, seemingly healing and protecting it. Magic was made of souls, after all... Perhaps the souls were acting as a shield against the raw power of magic?

If that was true, how would we defeat it?

Should I...

Transform Twain into a nimbus dragon so I could fly?

Why hadn't Jijo used his augmentation on me?

As the waves grew larger and larger, I realized the elder typhoon dragon was causing the storm. If I didn't get out of the ocean, I would be in trouble—and while abyssal dragons were strong, they couldn't breathe underwater.

I could burn through souls to heal, though...

I used another, and my arm *cracked* and *popped* as my flesh hurried to correct itself. The feel of a soul coursing through me caused me to shudder. Then the bone was set and *snapped* into place.

The rough waters then took me under. With two arms, swimming was manageable, but not easy. Struggling, I sensed the magical thread of the nimbus dragon and I pulled it. When my arcanist mark burned a second time, I knew I had what I needed.

The abyssal dragon strength...

It was slowly leaving me, but the empowerment of the soul wasn't immediately lost.

I swam for the surface, and when I broke through the water, I attempted to manipulate the wind. I flew upward—clumsily—and then went straight for the ship.

Heena, with her behemoth magic, was grabbing at the arms of the typhoon dragon. She was somehow ripping flesh from the dragon's body as though it was clay. The bloody mass of damage she was inflicting was quite impressive.

Jijo shot around the dragon, diving in and out of storm clouds, practically teleporting around. He had two daggers in his hands now. I wasn't entirely certain where he had gotten them, but he was using them to slice and dice through the dragon's body.

Lucian was high in the air, seemingly manipulating the weather. The elder typhoon dragon and him were in a war to keep the storm at bay—to prevent it from fully destroying our ship.

Sorin was on the deck of the ship, using his shadow tendrils to yank all the sailors out of danger. He tossed them overboard, but many of them then soared into the air, away from the thrashing waves.

Anyone who *couldn't* fly, Sorin kept them out of harm's way.

However, my brother wasn't yet a fully trained knightmare arcanist. He couldn't fight and protect the ship's crew. It was either one or the other—and my brother chose to make sure no one would get hurt.

Phila was also saving the crew. She manipulated the winds as well as she could, helping the flying sailors get far from the chaos of the battle.

To my surprise, even Exie was helping. She held up her hand and evoked searing light. It wasn't as powerful as the abyssal dragon's raw magic, but it was enough to cut through clouds and scorch the typhoon dragon.

"Get out of here, you *monster*," Exie shouted.

Her erlking also evoked white beams at the dragon, darting around like only a fairy could.

"Twain!" I shouted. "Where are you?"

As a tiny nimbus dragon, it was almost impossible to see him with all this commotion going on. Thankfully, my eldrin heard me. He darted through the sky, slithering as he flew straight for me.

"Gray!" he called out.

I held out my newly fixed arm, and Twain landed on it. He snaked his body around my elbow, clinging to me.

"Fly above the typhoon dragon," I commanded. "Don't stop flying! Get as high as you can! Hurry!"

Twain nodded once, determination in his eyes. Then he

shot into the air. He soared through the clouds, and snaked his way to the area above the dragon.

I had to wait—he had to be higher.

Then the ship rocked and began to snap. The typhoon dragon's long body was wrapping around the vessel as it clung to the shattering hull.

"*You can't defeat me,*" it roared. "*You're nothing but food!*"

Higher and higher Twain went. For a brief moment he hesitated, but then he kept going, just as I had asked. It became difficult to track him—difficult to watch his tiny body. But I waited, the ship creaking, my footing becoming unsteady.

Sorin saved the last of the sailors from the ship and then turned his magic tendrils on the typhoon dragon, but he just wasn't strong enough.

Once Twain was high enough, I tugged on the thread of magic that led back to the gabbro dragon.

It was a three-hundred-pound hatchling—a dragon known to be *indestructible.*

So when Twain plummeted, it was at such incredible speed, and such force, that he might as well have been a boulder from a catapult. His body was practically metal, and the little dragon didn't suffer from force damage like normal creatures.

But typhoon dragons sure did.

Twain crashed into the skull of the elder dragon, and there was no way the souls it had consumed could save it from having its skull pulverized.

CHAPTER 20

A KROSS WELCOME

Due to Professor Jijo's quick thinking, none of the ship's crew was harmed.

They were gathered back up, and set down on the deck, but we were now limping along through the ocean, taking on water. None of the other arcanists seemed worried, so I trusted we would eventually reach land without a problem, but it was clearly going to take longer than usual.

I waited at the shattered railing of the ship as Twain dried himself off. He stank of salt water, and his orange fur was matted. Nothing irritated him more than being wet.

My brother stood next to me, his knightmare swirling around his feet. The crew came by, one after another, thanking him, praising him.

"You're a real knight," one of the sailors said.

"Thank you, thank you," another added with a quick bow of his head.

Sorin waved away their praise. "It was a team effort. I couldn't have done anything without the others."

I had to admit—I was a little irritated. Who had defeated

the elder monsters? Me. Practically by myself. But no one was walking over to thank me.

Though, my thoughts quickly turned to the elder creatures. They had consumed so many souls, they were almost unbeatable.

"You have souls on your abyssal dragon," I whispered to myself, speaking to Deimos. "Why aren't you just gobbling down souls like those elder beasts?"

Deimos's irritation was quick and thorough. "Those elder creatures eat any soul they come across. The souls I bind to my dragon are those who deserve punishment. Murderers. Abusers. The scum of humankind who cannot be allowed to reincarnate. That is one of my duties as Death Lord, after all."

"Oh, I see. So when you use souls for your magic, that's the soul's punishment?"

"Correct."

I hadn't known that. What a dark powerset. Then again, I supposed no one wanted a serial child murderer to be reincarnated. This was probably the best outcome for humanity.

Although... Deimos was the only one doing his Death Lord duties anymore. Surely he wasn't catching *everyone*.

"*You!*"

Heena stormed over, avoiding the hole in the deck and the frantic sailors trying to right the ship. She glared straight at me, which was just my luck. No thanks for any of my heroic actions, and now I had *this* lady angry?

Before she reached us, her mammoth of an eldrin crawled itself onto the deck of the ship. It wasn't graceful about it—the behemoth was more lumbering and lummox-like than anything else. It broke some more of the deck's planks as it scrabbled up into the light, its black horns glistening under the sun.

What a bizarre eldrin.

It really had a head shaped like a cow, the scales of a snake, the claws of a lizard, horns of a goat, and the body shape of a hippo. Its body was just... awkward.

Heena stopped right in front of me, blocking my view of her strange eldrin.

"You," she repeated. "Mimic arcanist."

"My name is Gray," I said.

She shushed me with a snap of her fingers. "Your eldrin just now—it transformed into an abyssal dragon. You're *that* mimic arcanist? The one the headmaster wrote about?"

"No, I'm his twin," I quipped.

Sorin snorted back a laugh, but Heena clearly didn't find that funny.

The woman adjusted her thick-rimmed glasses, her whole demeanor stiff and serious. When she stared at me now, she reminded me a bit of Exie, and I could see how they were related. While Heena was dressed like a madman—with a giant coat and pockets filled with things—she had a beautiful face, and her bun of chestnut hair was quite luscious.

She was a gorgeous researcher, hidden under a layer of madness.

"I didn't realize I was on the same sailing boat as you," Heena muttered. "I want you to transform your mimic back into that abyssal dragon this instant."

Her behemoth finally joined us. The beast stomped to its arcanist's side, its weight threatening to shatter more of the deck. Fortunately, the ship was finely crafted. Everything creaked under its weight, but nothing more broke.

The behemoth snorted, its breath reeking of grass.

"My mimic is tired," I said. "He needs some rest."

Twain shook himself, a cloud of ocean water spraying from his orange body. Afterward, he puffed out until he was almost a perfect circle. With a glower, he huffed. "I'm *not* in a good place right now. Come back after we've had some fish. And milk. And a massage."

"I have some milk," the behemoth stated, its voice both masculine, and feminine, combining into one powerful voice.

Twain, Sorin, and I all cringed and leaned a bit away. I didn't see udders on the behemoth, but I also didn't doubt that it had them. Maybe they were tucked up in the fat folds of its body.

Heena held up a hand. "Enough games. Have your mimic transform. I want a piece of the dragon."

"Whoa." I stepped between her and Twain. "You can't have a piece of him. Not now. Not ever."

Sorin also stepped forward, his expression grim. "I appreciate you having me at your estate for as long as you did, but you can't hurt my brother's eldrin."

Heena exhaled. She wasn't as tall as Sorin, but that didn't intimidate her. She stood close to my brother, glaring up at him.

"Do you know what behemoths can do?" She crossed her arms. "They can breed with almost any mystical creature. All they need to do is eat a bit of the flesh of the creature they want to imitate in order to do so."

This information...

I really didn't need to know any of that.

Sorin nervously chuckled. "Uh, okay? So you want your eldrin to be able to breed with abyssal dragons? I don't think they're that kind of creature."

"*They aren't,*" Deimos answered through me, his tone angry. "Abyssal dragons don't lay eggs. Instead, they're born from the oblivion in the fifth abyss. It happens every one hundred years, and they must make the dangerous climb to the first abyss before they bond. This is known."

Heena shook her head, smirked, and then waggled a finger. "No. *You* don't understand. A behemoth can mate with almost anything because *it* lays the eggs, not the other creature."

"Even fable-born creatures?" I asked.

Heena slowly nodded. "Well... it depends. Not always. I don't know what it'll take to create the egg of an abyssal dragon—but I can't wait to find out." She pointed at Twain. "Hurry and transform your kitten. I have things I want to discover."

Twain hissed and then leapt to my shoulder. His whiskers twitched with his growing irritation.

Heena and her behemoth didn't back away, though. They loomed close, and my brother positioned himself directly between us.

"Auntie!"

I never thought this would happen, but Exie came to save me.

With the ocean winds in her hair, Exie stepped around the sailors and sauntered her way over. Her erlking fluttered close, his little arms tightly crossed over his chest.

"Leave the Lexly brothers alone!" Exie moved around her aunt and came to a stop next to Sorin. "What did I tell you? *Stop embarrassing me.*"

"And what did I tell *you*?" Heena snapped. Then she motioned to the ship's crew, and even to Lucian, Jijo, and the distant Phila. "You should be mingling with the others. Coyly, like I taught you. Winking occasionally. Saying sweet things."

Exie's face brightened red faster than a match catching fire in a dry forest. And it wasn't just embarrassment—there was a lot of *pure rage* in her expression.

"I. Already. Told. You." Exie pointed at her aunt, her teeth clenched. "*I don't want to do that.*"

"You'll never have a true form erlking unless you do," Heena shot back. "And a true form erlking is much more valuable."

"Stop. I'm done." Exie grabbed Sorin's arm. "Come. We're all leaving. My aunt doesn't know when she's crossing boundaries." She yanked my brother away as quickly as she could walk.

Her erlking, Rex, flew over to me, grabbed my torn and bloody sleeve, and then did the same thing. He tugged me away as though we should all be outraged as a group. Frankly, I wanted to go, so I allowed him to direct my path. Twain didn't seem to mind, either. He hissed and spat at the behemoth as we passed the beast, but otherwise didn't say a thing.

"Your aunt wanted you to flirt with the crew?" Sorin asked, obviously confused.

Exie huffed out an indignant laugh. "*It's a long story.* I don't want to talk about it."

She didn't need to say anything—I already knew thanks to the bestiary.

Exie's aunt wanted her to flirt with people so they fell in love with her. Apparently, if she got enough people to do so, her erlking would achieve its true form.

That was, in my humble opinion, extremely bizarre, but her true form requirement was *much* easier than mine, so perhaps I was just jealous.

What intrigued me was that Exie didn't want to do it. She was so fixated on having my brother, I just figured she wouldn't mind everyone falling for her.

We made our way to Phila and her coatl eldrin. They were helping the sailors gather up all the torn rigging, and switch out the ripped sails for new ones. When we neared, Phila perked up, her smile spreading across her face.

"Oh, don't worry," Phila said. "We're almost done, and apparently, we'll be sailing faster than ever. Lucian is going to use his magic to speed us toward the mainland."

"We're escaping my crazy family," Exie declared. She kept her grip on Sorin's arm, even after she stopped walking. "I want to think about anything other than this stupid boat. When will we arrive at the Kross family compound?"

Phila tucked her strawberry blonde hair back behind her ears. "I don't know. I assume soon?"

A horn sounded in the distance.

Well, maybe a trumpet?

The ocean swelled, and the ship rocked with the increase in the waves. We all had to adjust our footing as the ship groaned with the new movement.

"Look, Gray," my brother said. "I think... your fiancée has come to get you."

I glanced over the port-side of the ship. Sailing toward us, at high speed, was a fancy ship with three blue sails, all with crosses decoratively sewn into the fabric. A dragon swam in the waters—a familiar sight.

It was a typhoon dragon. A normal one. Its blue scales glittered in the daylight, even though it was several feet beneath the surface. Its fins jutted above the waves, like a shark's.

"I think you're right," I muttered.

I'd finally be reunited with Ashlyn.

My future wife.

CHAPTER 21

THE KAPPA ARCANIST RETURNS

The Kross ship sliced through the open sea, cutting a quiet, steady path through the endless expanse of water and heading straight for us. The faint wind wasn't enough to swell through the sails and carry the ship, which meant it was moving solely through the magical abilities of the typhoon dragon and its arcanist.

Once the ship was close, sailors began throwing ropes over to the other crew, and carefully setting up gangplanks and braces, so that the two vessels wouldn't collide.

A man stood proudly on the deck of the other ship.

I recognized him.

Archduke Septimus Kross, Ashlyn's father.

He stank of condescension, and even gave our crew a few judgmental glances when they took too long tying everything down.

Archduke Kross wore his blond hair short, probably the length of just half my thumb. His arcanist mark was prominent on his large forehead, like he was hiding his receding hairline with the magical marking, a seven-pointed star with a typhoon dragon wrapped through the points.

He also had a scar on his face—a slash from a weapon. Arcanists didn't normally scar, since they healed so quickly, but wounds from abyssal coral didn't seem to follow normal rules. I had given Archduke Kross the injury that led to his face being marred, back when we had our little duel.

I hope he didn't resent me for it.

His pale skin didn't suit the setting. The sun looked as though it were trying to cook him. And his black robes didn't help the matter.

The archduke strode to one of the gangplanks and then scanned his gaze over our ship. He stopped when he spotted me, and I knew he was about to shout at me, but that was when Lucian stepped in.

"What're you doin' here, Septimus?" Lucian had an edge to his voice. He was genuinely angry.

Archduke Kross sneered. "Doing *your* job, obviously."

"*My* job?"

"The headmaster of Astra Academy tasked you with bringing the boy to a safe location, didn't he? What does this look like to you?"

Archduke Kross sarcastically gestured at our ruined vessel. In that moment, I almost wanted to agree with him. We *were* in a lot of trouble just a little bit ago.

Lucian stomped over to the gangplank. His Source of the Storm sat perched on his shoulder, its white feathers fluffed up in indignant rage.

"*Do you even know what we're dealing with, Septimus?*" Lucian shouted so loud, the ocean practically shuddered. "Do you remember the arcane plague? Do you remember the corrupted monsters we had to fight? This is worse."

"*Nothing* is worse than the plague-ridden monsters," Septimus spat back, his words like daggers. "And do you hear yourself? They call you a *hero* of the God-Arcanist's War, yet here you are, blubbering like a baby because some *monsters* assaulted you."

The winds around us whipped up into a noticeable cyclone. It wasn't enough to carry a person away, but my black hair fluttered in every direction, and Twain had to cling to my shoulder to maintain his balance. Was this Lucian? Was his magic causing this?

"You know nothing," Lucian stated, icy cold. "You were a paper-pusher during the war. You didn't fight our enemies like I did—*you didn't fight at all.* Don't tell me what's a threat and what's not."

The archduke looked as though someone had slapped him across the face. His face went so red, it contrasted wonderfully with the blue skies.

His typhoon dragon, Enki, swirled through the ocean waves around both boats, as though his arcanist's anger was his own.

"I fought our enemies in more important ways than you could ever imagine." Septimus's nostrils flared. "And you question my honor while barely keeping your ship, crew, and ward alive? You would've sunk down to the abyssal hells had I not come to fetch you!"

"*We were perfectly fine!*"

"The smoke from your vessel could be seen from the mainland!"

They were just... shouting at each other now. Full on, no wit, no wordplay—just yelling. It was almost disgraceful. I decided this needed to end.

I leapt onto the gangplank between boats and held up a hand. Both men stopped their tirades and turned their attention to me. So did the crew on both ships, and so did all the other arcanists, including my brother.

"Gentlemen," I sardonically said. "Am I getting married? Or are you two? It's difficult to tell."

My brother laughed. It was just a few laughs, and then he quieted himself. His reaction was the only one. Dead silence followed afterward.

I walked along the gangplank until I was almost on the archduke's ship. "Listen, does it really matter who did what in some old war? Not really. All that matters is that we get out of the water so we don't have to fight any *more* elder creatures that might be lurking in the depths. We can all agree on that, right?"

Archduke Kross smoothed his clothing and then straightened his posture. "Come. *I* will be your escort for the remainder of the trip."

"Is Ashlyn here?" I asked.

"Of course not. She's waiting at our compound. *Now come.*"

The wind howled as Lucian leapt from his ship over to the archduke's. It was so powerful, I stumbled a bit, and almost fell from the gangplank and into the ocean with Twain latched onto my shoulder. Thankfully, Sorin stepped into the darkness, shot over to my side, and then stepped out of the shadows in time to catch me.

"Careful," he said.

My heart slammed against my ribs as I glanced down.

It was quite a fall.

I almost laughed at myself. Not too long ago, I was fighting two elder creatures to the death, and I wasn't afraid, yet a little fall got me wound up?

I needed to defeat my fears no matter what. This was getting silly.

Sorin kept his hands tightly gripped on my upper shoulders until I was steady. Then we walked over together.

Lucian was face-to-face with Archduke Kross, the men so heated, I thought they were about to kill each other. While they angrily growled things at one another, the other arcanists crossed the gangplank. Exie, Phila, Heena, and even Professor Jijo.

When the professor came over, I turned to him. "Thank you for helping the crew, by the way."

He ran a hand over his bald head and smiled. "It was nothing." Then he leaned in closer to me. "Like Lucian, I've seen my fair share of warfare." Then Jijo leaned away and continued on, as though that interaction never happened.

Deimos, who hadn't been interested in anything until that moment, seemed to flare with anger. "I dislike that man," he said through me.

I shrugged. "He's on our side, right? I don't think we should push away allies."

Twain nodded along with my words. He kept his claws hooked into my robes, so he could stay on my shoulder, and even pressed his whole body against the side of my neck for support. "I also like Jijo. He seems to know what he's talking about when it comes to combat. And he helped Sorin!"

"That's true," I said.

This new vessel was quite the beauty. Someone loved the color blue, because all the doors had blue silhouettes of dragons painted onto them, and the barrels all had blue crosses painted on the outside. The deck even had blue planks over the hatches down to the hold, which was interesting. I had never seen anything like it.

As Lucian and Archduke Kross stood with their noses practically pressed against one another, I decided to glance around.

The archduke's crew was carrying over supplies to Lucian's ruined vessel, including repair boards and food, likely to help them limp back to land.

But then I saw it. One of the deckhands was a woman.

That wasn't too out of place, as I had seen lady sailors in the past, but that wasn't why I took special notice. It was because I knew the woman. I had seen her before. Unfortunately, she was wearing a hood, hiding half her face, so I didn't know exactly who she was.

"Hey," I called out, curious.

The moment the woman heard my voice, she straightened and then hurried to one of the doors into the ship's galley. Was she... avoiding me? She must've heard me call out—all her fellow sailors did. They stared at me with bewildered expressions.

With a huff, I chased after the woman.

I slammed through the door and entered the ship's galley. There was one cook, slaving over a pot and watching the fires closely. He glanced up, his beard singed, his head bald and sweaty.

The woman was already on the far side of the galley, behind the table. She was tugging on the handle of another door. Clearly, it was locked. Her escape route had been cut off.

"Hey!" I shouted at her. Then I leapt over the table and landed a foot away from her before she could scurry away.

The woman whirled around and pressed her back to the door. Her forehead was covered with a bandana, but that didn't matter. I recognized her now that she was close.

Rosella Silvers.

She was a kappa arcanist who worked with Deimos's brother and was one of the crazy cult people who worshipped Death Lords—specifically, Deimos himself, not the other lords. The same crazy cult people who either tried to kidnap me or kill me.

She was a woman with long dark hair, the ends of which were uneven and matted. She had equally dark rings under her eyes, as though she hadn't slept in months, and her skin was paler than most. She must've hated sunlight.

I grabbed her forearm. "What're you doing here?" I barked.

Twain arched his back. "Yeah! Tell us or else!"

I used my mimic ability to sense the threads of magic nearby. Sure enough, I felt Rosella's kappa eldrin down below, probably hidden in the hold.

"Please," Rosella whispered. "I mean you no harm."

Last time I had seen her, she was fighting with her fellow cult members against Lucian and trying to prevent me from going back to Astra Academy.

"You're lying," I growled. "You were pretending to be one of the crew just now! You tried to hide from me. You're obviously up to something." I yanked her arm, trying to take her out of the galley. "Let's go."

Rosella pulled me back, but didn't attack or use her magic. I tensed, half tempted to pull my weapon and escalate this to a proper fight.

"Please," Rosella whispered. "I didn't mean to deceive you. I was only hiding until you came aboard—so I could find a moment to speak with you in private."

"Is everything okay over there?" the ship's cook asked.

"I have this under control," I said.

"Uh. R-Right."

The cook awkwardly turned around and stared at the pot of food.

Rosella stepped closer to me, and I gritted my teeth. I half expected her to attack me—to attempt to flee—but instead, she lowered her voice even further. "Please, Death Lord Deimos. I know you're fighting for control of that shambling body. I took the place of a crewmember in the hopes of finding you—and helping you."

With half-lidded eyes, in the most sarcastic stare ever, I asked, "Really? *Shambling body*? You know I'm my own person, right?"

Rosella shook her head. "I watched you fight Lucian to escape Lord Oto's compound. Only Death Lord Deimos would fight so ferociously. You are but a normal child—soon to be overcome by the Death Lord's will. I know it."

I rolled my eyes, but that was fine. She wasn't trying to hurt me, at least.

"Why are you here?" I asked under my breath, a little nervous with how close she was.

"I told you—you're the only one who can help me."

She seemed desperate now.

"Help *you*?" I lifted an eyebrow.

"I need to go to the abyssal hells. I have to speak to my son. I'll do anything—just allow me to stay close, so that whenever the Twilight Gate opens again, I may journey with you."

Ah. Right. I remembered her plight. She wanted to speak with her deceased child.

Deimos growled, but didn't actually articulate any words. When he was done being irritated, I released Rosella's arm.

"Fine," I said. "You can stay close—but you have to stay *real* close, got it? If anyone asks, you're my bodyguard now, type of close."

Rosella's eyes went wide with surprise. Her eyes were the same dark color as her hair, nearly black. She appeared hopeful now, though. I liked that. It was better than her standard depression.

"You *will* take me?" she asked, breathless.

I nodded once.

"The captain doesn't normally like passengers in here," the cook muttered. He didn't turn to face us; he just watched his pot as though it needed his full attention.

I motioned for Rosella to follow. "Come on—let's go see Lucian."

Rosella leapt forward and then grabbed my arm. "Please! Not him. He's an unforgiving monster. If he knows who I am, he'll—"

"Don't worry," I said. "I'll handle everything."

CHAPTER 22

THE KROSS FAMILY COMPOUND

"*You'll handle everything?*" Twain whispered into my ear. He clung to my shoulder, even when he glanced backward to cast a suspicious eye at Rosella. "How are you going to explain away her presence? She's bad news."

I patted his orange head. "Hey, not only have I done the impossible—by getting into the abyssal hells—but I've done it *twice*, by also escaping. I think I can handle explaining away Rosella's presence on the ship."

"Mm-hm." Twain waggled his whiskers, his eyes narrowed.

He didn't believe me.

With a chuckle, I made my way across the deck and went straight for Exie. She stood near the railing of the archduke's ship, her beautiful brown hair fluttering in the wind. It was too short to go too far, but it was long enough to throw locks into her eyes. She constantly smoothed it down and stared into the wind, trying to keep it all under control.

"Oh, there you are," I said as I slid up next to her.

With a deep frown, she crossed her arms. Her erlking, Rex, fluttered around her head. "Yes?" she asked, curt.

"You're just the person I wanted to see."

"*Exie?*" Twain asked, shocked.

"*Exie?*" Rex asked at nearly the same time.

Exie pressed her lips together into a tight line. "I haven't spoken to your brother, thank you very much."

I waved away the comment. "No, no, no. I'm not here about that. I came to ask a favor." Then I motioned for Rosella to step close. "If anyone asks, I want you to say this is your cousin who got mixed in with some bad people and used to go to Astra Academy and is now returning?"

"Why can't I just pretend to be *your* cousin?" Rosella whispered.

"Because I was born to a candlemaker, and no one would believe I had cousins who went to Astra Academy," I sarcastically whispered back.

"Ah, such humble beginnings for the vessel of Death Lord Deimos," Rosella said, basically to no one.

Exie's irritation didn't fade. "Why should I?"

I shrugged. "I know about your aunt—and about the true form requirement of your erlking." I pointed at her. "You just want my brother to fall for you because it'll help you gain magical power. And if you don't want me spreading that around, I think you can help me with this teeny tiny favor."

I thought I had caught her red-handed, and that she would immediately capitulate, but the instant I brought up her true form requirement, Exie grew red in the face and practically shook with visible anger.

"*Tsk!*" She stomped her heel and turned away in one dramatic movement. "You know *nothing*. Tell everyone on the damn ship about the erlking and how it requires its arcanist to gain the love of three people. Go on. I don't care one bit because I'll *never* do that. Not now. Not ever."

Rex fluttered around her head. He just frowned. He

didn't add to the conversation—neither affirming nor denying Exie's claims.

"Why not?" I asked.

"Because I want just *one* person to love me." Exie stomped her foot again, all drama. "I want *true love*. Beautiful love. Perfect—like a fairy tale."

I almost made a sarcastic comment about how breaking up my brother from Nini wasn't anything like a fairy tale, but I decided to keep that to myself.

"I can't have true love if I'm always moving on to the next man." Exie's tone had softened. "And I won't do anything my aunt says. She's weird. Too weird. I think she *only* loves mystical creatures and strange magic."

"Okay, then how about this." I stepped in close and lowered my voice. "Sorin once wrote a poem about true love. If you do me this favor, I'll tell you all about it."

Exie turned back to face me. "He... did?"

Technically, Sorin had written like fifty poems about true love, but I wasn't about to admit that. "Yes," I finally said.

"And it was beautiful?"

"So beautiful."

Twain nodded. "I agree. It was one of his better poems."

Exie fixed her hair for the hundredth time as she mulled over my proposal. Before she managed to speak, however, Lucian himself came stomping over to us.

I loosened my posture, trying to look relaxed, but Rosella immediately grabbed my arm like she was in danger—which looked more suspicious than the fruit in the abyssal hells. Lucian immediately homed in on it, eyeing her as he approached.

His Source of the Storm puffed up his white feathers, and gave us all tiny angry eyes, glaring in an adorable manner.

"Who is this?" Lucian demanded. "Is this one of the cultists from Lord Oto's compound?"

I opened my mouth to speak, but Exie beat me to the punch.

"Don't talk to her that way," she snapped. "She's of House Lolian and you will be civil to her." Exie took Rosella's arm and pulled her off of mine. "She's my dear cousin. We thought we had lost her, but she's come to her senses and wants to return to the Academy posthaste."

Exie's indignant rage sold the whole thing.

Lucian rolled his eyes as he glanced away from Rosella. "Very well, but if *anything* happens involving her, I'll throw her into the water." He shot a glare at her arcanist mark. "I know kappa arcanists can swim just fine—unlike their children."

Rosella tensed, her face losing color.

"How dare you," Exie snapped. "Is this what you consider *civil*? I thought you were a war hero."

Somehow, Lucian always seemed to anger whoever he was talking to. It was his special ability.

"Listen," he snapped, "just stay on this ship. I couldn't talk any sense into the archduke, so that means you're all to stay in the cabins until we reach House Kross, do you understand? I don't want anyone splitting up, or going on any unsanctioned adventures, or anyone secretly attacking someone else—*just stop causing me problems and be good little students until you reach your damn school.*"

There was a moment of silence after his tirade.

I couldn't help myself.

"But we're allowed to go on *sanctioned* adventures?" I quipped.

Lucian's glare could kill.

He did *not* like my sense of humor.

I almost wanted to say, "*Let's turn that frown upside down, Grumpy!*" but I was pretty certain he would throw overboard for that.

"How long will it take us to reach House Kross?" I asked.

Lucian exhaled some of his anger. "In this vessel... before nightfall."

Exie fiddled with her hair and sighed. "Very well. We'll wait in the cabin." Then she clapped her hands. "Cousin—come with me."

Rosella offered me a nervous glance, but I subtly motioned for her to go. Exie and Rosella then hurried away, leaving me alone with Lucian.

He jabbed a finger into my chest. "Don't. Do. Anything. You stay in the cabin. Understand?"

"Aye, aye." I sarcastically saluted him, and Twain did the same thing.

The cabin was quite luxurious. Archduke Kross had spared no expense. The rooms didn't have cots or hammocks—there were actual beds with soft mattresses. How did he keep them dry and not lumpy? Most ships could never manage it.

Sorin, Phila, Exie, Rosella, and I all shared a single cabin, and for the most part, it was dead silent. The cabin was meant for two people, as it only had two tiny beds, and a few chests for belongings, which meant we all had to sit in awkward locations.

Sorin sat near the porthole, staring at the waves. Phila sat on the edge of one bed, playing with her coatl, practicing her wind manipulation. Exie sat on a trunk, one leg crossed over the other. Rosella stood next to her, like an attentive servant. I was spread out across the other bed, half staring at the ceiling, trying not to think too much about Ashlyn.

Nerves were starting to set in.

Phila managed to lift a large chest off the ground for a long while, but the whirlwind of air was rather irritating in a confined space.

"Sorry," she whispered, and then stopped. The trunk slammed down on the floor with a hard *clunk*.

"Who are you again?" Sorin asked as he tore his attention away from the waves and stared at Rosella. "I get this feeling like... you shouldn't be here."

"I'm a humble servant to House Lolian." Rosella bowed again. "I'm here to carry luggage."

"What a blatant lie," Thurin said.

My brother's knightmare was nothing more than a puddle of shadow around my brother's bed, but whenever he spoke, the edges of the shadows fluttered like bat wings, betraying their supernatural qualities.

I held up a hand. "Calm down, Thurin. Everything is okay. This, uh, new servant is here because she's a friend of mine."

Rosella gasped.

Everyone in the tiny cabin turned to her.

"Death Lord Deimos... considers me a friend?" Rosella smiled slightly, her lower lip quavering. "I'm honored."

Oh, jeez.

Thurin rose out of the darkness. As a suit of armor, he was rather intimidating, even if he was missing a few pieces. His feathery cloak fluttered as he pointed at Rosella. "You're one of the *cultists*."

I stood from the bed and held up both hands. "Hey, hey. She is, but that's okay. You see, she *also* wants to get to the abyssal hells and it's for a good cause."

"What is a good cause? There can be no good cause to infiltrate the land of the dead."

I shook my head. "She wants to speak with her dead son. Isn't that noble? Or at the very least, beautiful?"

Thurin didn't reply to that. And since he was just hollow

armor, with no face or expression, it was difficult to know what he was thinking.

"Plus," I said, holding up a finger, "she's also a kappa arcanist, so that means she can be a valuable asset."

"A *kappa* arcanist?" Thurin scoffed. When he lifted his hand, my brother's black trident lifted out from the shadows as well. It flew up into Thurin's gauntleted hand and he grabbed it with the firmness of a warrior. "No wonder she wants to speak with her dead son."

Rosella tensed, her eyes wide with shock. "Y-You know?"

"Everyone knows the kappa's Trial of Worth."

Everyone in the cabin—besides Rosella and Thurin—tilted their heads in the universal sign of confusion.

Had we learned about the kappa in class yet? I couldn't remember. Fortunately, I still had Exie's aunt's bestiary, so I could check, but I didn't know the kappa's Trial of Worth off the top of my head.

"It involves—" Thurin began.

"*Stop!*" Rosella practically screamed the word. Then she covered both her ears with her hands and turned away. Her shoulders shuddered and she stepped into the corner of our cabin. "I don't want to hear," Rosella said through clenched teeth.

My brother leapt away from the porthole. "Thurin—enough. There's no need to distress her."

The knightmare, his emotions still a mystery, simply slipped back into the darkness.

I made a mental note to check the bestiary later.

"Oh!" Phila also leapt to her feet. "Look there!" She pointed at the porthole window, a smile wide on her face.

I walked over, as did Sorin.

Through the small window, I peered out across the sapphire blue of the ocean. A dock and house were on the horizon, clearly in view, dark against the horizon.

The Kross Family Compound.

The compound was a thing of beauty, built into the landscape with a fierce grace. The roofs of the buildings were sleek and curved like dragon wings, their tiles glistening from the salt spray that constantly battered them. The high walls of dark stone were draped with creeping vines, as though even nature itself sought to contain the power housed within.

Typhoon dragons, carved from black granite, each one poised mid-dive, decorated the edge of the port.

The archduke's ship slid into the sheltered bay of the compound's port, the water beneath it turning a deep, inky blue. Here, in the shadow of the cliffs, the wind was still. Fortunately, the archduke's very own typhoon dragon could manipulate the water. We were brought into the port without any trouble, guided by a magical current.

"This is amazing," Sorin whispered.

I nodded once. "I guess this is my new home."

"It's impressive."

The typhoon dragons were more than just creatures to the Kross family—they were clearly symbols, embodiments of the raw, untamed power. No wonder the archduke liked them so much. They were seemingly carved into everything that allowed their shape.

The archduke's ship gently bumped against the dock, and I heard the busy footfalls of the sailors as they unloaded everything. I even heard Archduke Kross shouting orders— the man was not quiet.

"Okay, it looks like we need to gather our belongings." I whirled on my heel, happy to be off the boat, but my attention fell on Rosella.

She was still in the corner of the cabin.

I quickly walked over to her, tapped her on the shoulder, and then motioned to the door. She slowly removed her hands from her ears, her body still shaky.

"Are you okay?" I asked. "Thurin didn't say anything." I held out my hand. "You don't have to worry—Death Lord Deimos is here, remember?"

I said that last part as more of a joke, but then Deimos actually spoke through me. "I know of kappas and their requirement. You needn't fear judgment from other mortals— only the voice of your son matters at this point."

Water welled in Rosella's eyes. "Y-Yes. You're right... I... I need to speak with him. It's more important than anything else."

Now I was *extra* curious. What did kappas require?

But then I heard the whistle. It was the signal to disembark.

CHAPTER 23

TRUSTING YOURSELF

--Nini's Perspective--

Time became meaningless.

I walked until my legs ached, until my fingertips were raw from running them along the walls.

And yet, I continued. Not out of hope—I had abandoned that long ago—but out of stubborn defiance. Each step forward was an act of rebellion against the oppressive will of the labyrinth, a refusal to give in to the suffocating darkness. Sorin wouldn't give up, and I couldn't let him down. I had to keep going.

But every corridor appeared to be the same as the last.

Every. One.

And my bell did *nothing!* I didn't know how to use it, and in frustration, I wanted to throw it away.

"*This is a place people come to get lost,*" Waste said. "*It is a place for souls to wander, seeking answers they will never know.*"

I turned my attention upward. The blue motes of light that faintly danced around overhead were souls, that I knew, but I didn't understand what kept *them* here. I couldn't fly over the walls, lest I lose my eyesight. The souls didn't have eyes, though. What kept them here?

After shaking my head, I pressed on. I kept the bell in my hand, just in case it did something useful, and just focused on the corridor.

I also whispered small prayers to the good stars, not for deliverance, but for the strength to keep my legs from giving out. There was no sense of progress, no promise of an end, only the cold certainty that the labyrinth would win if I faltered.

"Ah!" I cried out as my foot found nothing solid. I nearly stumbled forward, caught by surprise. When I glanced at the floor, it was the same mirror-like surface. When I inspected further, I realized there was a loose tile—perhaps a trap?

Could I fall out of the labyrinth? Or perhaps... it would lead to death...

Then I heard the scrap of claws and clop of hooves. Were they in my imagination? I doubted it. I stood tall and backed away from the loose tile.

Then I held out my hand, and my scythe flew straight into my grip. The gold weapon gleamed as I slowly turned around to face the sounds of the approaching creatures.

I had been correct. Two beings rounded a corner and came into my section of the labyrinth. It was an elder golden stag and an elder basilisk. The stag was bizarre when compared to the other creatures. It didn't have a mane of souls; instead, it had bluish souls clinging to its majestic antlers.

The souls themselves looked like paper that had been blown into the prongs and were then caught. The flailing arms of the once-humans were wrapped around the antlers, dangling, struggling, their faces contorted.

It appeared as though an invisible wind was blowing them

upward, and if they let go of the antlers, they would fly away and never be seen again.

"It seems we found you," the elder golden stag said, his voice deep and regal. When he strode forward, his cloven hooves clopped louder and louder. He stopped once he was about thirty feet away. "Reaper arcanist—why do you walk in circles?"

The basilisk snaked its way up behind the stag. It was monstrous, and muscled, and its mane of souls seemed much bigger than the other basilisks who had attacked me. Flashing its fangs, the creature asked, "Are you lost? How ironic."

"Get away from me," I said, my dry throat raspy, Waste's voice more prominent than my own.

"Xuandi's offer still stands," the stag said, lowering his head as though half bowing to me. "You can stay merged with your reaper and join our ranks. Come, young arcanist. Come with us. You look lost and hurt—I can heal all your injuries and bring you soothing comfort."

I readied my scythe. There was no chance I would go with them.

The elder basilisk hissed as it moved in front of the stag. Standing up on two legs, and flexing its other four claws, the beast said, "Xuandi said I shouldn't bite you—that you're immune to death magic—but that doesn't matter. You're out of time, arcanist. Soon, your soul will wander these halls for eternity."

"Unless we decide to eat it," the stag muttered, his tone now icy and serious.

I took a combat stance, Waste's magic flowing through me as much as adrenaline.

The elder basilisk stepped forward, fangs bared. When the beast rushed me, it was on all six legs, its body moving concertina, like a snake.

I held out my hand and evoked my terrors. One basilisk didn't frighten me.

My mental horrors bombarded the basilisk's mind. It stopped halfway to me, screeching as it whipped its head from side to side.

"That won't work here," the elder golden stag said.

The stag evoked something, and the corridor of the hallway felt more... tranquil. Even my own anger and frustration seemed to be at ease.

The basilisk refocused on me and then lunged. The stag's magic must've cancelled mine out—but I was still prepared. I leapt out of the way, the golden chains of my reaper helping me move. Like the extra legs of a spider, the chains stretched and carried me along. They clattered whenever they struck the floor or the walls.

When the basilisk turned and slashed with its claws, I answered with my scythe. The blade pierced its scales and went deep into the basilisk's shoulder. It cried out, but maintained its confident smile. When I yanked my weapon out, blood gushed to the floor.

The stag waved his head, and the corridor felt... strange.

The basilisk's injury healed right before my eyes. Its shoulder—which once had a hole—was now as muscled and firm as it had been before I struck it.

Mystical creatures couldn't normally heal that fast...

"You have a death wish," I said, shifting all my focus on the golden stag.

The chains lifted me high and then I used them as four long legs, the lanterns almost acting as feet. I thought the glass might break, and the flames might go out, but they never did. They seemed harder than steel, and *banged* on the floor as I scurried over like a spider wielding a scythe.

I swung for the stag, but it was *fast*.

The majestic creature nimbly leapt away. Its cloven hooves

clip-clopped on the floor as it danced around me, avoiding my scythe whenever I swung.

I held out my hand and evoked my terrors, hoping to frighten it for just a moment, but they had no effect whatsoever. Was the stag immune to fear?

The basilisk slammed into me from behind. It dug its claws into my cloak and then through my back, tearing Waste's red fabric and my fragile flesh in one terrible blow.

I manipulated the blood dripping on the floor and sent a hundred little daggers of hardened crimson straight into the air. They *thwipped* through the basilisk, slicing its flesh in a dozen locations.

But then it instantly healed, the elder golden stag repairing its wounds long before I could capitalize on them.

"Waste," I said as I backed away from the basilisk. "I..."

"My arcanist, rely on my calm. If we can create an aura, we might be able to win."

I had never created an aura before. That wouldn't work.

The basilisk leapt for my face, its claws outstretched. My chains moved me out of the way, but my body felt as though it were on fire. Agony lanced through me. I didn't know how much more of this I could take.

The basilisk laughed as it went for me again, and I was forced to retreat.

"Reapers create an anemia aura—it prevents healing and even causes old injuries to reopen. Please, my arcanist. Focus."

An anemia aura?

It sounded as though it would work, but my poor body couldn't handle much more. The corners of my vision darkened, and my hearing grew worse. I feared I would collapse soon.

"If you cannot summon the magic to create an aura, then you must run."

Run?

But where?

At first, I thought that was futile as well, but then I remembered the tile in the floor. I turned toward it, rushing down the corridor. The basilisk gave chase, its laughter growing bolder.

"*You can't escape,*" the basilisk said with a chuckle. "Sooner or later, I'll catch you!"

I waved my hand and manipulated the blood on the floor. Instead of making them into weapons—and going for the kill —I created a wall of scarlet. The wall lifted up between me and the two elder creatures. The basilisk slammed into it, cracking my creation. Then it dug its claws into it, its growling echoing throughout the corridor.

It would break it. And soon.

But I didn't care.

While they were on the other side, and unable to see me, I used a chain to lift the tile in the floor. I slipped under it, entering a dark underground tunnel. Then I slid the tile back into place overhead, leaving me in the dank environment.

My four lanterns kept the area illuminated, but it reminded me of a sewer.

Was this part of the labyrinth?

I heard the click of hooves and the scrape of claws, but not their voices. The elder beasts ran back and forth for a short moment before leaving.

"I think we're safe," I whispered.

"*This tunnel... It goes a long way.*"

I turned around. Waste was correct. This tunnel was massive—at least seven feet from the floor to the ceiling—and it went on so long I couldn't see the end. It was just darkness beyond my lantern light. Well, not *just* darkness. There were bluish motes of light, drifting aimlessly.

And it was damp, as though water were seeping through the walls.

Blood slowly crept down my back, soaking into my clothes and then dropping onto the floor near my feet. The basilisk had dug furrows through my flesh, and they burned with agony. I exhaled, thankful to still be alive.

"*We must press on,*" Waste said.

I nodded. "We can't give up."

No matter what, I'd find my way out of here.

CHAPTER 24

ASHLYN KROSS

As I stepped onto the wooden gangplanks, the familiar scent of land filled my nose. I gazed up at the towering walls of the Kross compound, my heart quickening. It wasn't because of fear—it was anticipation. It felt like *forever* since I had last seen Ashlyn.

Plus, this *was* my new home.

I didn't really like that thought... Especially not with the shadows of typhoon dragons looming above me. This place had all the welcoming warmth of a meat grinder.

Sorin walked down the gangplanks with me and Twain. My eldrin sat on my shoulders, and Sorin's skirted around in the darkness near his feet.

"This place inspires me," Sorin muttered. After he cleared his throat, he spoke in his poetic manner. "*Beneath the waves, where silence reigns... Typhoon dragons swim watery plains... Majestic tails sweep currents wide... They ride the tides with graceful pride.*"

I wanted to make a quip about the last line, but my words were cut short when Archduke Kross walked down the gangplank. He practically stormed down, and his eyes were already narrowed.

"Was that *poetry?*" he asked as he stepped around my brother. "What they teach at that Academy baffles me," he muttered under his breath before turning his attention to me. "*You.* Come. The rest of your classmates will be dealt with separately."

I held up a hand. "But—"

"*We haven't much time,*" the archduke barked. "Now follow me."

He walked down the little dock, straight to the dragon-themed compound. I glanced over at my brother, and we shared a silent conversation. He motioned with a tilt of his head, telling me it was okay to go. I nodded, and then headed off to follow the archduke.

The others walked off the ship as I left, and I wished I could've stayed.

I kept pace with the archduke, even though his gait was long, like he wanted to rush into the house and get everything over with.

"You'll only be here a few days, and then it's off to the Academy to start your second term," Archduke Kross stated. "Do you understand?"

"Yup," I replied.

"Don't be flippant with me, boy. I'm soon to be your father."

That statement caused me to internally cringe. I decided to ignore it.

We walked through the front gate, up the steps to the front door, and then entered the massive compound. The first thing that greeted me was the faint, rhythmic bubbling of water. Fish tanks, dozens of them, lined the walls in every direction.

Schools of vibrant fish darted through the water, their

movements as fluid and graceful as the gentle current that swept through the tanks. Servants hurried through the halls, carrying white lilies and decorating for a celebration. It was as though the entire compound was alive, not just with people, but with the constant pulse of aquatic life.

"You have a nice home," I said, trying to start a conversation.

Archduke Kross sighed. "Consider it your home, too." He didn't enjoy speaking a single word of that sentence.

"I love this place," Twain whispered into my ear. He pointed with a paw at a fish tank filled with orange and white fish. "That's my bedroom."

I smiled. "Calm down. You're going to get me in trouble if you massacre a school of fish the first night here."

As we walked further into the compound, the air shifted, becoming warmer and more welcoming. The heart of the home revealed itself—a large, open library filled with floor-to-ceiling shelves. The spines of old and new books were meticulously arranged, some worn and familiar, others pristine and unopened.

In one corner of the room, I spied a cozy reading nook. Cushioned armchairs surrounded by soft pillows sat tucked beneath a wide window that overlooked the largest of the fish tanks—one that had a gigantic green parrotfish within.

"It *feels* like we're underwater," Twain said, his large ears perked.

"It kinda reminds me of the abyssal hells," I replied.

Archduke Kross stopped and whirled on his heel to face me. His frown was quite prominent. "*Mind what you say*," he hissed through clenched teeth. Then he motioned to the reading area. "Stay right here. I'm going to make sure your room is set. Then you rest and prepare yourself for the wedding tomorrow."

"It's *tomorrow*?" I asked, shocked it was so soon.

The archduke replied with a curt nod. "You will have one day to stay here with Ashlyn, because after that you depart for one of the Gates of Crossing. Any further questions?"

I shook my head. "No, sir." I sounded more sarcastic than responsible.

The archduke didn't like that.

With a huff, he turned and headed deeper into the compound. I watched him go before meandering around the cozy little reading nook. To my surprise, a few books were left open, one about influential arcanists. It looked more like a fairy tale book, complete with pictures and great deeds written like an epic.

"Gray?"

Both Twain and I practically leapt out of our skin. I turned, and Twain had his claws locked into my shoulder.

Ashlyn stood next to me in the reading nook.

I caught my breath, suddenly losing my words.

Ashlyn was beautiful—she had always been beautiful—but today something was different. Her blonde hair hung loose and flowed over her shoulders. The arcanist mark on her forehead was prominent, with the seven-pointed star and dragon laced through the points as striking as her other features.

Her athletic frame was clothed in a white dress that hugged her nicely. Probably too nicely, but I didn't dare give her the once over—I just met her blue gaze and half smiled.

"I don't think your father wants me spending time with you before the wedding," I said.

"Heh, he's your father too, now, remember?" Twain huffed a laugh.

I glared at him. "You're making this weird."

Ashlyn didn't say anything—she just ran over and threw her arms around me. She hit me with such force I stumbled back on one foot, shocked. Twain leapt off my shoulder and landed on the nice seat, his orange fur puffed in surprise.

I slowly wrapped my arms around Ashlyn. "Yeah," I awkwardly said, chuckling. "I missed you, too."

She was warm. And soft. But also firm. It was hard to describe without going into the specifics... I brought a hand up to caress her silky hair. She smelled of cherries, for some reason. I loved it.

When she stepped away, I almost pulled her back into the embrace.

"I wish you would've gotten here sooner," Ashlyn said in a playful tone.

I shrugged. "I'm sorry. I've been takin' my time getting here. I had to see my own family, and get my brother, and learn about my powers, and—"

Ashlyn stepped close and put a finger to my lips, halting my excuses. I stopped talking, especially as she leaned in close.

"What's your favorite color?" she asked.

"Gray," I said with a laugh. "For obvious reasons."

Ashlyn brought her lips to the shell of my ear. "Then that's the color I'll be wearing underneath my dress tomorrow."

My heart skipped a beat. It felt like it flipped a little, really. All my thoughts came to a halt—except for the fact that I regretted answering "gray" to her question.

Ashlyn stepped back, giggled, and grazed her knuckles over my hot cheek. "You're cute when you blush like this."

Before I could gather all my thoughts, Ashlyn stepped around me. She headed in the same direction her father had gone. After a few steps, she glanced over her shoulder.

"I can't wait for tomorrow," Ashlyn said.

My chest felt knotted. "I look forward to it as well."

After Archduke Kross left me in my new room, I paced for a few hours.

The walls of my room were adorned with paintings of the ocean—waves crashing against distant shores, stormy skies, and the deep, quiet blues of the sea. The bed was draped in plush white linens, the headboard a deep blue wood that matched the color of the rest of the house.

I also had a personal hand-knitted blanket embraided with the images of typhoon dragons eating fish at the foot of my bed. Apparently, Ashlyn's grandmother had made it for our wedding night—and as a blanket for our first child.

The Kross family didn't mess around, it seemed.

Twain sat on the pillow of my bed, watching me as I walked back and forth.

"Are you nervous?" he asked.

"No," I quickly replied. "I have bigger things to worry about than my wedding, thank you very much."

"You seem nervous to me."

I shrugged. Then I eyed him. "Do mimics breed? I mean, like, do they make kittens in the old-fashioned way?"

"I was born from the Mother of Shapeshifters," Twain replied matter-of-factly. "So, I don't think mimics make children like humans do."

Thankfully, I still had Heena's bestiary. It was brought to my room along with what few belongings I had. I walked over and opened it up to the section about mimics.

Mimic

A mimic is a mystical creature who regularly changes shape—transforming into other mystical creatures, but only those close enough for the mimic to feel their magic. However, when a mimic is in its natural form, it appears to be a domestic housecat. The color of their fur in their "cat form" is either gray, pink, orange, tan, or a light blue. All mimics have heterochromia, and the colors of these eyes are limited to the same as the mimic's fur colors.

Trial of Worth

In order to bond with a mimic, one must gain the approval of the Mother of Shapeshifters by claiming they are "afraid of nothing." Those who fail to give the correct answer are killed and made into doppelgängers.

Tier

1 to 4—mimics are whatever tier of creature they transform into is, up to tier 4. They cannot mimic god-creatures and it is unknown whether they can mimic unique creatures, such as the Mother of Shapeshifters or the Source of the Storm.

Reproduction: Progeny

Mimics are born from The Mother of Shapeshifters, a unique mystical creature who has birthed all mimics and doppelgängers that exist. The Mother of Shapeshifters is the only creature who can birth mimics.

Well, here was my answer.

But then I flipped to the page about the typhoon dragon, my thoughts continually returning to Ashlyn. Her true form requirement caught my eye again, and I wondered if I should give her my gift before or after the ceremony.

Logically, I would give her a gift *during* the ceremony, but my heart said I should go find her now.

It was night—the moon shone through the far window, and the glowstones built into the ceiling offered a warm yellow glow that made everything cozy. This was the perfect atmosphere to be romantic, wasn't it?

Of course.

And any reason to see Ashlyn early was a good reason in my book.

I shut the bestiary. "Twain, we should go find Ashlyn."

He stood straight and stared at me with wide eyes. "R-Really? Is that allowed?"

"Well, we can sneak around and go find her."

"How are we going to do that?"

I tapped the side of my head. "We'll be clever."

I felt for magic in the nearby area, sensing the threads of power that connected me to all things mystical. I sensed three typhoon dragons nearby, each one more powerful than the last. I also sensed Phila's coatl, and Exie's erlking...

But as soon as I sensed Sorin's knightmare, that was all I needed.

I tugged on that thread, and Twain transformed into a shadowy suit of hollow armor, his cat form bubbling upward and shifting black. Once his body fully formed, he resembled Thurin in almost all regards—and now he was standing on the middle of my bed with his full plate boots.

My arcanist mark burned as a shield and a cape appeared in my seven-pointed star.

With a dramatic sweep of his feathery cape, Twain stepped down onto the floor and chortled. "Ah. We'll sneak through the shadows. How convenient."

"And we can slip under doors with the knightmare's ability to step through shadows," I said with a smile. "Perfect for looking around, I'd say."

"Excellent."

CHAPTER 25

MY WEDDING GIFT

I stepped out of my new room and into the hallway.

It was still bizarre to me that this was my new home. The blue rugs and white walls were very ocean themed, and it wasn't exactly my aesthetic. However, it was *much* better than my family home on the Isle of Haylin, so what did it even matter?

"C'mon," I whispered.

Twain, still wearing the skin of a knightmare, stepped close to me, his darkness plate armor quietly clinking with each step. He stepped close to me, his feathery cape fluttering behind him.

"Where is Ashlyn's room?" he asked, keeping his tone low.

With my mimic magic, I sensed for the typhoon dragons a second time. The strings of magic were all different, even if they came from similar mystical creatures. I could tell if one was older, or more powerful. Ecrib, Ashlyn's dragon, was younger than her father's and brother's, so I sensed for the weakest typhoon dragon thread.

I found it—in a room one floor below us.

For some reason, all my friends were on the same floor as

me—the second story, basically—and all the Kross family members were below us.

I motioned to Twain to follow me back into my room. He tilted his head, and although knightmares didn't have faces, I knew he was confused. I went straight to my window, opened it a tiny crack, and then slid into the darkness.

Knightmares were strange, and powerful, and I never got used to stepping into shadows. It was like sinking into water, until I was completely submerged in the void, unable to see. I had to sense the world around me as I slithered as a puddle of darkness through the open window and across the outside wall of the compound.

Twain followed me as the same kind of darkness creeping along the wall.

With surprising speed, I darted down to the ground floor and then stepped out of the darkness, emerging head-first and walking up as though there was a set of stairs in the shadows I was slowly ascending.

Once again, Twain followed my example, clinking as he also emerged from the depths of the void.

"Follow me," I said.

With my mimic magic, I headed around the outside of the compound. The warm glow of lights shone through most windows, illuminating the bushes and gardens. I ducked under each window, hoping I would avoid detection. If someone found me, I was certain they would ask questions, and I didn't want to tell them I was sneaking into Ashlyn's room the night before our wedding.

The archduke would be upset.

Creeping through the garden of my future home made me feel both silly and rebellious. Thankfully, I didn't get to dwell on it long—Ashlyn's room was located at the corner of the main compound building.

There was a balcony connected to her room, and it was the

cutest little thing I had ever seen. Firstly, it wasn't very high up. It was five feet above the garden, and it was mostly a pool of water. Sitting in that balcony pool was none other than Ecrib, Ashlyn's typhoon dragon eldrin.

He had gotten large and was now nearly the size of a full-grown horse. Ecrib's scales came in every shade of blue, from the indigo of twilight, to the deep aqua of the ocean. He was a dragon of the water, which meant he didn't have wings, but instead, he had enough fins to make a whole gang of sharks jealous.

His gold eyes shone from the illumination of the glowstones, and he lazily rolled through the water, basically bathing himself.

I crouch-walked over to the balcony and then dove through the darkness, shadow-stepping my way over the outside wall of the compound, and up to Ecrib's pool. When I emerged from the dark, Ecrib's scales flared, and he flashed his impressive fangs while letting out a deep, guttural growl.

"Whoa, whoa," I said, holding up both my hands. "It's me. Your second-favorite arcanist."

Electricity crackled around Ecrib, but he eventually took in a deep breath, calming himself. His scales flattened against his body, and he narrowed his eyes to glare at me.

"What're you doing here? The wedding isn't until tomorrow."

Ashlyn's voice rang out from inside her bedroom. "Ecrib? Is everything okay?"

"I'm here to see her," I whispered. "Do you mind?"

Twain shifted through the shadows and emerged next to me. While still in knightmare form, he sarcastically saluted Ecrib.

"Feh," Ecrib finally said. Then he returned to rolling through the outdoor pool and cleaning himself.

He halfway reminded me of a cat in that moment...

But I ignored that thought and hesitantly knocked on the door that connected Ashlyn's bedroom to the balcony. A moment later, the door swung open.

Ashlyn stood before me in a simple outfit—a pair of riding shorts and a thin white tunic. No matter what she wore, she was beautiful, but she was most like herself whenever she appeared athletic and adventurous.

"Fancy meeting you here," I playfully said.

Ashlyn quickly glanced around me. Then she grabbed the front of my shirt and pulled me inside. Under her breath she hissed, "*What're you doing?* We shouldn't see each other the night before the wedding!"

Twain slid through the darkness in order to bypass the closed door. When he stepped up into the room, he transformed back into his mimic form, his body bubbling and shaping itself back into the form of an orange cat with a bobtail.

I lost the knightmare magic, and the mark on my forehead went back to being just a seven-pointed star.

Ashlyn's room...

I had never seen it before.

A small collection of books rested on a bedside table, and more were scattered around the room—on shelves, on the floor, as if they had been pulled out in haste but never returned to their proper place.

The walls were adorned with fragments of her life— pictures, old drawings, and notes tacked up in a way that told me she had grown up here, in this very room. A vanity by the window had scattered knickknacks, like seashells and jewelry.

But the most striking feature was her bed. It was covered in stuffed animals of various shapes and sizes. She had a fluffy dog, a large blue shark, a whale the size of a chair, thirteen teddy bears, a squirrel, three rizzels, five owls, a starfish, and even a stuffed typhoon dragon. They were piled neatly like a pyramid, with the largest on the bottom and the smallest on top.

When she made her bed in the morning, did Ashlyn stack them all each time?

Ashlyn must've noticed me staring, because she dramatically jumped in front of me, blocking my view of the stuffed animal pile.

"W-What're you doing here?" she asked, her cheeks pink. "You weren't supposed to see any of this."

I shrugged. "What? You're not going to bring your stuffies with you when we live together? I was going to see them at some point."

Ashlyn turned away from me, her face growing redder. "What? No. Of course I wasn't going to take them with me. I was... going to leave them here. Or give them away to my cousins, who are much younger."

"Why?"

"Because." She shook her head. "They're childish. I... I know I shouldn't have them at my age."

I walked around until we were facing each other once again. I took one of her hands and half-shrugged. "Do the stuffed animals make you happy?"

Ashlyn stared into my eyes. She didn't answer verbally, but her expression said it all—she liked them.

"Then just keep them," I said. "Anything that makes *you* happy makes *me* happy. And I won't tell anyone if you don't want me to."

I hadn't visited her room expecting to see anything embarrassing, but I supposed I was glad I did now—I'd hate to imagine that Ashlyn gave up all her favorite things because she feared my judgment. I wouldn't think she was childish. Not now, not ever.

Ashlyn's gaze fell to the blue rug across the floor. "My father thinks they're silly."

I wanted to say, "*Your father can go suck a cucumber,*" but I held that back and instead said, "Good thing you're not marrying your father, because he sounds like a bore."

That made Ashlyn honestly laugh. She shook her head and stared back at me, smiling this time.

Before we could be distracted by anything else, however, I reached up to my collarbone and grabbed Vivigöl. The weapon *click-clicked* as it transformed from jewelry around my neck and shoulders, into a trident.

Ashlyn took a step back, her brow furrowed in confusion.

"I came to see you because I wanted to give you a wedding gift a little early," I said. Then I showed her the weapon, slowly turning it over in my hand. "I did some reading about typhoon dragons, and I found out that they reach their true form when they eat abyssal coral."

Ashlyn nodded once.

I pointed to Vivigöl. "This is made out of abyssal coral. I figured... Ecrib could take a bite out of it and gain his true form."

Ashlyn said nothing.

We sat in silence for a moment.

Out of the corner of my eye, I spotted Twain leap onto Ashlyn's bed. He searched around the stuffed animal pile before finding a comfortable spot and curling up like he belonged.

"Won't your weapon be broken then?" Ashlyn finally asked.

"Well..." I shrugged. "I don't know. It, uh, kinda rearranges itself, so I figured it wouldn't be *broken*, it would just be *smaller.*"

Ashlyn stepped close. I held the trident away from her.

"It'll hurt you if you touch it," I said. "I figure typhoon dragons must have iron stomachs or something, but normal arcanists will have their soul slowly damaged if they touch abyssal coral too long."

"Right." Ashlyn pushed back her blonde hair, tucking some of it behind one ear. "Gray... This is very generous of you."

I smiled. "Well, you're about to be my beautiful wife, and that means you deserve the very best."

She chuckled, and then shook her head. "I'm sorry. I don't think I can accept this."

"What?" I tensed. "Why?"

"Isn't that actually Death Lord Deimos's weapon?" Ashlyn tilted her head to the side. "And don't you need to prepare for your dive into the abyssal hells? You need all the advantages that you can get—and that means having a weapon that isn't broken. Or smaller."

I lowered Vivigöl, unsure of what to say.

"Besides," Ashlyn continued, "I'll be with you in the abyssal hells, and we'll find more coral there, right? Ecrib can eat some then—and I'll get a true form typhoon dragon."

A small piece of me didn't want Ashlyn to endanger herself in the abyssal hells. However, knowing she was planning to stay by my side no matter what gave me a lot of confidence. Ashlyn was amazing—practically perfect in all ways—and together we could definitely solve whatever problems Deimos and the other Death Lords were having.

"All right," I whispered. Then I changed Vivigöl. It *click-clicked* back into place around my neck and shoulders, once again becoming jewelry.

Ashlyn smiled wider and then happily leapt over to the bedside table. "I have a gift for you, too. I was planning on giving it to you tomorrow, but since you're here..." She withdrew a small wooden box and then hurried back over to me.

The box was the size of my hand, and when I took it from her, I realized it was rather heavy.

"What is it?" I playfully asked as I opened the box.

Inside was the strangest thing I had ever seen.

It was a golden-orange orb the size of an apple. It glittered bright, practically glowing, and around it swirled darkness, as though the shadow it cast had a small life of its own. What was this?

I grabbed it and lifted it out of the box, my whole arm surging with intensity, like a pleasant static shock. It felt like cold metal, and it weighed as much as a steel ball. The object pulsed with power, though. Like a heartbeat.

I had never felt anything else like it.

"What is it?" I asked again, this time serious. "It's a drop of blood from the corona phoenix," Deimos said through me, like I was a madman talking to myself.

Ashlyn quickly nodded. "Yes. It is! The corona phoenix was a god-creature that fought in the God-Arcanists' War, and my family was given some pieces of it as a reward for helping during the fighting and reconstruction afterward. It's, uh, super unique. The corona phoenix died, so it's not like we can get more of these."

I held the orb close, my eyes fixated on the glow. "This is a drop of *blood*? It's so solid."

"Apparently, the corona phoenix was so hot, molten metal was its blood." Ashlyn shrugged. "Or so the legends say. I never saw it."

This...

"Are you sure you want to give it to *me*?" I asked with a nervous laugh. "I mean... I think you should have it. This is really powerful. And rare. And should be used by one of the Kross family arcanists."

"You're a member of the Kross family now, remember?"

Ashlyn poked me on my chest. "You'll be *Gray Kross* tomorrow. So, I think it's fitting if you keep it."

It still didn't feel right.

"What should I do with it?" I asked, still staring at the object.

"Make it into a magical item," Ashlyn replied. "Into a trinket or an artifact. You just need some star shards. They're really expensive, but I think I can convince my father or mother to give us some as a wedding gift, and then you can make armor or something else to help with the abyssal hells."

Ah.

Now I understood.

"You want me to be safe," I said, my tone quiet.

Ashlyn nodded along with my words. "Of course. I saw the abyssal hells, Gray. I... know it's dangerous." She pushed the corona phoenix orb closer to me. "You should definitely make an item that will protect you while you explore. Okay?"

"This seems like... too much."

I didn't know what else to say. Ashlyn was worried about my safety? So much that she was willing to give me one of her family's treasures just to help protect me?

"Well, you're about to be my handsome husband, and that means you deserve the very best," Ashlyn said, mimicking my voice as she used my own logic against me.

Still...

I forced a smile. "Thank you."

We stood there in silence for another few moments before Ashlyn hesitantly motioned to the balcony. "I think you should probably go. If my father finds you here..."

"Yeah," I said. Then I inched over toward the balcony. "Uh, thank you again. This is amazing. I'll try to live up to it."

Ashlyn nodded once. "See you tomorrow."

CHAPTER 26

MY WEDDING CEREMONY

I stood in a large circular dressing room. Mirrors were placed in various positions around me, and I stood on a small little stage, examining my outfit. Today, I would be dressed in dark blue from my shoulders to my feet.

On the Isle of Haylin, we used honeysuckles as a motif. The Kross family, on the other hand, *really* liked the ocean. Typhoon dragons, turtles, fish, sharks—the colors and shapes of these creatures were everywhere.

I wore a long robe and the sleeves reminded me of dorsal fins. My belt, which was a deep bluish-green, resembled silky kelp. My boots were slick, like fish scales.

"I look ridiculous," I muttered.

Sorin stood in the room with me. He was beside the stage, examining me thoroughly. Occasionally, he squinted at something. Then he sighed. "You seem fine to me. Everything is in place. Your hair is perfectly combed."

I lifted both my arms and frowned. "I feel like a tent."

The robes were quite long. I was swimming in this outfit. Perhaps that was the intention—I could blend in with the waves of the ocean.

Thurin shifted through the shadows on the floor, circling my brother's feet. His voice echoed out of the depths of the darkness. "I attended a wedding once. Everyone was a warrior —they wore their most bloodstained armor to the ceremony."

"Yikes." With half a smile, I whispered, "What about you, Deimos? You ever attend weddings? What were yours like?"

"I never wed," Deimos said through me. "Most marriages were arranged—for political and magical power. My twin brother and I were seen as undesirable for most of our lives."

Sorin leaned in closer, clearly listening. "But surely you *saw* a wedding? What were they like?"

"The couple to be wed would burn food, incense, and small animals in a pyre built by their families. It was a sign of sacrifice, to show they were willing to overcome any obstacle. Then there was feasting, music, and dance until the sun arose the next day. That part, at least, was amusing."

I lowered my arms and scoffed. "Well, at least my wedding won't involve animal sacrifice. That's a win in my book."

Twain, who had been hiding behind one of the mirrors, poked his orange head around. "I agree. Animal sacrifice is weird. And gross. It makes me sad thinking about it, to be honest."

"Maybe we should stop talking about this," Sorin said. "Remember what Dad said about bad omens? I think talking about burning animals on your wedding day is a pretty bad omen."

I nodded along with his last statement. "You're probably right. Let's go back to talking about how I look like a buffoon."

"How about we discuss our birthday." Sorin stepped up onto the stage with me, smiling. He was still taller than me. What a disappointment.

"*Our birthday?*" I muttered. "It was two days ago. We were

stuck at sea, traveling. I didn't even mention it to the others because it would've been depressing."

Twain leapt around the mirror and then rushed over to the stage. He, too, leapt up, his fur standing on end. "Wait! You didn't tell me it was your birthday a couple days ago! I'm your eldrin. W-Why wouldn't you mention it?"

I shrugged. "Calm down—I have a lot on my mind lately. It wasn't that big of a deal. Sorin didn't even mention it, and it was his birthday, too."

Twain lifted a paw, unsheathed his sharp little claws, and then swiped at me. I pulled my leg out of the way just in time, protecting my flesh *and* my wedding outfit.

"What's wrong with you?" I asked.

"You're constantly talking to Deimos, and now you didn't even tell me about your birthday?" Twain laid his large ears back on his skull, frowning. "We're. Supposed. To be. A team."

I opened my mouth to protest, but within a fraction of a second, I knew Twain was right. I swallowed my words, carefully folded my robes as I knelt, and then looked him dead in his differently colored eyes.

"You're right," I said. "If you're gonna swipe me with your claws, at least do it on my face, where I can heal, because I have to marry Ashlyn in an hour, and her family will probably kill me if I ruin the clothing."

Twain lifted his paw. Then he struck me in the cheek with his toe beans—no claws. It was a simple little *bap*, nothing more.

He glared at me. "Bad human. Don't do that again."

I snorted out a laugh. "Okay, okay. I got it. I'll be better. I promise."

Sorin grabbed my upper arm and hauled me back up into a standing position. "Gray—I was trying to tell you something happy. Remember how you have that occult ore? The stuff Phila gave you."

"I remember," I said.

"Well, Lucian and Professor Jijo said they could both ask the Mother of Shapeshifters arcanist to come give you a rune. They said he would do it at the Academy—I wrote a note and everything, telling them you needed it."

"Really?" I was a little shocked—I had wanted a rune from the Mother of Shapeshifters, because her magic was so unique and interesting. I had told Sorin that, but I hadn't known he would act on it. "You did that?"

"For our birthday, yeah." He nervously chuckled. "I don't have a lot of coin or anything—and life has been so hectic ever since you were attacked by Deimos... This was the best I could come up with."

First Ashlyn giving me the blood of a literal god-creature and now Sorin going out of his way to make sure I could get magical runes?

"Did you... do this because you're worried about me?" I asked in a quiet voice. "Because the rune will help protect me?"

Sorin caught his breath. Then he playfully punched me on the shoulder. "Well, of course. I mean, if anyone needs extra protection, it's you. Who else has almost been killed half a dozen times? Who else is carrying the soul of a Death Lord?"

It felt weird...

Everyone fretted so much.

It was making *me* worry. And it bothered me. Was I so weak that everyone thought they needed to step in on my behalf? If I were stronger, they wouldn't feel this way. I could make *them* feel safe.

After a short sigh, I met my brother's gaze. "Thank you. Also, uh, I thought about your gift, but I haven't had time to get it."

"I understand," Sorin quickly said, before I could say anything else. "Even my gift isn't really *tangible*. It's just a promise."

"Then I promise I'll get you—"

Sorin lifted his hand, cutting me off before I could finish. "Just promise me you won't forget about Nini. We have to find a way to help her."

"I already promised that," I said.

"Promise it again. Promise it whenever you can. All right, Gray? That's all I really want."

I nodded once, allowing his words to sink in. "I got it."

The door to the dressing room burst open with a slam. Sorin and I whirled around, the shadows in the room shaking as Thurin rose to stand by his arcanist. Twain leapt to my feet, his back arched. All our panic was for nothing, though—in strode Archduke Kross, like he owned the place. Because he did.

The man gave me one quick glance and then frowned. He didn't say anything afterward—no critique of my clothing, no snide comment. The archduke simply walked over to me, straightened my green-kelp belt, and then smoothed my sleeves.

"Are there a lot of people here for the wedding?" I asked.

"No," Archduke Kross immediately replied. "Just *some* people. Your family, some of my family, and a handful of noteworthy individuals. That's it."

"I thought there would be—"

"Many nobles have already headed to Astra Academy. The headmaster summoned them once he learned of everything. We could've delayed the wedding, to accommodate other prominent arcanists, but my daughter insisted we do this as soon as possible."

Once Archduke Kross was done fixing my outfit, he gave Sorin an odd glance.

"I'm Gray's twin brother," Sorin stated. "Remember? We, uh, met at Ashlyn's cotillion."

The archduke sneered. "I remember." He motioned to my brother. "You shouldn't be here. You should be out with the others, waiting for the ceremony to begin."

"R-Right."

Sorin met my gaze, half smiled, then headed for the door. Thurin followed behind him, clinking the whole way. Once the door shut, silence descended.

Archduke Kross cleared his throat, ending the awkwardness between us. "You know what to do, yes?" he asked, practically a demand.

"I assume the answer is, *don't embarrass you*?" I quipped.

He narrowed his eyes into a cold glare. "Do you speak to your father in such a disrespectful manner?"

"This is how I always speak."

"Well, for your wedding, you are to enter the room, *say nothing*, wait until my daughter is with you, and then recite your oaths of commitment. You do know the oath, don't you?"

I nodded once. "Yeah. They gave them to me this morning."

Apparently, the Kross family had recited the same oaths for hundreds of years. Every married couple said the same things to each other at every wedding, no exceptions. It seemed a little impersonal to me, but I wasn't about to argue. Whatever made Ashlyn happy.

"And you memorized them?" the archduke asked. "If you have to read them from a paper, it will embarrass the whole family."

Twain huffed, drawing Archduke Kross's gaze to my feet. My eldrin puffed himself. "Gray memorized them fine. They're not even that long!"

"I'm just trying to ensure everything goes according to plan," Archduke Kross stated.

The man wore a long coat that practically went to the floor. His black pants, and black button-up shirt, were smooth and pristine, as though never worn before. He seemed elegant and fashionable, without being flashy.

"Well then, wait here until you hear the bells, then exit and head down the hallway." Archduke Kross walked away from me and headed for the door. He stopped before exiting, his fingers over the handle.

I waited, silent.

He didn't turn around when he spoke next. "Ashlyn was sickly as a child."

I hadn't expected him to say that. "I heard."

"I worry she'll become sickly again."

"She seems pretty strong and healthy to me," I said. "And determined. Even in the abyssal hells, she held herself together."

But the archduke didn't reply. He didn't even really move, like he wanted to say something else—or maybe he was thinking of the right words, I didn't know.

"Ya know," I finally said, "even if she does get sick—for whatever reason—she'll have me to help her. I'd go anywhere, do anything, to make sure she was safe and happy."

The archduke relaxed a bit after my statement. He grabbed the door handle and pushed it open. "Just remember the lines to your oath, boy. We'll have time to discuss it after the ceremony."

When the bells rang, I was ready.

Apparently, for the Kross family weddings, arcanists did the ceremony with their eldrin by their side. I liked that aspect

—some places had the eldrin separate, or even had the eldrin perform their own ceremony together—but I liked being with Twain.

He leapt onto my shoulder, and I exited the dressing room. What had the archduke said? Walk down the hall?

I followed all the flowers and markers, and headed for the ballroom. It wasn't far, but my heart was already pounding by the time I reached the door. I hadn't thought I would be getting married so early in life. I was lucky, really. Ashlyn was amazing.

That didn't change the fact that, in the short time I had been alive, a lot had happened. Sometimes it felt like I was speeding through life, tackling more problems in a week than some people had in a lifetime.

"You overthink things," Deimos said through me as I placed my hand on the door. "It would be better—for the both of us—if you quieted your mind and just *experienced* this moment."

I swallowed hard and pushed open the door.

My steps were slow and deliberate as I entered, my gaze straight ahead, even though the ballroom was gorgeous. I had seen several ballrooms in my life, from the Academy to random noble houses, but this one had windows that went from the ceiling to the floor. The light shining through played across my blue robes, catching silver threads woven throughout, and making it seem like I was actually wearing water.

Maybe that was why they had insisted I wear this particular outfit...

The ballroom itself was hushed, filled with only a handful of faces, and all turned toward me with quiet expectation. Everything was styled after the sea: the soft blues and whites, the subtle scent of saltwater woven into the silk draperies, the coral sculptures, a spray of white orchids resting in large vase, and even iridescent conches at each corner.

Twain marveled at the decorations, his mouth open.

"Do you think Ecrib helped gather some of this stuff?" he whispered in my ear as I walked.

"Shhh," I replied.

Chairs had been placed in a semi-circle in front of a pair of massive glass doors. Dragon sculptures stood on either side of the doors. And not just sculptures of rock—sculptures made of flowers and seashells were also here.

The glass doors overlooked a sweeping view of the ocean itself, where waves crashed gently against the cliffs that surrounded the Kross compound.

My heart hammered harder as I made it to the doors. They remained shut, tied with string, and once I was near, I came to a stop.

It was only then that I chanced a glance at the audience. My father was here, as well as my stepmother. My classmates were here, too—at least the ones that had traveled with me. Exie wore an outfit that also matched the sea, the blue silks glittering, stealing my attention away from everyone else.

She was a showboat.

I also spotted Ashlyn's father, brother and mother, but I didn't dare stare for too long.

Her brother was glaring.

I spotted a few eldrin, including a couple of typhoon dragons, off to the side. They were too big to sit in the seats, but small enough that I knew they weren't adults. The archduke's typhoon dragon had to be outside.

Everyone else who had smaller eldrin, like Phila and Exie, had them close, sitting in chairs next to them.

To my surprise, I spotted Rosella...

She sat near my family with her kappa eldrin in her lap. The kappa was a small fish-person with needle-like teeth and giant yellow eyes. The creature had scales and fins and webbed hands.

And he also wore a little outfit, like a mortal human. He wore trousers and a shirt, and even a small hat atop his bulbous head.

Most mystical creatures didn't wear clothes. From what I understood, they didn't like them. I had seen Rosella's kappa wearing clothes before, though—back when I was with the cultists. I wondered why she would bother to dress up her kappa like that.

People spoke to one another, whispering, but all I heard were the bells chiming from outside. I was too anxious to focus on anyone's words. They were nothing but a low buzz in the back of my mind.

The far door opened, silencing all conversation.

Then she emerged, entering the ballroom like a cool breeze on a hot summer day.

Ashlyn.

She wore a pale blue gown, layers of sheer fabric flowing around her like gentle waves, each step sending ripples through her outfit. Her golden hair fell in loose curls, adorned with tiny glimmers of silver, pearls woven through like drops of morning dew on a spider's web.

As she walked, the fabric of her dress seemed to float around her, light and unbound by gravity.

Ashlyn met my gaze as she walked, her blue eyes bright. I swear the room fell away at that moment, leaving only the two of us. I couldn't even feel Twain on my shoulder, that was how transfixed I was.

Sunlight continued to filter in through tall windows, casting patterns of dappled light that danced along the polished marble floor, and also over Ashlyn's dress. Just like my outfit, it was as though she wore water itself.

I hadn't even noticed Ecrib until she was halfway to me.

The typhoon dragon walked behind her, his head raised. He, too, was beautiful in the light, his dragon scales sparkling.

Once Ashlyn reached me, she stopped and turned. Ecrib took his place behind her, and I found myself unable to breathe.

Silence settled around us, a stillness so thorough that I heard the faint rustling of silk and the distant call of seabirds from outside.

Ashlyn's gaze was steady, a soft smile curving her lips as she stared into my eyes.

We had a silent conversation between us. She slightly nodded, basically asking me if I was ready. I subtly returned the nod, letting her know I was fine.

Then she motioned with her eyes.

I was supposed to start the oath.

Right. Yes. Me. The first lines came from the person entering the Kross family—which was me.

Me.

What were my lines?

I... had forgotten them. The moment I had laid eyes on Ashlyn, everything else had left my mind. She was stunning— too stunning, apparently.

Dammit.

Ashlyn must've sensed my building panic, because she tried to mouth something. She probably knew my lines as well as hers, but I couldn't remember, and I wasn't able to read the exact words she was trying to silently form.

Murmuring in the audience only worsened my stress.

Twain's ears twitched, jarring me from my frozen state.

"You have to say something about bonding, and the Kross name," he whispered.

That sounded familiar. Would they be angry if I just made something up?

Yes. Definitely. I didn't even need to ask.

Then, with an emotion that was a mix of vexed and amused, Deimos spoke through me. "I stand here before you, as the sea meets the shore, where earth and water find their bond unbroken. With my heart and soul, I swear this oath—in times of calm and in times of storm, I will be there for you. I pledge myself to the Kross family name, unwavering."

That was it! That was the start of the oath!

Deimos had memorized it, too?

Ashlyn, relief washing over her, smiled wider. "And I offer my strength and my love. Through waves and stillness, in sunlight and shadow, I bind myself to you and bring you into the Kross family. Together, we are made stronger, and supported by all those who have come before us."

I remembered the rest. Before Deimos could take over, I said, "By this oath, I claim my place beside you, entwined by destiny and blood."

"By this oath, I seal my heart, my name, and my life to yours. As the Kross family has endured, so shall we endure, a bond woven by the ages, deeper than the ocean and as everlasting as the stars."

"In this life, and in the next," I said, quieter now, truly staring into Ashlyn's eyes. "We shall be held together through honor and devotion."

"You are welcomed into the Kross family," Ashlyn said, "my beloved."

I leaned forward, and Ashlyn met me halfway, her soft lips pressing onto mine.

She was so beautiful, strong, and compassionate. It was all I could think of as the ballroom erupted with clapping.

CHAPTER 27

MY WEDDING NIGHT

I want to say that the festivities were wonderful and memorable, but that wasn't the case.

We had a quiet meal in the banquet hall, and then Archduke Kross led us to the gardens for an evening of dancing and music. Apparently, several members of the house were talented musicians, and their songs livened up the night.

It all went by in a blur. I had food. We went to the garden. Eight hours must've passed, because my feet hurt from walking around and chatting, but I barely paid attention to any of it.

Because Ashlyn kept glancing over at me and smiling.

It was different from how she smiled before. In her own silent way, she was telling me that this was exactly what she wanted, and I kept smiling back—probably like an idiot— replying, without words, that it was what I wanted as well.

However, as the night grew cold, and people began turning in, I noticed Lucian and his Source of the Storm near a large rose bush. He was sipping a glass of wine, and staring up at the stars like they might do something interesting. I had no idea what he was looking for.

But I did want to speak to him.

I left Ashlyn's side, whispering about how I would be back, and then walked over to the man.

Lucian was so fixated on the sky that he didn't turn to meet my gaze until I was mere feet from him. Despite the festive occasion, he wore heavy boots, long dark pants, and armor under his white button-up shirt. He also wore a cloak over his shoulders that fell all the way to his ankles. It was classy, but in a warrior way.

The man just liked to be intimidating, didn't he?

"I didn't see you at the wedding ceremony," I said, lifting an eyebrow.

"Septimus didn't invite me," Lucian stated.

Septimus. That was Archduke Kross's first name. Should I be using that now that he was my father-in-law? It made sense.

"Why are you here if he didn't invite you?" I asked.

"Because he can't keep me from wandering around his damn compound," Lucian snapped. "I have to be here because I'm not leaving your side, so if I want to wander the gardens, I will."

I held up both hands and shrugged. "Whoa, whoa. It's okay. I would've *preferred* you were at the wedding, but good ol' Papa Septimus didn't ask me."

Lucian snorted as he crossed his arms. The Source of the Storm puffed its tiny white feathers until it looked like a ball resting on Lucian's shoulder.

"I actually wanted to speak to you," I said. "You were a god-arcanist, right? Bonded to one of the god-creatures?"

Lucian curtly nodded.

"Were you bonded to the corona phoenix, by chance?"

"I was not. Why would you even think that?"

I pointed to the little bird on his shoulder. "I don't know. You seem to like birds. I thought it was a logical guess."

"Have you forgotten his title was the *Dauntless*?" Deimos

said through me, his tone irritated. "It is only bestowed upon individuals who bond with the tempest coatl."

Lucian eyed me as though I was just plain weird. "Yes. I was bonded to the tempest coatl. But I knew the god-arcanist who was bonded with the corona phoenix quiet well. She was known as the *Solstice*."

"Oh. Good. Well, I wanted to ask about the phoenix's magics. If someone had a part of the phoenix, for example, what would it best be used for? Fire-based something, I assume?"

This question seemed to bother Lucian. He frowned and shifted his weight from one foot to the other, his gaze slowly slipping back to the sky. At first, I thought he wasn't even going to answer. Was it an offensive question?

"The corona phoenix was a creature of pure light and darkness. Her god-arcanist didn't use her fire as much, though. She focused on her ability to control shadows. She evoked impossibly black shadows that blanketed the area in complete and utter darkness."

"Like knightmares?" I asked.

Lucian's expression flickered for a moment. Then he finally whispered, "Yes. Like knightmares. But hers... Her shadows were glorious."

"You sound like you really liked her."

Lucian snapped his gaze back to my own, his eyes narrowed into a glare. "Listen—the corona phoenix's shadows weren't harmed by light. They were the darkest of void, and the god-arcanist even managed to manipulate shadows with such skill, she created *creatures* from the darkness. If you're going to make an item or artifact from the corona phoenix, I would suggest you capitalize on indestructible darkness."

"My brother is a knightmare arcanist," I muttered. "Maybe he could help me come up with something."

Lucian softened a bit. Then he nodded. "Sorin. Yes. He's a good man. Perhaps you should ask him."

After that, he stopped all conversation. Lucian returned to his stargazing. Even his eldrin did the same, the both of them transfixed by the sky. I glanced up, just to see if anything interesting was happening up there, but it was just a bunch of stars.

Nothing else.

"Well, uh, good talk," I said, turning away.

Lucian didn't reply. I wondered if he had even heard me.

As I strode away from the man, Deimos had a lot more to say, though. Slightly angered, he said, "The corona phoenix is a creature of extremes."

"Why do you know so much about the god-creatures?" I asked. I almost stumbled over my wedding robes as I walked. They were long and flowing and somewhat in the way. The sleeves bothered me to no end.

"The god-arcanists have souls unlike any other that enter the abyssal hells. And the god-creatures themselves have pure magic that dwells in a special location known as the *Spire of the Gods*. Every Death Lord knows of them, and their abilities. They are possibly the only arcanists with magic that rivals or exceeds that of the abyssal dragons."

"Someone sounds jealous," I said with a grin.

"Feh." Deimos's irritation almost felt playful. "No arcanist has lived as long as a Death Lord. I'm secure in my place in the world, but that doesn't mean I don't respect the power of the god-arcanists and their purpose in the cycle of life."

"Jealous," I whispered, in an attempt to playfully get under his skin.

Deimos just laughed.

I returned to the wedding parties, but it was clear they were basically over. Once I took Ashlyn's hand, she motioned with a tilt of her head to the compound. I nodded. This was it —the end of the night.

I would be lying if I said I wasn't nervous.

Ashlyn and I had our bedroom.

Apparently, Twain and Ecrib had their own room adjacent to ours, complete with a balcony pool, plush beds, and a scratching post. I suspected the post was a last-minute addition by the Kross family in an attempt to make Twain feel more at home. Since most people here had no idea what mimics liked, they just doubled down on the fact that he was a cat and ran with it.

Fortunately, that meant he got lots of fish, which he was excited for.

I left him and Ecrib in their room before heading to Ashlyn's and mine.

When I entered, I took note of the spacious accommodations. A reading couch. A bookshelf. A large dresser and wardrobe. A beautiful window overlooking the ocean.

Really, I tried to look at everything other than the bed first, mostly to be polite. I didn't want to seem like I was too eager.

"So, what would you like to do?" I playfully asked. "Card games? A hiking trip? A six-hour board game that simulates capturing territories during a war?"

Ashlyn stepped close, threw her arms around my neck, and brought her mouth to mine. Then she bit my lower lip, surprising me. She slid her tongue over it like a sensual apology, and I had no more jokes. No more quips.

I picked her up, and Ashlyn giggled as she wrapped her legs around my waist. Her gown was getting in the way, and we probably looked ridiculous if anyone was watching, but no one was, so this was—

I stopped halfway to the bed, almost stumbling in my haste. Ashlyn held on tight—she had the core strength to just cling to me like a monkey, if she wanted.

"What's wrong?" she whispered. "Was I... too rough?"

"No, no, no." I shook my head. "I just, uh, need to wash up first. You don't mind, right?"

Ashlyn slowly unraveled herself from me, still smiling. Her cheeks were slightly red, and she brushed her blonde hair back. "I'll wait here."

"Right here? Here, here?"

"I won't move."

I chuckled as I stepped backward and then turned. Our room had its own bathing room attached, and I went straight there. I shut the door between the rooms and then leaned my forehead against it.

I didn't need to wash up. I needed to make sure we would be alone.

"Deimos," I whispered. "Can you leave us alone for the night?"

"Of course," he sarcastically replied through me. "I'll take a short vacation away from this soul cage and allow you both the privacy you deserve."

"Dammit, I'm serious."

He didn't reply, but I felt his sardonic attitude to the whole situation.

"Just close your eyes, and don't say anything, all right? And also never speak of this to me, or anyone, for the rest of your life."

"It'll be my wedding gift to you," Deimos quipped.

I couldn't help but smile. Was Deimos getting funnier because of me? Maybe I was having a positive influence on him—that was what I liked to believe, anyway.

"I'm really serious," I said. "This is... my first time... and I don't want to constantly think about you also being there, got it?"

Deimos didn't reply.

I took it as his way of saying he would remain quiet.

After that, I exhaled. My hand went to my collar bone and I felt to make sure I wasn't wearing Vivigöl. I wasn't, because I had taken it off before the ceremony, but I kept worrying about it regardless. I didn't want anything to go wrong between Ashlyn and I tonight. It had to be perfect. I couldn't be disappointing, or somehow hurt her on accident—it had to be great.

Had to.

"Okay, show time," I said to myself. Then I exhaled and returned to the bedroom.

Ashlyn was waiting for me in the same spot as before, just as she had playfully promised, but now she wore a necklace—and nothing else.

The necklace had a pendant with some sort of stone that sparkled a blue-gray, much like my eyes. So, she hadn't been lying about wearing my favorite color.

Not that I was focusing much on the necklace, mind you.

Without words, I made my way to my wife, and we picked up where we had just left off.

In the early morning, I lay in bed, staring at the ceiling.

Ashlyn was beside me, equally as awake. We sat in relative silence for a long time, soaking in the pleasant moment. Unfortunately, my own thoughts were my worst enemy. They wouldn't allow me to stay happy for long—they always had some worry to dwell on.

"You okay?" Ashlyn whispered.

She ran a hand over my bare chest, her fingers trailing over the grooves of my scars. Deimos had given those to me, back when he tried to enter the world of the living...

"I need to get stronger, and it's taking too long," I finally replied.

"What's taking too long?"

I rolled onto my side so I could stare Ashlyn in the face. She was snuggled in the blankets, like an adorable dumpling, her hair pooled around her like honey.

Maybe I was hungry... It was almost breakfast, after all.

I pushed that random thought to the side and continued my explanation. "In order for me to achieve a true form with Twain, I have to defeat fear."

"Okay," Ashlyn said.

"I'm prepared! I think I know what I need to do—I need to defeat the soul catcher arcanist, prove myself capable of overcoming any obstacle, and embracing inner tranquility."

She nodded once. "Are you frustrated because you haven't done that yet?"

"Sort of. Yeah. I don't know." I let out a long sigh, trying to return to the blissful moments of before. "I don't want anyone to worry about me. I want to be... powerful enough to stop all these problems."

"And a true form mimic will help you do that?"

It was my turn to nod.

Ashlyn cupped my cheek with her hand. "All right. Then I'll be there to help you."

"I have to do this on my own. *I* have to be the one who defeats fear."

She lifted her perfect eyebrow. "Well, maybe you could befriend it instead, hm? They say that's the only way to get rid of an enemy."

"Friendship?" I snorted out a laugh. "Who said that?"

"I think I saw something like that carved into a stone at

the Academy. It said something like... *Friendship. Without it, we cannot truly defeat our enemies.*"

While it was a nice, albeit strange, phrase, I suspected it wouldn't help me, not even in the slightest. Was befriending someone the same as defeating them? How could you even befriend *fear*? It was a concept—an emotion.

No. I had to focus on defeating the soul catcher arcanist.

"Gray, no matter what, we're a team, all right?" Ashlyn had an infectious confidence. "I'll think of some ways to help you with your problem."

I grabbed her hand and smiled. "Thank you, Ash."

That got her smiling.

CHAPTER 28

A NEW YEAR AT ASTRA ACADEMY

Normally, married couples took time to visit their arcanist relatives—even the ones in different cities —to announce the new member of the house. I was a Kross arcanist now, after all, and everyone with the same last name wanted to meet me.

Fortunately, that wasn't our plan. Ashlyn and I needed to get back to Astra Academy before the start of the next academic year, and that was happening tomorrow.

So, in order to get there on time, we all piled onto Septimus's ship and prepared for the trek to the Gates of Crossing.

Ashlyn and I boarded together, but as soon as Phila and Exie stepped onto the deck, they rushed over, wide eyes and squeeing.

"Ashlyn!" Phila said, smiling wide. "You simply must spend time with us on the trek to the academy. We can have a girl's tea party."

Her coatl, Tenoch, circled around her feet. "Am I allowed, my arcanist? Even if I am a boy?"

"Oh, of course, Tenoch! I'm sorry, I didn't mean to

exclude you. We are bound by magic, and do everything together."

Phila picked up her eldrin. Tenoch's snake body immediately wrapped around her arm, clinging tightly.

Exie motioned her erlking to rest on her shoulder. "Yes, Rex, you will have a tea party with us, too."

Ashlyn gave me a sidelong glance. In half a second, I already knew everything. She was going to join them. She didn't want to, but at the same time, she thought there was a possibility it could be fun. I nodded in complete agreement.

"I'll join you," Ashlyn said, separating from me. "And you know what's odd? I just realized all three of us have eldrin who are male. Does that happen often?"

Exie shrugged.

Phila held a hand over her mouth as she giggled. "I don't think so. Perhaps we're special."

The three of them wandered off, their male eldrin in tow, including Ecrib.

Septimus's ship left the dock, and instead of searching anyone out for company, I went to the railing and watched our journey. It wouldn't be long until we arrived at our destination, and I wanted to see Astra Academy the moment it came into view.

Twain bounded around the deck until he noticed me by the railing. Then my mimic darted straight over and leapt to my shoulder. He purred—which was rare these days—and nuzzled against my neck. I patted him as the ship leapt over the waves, speeding forward with a force far beyond the strength of the wind.

Beneath us, the water churned, a relentless current pulling us onward. It was as if the sea itself had taken an interest in our journey, propelling us with an energy that was both thrilling and unnerving. But I knew better. It wasn't the sea or the wind driving us, but the will of Septimus's typhoon dragon, Enki.

Somewhere beneath the rolling depths, unseen but palpable, Enki swam alongside us, twisting and coiling, bending the tides to his whim. Every now and then, I caught glimpses of him—a flicker of scales shimmering through the water, a ripple that was too deliberate to be a mere wave.

The horizon began to change, brightening, as if we were racing toward summer itself. Then, rising from the sunshine ahead, I saw it—the Gate of Crossing. It loomed out of the water, impossibly vast, its towering circular form large enough for ships to pass through. It was made out of metal, and imbued with rizzel magic.

The ship slowed as we neared, but not from lack of speed. One of the crew members brought out a star shard from a secure lockbox, and placed it on the ship. Then Enki swam close, his fins bursting from the waves, and he physically grabbed hold of the vessel.

"It's time," Twain whispered, excitement in his voice.

I held my breath as we drew closer, the world narrowing to the sight of that vast archway. We were at the edge of something that could whisk us across oceans in the blink of an eye, and as the magic shimmered within the circle arch, it reminded me of the abyssal hells.

"Twain," I said, breathless.

"Yeah?"

The ship sailed forward, lazily passing into the Gate of Crossing, the metal ring glowing bright white.

And then we teleported. The shift of position was jarring. Thankfully, I had experienced it before and was prepared. A second later, when I opened my eyes, we were no longer on the ocean but in the middle of a pure and beautiful lake.

But...

I doubled over, clinging to the railing. Twain dug his claws into my shoulder to hang on, his orange fur puffing out.

"G-Gray! What's wrong?"

It had been... so painful...

I rubbed my chest, my teeth gritted. That was strange. Teleporting through the Gate had never hurt like that before. The sway of the ship as it glided toward the shore was almost too much.

But I took a deep breath and shook it off. The pain was already dissipating and I still wanted to see the Academy.

I stood straight. "The teleporting hurt, but I'm better now. Thank you for worrying about me, Twain."

Twain nuzzled my neck again. "Thank you for telling me what was wrong. One step closer to you talking to me about *all* your problems."

I rolled my eyes. "Don't get sappy." Then I glanced around.

Our Academy had defenses—the first time I arrived, I had taken note of the six massive cannons that were mounted into the rock around the Academy's estate.

They were still here, and they were heavy, formidable weapons—the sort meant not just to ward off but to utterly destroy—but they weren't the most impressive defense now.

Astra Academy was surrounded by shimmering shields of magic. They were transparent domes that covered the mountains, shimmering in the afternoon light, their creation stemming from metal rings built into the mountains. Much like the Gates of Crossing, these were *gigantic* artifacts, and probably made with so many star shards I couldn't comprehend their cost.

"Wow," I whispered.

"That's amazing," Twain said.

My mimic magic allowed me to sense magical types, and

these shields were made by atlas tortoise or atlas turtle magic, though I wasn't entirely sure which. Tortoises walked the land and turtles swam the ocean, but they were both gigantic creatures with shells so large you could build things upon them.

I lifted my eyes to the peak of the mountain, gazing through the barrier. A forest of tall, proud pines spread across the base—a deep green sea of pointed tops and rough, prickly leaves. Rising from the trees, the slate-gray mountainside stretched upward. And there, at the plateau, stood a castle-like building, its walls dark and strong, made of black bricks and steel, with accents of ivory that gleamed against the hard rock.

Astra Academy.

The black bricks took me back, stirring memories of my first arrival here. The academy seemed to reach, impossibly tall, as if it were striving for the stars.

Mountains stretched out in every direction, the barriers covering most peaks. Farther along those mountains were other dark structures, distant but distinct. Those buildings were other parts of the Academy, equally protected.

Headmaster Venrover wasn't joking about changing this place for the better. We wouldn't have random people sneaking in anymore.

A long, winding road led up to the Academy's front gates, and Septimus's ship went straight for the dock at the base.

"Gray!"

I whirled on my heel. Sorin ran over to me, smiling, though not in his usual way. It seemed forced.

"We're back," he said. "This is it. Our second year. Aren't you excited?"

"Yeah. It feels great to be back."

New arcanists, and hopeful arcanists, had to visit the courtyard and the Menagerie for their first-year orientation, but as second-year students, we had to head to the auditorium.

Phila, Exie, Sorin, Ashlyn, and I all met up with other second-year students in the hall. My class hadn't been the only class last year, and there were dozens of people heading for the auditorium.

Our eldrin were of all shapes and sizes, but that wasn't a big deal. A massive tree grew around the outside of Astra Academy and connected most of the large windows with branch-walkways that the larger mystical creatures used. If anyone's eldrin couldn't fit through the hall, they could walk on the pathways outside to get to the same place.

"I think everyone is here," Sorin whispered, frowning. "Except for Nini."

Our class had been small—we only had nine students—and Sorin was correct, the other eight of us were here. Raaza was easy to spot in the small crowd, his kitsune eldrin difficult to miss. The kitsune had flames on her paws that lit up whenever she took a step, and that was often. She pranced around her arcanist, her tail swishing.

Raaza stood tall in the group, his dark tanned skin slightly scarred, especially on a part of his face. His dark eyes scanned his surroundings until his gaze landed on me—then Raaza perked up and hurried over, his kitsune following close.

"Gray," he said, grinning. "You made it okay."

Miko, his eldrin, laughed. "We thought you might get whisked away to the abyssal hells again! I'm glad you didn't."

Twain bounded over and sat between my legs. "We're too good to get caught twice, thank you very much."

Raaza wore a plain outfit that matched a lot of Astra Academy. He had a white button-up shirt, black trousers, and boots that shone with care. His black hair didn't cover his arcanist mark, which was the seven-pointed star with a fox woven through the points.

"Raaza, good to see you," I said.

Then he threw his arms around my neck and hugged me tightly. That was a bit of a surprise. I chuckled and patted his back.

"Uh, it's only been a few weeks, ya know."

Raaza released me. He was toned, and physically fit, and his expression was always set to serious. The man looked a little scary, even in the plainest outfit around.

"I'm just glad you're here," he said. Then Raaza spotted Sorin and headed to my brother—but only after patting me on the shoulder.

He was a good guy. I liked him.

Nasbit was also milling about, his portly frame giving him a unique silhouette here at the Academy. He muttered apologies as he stepped between people, making his way over to me.

Nasbit's arcanist mark was the same seven-pointed star I had, but his had a stone golem wrapped around the points. And Brak, the golem, stood by the far wall, his sandstone body massive and imposing. His shoulders were boulders, and his stone body was held together with magical threads.

When Nasbit finally made it to me, he quickly waved. "Gray. It's so good to see you. Where is Phi—" He stopped himself midsentence when he answered his own question.

His dark eyes locked onto Phila, and that was when he stood a little straighter and smoothed back his dark brown hair. He wore a cape—a classy one, blue and white—along with a white shirt and dark trousers. He seemed like a proper noble, even if he was soft.

"I'll be right back," Nasbit whispered as he headed over to speak with Phila.

"Good to see you, too," I sarcastically said as he went. Then I just smiled to myself. I didn't blame him for heading straight over to Phila—I probably would've done the same.

The last member of our class was Knovak.

And he was... interesting.

Knovak had traveled with me to the abyssal hells, and ever since then he hadn't been the same. Sure enough, when I spotted him in the crowd, he wasn't happy to see me. It was the opposite—he immediately avoided eye contact.

He didn't look like himself, either. He normally had a plain look about him—someone who bordered on forgettable. Paler skin, sandy brown hair, no distinguishing marks, and eyes that almost seemed dull.

Now Knovak was *very* distinct.

While everyone had an arcanist mark on their forehead that was rather standard, he had a star that appeared melted. The lines of his mark cascaded down around the sides of his eyes, and somewhat down his nose, creating a terrifying mask effect.

He was a unicorn arcanist, but I couldn't make out the unicorn shape anymore because it was too distorted.

"What a freak," some of the other arcanists whispered. "What happened to him and his eldrin?"

"I heard he was kidnapped or something. So much for the mighty Gentz family. Ha!"

I pushed my way through the crowd. "*Hey*," I barked. "Is that really how you should be talking about another arcanist at this Academy?"

They all turned away from me, pretending they hadn't said a thing. When I glanced over to Knovak, he finally acknowledged I was there. He was red in the face—from embarrassment or anger I wasn't certain—but quickly looked away.

Rubbing his upper arm, Knovak strode into the crowd of

other arcanists and headed for the auditorium door, never saying a word.

"Do you think he's still angry with you?" Twain whispered.

I *had* taken Knovak away from the Deimos cult. He had liked it there, and he had been training to become powerful... I hoped he realized what I did was for everyone's best interest.

Where was his unicorn, Starling?

I worried about them both. Ever since Starling ate souls in the abyssal hells, neither of them had been right.

Starling, especially. Unicorns were graceful, beautiful creatures of speed and power, but after Starling ate that soul... he was different.

"Gray!" Twain leapt up to my shoulder. "They're opening the doors. Let's go!"

I held Twain as I headed for the door. Sorin moved to be by my left side, and Ashlyn to my right. I offered them both a grin before we all stepped forward.

The auditorium was vast, high-ceilinged, with arched beams that went at least twelve feet high. Glowstones lined the walls, their brilliant gold hue creating a cozy atmosphere.

In the middle of the auditorium were six marble statues, each in the shape of an impressive arcanist. I was certain they were famous figures from history, but I wasn't the best at history, so they were just six impressively dressed people to me.

Guardian Captain Leon stood next to the statues, his cerberus eldrin right at his side.

The man was rather pleased with himself today. He had short white hair, a white beard trimmed equally short, and a demeanor of confidence and authority. He wore silver armor that gleamed in the glowstone light, and his arcanist mark was prominent on his forehead, the three-headed dog wrapped through the points of his star.

"Welcome, second-years," he said, his voice loud and gruff

enough to boom through this massive area. "You all remember me, yes? If not, I'm Guardian Captain Leon. Headmaster Venrover is welcoming the first years as we speak, so I will help you pick your major for the rest of your time here in Astra Academy."

The other arcanist students in the room whispered, their tones a mix of excitement and apprehension.

"You will have all afternoon to mull over your major," Leon said before motioning to the statues. "And once you've come to a conclusion, you will write your name on the stone here. Tomorrow, your classes will begin—a journey toward your rightful place as an arcanist in this uncertain world."

"What are our choices?" someone asked.

"Are you daft?" another person hissed. "Don't you remember when they told us this at the beginning of our first year?"

"I don't remember that long ago! Sheesh."

Leon held up a gauntleted hand. "Calm down. I'm here to guide you." He lowered his hand and then paced in front of the marble statues, taking a moment to glance at each one as he passed. "From here on out, Astra Academy will no longer offer five majors. We are now offering six."

"Wow," a girl in the room whispered.

"You can either train to be a knight, an artificer, a mystic guardian, a cultivator, a vizier, or... an abyssal sentinel."

The last option got everyone's attention. Most people in the auditorium hadn't heard that option before, but I had. Headmaster Venrover had met me at the Dodger Family compound and explained to me that this major would be to deal with the threat of the abyssal hells.

All the classes would revolve around preparing for our eventual dive into the brackish waters that filled the land of the dead.

"Each statue represents the major. It explains what you will learn, and I invite you all to come up and take a look at each." Leon motioned us forward. "Come, come. We haven't got all day."

CHAPTER 29

ABYSSAL SENTINELS

While the other second-year arcanists stepped forward, I stayed behind.

I already knew which path I would be picking —and it was abyssal sentinel. It was the *only* choice for me, because it had been specifically crafted after I told Headmaster Venrover all about the myriad of problems in the abyssal hells. If I didn't pick this, who else would?

Plus, I had a fragment of Death Lord Deimos's soul in my own. Couldn't ignore that.

The others in my class, however, could easily choose something else.

Phila walked forward with other arcanists. Nasbit hurried alongside her, as happy as could be. Had he gotten taller? I didn't remember Nasbit being notably taller than Phila before, but it seemed to be the case now. Funny how things changed in the blink of an eye.

"Look at these," Phila said, gawking at the statue of the knight.

On the base of the statue was written: *Justice will prevail when reason has failed.*

The marble statue of the knight was an imposing figure clad in glinting armor. His face was lined and scarred, yet noble, and his stance held the unyielding strength of the mountains. His arcanist mark was that of a knightmare, which seemed rather fitting.

"Arcanists who choose to study with the knights will learn a great deal about combat, law enforcement, and the various nations around our continent." Leon moved around behind the statues as he spoke. He said every word as though it were a proclamation, his tone grand. "At the end of your studies, you will even have an opportunity to serve the ruling leaders of a nation."

Exie seemed to ignore that entire speech as she walked over to the artificer.

The base of the statue had the motto: *Better living through magic.*

The statue was a slender, sprightly figure with gears in her hands. Her robes, stitched with intricate patterns of copper and brass, seemed to hum with restrained energy. There was a glimmer of curiosity in her eye, a spark that promised knowledge of the deepest secrets.

I almost wanted to know who carved these damn statues —they were clearly talented.

"My aunt said she is teaching this course," Exie declared.

Leon exhaled, but then quickly regained his excited demeanor. "Arcanists who decide to study with the artificers will learn all about item creation and enchantment. You'll make trinkets, runes, and some of you might even be able to make artifacts."

A lot of the students whispered excitedly. At least a dozen of them walked over, marveling at the marble statue.

"If you know you want this path, you can write your name on the statue right now." Leon shrugged. "But I do encourage you to research the others. At least a little bit."

"I'm ready," one girl said. She stepped forward and then frowned. "Do you have a pen? Or some charcoal?"

"You write your name with your finger, lass."

The girl—who had an arcanist mark laced with a bird-like figure—blushed a bit. Then, with a shaky hand, she touched the statue. Using her pointer finger, she traced the letters of her name.

To everyone's delight and surprise, the stone molded to her touch and then glowed golden. Someone gasped, but before any questions could be asked, her name sank beneath the stone.

"Excellent choice," Leon said. "Now you can relax in your second-year dorm until tomorrow. And make sure to get plenty of rest."

Leon walked over to another statue. "This is the path I teach," he said. "These are the mystic guardians. I train arcanists to venture out into the wilds and find rare mystical creatures to bring back to civilization. That, and we stop people from stealing or endangering mystical creatures. It's a noble profession that is as old as arcanists themselves."

He stood tall and smiled.

It sounded like an amazing profession.

The base of the statue had a motto etched into it as well. It read: *We venture where others won't.*

The statue reminded me a lot of Leon, actually. It was a tall figure wrapped in a cloak. The statue's gaze was distant, a pair of deep-set eyes that looked at us yet seemed to peer far beyond, and the beard the man had was impressive—it went down to his collarbone.

"Personally, my favorite is the cultivators," Nasbit said as he wandered over to that statue. "You see, *cultivation* is the word used for constant improvement and development. Arcanists who have studied on this path typically go on to help nations improve their crops, currency, or even legal systems. They do it all with their magic, mind you. Very innovative."

"Oh," Phila muttered, her attention still on the knight.

"A-And the statue here is modeled after a famous sovereign dragon arcanist named *Marigrave Velleta*."

The statue was one of the tallest. It was a woman with a long cloak, her arms outstretched. Her hair, braided with vines and tiny blossoms, went all the way to her waist. She looked powerful yet caring, which was a surprise. Weren't dragon arcanists usually a little aggressive?

I glanced over at Ashlyn. She met my look with narrowed eyes, as though she knew my thoughts exactly.

The base of the cultivator statue read: *Improving the foundation of civilization.*

"I like the vizier's statue," Raaza whispered.

I nearly jumped as I whirled around. The man and his kitsune were standing behind me. He had his arms folded, and he rested back on one foot, as though he had been there for quite some time. He probably had; I just hadn't been paying attention.

"The vizier's, huh?" I asked, calming down.

"Look at him."

I did as he asked, curious.

The vizier statue was a little... intense. The statue depicted a man who was a relickeeper arcanist. He wore long robes, but his sharp eyes were something else. He stared upward at the ceiling, and his hands were scarred. He almost looked as though he would ascend into the sky at any moment.

The base of the statue read: *Granting the wisdom to govern.*

"Why do you like that one?" Ashlyn quietly asked.

"All these other statues are staring straight at us, but the vizier appears to see something bigger and better. I like it." Raaza shrugged. "I think... I want to be like that."

"Are you going to take that path?" I asked.

That was when Raaza glowered at me. "Of course not. I told you I'd be with you in the abyssal hells—I won't be joining any other class but yours."

His confidence was surprising. Raaza had said he would be with me, but I figured he might change his mind. His tone told me he wouldn't, though. Not now, not ever.

Leon walked over to the last statue.

It was...

"Gray, is that you?" Sorin whispered. "It looks *just* like you."

All the statues wore outfits that were robes or cloaks, and the abyssal sentinel was no different. However, the statue was the youngest, and the star on the man's forehead was blank, like mine. A mimic arcanist.

It was also holding a trident, the three tines pointed at the ground.

The base of the statue read: *Protecting the circle of life.*

"That seems more noble than what we're actually going to do," I muttered.

"Yeah, we're going to go down and punch some Death Lords in the face," Twain said with a snicker. "But I guess this would be a weird path to pick if the motto was, *breakin' some jaws while tourin' the underworld.*"

Leon motioned to the abyssal sentinel statue. "This path is new, and not for the faint of heart. We'll need arcanists to study the bizarre nature of the abyssal hells and prepare themselves for confrontation. Surely, you've all heard of the strange monsters emerging from the Gate fragments?"

There were murmurs of affirmation. No one seemed too thrilled, though.

"The headmaster wants arcanists who are prepared to put their life on the line and face the unknown. If the abyssal hells reopen, many arcanists from around the world will need to confront an enemy we've never seen before." Leon frowned after that last statement.

The auditorium grew quiet.

And while I was afraid of heights, I wasn't afraid of this.

I strode forward, confident. When I approached the statue —my statue—I held out a finger and quickly drew my name.

This was the first time I was writing my new name. Gray Kross. It felt awkward, almost silly, like this was all pretend. But no, that was my name now.

My finger molded the stone, and my letters lit up gold. Then my name sank into the statue, disappearing a moment later. There was no other path for me.

Ashlyn stepped up next to me a moment later and she did the same thing. She signed her name and then offered a smile.

Sorin walked over next. When he lifted his hand, I grabbed his wrist.

"Sorin, you don't have to do this," I said. "I mean, the knight major sounds like you, and apparently a knightmare arcanist might be one of the teachers."

"I have to save Nini," Sorin said, no hesitation.

Ah. Right.

I hesitantly released my brother and sighed. "Okay. Let's do this."

He wrote his name—Sorin Lexly—and then stepped back, pleased with himself.

Exie, Raaza, Nasbit, and Phila walked over next. They crowded around me, and the abyssal sentinel statue, all forming a line to sign their names.

"You all don't have to do this," I said, getting in the way before they could sign. "Sorin, Ashlyn, and I can handle this."

"We're not going to abandon you now," Phila said in a dreamy tone. With a beautiful smile, she added, "We're good friends, and we know exactly what you've gone through."

"You four didn't go into the abyssal hells with me," I

muttered. They didn't need to risk themselves. "It's dangerous. Way more than you all know."

Nasbit held up a finger. "Actually, I *do* know how dangerous it is. Remember? You told me about it in great detail. Plus, I have spoken to Knovak, and he's given me plenty of information on the hazards we will all face."

"Really?" That was genuinely shocking to me.

"Headmaster Venrover even asked me to be a personal assistant to the professors who will be teaching this route. I can't let the headmaster down."

I turned my attention to Exie. There was no way she wanted to risk her life for me. Why would she be here?

"Don't you want to be an artificer? Or a vizier?"

Exie crossed her arms and huffed. Her erlking landed on her shoulder and did the exact same thing—folding his little arms and glaring at me.

"For your information, erlking arcanists are known for being great cultivators." Exie stepped close to the statue. "But I don't care about that. I *am* friends with you. And Sorin. I'm going to help you no matter the danger."

Ah. It all made sense now. I almost sighed in frustration, but I supposed she *was* helping my brother... I couldn't take that from her.

Raaza smacked me on the shoulder as he joined Exie. "I already told you I'm not leaving."

That meant seven of us were going to be in this new class. Second-year students taking on a major no one had ever done before.

"They're crazy," someone whispered from the group of arcanists behind us. "Who wants to fight in the abyssal hells? Isn't that a place of unrelenting death?"

We probably *were* crazy. That was fine. Someone had to set the world right, and it wasn't going to be *those* cowards.

But they would thank us later, when we solved this whole mess.

"I'm really proud of you all," Leon said as he walked around the abyssal sentinel statue. "It takes a great deal of courage to put the needs of the many before your own. I can't wait to hear of your progress as you all advance through your classes."

CHAPTER 30

THE INEVITABLE AURA

While most people went to their new second-year dorms, technically married arcanists had their own rooms. I thought that meant Ashlyn and I would have luxury accommodations befitting royalty, but...

"It's charmingly compact," Twain said as he leapt off my shoulder and landed on the ground without much of a noise.

The walls seemingly pressed in with eagerness, and the bed was barely larger than the one I was used to in my old dorms. Could it fit two people? I supposed, as long as neither of us breathed too heavily.

The single window let in a sliver of light, and the gray stone walls were a dull color that only added to the drabness of the place. We had a wardrobe, but that took at least forty percent of the available floor space.

"I think this used to be a closet," Ashlyn muttered.

"I think they forgot a mop in the corner," I said, pointing.

"R-Really?"

"No." I chuckled and then elbowed her. "We're fine. It's just cozy."

Ashlyn rolled her eyes as she took a seat on the foot of the bed.

I grew up in a small room. This wouldn't be a problem. Plus, I'd love to cuddle close to Ashlyn every night. Who wouldn't? I was certain every arcanist in the Academy was jealous of me. That was a new development, but one that I rather enjoyed.

"I'm still allowed to stay with you, right, Gray?" Twain stared up at me, his ears fully up.

He *had* stayed with me in the first-year dorms, so I understood why he wanted to stay now. The second-year dorms for men, the one Sorin was staying in, was just down the hallway, and I almost suggested Twain go there, but I couldn't do that to him.

He was my eldrin.

"Of course you can stay," I said. Then I quickly turned to Ashlyn. "Right?"

She nodded. "Seems reasonable."

"Yes!" Twain leapt up to the top of the wooden wardrobe. He surveyed the tiny room like a lion taking in his kingdom. "I will keep watch over you in the night."

"Thank you," I said.

Ashlyn lay back on our small bed. "We should get some rest. Tomorrow is going to be a long day."

A moment after I closed my eyes, everything felt arid, like a hot breeze had wafted through the room.

I opened my eyes and almost gasped. This wasn't my new bedroom—I wasn't even lying down. I stood in the middle of a desert, the sky a sickly crimson, the sands a mix of pale blue and gray.

The third abyss.

Nothing lived here. No sun touched this barren expanse, and yet it was hot—an oppressive, dead heat that seemed to suck the breath from my lungs.

Scattered across the desolation were castles, their dark silhouettes cutting stark shapes against the horizon. They were empty, silent, left to the mercy of the desert winds that had long ago eaten away at their edges, wearing down turrets and towers until they looked like hollow teeth jutting from the dunes.

Each castle was so distinct, as though they had been plucked from different times and places, dragged here by some unseen hand and abandoned to the endless drift in the abyssal hells.

When the wind rushed by, it carried whispers.

Ghostly wisps flickered in and out of sight, some small, like birds, and others as large as a dog. They had tortured faces, but they vanished just as quickly as they appeared.

When I took a breath, it was with power and confidence. I was... taller. More muscled.

I was Death Lord Deimos.

He wore plate armor over most of his body, though no helmet. The bone and metal of his attire was striking and surprisingly lightweight. When it moved, it clicked in a way that reminded me of Vivigöl transforming.

"What's going on?" I asked, speaking through *him* instead of the other way around.

Deimos growled, his irritation spiking the moment I said anything. "What're you doing here?"

"I don't know. I don't even know where we are."

It was bizarre to be the observer, but this had technically happened before. I had used Deimos's ability to astrally project my soul into his, and see things through his eyes. Why was I doing it now? Was it because I was sleeping?

"We are in the *Graveyard of Empires*," Deimos intoned.

Then he strode forward, his footing steady, despite the shifting sands. "Beyond it is the Spire of the Gods—which is where I'm heading."

"Is that why you've been quiet for a while?" I asked.

It was odd using his voice.

Deimos ground his teeth. "Feh. I've decided I can't wait. I'm growing weaker by the minute, and I need to reverse this, lest I succumb to final death."

A shadow passed over Deimos. Well, it passed over *us*, since we were one person, but it was strange to think that way. Something I'd just have to deal with.

Deimos glanced up and caught sight of his eldrin—the powerful abyssal dragon, Hektor.

He was as monstrous as he was gigantic. The dragon's wings were made of grafted souls cobwebbed together and a bright, sickly blue that reminded me of the sand around us. Human faces dotted the wings, their eyes circles, their mouths open as they softly moaned and cried.

Hektor flapped his transparent wings like any normal dragon would, but the souls screamed louder whenever he did so.

In a wide arc, the abyssal dragon circled and then landed in the sand before us. He practically *crashed* into the dune, sending the blue-and-gray sand into the air.

Things wiggled around under the surface of the sand, like there were worms just out of sight. They squirmed, digging deeper into the ground, away from sight. I never quite saw what they were, but they were at least the size of a human arm.

Hektor exhaled, his breath reeking of coppery blood. He turned his head, his six eyes all shifting to give Deimos his full attention.

"The Death Lords know you've left the Requiem Throne." Hektor snorted. "The souls here speak of one's approach. I'm not certain of which."

"Then we haven't much time," Deimos replied. "Search harder. It must be here."

Abyssal dragons were creatures of decay. Their scales were mottled and cracked, and their muscles glistened with the sickly sheen of mucus that dripped and pooled in stagnant, nauseating puddles.

But Deimos's eldrin was in a condition even more nightmarish. One of Hektor's front legs ended in a jagged stump just below his wrist, where the remnants of torn muscle clung like rotting strips of cloth around the exposed nub of bone.

It looked better than when I saw him last time. Before, Hektor's arm was missing, but now it was just his clawed hand. He was regrowing his damaged body, likely using human souls to fuel his regeneration.

His arm had been cut off in Astra Academy, and every time I saw Hektor since, I felt bad.

"Enough," Deimos snapped.

His eldrin lowered his head. "My master? Have I offended you?" His voice was laced with the soft moan of souls.

"You haven't offended me. *It's the boy.*" Deimos placed a hand on his face and groaned. "Enough of your thoughts. I need to focus."

"On what?" I asked through him.

Hektor snorted, blue mucus spilling to the sand for his efforts. "I see now. Your soul is breaking apart. You're losing stability."

After that disturbing statement, Deimos took a moment to breathe. He placed a hand on the chest piece of his armor, seemingly to settle himself.

"Why is this happening?" I asked.

It took Deimos a while to reply. He closed his eyes as he said, "A piece of my soul has been missing too long. It's like a wound that's never been treated... I've just been bleeding out, and it gets more difficult with each passing day."

"Can't you use your abyssal dragon magic to stop this? I thought you could manipulate souls or something? O-Or at the very least, I thought you could use human souls to heal yourself?"

That was all true—I had seen Deimos do it in the past. The many human souls grafted to his abyssal dragon eldrin could be used to empower him, both physically and magically. Why couldn't he just... stitch himself back together?

"Have you ever seen a physician operate on themselves?" Deimos darkly quipped. "I haven't the strength to fix what's wrong with me—Hektor cannot do it on his own—and none of the other Death Lords would allow me to live if I submitted myself to their mercy."

Screeching pierced the air. The haunting landscape seemed more sinister than before, and the crimson "sky" grew darker in color.

Three birds appeared above use, zipping in at speeds I didn't think were possible.

They weren't normal birds—they were mystical creatures the size of a house. They had golden feathers, lightning crackling off their wings and sizzling the air. Their tails were long and zigzag, the feathers ending in a plume of bluish souls.

They had two eyes in the normal spots, but then each of them had a third eye in the center of their head, and it glowed the same pale blue.

These were elder thunderbirds—a normal thunderbird wouldn't have such bizarre soul-infested features.

Thunder boomed overhead, and the three elder thunderbirds soared down toward Deimos.

With confidence I had never felt before, Deimos turned on his heel. He met the gaze of the closest bird—the one diving straight for him with talons that crackled with raw power—and then lifted his hand and evoked raw magic.

A beam of bluish-white energy burst from his palm and sliced a hole straight through the chest of the thunderbird. Despite that obviously grievous wound, the souls on the creature's tail fluttered over its body and went straight to the injury. The souls sank into the hole, filling it within a moment, mending the elder creature before it died outright.

It was still injured, though. The thunderbird crashed into the desert, sending a dune's worth of sand into the air. Some of it washed over Deimos like a rough wave.

He didn't care.

When the second and third thunderbirds swooped in, they didn't aim for him—they aimed for Hektor.

The abyssal dragon opened his rotting maw and also evoked raw magic, but this time, the birds were ready. They *zipped* through the air, practically teleporting with their speed, and then were behind the dragon.

Their talons carved through Hektor's body, gouging out scales, mucus, and muscle.

Deimos turned and fired more of his evocation, but the two birds dodged again. They *zipped* through the sky like a streak of lightning.

The third bird leapt from the sand and went for Deimos.

"*Die, traitor!*" the elder beast screeched.

Deimos—probably through battle instincts—barely moved but somehow dodged the entire talon that had threatened to take his head. With controlled movements, he backed away, his heart rate steady, his focus perfect.

I wished I knew how to fight like this.

The thunderbird landed next to Deimos, its wings spread wide, its three-eyes wide open. "Death Lord Kallikore commands an army," the elder thunderbird rasped. "*You have nothing*. Why do you keep fighting? Why won't you just *die*?"

"I never lose," Deimos confidently stated.

Then his magic filled his body and spilled outward.

I knew this! I had learned it in class and read all about it in the books—and I had seen it in action on many occasions. It was an arcanist's *aura*, one of the most difficult magical techniques to pull off.

Deimos's aura spilled out of him. Then the area went black and white, all color draining away. The crimson sky, the blue-and-gray desert, the dark castles, the golden wings of the birds, the blue of the souls—it was all gone. All that was left was a world devoid of color.

"You're all dead," Deimos stated.

And while he didn't articulate what his aura did, I had access to his thoughts.

This was *the inevitable aura*, something only an abyssal dragon arcanist could create. All living beings who weren't immune to instant death effects would die if they stayed within the inevitable aura for longer than sixty seconds.

That was... a powerful ability.

The three thunderbirds screamed.

"You'll be dead before this works!" The elder thunderbird closest to Deimos went to attack. It flapped its wings and jumped, talons first.

Deimos waved his hand, and the sand answered his command. The desert reached up and grabbed the thunderbird midair, stopping the attack. The sand itself was shaped like a hand, and it hardened around the bird, trapping it in place.

The thunderbird opened its beak and lightning crackled outward, heading straight for Deimos. Again, through sheer battle-tested ability, he quickly sidestepped out of the way. He *barely* moved, and the lightning went sailing by his ear, sizzling so loudly I heard it as it went by.

Why could he manipulate the sand?

The souls...

This was the abyssal hells. The souls—and fragments of souls—were everywhere. In this realm, he practically had complete control of the environment.

The other two thunderbirds picked up their attacks on Hektor, clawing him and flinging their own lightning. Hektor chomped his massive maw down on the neck of an elder thunderbird and then slammed it into the dunes.

The last thunderbird jumped on his back, clawing with talons and pecking with its beak. Deimos held out his hand and his beam of raw magic shot out so fast, and so precisely, that the bird couldn't dodge.

It was struck through the chest and hit the sand.

In this colorless world, the beam of raw magic seemed pure white. It was beautiful—in a dangerous and frightening way.

"I thought you were too weak to do any of this," I said through Deimos. "Your aura, this magic..."

"I've learned to make do," he curtly replied.

But that was when I noticed the souls across Hektor's body...

They were popping out of existence, snuffed to fuel Deimos's body and magic. One, two, three—way more than he ever used before to do a simple fight. Fortunately, there were hundreds woven throughout Hektor's wings, but if this kept up, Deimos would be in trouble.

"It's over," he said.

The thunderbird trapped in the sand, the one held down by Hektor, and the last one struggling to stand—they all died instantly.

Color came rushing back, filling the sand, the birds, the sky with all the colors that had been there before, but that explosion of radiance stole the lives of the elder thunderbirds. They didn't even have a chance to scream.

They just stopped moving.

All of them fell over, slumping lifelessly where they stood.

The inevitable aura...

It was so powerful.

But then Deimos doubled over, pain flaring through his chest, knotting in his lungs, and sending spikes of agony through his heart.

"*Arg,*" he said through gritted teeth, his eyes closed.

I tried to speak through him, but it was impossible. The pain was too much.

What could I do? He felt like he was having a heart attack. There had to be something.

There had to be!

CHAPTER 31

A SIN AGAINST NATURE

Using my mimic abilities, I felt around for threads of magic. Even while I was "in" Deimos, I still had access to the magics I personally possessed, so I figured there had to be *something* nearby that could help.

In my panicked desperation, I grasped at threads and discarded them without much thought. Threads from both the abyssal hells *and* Astra Academy were at my disposal, as though I was somehow physically in the third abyss with Deimos. I technically was, but it was still disturbing...

I felt the magical threads of creatures hidden in the sands, and of beasts in the far-off castles.

What were they? Their magic seemed warped and disturbing, and I suspected I couldn't actually use them. They were likely elder creatures—mystical creatures who had gobbled down one too many human souls and were now distorted.

So, I quickly sifted through the threads of Astra Academy.

A knightmare.

A kappa.

A typhoon dragon.

A cerberus.

A kitsune.

A golem.

There were too many! Deimos's chest twisted with more agony, and he fell to one knee. Was he even breathing? His lungs burned, and even Hektor was concerned. The massive abyssal dragon lumbered over, despite his stump-leg, and observed his arcanist.

I couldn't just search around for creatures. I had to narrow my focus. What creature did I *know* could heal individuals? Or at least subdue pain?

Astra Academy had... a physician. He was an older arcanist.

Doc Tomas!

He was bonded to a golden stag! He could heal people—he healed before, didn't he? Was he close enough for my mimic magic to copy his eldrin?

I stretched my thoughts and focused, ignoring all other magical threads as I attempted to find the warm and caring magic of the golden stag.

Then I found it. It was far, but not too far. With all my concentration, I tugged on the thread, and then golden stag magic flooded me.

How did it work? I assumed the stag's augmentation would heal, because that was how it was with other creatures who mended injuries. I focused on the pain in Deimos's chest, and I tried to imagine myself with a physical body here, helping him recover.

For some reason, a sense of calm came over me as the magic answered my will.

So tranquil...

It must've affected Deimos as well, because he relaxed and managed to take a small breath.

Then the healing coursed through his body. Something

about his heart, and perhaps his lungs, had been damaged, but now they were mended.

Deimos took in a deep breath. Then he stood.

"Are you okay?" I asked through him.

"Master?" Hektor asked, his voice haunting.

Deimos shook his head. "I'm well. Let us continue our search."

"Hmm." Hektor's growl rumbled this whole section of the desert. "Perhaps you should go ahead, to the Spire of the Gods, and I will scour the dunes. You should rest."

"*I'm not so weak,*" Deimos snapped.

The mighty abyssal dragon lowered his head. "If you had been your usual self, you wouldn't have broken apart like you just did. And even then—you would've healed yourself with a soul. You need to be mindful of the damage you're taking. Your soul can't handle much more. It's not complete."

Deimos listened to his eldrin's words, but he responded to none of them.

Deep down, he felt... remorse? Sympathy? Understanding? It was *something*. An emotion that told me that Deimos knew his eldrin was correct. He couldn't be flippant. His body and soul weren't in the condition for it.

"I'll wait for you at the Spire of the Gods," Deimos eventually stated.

Hektor snorted and nodded his head. "By your command."

With a few flaps of his soul-stitched wings, the dragon took to the hellish-red sky. Deimos didn't watch him go. Instead, the Death Lord started his way forward, marching through the sands with a single-minded focus.

As much as I could, I took in the sights. There wasn't much, but I wondered about the empty castles in the distance, and the many dunes around us that looked as though creatures were writhing underneath.

Eventually, I released the golden stag magic.

"You can say *thank you* at any time," I sardonically stated.

"Feh," was Deimos's only reply.

"I *did* save you. Just now. With healing magic."

"And how many times has my magic—or my skills and knowledge—saved *you*?" Deimos growled. "We are hardly even. Perhaps once you've helped me a couple dozen more times, I'll deign to thank you."

"You're always so grumpy, Dee," I playfully said. "Maybe you need to take a nap."

After a long sigh, Deimos went silent. He stormed through the sand a little faster, heading toward a goal I couldn't see. Was he even heading in the correct direction?

"I'm, uh, going to be studying the abyssal hells now that I'm back at the Academy," I said. "I'm hoping that the headmaster brings in some real experts."

"*I'm* already an expert on the abyssal hells," Deimos drawled. "I don't need you to learn what is already familiar knowledge to me."

"We could learn how to kill Death Lords quicker. Or maybe how to negate their magic? What if we had a way to deal with elder creatures?"

Deimos strode over a dune and then slid down the other side. His footing was perfect, despite the uneven sand. He moved with such purpose and confidence that I remained impressed.

"If you find something, I'm certain I'll see it," he finally muttered.

"So, you're *always* paying attention to what I'm doing?" I asked.

"Unfortunately," he quipped.

"It can't be all bad," I said, trying to lighten his mood.

When Deimos stepped over the next dune, creatures in the bluish-gray sand slithered away, digging deeper and then becoming still. Was everything afraid of him? I supposed Death Lords were quite spooky. His inevitable aura was devastating.

"It's not all unpleasant," Deimos murmured, his thoughts becoming distant. "You brought my soul closer to my brother, which I am grateful for. You also have seen the world, and I'm shocked by all the changes."

"Really?" *That* was a surprise.

"It fascinates me."

Now we were getting somewhere.

"I do appreciate your own twin brother," Deimos said as he went over an even larger dune. "And your woman is... acceptable."

"You're jealous of my wife?" I asked. "*You*?"

Deimos rolled his eyes and then headed across a large straight flat of sand. "Did it occur to you that I can feel *your* emotions, too? You bombard me with feelings of lust, affection, and obsession whenever you look at her."

"Well, I'm sorry, but she's taken."

Before Deimos could snap back with anything, something bizarre happened.

A mirage shimmered before us. Well, I thought it was a mirage at first—some sort of trick of the heat over a desert—but the longer Deimos walked toward it, the more I realized it was a building fluttering into existence.

No, not just a *building*.

It was a tower so tall it seemingly pierced the blood-red sky.

The outside was made of smooth obsidian, and it shone in the eerie light. There were no windows or doors, but there was a small set of stairs that led up to the stone wall.

The Spire of the Gods.

It was large enough to fit a grand redwood tree within, and then some. When Deimos stepped up the stairs, heading straight for the wall, he seemed small, like a cricket on an oak tree. Inches from colliding with the obsidian, the tower shifted and moved, a door shaping itself out of the stone.

It opened without words or magic.

Deimos walked into a strange hallway where the ceiling glowed pale blue, and the walls were nothing more than carvings of massive creatures. There was no rug, but the stone floor beneath Deimos's feet was somehow soft—Deimos's footfalls made no noise here.

"What is this place?" I asked through him, my voice barely above a whisper.

"I told you what it is," he snapped.

The door behind him closed, leaving us with just the glowing ceiling and the many carvings. They were mystical creatures—one a giant serpent, one a wolf, one a bird, another a dragon—but they were depicted as gargantuan. The wolf was big enough to crush trees under his paws, and the serpent was effortlessly wrapped around a sailing ship.

"Are these god-creatures?" I asked.

Deimos huffed and then nodded.

He walked by the carvings, ignoring all of them, which was a shame. I wanted to get a better look—I had never seen a god-creature before. Supposedly, there had been twelve that had fought in a war, but that was decades before my time.

To my surprise, as Deimos fully passed a carving, it began to glow. The serpent sparkled with green light. The wolf glowed white. There was also a slug? At least, I thought it was a slug. It glowed pale red.

"Deimos," I whispered. "I can feel their threads of magic."

A piece of me got a little excited. As a mimic arcanist, could I... mimic a god-creature?

I could've asked Deimos, but I decided I didn't even want to wait. I tugged on one of the new threads.

But nothing happened.

The tether of magic didn't answer my call. I couldn't pull it to me—I couldn't do anything with it. It was like a child trying to lift a fallen tree. It was just beyond me.

"All the god-creatures are born here," Deimos stated as he continued to walk.

More creatures. More colors.

"When the world needs magic capable of changing *everything*, then the god-creatures are born. A light emanates from the Spire of the Gods, pierces the abyssal hells, and then the very heavens, before descending back to the realm of the living. When the god-creature dies, most of its magic returns here, so that it can be born again later."

"Are you here to take their magic?" I asked.

Deimos chuckled. When he finished walking past the last god-creature, and the hallway was more colorful than a rainbow, he found himself in front of another door.

"No," Deimos said. "I cannot take god-creature magic. However, the souls of the god-arcanists are much different than others. They are souls that have touched raw magic, and unlike other souls, they come to the spire for their final judgment."

"I thought Death Lords helped souls reincarnate?" I asked.

Deimos nodded. Then he placed a hand on the door. It didn't open.

"They do. Except for god-arcanists. Their souls... are here. They reincarnate differently."

"So, if you don't help them, why are you here?"

"To take the souls for myself," Deimos intoned, dark and without emotion.

I wasn't an expert on souls or the abyssal hells or even the duties of the Death Lords, but I knew in my gut this was a terrible idea. If there was a whole hidden building in the abyssal hells dedicated to ancient world-altering magics, and homes for god-souls, I seriously doubted it was meant to be disturbed.

"Why hasn't Death Lord Naiad come for these souls?" I asked. "Didn't she start collecting Death Lord souls, and that was how she got so powerful?"

"She can't get in." Deimos ran his hand down to a groove on the door. "Only an individual with the lotus diamond runestone can enter the heart of the spire. It's meant as a last sanctuary, and a sacred place that none should step foot on."

"Is that what you and Hektor were looking for in the desert? A runestone?"

"If I can graft the souls of the god-arcanists to Hektor, he'll gain power unlike any we've seen," Deimos stated. "The pure magic the god-arcanists touched will help me win this war. *And nothing matters more than that.*"

His vision blurred at the edges, and Deimos had to rest against the cold obsidian of the spire. The pain was creeping back.

"But this door is locked for a reason," I muttered through him.

"It is a sin against nature to take these souls from the Spire of the Gods. But I have few other options."

"A *sin against nature*? Do you hear yourself? C'mon, Dee. Pull it together. You can't do this."

Deimos said nothing.

"Look, one of the reasons I want to help you is because you *did* seem like the only Death Lord who hadn't gone completely insane. Death Lord Kallikore grafted his own dragon's body onto his own! Death Lord Naiad is the original serial killer! Death Lord Umbriel is apparently praying to oblivion! You're the only one left who's still doing his job. If you gobble up a bunch of god-arcanist souls, and disturb whatever cycle is going on here, just for some quick power— you're going to be just as insane as all the others."

"I'm. Running. Out. Of. Options." Deimos ground out each word through clenched teeth. It was getting difficult for him to breathe, and I wondered if his injured soul was just causing his body to give up on him.

"Don't do this," I said.

Deimos slumped down onto one knee. He was in pain, but I could also sense his resolve fading. He didn't want to do this plan—he was just desperate.

And I could understand.

He was dying.

If he didn't get his piece of soul back, or he wasn't properly healed, or he didn't get an influx of power, he was definitely going to lose against the other Death Lords.

"I told you—I'm going to help you," I said.

"Unless you're here, there's nothing you can do," Deimos snapped. "And you get further away with each passing day."

"I helped you just now, didn't I? I healed you, remember? Maybe... Maybe I should just reverse haunt you more often."

"Reverse... haunt?" Deimos scrunched his eyes closed and darkly chuckled.

"I like to think you're haunting me," I joked. "So, you know, I'm reverse haunting you, and I'll lend you *my* skills. At least until I return to the abyssal hells, okay? And that won't be long. Your brother said he was looking for a way, and Headmaster Venrover has all the best arcanists coming to help him. You'll see. We'll do it."

Deimos didn't reply.

"Please, Dee. C'mon. Get away from the door. Leave this place. Don't look for whatever runestone gets you in there— just forget about this. You need to remain the only sane Death Lord left. For the world's sake."

CHAPTER 32

BACK TO CLASS

"You know, when this is all over, I'll ascend to the realm of the living and rule over my own nation, as my right as a Death Lord who has served his time," Deimos said.

"Well, I was hoping by then that you wouldn't be a crazy warmonger," I replied through him. "You've seen the way the world works now—you just told me that! Wouldn't you want to, I dunno, find an Ashlyn of your own and settle down?"

Anything but start a war with some other nations about a millennia-old promise that was made to him by individuals who weren't even around anymore. I *actually* wanted Deimos to be seen as the good guy in all this, and if he rose from the depths of the abyssal hells, only to start sending people there en masse, I knew I'd also be in trouble.

"You could live a peaceful life with your brother," I added.

Deimos shook his head. Then he managed to stand.

"Very well." He turned on his heel. "I'll leave this place. And I'll allow the souls to rest."

"Thank you," I said.

For some reason, this interaction reminded me of Sorin. Normally, it was *him* asking *me* not to do things that were questionable or unreasonable. Now I was doing that with Deimos? Perhaps my brother had rubbed off on me.

Then I sensed something. A new thread of magic that reminded me of Twain, but also of the thunderbirds.

"Someone is here," I said.

Deimos turned around and glowered at the glowing hall of statues. When the far door opened, the statues themselves seemed to melt away into the walls, disappearing from sight— like raindrops merging into a puddle of water and becoming one.

Their magic was still *here*, but the representations of their bodies had vanished.

Whoever was at the front door wasn't a Death Lord, and the Spire of the Gods seemed to know that fact. Was this place alive? Was all of the abyssal hells alive?

I was starting to suspect that was the case...

There wasn't anyone at the front door, though. The doors opened and revealed nothing. The thread of magic remained —whoever was here had just declined to enter. They were outside.

"Why don't you use your inevitable aura?" I asked. "You could probably kill whoever it is without even going outside."

Deimos shook his head. "My aura won't work on mystical creatures or arcanists who are immune to instantaneous death. All Death Lords are immune to the aura, as are true form reaper arcanists, and—"

"Our visitor isn't any of those," I interjected. "I would know. I'm a mimic arcanist."

"Feh. If it isn't a Death Lord... then it's likely my new ally."

"New ally?"

Deimos strode down the empty hallway, the soft blue glow

of the ceiling somehow comforting. Then he stepped out into the desert, and the harsh winds of decimated kingdoms washed over us.

A man stood out here—one who was freakish and unwell. He was humanoid, but not *human*. He had arms like a bird's legs, his hands nothing more than talons. His whole body was covered in gold and white feathers, most of which were patchy. His back was adorned with golden wings, but they were ill-defined and hung limp, the feathers dragging in the sand.

And his face...

Feathers hung forward, blocking most of his features. I saw his mouth, but no eyes, because the fluff of feathers was too clustered.

His legs were the same bird-like limbs, complete with taloned feet.

"Everett!" I said through Deimos, excitement in my voice. "You made it!"

He had helped me escape the abyssal the last time I was here, and I was so happy to see he hadn't died fighting Death Lord Kallikore. Apparently, he had gotten stuck in the abyssal hells due to strange circumstances that dealt with the followers of Death Lord Umbriel.

The bird-man lifted his head, though I still couldn't meet his gaze.

"Death Lord Deimos?" he asked. "I don't understand. You're happy to see me?"

Deimos growled something at me before taking over the conversation. "Everett—did you find anything?"

"No," Everett replied.

"Then why have you come here?"

"Death Lord Umbriel is ascending through the abyssal hells. She's in the fourth abyss, and I thought I should warn you."

Deimos exhaled, his vision on the distant horizon. "And what of Nini? Has the woman returned from the labyrinth?"

"She has not."

The way they both spoke told me that Nini had been there for some time. Anxiety welled up within me. Sorin wouldn't like this.

"We need to retreat to the Requiem Throne," Deimos finally stated.

Everett scratched his feathered face with his sharp talon hands. "I thought you said what you needed was deep within this building? Shouldn't we continue to search for your runestone?"

"No. I've had a change of heart. We'll regroup in a location of safety and go over our options there."

"Very well."

Everett had a sort of confidence that I liked. Although he was speaking to a Death Lord, he never seemed intimidated or in awe. He just spoke to Deimos like he was an equal—even though he was a freakish monster.

"I gave your necklace to your husband," I said through Deimos.

That was when Everett tensed. He used his talon-hand to push the feathers up, revealing his eyes. They were gigantic and black, much like a bird's, but still human.

"You... what?" he breathed.

Deimos gritted his teeth. "The mimic arcanist, Gray Lexly—"

"*Kross*," I interrupted.

"—speaks through me."

"You gave the necklace to Lynus?" Everett trembled for a moment, his face twisting into something pained. He allowed his feathers to fall back over his eyes. "Is he okay?"

"He misses you—and he declared he would rip down the gate between worlds to get you back."

"*What?* No. He can't come here. He can't see me like this. I'm... not myself anymore."

After a nervous chuckle, I said, "I don't think I can stop him. He went berserk when I told him about meeting you. He might have an anger issue."

Everett shook his head. "It's dangerous. He should stay away. If he also ended up like me... I would never forgive myself."

And while I wanted to continue this conversation, because I had more to ask, something felt off. My mind grew foggy, and Deimos's presence seemingly slipped from me. Everything went dark, and at first, I grew terrified. What if our souls were separated?

Thankfully, that wasn't the case.

I was being shaken awake, and when I managed to open my eyes, I was back in my room with Ashlyn. She was jostling my shoulder and staring down at me.

"What's going on?" I asked, groggy.

"Twain broke our wardrobe," Ashlyn answered, her tone as calm as ever.

"He... what?"

She pointed to the wardrobe. My eldrin sat on a pile of splintered wood, his lynx-ears standing straight up, his eyes giant and round.

"I just... turned into a stag *out of nowhere*," he said. With a frown he added, "I guess I was sleep transforming... That's, uh, totally normal, by the way. I'm sure every mimic goes through it."

I couldn't help but laugh. Ashlyn and Twain stared at me while I got my mirth out, and I quickly shut it down to regain my composure.

"I'm sorry. This is my fault." I sat up in my bed and sighed. "Let me explain everything."

I spent so much time telling Ashlyn everything that we both missed breakfast. That was fine—I didn't feel hungry. I was enthusiastic. There were several things I had to do. First, get my true form. Second, get a lot of skills to help Deimos. Third, find a way into the abyssal hells. Fourth, stop all the Death Lords and set the world on its correct path.

And I couldn't do all that if I was concerned about breakfast.

Bells chimed through the hallways of the second-year section of the Academy. Class was about to begin.

"We need to go," Ashlyn said as she quickly dressed. "Hurry, Gray."

I slipped into my clothing much faster than she got into hers. "I am the superior dresser."

She rolled her eyes, shoved her legs into her trousers, and then headed for the door. "If I had known you were going to turn this into a competition, I would've dressed circles around you."

Twain chortled as he hurried out of the door. "We'll have to race tomorrow morning."

I laughed as I followed my eldrin. Ashlyn did, too—nothing got her more fired up than competition. It was one of the many things I loved about her.

Speaking of competition... Ashlyn raced by me down the hall, and I knew she was trying to beat me to class. I huffed and dashed forward. I couldn't just let her win! No, my pride wouldn't allow that.

We raced through the hallways, passing other arcanists as we went. At one point we saw a man with a humanoid-looking eldrin, a little statue creature where all his limbs were held together with magic threads. At first, I thought it was a golem, but when I dashed by, I saw the spooky face and the gold chest it had inside its chest piece. Housed within the cage was a glowing gem.

It was a gemstone effigy, a rare little creature that Professor Helmith loved to talk about.

I craned my head to get a better look at it—the thing was only two feet tall—and that cost me some speed.

Ashlyn passed me, laughing the whole way.

"Hey," I barked.

Twain also ran by. "You have to keep up, Gray!" He taunted me with another laugh.

We recklessly flew down the hallways, and then up a set of stairs. I didn't actually know where we were going, so I just trusted Ashlyn to lead the way.

Unlike Ashlyn, I did have Deimos's help when it came to physical activities. I ran, and breathed, in such a way that I didn't get winded as fast. She was huffing and puffing at the top of the stairs, like any normal person, but I was still energized. I went by her and then started looking for familiar people to find my room.

Wait...

I used my mimic magic to sense my brother's knightmare, Thurin. His was the only knightmare in the whole Academy! I was sure to find our classroom without a guide if I followed his thread of magic.

Thankfully, they weren't too far from me. I pushed myself until I slammed through a heavy wooden door and into a lecture hall.

The air was thick with the scent of old parchment as I gulped down a breath. Glowstones were positioned between windows and across the ceiling, giving the room a warm glow.

Shelves lined the walls, stacked high with ancient tomes bound in leather and metal, some humming faintly, others silent and still but radiating a sense of weight and presence that made me feel small. What a strange classroom.

Sorin, Exie, Phila, Nasbit, and Raaza were already here. They sat in seats that resembled a stadium. Down at the lowest point of the room, in front of all the seats, was a podium for a speaker and a single chalkboard.

Sorin and the others all sat close together, their eldrin all in seats next to them, including Thurin, who was usually hidden in the darkness. Brak, Nasbit's golem, was seated so carefully, he almost looked like he would topple over at any second. The rows of seats were just stone benches, and the long wooden tables before them glistened with polish.

Two other people were here that I hadn't expected...

Knovak and Rosella.

Knovak sat by himself on the other side of the room, and Rosella sat closest to the door. When she spotted me, her eyes lit up. She stood from her spot and waved me over.

"What're you doing here?" I asked in a harsh whisper.

She shook her head. "I had to explain my situation to the headmaster, and he said I could join your class. Isn't that wonderful, Death Lord Deimos?"

Her kappa, Rooks, sat on the bench next to her. The fish-man was just tall enough to see over the desk, his huge eyes staring. Today, he wore a white cloak, black shirt, and white trousers. He was almost a little student here at the Academy.

The kappa waved to me. I waved back.

It was awkward.

Ashlyn dashed into the room a moment later, followed by Twain. She nearly ran into me, but then gracefully twirled around as she dodged.

"What's going on?" she asked between heavy breaths.

"This is our new classroom," I said, my voice almost echoing.

The ceiling was tall, and this place was built so that at least fifty people could listen to a single lecture at a time. It was massive, and quite open. Was that so some mystical creatures could still fit inside?

Even as I had that thought, it was proven correct. Ecrib, Ashlyn's typhoon dragon, came walking in through the window. A part of the Treehouse was connected here, which meant the branch walkway was visible if one looked outside.

Ecrib sauntered in, stepped into the seating area, and then glanced over at his arcanist.

"Ashlyn?" he asked.

She grabbed my arm. "C'mon. Let's get seated."

Watching me intently, Rosella sat back down, her expression downcast. I tried not to pay too much attention to her.

"One second," I whispered to Ashlyn. "I'll be right there."

Ashlyn released me and went straight over to my brother. Before taking a seat, I headed over to Knovak. In a way, I felt responsible for his condition, so I wanted to make sure he was okay.

Besides, what was he doing here? Had he signed up to be an abyssal sentinel? After what happened to him? His unicorn was nowhere to be seen, and the man wore a hat today, mostly covering his melted arcanist mark.

When I drew near, he turned to face me, his arms crossed over his chest. "Gray."

"Hey, Knovak." I leaned onto one of the benches, trying to seem causal. "We haven't spoken in a while. I didn't even know you signed up for this. Are you, uh, sure you want to go back to the abyssal hells?"

Knovak smirked. "The abyssal hells were the best thing that ever happened to me." He spoke every word with cold certainty.

"Right," I murmured. Then I cleared my throat. "What's your stance on *therapy*? Positive? I sure hope it's positive."

His face reddened and he tightened his hands on his arms.

"*Gray*. You're never serious. It's an unfortunate trait of lowborns, I suppose. Get away from me. I'm a powerful arcanist from a rich merchant house and I don't need you as one of my associates."

Since when had he become so snobby? Knovak had always been one for dressing nicely and being fancy, but not like this.

I gritted my teeth and pretended not to have heard all the words he just vomited.

"I should be getting back to my beautiful wife," I said, pushing away from the bench. "Ya know, because I'm an arcanist of the Kross family now." I gave him a sarcastic salute. "See you around, Knovak."

He said nothing as I took a seat next to my brother and the others.

"Psst," Sorin said. "Gray—are you paying attention?"

I glanced over to him, and then to the empty podium. No professors were here. Then I shrugged. "Paying attention to *what*?"

"The chalkboard."

Huh?

I turned my attention to the front of the class.

The chalkboard was rather massive, and it almost stretched from floor to ceiling. The dark surface swirled with ghostly images that shifted and blurred—a diagram here, a constellation there, the slow march of stars across some distant plane.

Then words appeared. It read:

> Today we will be learning about abyssal
> dragons.
> A year ago, the leg of an abyssal dragon
> was left in the basement of Astra

Academy. The headmaster has carefully dismantled it so we now have its skin, scales, sinew, muscle, and bone.
We will be using these parts to craft trinkets and artifacts to help survive the abyssal hells.

CHAPTER 33

ABYSSAL DRAGON MAGIC

An abyssal dragon leg? That had to be Hektor's. I felt bad for him... It had been cut off when we forced him back through the closing Gate of Crossing—the whole limb was just *hacked* straight off.

"Who is writing on the strange chalkboard?" I asked.

My brother shook his head. "I don't know. It just started forming words, so I think it wants us to pay attention."

The chalkboard kept going, the words vanishing from the surface. Well, they didn't just *vanish*—the words seemingly sank into the darkness of the board, like a stone sinking into deep waters. When more words appeared, they surfaced in similar fashion, rising to the surface one letter at a time.

Abyssal dragons are creatures made from brackish waters, souls, and the oblivion found in the fifth abyss. Not much is known about them, as it has been thousands of years since one was seen.

We know they evoke raw magic, which is a powerful force that can cut through flesh and blast through stone.

We suspect they manipulate and augment souls, but we don't fully understand the limitations.

We don't know how an abyssal dragon gains its true form, nor do we know the aura it can create.

I raised my hand. Could the chalkboard see me? I didn't know, and I felt foolish just silently waiting, so I cleared my throat instead.

"Uh, excuse me? Mr. Chalkboard? But *I* know what kind of aura an abyssal dragon creates." Everyone else in class turned to me. I smiled. "It's the *inevitable aura*, and anything caught in its sphere of influence will die sixty seconds later—as long as the aura maintains the whole time. If the arcanist fails to hold their magic, people won't die."

"Death Lords can just instantly kill people?" Sorin asked.

"Of course they can," Rosella interjected. Everyone turned to face her. She hesitantly glanced over, and then smoothed her hair. "They're lords of death," she said as though it was obvious. "Killing is their very nature."

I nodded. "It's, uh, their aura, though. And it doesn't work on other Death Lords."

The chalkboard must've heard everything we said, because new words floated to the surface. They read:

Fascinating.

That helps to explain abyssal dragon magic a bit, as all trinkets and artifacts made with the creature's body parts has now created either items that detect someone's impending death, or granted them complete immunity to instant death magics.

I snapped my fingers and pointed at the chalkboard. "Yes! Deimos told me that." My heart raced as I thought of a few possibilities. "Wait, could we create items that made it so people could explore the abyssal hells without dying?"

"People die if they explore the abyssal hells?" Raaza whispered.

I nodded. "Yeah, when I was stuck there with Ashlyn, Knovak, and Nini, they were slowly dying the whole time. Well, not Nini, because she's a reaper arcanist, but everyone *else* was. The abyssal hells drain you of your life, and if we hadn't escaped, then Ashlyn and Knovak would've died."

Exie stared at me with wide eyes. "Oh my."

"That is quite the predicament," Phila said. "I remember you telling us about that." She turned her gaze on the distant Knovak. He didn't glance over, or even really pay attention to what we were doing. "Were you scared, Knovak?"

Knovak still had his arms crossed. He leaned forward and glared. "No, I wasn't scared. Starling and I heroically made our way through that nightmare land and escaped."

Phila nodded along with his words. "Oh. That must've taken some bravery."

Perking up a bit, Knovak nodded. "It did."

Ashlyn rolled her eyes, but I motioned for her not to get too dramatic.

"I even emerged more powerful," Knovak said, so loud his voice bounced around the room. "Starling ate some of the soul fruit there, and now I *won't* die in the hells. At least, that's what Starling thinks."

He had spoken with an arrogant *huff* the entire time that acted as a sort of negative charisma. Why were so many of my classmates irritating twats from time to time? Couldn't they keep their insecurities and lunacy to themselves?

Sorin leaned forward and motioned to Knovak. "Hey— why don't you come sit with us? We have plenty of room on this side of the classroom."

I snapped attention to my brother, giving him the most baffled of looks. "*Why?*" I silently mouthed.

"*Because he seems upset,*" Sorin silently replied to me. It was easy to read Sorin's lips—he was an open book in many ways.

"Why do you want me to sit with you now? Is it because I have a powerful eldrin?" Knovak shifted his body so that most of his back faced us. "You never wanted to me to sit with you before."

"We sat together all the time," Raaza snapped.

"Because we were forced to. You made fun of me just like the others. I was weak, pathetic Knovak—and now that I'm not, suddenly you want to be friends? Pah." Knovak waved us all away.

"Has he been day drinking?" Raaza sarcastically asked, keeping his words quiet.

Sorin shrugged. "He's been like this ever since he returned. He won't even talk to me. Calls me *lowborn* under his breath and then shoves off."

"Does he think we *all* made fun of him?" Phila asked. She leaned closer to our group. "Because I never did that. I wanted him to spend more time with us."

Nasbit rubbed at his stomach. "He doesn't seem like himself."

"*I know you're all talking about me*," Knovak shouted, his voice echoing throughout the lecture hall. "Well, *fine*. Get your laughs in! You won't be laughing in the future. *You'll see*." Then he stood from his seat and stormed out the door.

Phila muttered some sort of apology, but it was too late. Knovak was gone. Since when did he have such a short temper?

Rosella watched this whole interaction as though it was a stage play. She appeared fascinated and had almost laughed when Knovak stomped out of the room. Her kappa watched with wide eyes, and even sniggered.

The chalkboard, silent but still "talking," had more words appear across the surface.

When you create trinkets and artifacts, you mix your magic into the base material being used.

Since the purpose of this newly formed course is to prepare you all for the abyssal hells, the students with magics most advantageous for fighting against the legions of monsters in the depths will be needed to help create the most items.

Nasbit held up his hand.

Unlike me, he waited to be called on.

The chalkboard never noticed him.

Your first task as students in this

course will be to identify which of you has the best defensive magics.

Since most of the abyssal hells is an unknown, Headmaster Venrover wants to prepare everyone for the worst. Armor, healing, and shielding will be crafted for everyone.

"Uh, Mr. Chalkboard?" I called out. "Nasbit has a question."

The chalkboard, which somehow had ears even though it had no eyes, did reply to that.

Nasbit?

He lowered his hand. "I was wondering if Astra Academy had enough star shards to make all these items? Creating even just a simple trinket is rather costly."

The Academy has over five hundred star shards for the purpose of outfitting all arcanists.
And not just you students—the Academy will be sending other arcanists into the abyssal hells as needed.

"O-Oh. I see." Nasbit leaned forward on his desk. "Can we make other items? Not just out of abyssal dragon parts?

Because there are several powerful artifacts that can be made that would help us. Caladrius arcanists have the best healing in the world. Imagine if we made something with their magic!"

This was Nasbit's area of expertise, it seemed. He *wanted* to make magical items.

Ashlyn and the others nodded along with this statement. Having a major healing artifact would make trekking through the abyssal hells a little easier, right?

The chalkboard swirled again, the words lifting to the surface with some hesitation. They were ghostly and faint at first, but then bolder as they went along.

Perhaps it is best you come to the labs...
We have much to show you.

We had to travel to the artificer's section of the Academy to get to the magic labs. It was interesting seeing how Astra Academy was segmented. All the second-years and higher had their own wing and rooms for all their specialized education.

Artificers had to become experts on making magical items, so it made sense their section would have all the star shards and mystical creature parts.

The larger eldrin, like Nasbit's golem and Ashlyn's dragon, went to the treehouse. Only the smaller creatures followed us down the halls.

Rooks walked alongside his arcanist, his fishy feet slapping on the stone floor whenever we left the rugs. He walked like a little human, upright, though he was only the size of a pre-teen child.

Rosella kept him close, whispering to him the entire way.

As a class, we entered the lab. Well, everyone but Knovak, who had disappeared entirely.

The air inside the lab was heavy, thick with the mingling scents of oils, metals, and something far less pleasant—human sweat masked by incense. The door creaked shut behind us, sealing everyone into this world of item creation.

At first glance, the lab seemed disordered, yet as I stepped further in, I realized that every object had been placed with meticulous intent. Shelves lined the walls, groaning under the weight of jars filled with oddities that shimmered faintly under the light of the glowstones.

There were so many things in those jars... A dragon's claw suspended in amber fluid, a vial of silvery liquid with a leathery wing floating through it, and then a jar filled with white bone fragments.

Interesting.

"Gray, do you see this?" my brother whispered.

I turned my head.

The tables were a jumble of tools and half-finished trinkets. A blade lay half-formed, its hilt carved from bone too smooth to belong to anything natural. Words etched into its surface shimmered faintly, and I assumed they were some sort of stamp—a signature the creature left.

Beside it sat a coil of what could only be the hair of an ifrit, its strands smoldering softly as though unwilling to die even in captivity. It would be amazing to having a sword that was always hot, or armor that repelled heat.

Probably wouldn't be useful in the abyssal hells, however.

Twain leapt to my shoulder. "This place is crazy. Do you feel all the magic?"

"I hadn't even thought to," I muttered.

As a mimic arcanist, this placed felt *very* strange. Half formed threads of magic were everywhere. How many mystical creatures did they have? And if I tugged on them, would

Twain transform? Of course—he could take the shape of magical items, even mundane ones, if he wanted.

Several tables in the room had tools on them, both mundane and magic. A hammer that glowed, tongs carved from obsidian, and a scalpel whose blade seemed to evaporate into mist at the tip were all fascinating, but I couldn't pay them much attention.

Cages hung from the ceiling, their contents obscured by thick, velvet drapes. Magic threads went to them, too. They weren't alive, though. Somehow, in some way, I knew that. The cages held more creature parts—not creatures.

Ominous.

"Hello, students," a familiar voice melodically floated through the room.

I had been so distracted by the magical lab that I hadn't realized there were three people in the room already. One of them was Professor Helmith. I recognized her instantly, and my eyes went wide when I realized how well she appeared.

Last I had seen her, she was... under the weather. From her fight with Death Lord Deimos. In my dream—when she had been trying to save me.

"*Professor*," I said as I rushed over.

Once close, I smiled. She answered in kind, her beauty ethereal.

She wore a long, sleeveless white dress that was practically weightless. It moved like feathers as she turned to face me fully. Her inky hair cupped her heart-shaped face, framing her cheeks and highlighting her lavender eyes.

Her arcanist marked glowed a gentle white—a sign she had a true form creature. Her mark was the standard seven-pointed star with a strange dream creature woven throughout. It was just a mishmash of creatures, from dragons, to cats, to birds.

And Professor Helmith's exposed arms bore blue and pink swirling tattoos that flowed across her skin down to her wrists.

The tattoos were runes—enchantments to her body made with occult ore. One was in the shape of storm clouds, stylized and glittering with power.

Professor Helmith didn't look like anyone else I knew.

"Gray, I'm so pleased to see you," she said. "It feels like it has been forever."

"Are you... teaching us?" was all I managed to ask.

Helmith nodded, her smile widening. "Oh, yes. My husband will continue to teach the first years, and I'll be teaching about mystical creatures found in the abyssal hells, as well as item creation. Heena Lolian will be assisting me."

Professor Helmith gestured to the woman standing next to her.

The behemoth arcanist, Heena. Exie's aunt.

Heena fixed her thick glasses and then straightened her chestnut bun. While Exie was stunning, her aunt definitely looked like a thirty-year-old pushing eighty. She was frumpy, but also intense, in all the worst ways.

"I'm very familiar with Gray," Heena said. "I wanted his mimic to transform into an abyssal dragon to use its parts—but that will no longer be necessary." She grazed her fingers over the parts on the table in front of her.

Several blue and gray scales were scattered in front of her. Some mucus was also in a jar—the same type of vile substance I saw on abyssal dragons all the time.

"You're going to be working for Astra Academy?" I asked.

Just as the words escaped me, the others in my class finally made their way over. They had been transfixed by the many creature parts in the room, but now they all had eyes on the scales. There were at least two dozen here.

"I will be working here," Heena said. "And you can refer to me as *Professor Lolian*. Isn't that grand? The Academy will *pay me* for all my experiments, which is practically a dream come true."

"You're going to be here *forever*?" Exie suddenly asked, her voice nearly a shout. "*Ugh.*"

The final person in the room—who I should've paid more attention to—stepped around the large scale-covered table. He was tall and lithe, but easily overlooked. He wore long robes of black and white, and his long hair fell straight to his shoulders.

His arcanist mark was a seven-pointed star with a sphinx woven throughout.

Headmaster Venrover.

"Please, arcanists," the headmaster said. "Such disrespect is unbecoming. Professor Lolian will be responsible for making sure each abyssal sentinel is outfitted for any situation that may occur. And believe me, that will be no simple feat."

CHAPTER 34

THE ANEMIA AURA

--Nini's Perspective--

I woke up in a tunnel.

My four lanterns stood around me like guardians against the darkness. Never before had I been happy to see the flicker of flames. When I sat up, I realized Waste and I were still merged. How long had it been? Weeks? Months?

Time in the abyssal hells was difficult to judge.

And I never needed to eat.

My stomach rumbled, but I never wasted away or grew too weak to walk. Death Lord Deimos had warned about eating any of the food, but he said the water in the fountains were safe.

"The abyssal hells slowly kill those who shouldn't be here," Waste telepathically said. *"But as a reaper arcanist, you are welcome. The magic of this place keeps you alive without sustenance. It will be a painful existence, but you will persist, even if we were to stay here for a hundred years."*

I didn't want that.

I wanted to see Sorin again.

So, I picked myself up, patted off my cloak, and then hobbled forward. The ambient magic that kept me fed also seemed to help with my recovery. The injuries to my legs, arms, and back didn't hurt as much as before... but they still stung. Walking was quite difficult.

Blue motes of light bled through the walls and ceiling of my tunnel. The walls were made of the same white alabaster as the rest of the labyrinth, but they were rougher here, less refined.

The tunnel went on in many directions, and I suspected it mirrored the labyrinth above. I could turn left, or right, or just keep going forward—there were so many four-way intersections that it became difficult to keep track of them all.

The bluish souls sometimes giggled as they floated by. At first, I thought them sinister, but after the third one laughed, I realized they weren't intimidating—they were the souls of children.

I lifted my hand and cupped the bottom of one small mote.

"Why are they here?" I whispered, my double voice still echoing throughout the tunnel.

"*These are children who were frightened when they perished,*" Waste explained. "*So, they got lost. But you shouldn't pity them—they will eventually find their way and be reincarnated.*"

"Aren't the Death Lords supposed to help them move on?" I stared down the tunnel, counting the blue motes of light.

There were hundreds here. Maybe more. They floated through the floor and then up through the ceiling, coming and going. It was too difficult to get an accurate number.

"*The Death Lords have forsaken their duties. All but*

Deimos. The souls here say Deimos occasionally visits to guide souls to safety."

Death Lord Deimos...

He did this all alone?

I tapped the tips of my fingers together, worried for the poor kids' souls. "Can we help him? I'm a reaper arcanist, after all."

"Only Death Lords can help souls reincarnate."

"You can understand the souls?" I asked, my eyebrows knitted under my face mask. "I don't hear any words."

"I hear them. As a reaper, I am one with death. If you close your eyes, you can hear them, too."

After a deep breath, I closed my eyes. At first, I heard nothing. It was just quiet in this tunnel of misery. Then I heard whispering—soft, scared words murmured by children.

"Where am I?" one asked.

"What happened?" another whispered.

"I want my mom..."

They were all pained, all confused.

"You'll be okay," I said aloud, hoping it would comfort them. I opened my eyes, surprised to see so many near me.

"We're lost," one whispered.

A few of the motes floated close. "Where is Death Lord Deimos?"

A couple danced around my head. "Are you also lost?"

"Stay close to me," I whispered. "I'm looking for a way out. Maybe I can take you with me."

I wasn't a Death Lord, but hopefully they wouldn't mind? Children shouldn't be lost in the abyssal hells, waiting to be reincarnated. It was cruel. They should've moved on already...

The motes stopped speaking and delicately danced around me. Were they happier now? The thought of helping them actually made me smile. Hopefully, I could lead them out.

With about a dozen motes in tow, I headed down the

tunnel. I still didn't know what I was going to use my bell for. I took it out of my pocket and stared at it again. This was worthless. But what else could I use to escape?

It was a real mystery...

A strange slurping caught my attention. Up ahead, in the darkness of the tunnel, the sound of hooves and claws mixed in with the slurps.

It was the elder basilisk and the accursed golden stag. They had somehow gotten ahead of me, and now they were eating something? What was that slurping?

The bluish motes continued to dance around me, seemingly unbothered by the sounds, or even my panic. Were they oblivious? They were just little souls—could they even fully perceive their surroundings?

Waste's scythe floated into my hands, and I waited, my shoulders tensed. With the faint light of the souls, and my lanterns, I spotted silhouettes of the elder beasts. They weren't rushing toward me—they were taking their time, stopping ever few steps—and seemingly searching the tunnel.

When one of the souls floated by the basilisk's head, the creature stuck out its tongue.

Slurp.

The basilisk somehow drew the soul straight into its mouth, eating the child's soul right before my eyes. It was disturbing—so disgusting—I felt my rage well in my chest like a scream I couldn't voice.

"*My arcanist,*" Waste telepathically said. "*You cannot rush in. Remember how they fought you previously? You must be strategic. Confident. Decisive.*"

I gripped the scythe as tightly as possible. I couldn't let these beasts eat all these souls. They were just children—they didn't deserve this. I had to protect them.

What would Sorin do? He would stop them. Somehow. He'd probably just charge in.

"What do we do?" I whispered in both my voice and Waste's.

"*You must use your anemia aura.*"

"We haven't done that yet. I don't know how."

"*You must fill yourself with your magic, and allow it to spill out of you, like a cup with too much tea. An aura affects the area around you. Your magic changes your surroundings. If you can do this, we have a chance at winning. If you can't, we must run.*"

I backed down the tunnel and around a bend. I didn't want the elder creatures to see me before I managed to manifest an aura—if I could manifest one at all.

Their slurping didn't stop, however. They continued to gobble down souls, even as they slowly crept closer to my location.

What monsters.

I took a deep breath and closed my eyes. Waste's strength was with me, and his cloak seemed to hug my shoulders. Could I create an aura? I hoped I could.

Focusing on my magic, and also focusing on my body, I imagined my magic as a liquid and my frame as a container. Filling myself with reaper magic was like augmenting something. I was *pushing* magic into my body—into my very flesh and bones.

With my eyes closed, the voices of the souls became louder.

"Where am I?" one asked.

"Where is my momma?" another chimed in.

I would've said their words were distracting, but when the slurps echoed down the tunnel, it had the opposite effect. I was so enraged, their voices actually helped me concentrate. I wasn't making an anemia aura for myself—I wasn't making one for class, or to impress someone—I was making it to save these children.

I *had* to do it.

There was no room for failure.

I swallowed hard and continued to fill my body with all the reaper magic I could muster. The only voice that threatened to break my concentration was one that asked, "Where is my sister?"

At first, I thought it was my brother's voice, but I quickly realized it wasn't. No—I was just tormenting myself again. I had to let that go.

And I would.

With my body tingling from the magic I had gathered, I pushed myself just a little further. I needed the reaper magic to spill out of me. I needed it to flood these tunnels and surround my enemies.

I scrunched my eyes shut as I struggled with the last bit. The clops of hooves and the scrap of claws were closer, but they didn't frighten me.

And then it happened. My magic—it was like it broke out of a dam, rushing from me.

I snapped open my eyes and held my scythe close.

The tunnels weren't normal. They were filled with a red mist, like a bloody fog had filled the labyrinth, and we were all caught within.

"*That is your anemia aura,*" Waste telepathically said. "*That is what it looks like when it manifests.*"

My anemia aura was disturbing, but not as much as those monsters. I wheeled around the corner, my scythe in hand, the bluish souls bobbing in the air. The elder basilisk and golden stag jumped when I made a sudden appearance.

"*You,*" the basilisk hissed.

"Kill her," the golden stag shouted, his voice echoing. "Her soul will be more delicious than these mere morsels."

I rushed forward and swung with my scythe. The tunnel was at least seven feet wide, which was narrow when wielding my weapon, but not narrow enough to stop me from fighting.

The curved blade struck square in the basilisk's shoulder, and the beast shrieked.

When I yanked my scythe from its flesh, blood gushed out with it.

The golden stag lowered his head, his soul-covered antlers shimmering. He tried to heal his ally—but nothing happened.

The basilisk hissed and then slashed with two of its six claws. I managed to sidestep out of the way of one, but the other caught my forearm. The beast's claws sank all the way down to my bone, but anger masked all other sensations.

"Leave... these..." I readied my scythe again, lifting it as high as I could. "*Children*... alone!"

I swung as hard as I could, my attack wildly telegraphed. Fortunately, the basilisk was big, and the tunnel wasn't large enough for the dastard to dodge. I struck it in the ribs, the blade of my weapon sinking deep.

The souls on the elder basilisk's mane reached out, as though trying to heal it, but the red mist that haunted the air got in the way. The basilisk *couldn't* heal—not naturally, not with the golden stag magic, and not with the souls it had consumed while in the abyssal hells.

"Die, you fiends," I said as I lifted my hand.

I manipulated the blood on the ground and created spears. They lanced upward, stabbing through the basilisk and even clipping the golden stag.

The stag snarled as he clopped around, trying to dodge. I threw more blood knives, and the beast nimbly evaded. He was smaller than the basilisk, and quite dexterous.

When I evoked terrors, nothing happened. The stag was completely unaffected.

The basilisk, skewered on the hardened blood, tried to squirm off, but couldn't dislodge itself. Within a few moments, it bled out, its magic unable to help while my anemia aura was up and running.

"You're not worthy of that reaper magic," the elder golden stag shouted. "*You should be with us!* You should be using souls for your own gain—your own power! They're already dead. They're just raw magic for the plucking!"

I held out my hand, and the four golden chains hanging from Waste's cloak launched forward. They acted like tentacles, and grabbed the golden stag before it could dance away. The chains wrapped around the creature's front legs and its antlers, the lanterns tethered tight against the beast's body.

"No more running," I breathed. "*You're an abomination that needs to be purged from the cycle of reincarnation.*"

"N-No! Wait!"

I swung with my scythe, aiming for the elder stag's neck. In one clean swipe, I managed to decapitate the stag. *Thwick.* The head came clean off the body, the antlers clattering when they hit the tunnel floor. The souls attached to them slowly separated and floated away, free.

I allowed my weapon to lower.

My arms hurt.

My back ached.

My heart hammered.

But they were dead, and I wasn't. That was all that mattered. I had stopped their vile evil, and saved these souls.

My anemia aura faded, the red mist dissipating.

"I think we need to rest," Waste and I said as one.

CHAPTER 35

PROTECTION ITEMS

Heena—I mean, *Professor Lolian*—stepped closer to the table with the many abyssal dragon parts. Her broad smile included teeth, and for some reason, she seemed unhinged.

"I can't wait to experiment with these abyssal dragon pieces. This is a dream come true." She turned her deranged smile onto us. "Who wants to go first?"

Phila grabbed Nasbit's arm and ushered him forward, bringing him right up to the other side of the table. "Can Naz try making a trinket?"

"W-What?" Nasbit's round face grew red and his eyes wide. "I'd rather just watch, I think. So I don't mess anything up."

"You were so excited before we entered! You should be the first. Everyone would agree."

The others were still focused on our surroundings. No one cared who went first, obviously, not when there were spinal cords in nearby jars to observe.

"Please try, Naz," Phila said as she squeezed his arm. "I'd like to see you try."

Nasbit somehow got sweaty in the blink of an eye. Despite his noticeable perspiration, he nodded. "Uh, right. Yes. I'll do that. For you."

Professor Helmith and Headmaster Venrover stepped closer to the wall to allow Heena the stage. All the students gathered around the large table. The many abyssal dragon scales were of various sizes, but most were the length of my thumb and as wide as three of my fingers.

Professor Lolian grabbed a wooden box off a nearby shelf and brought it to the table. "Normally, artificer students learn the importance of mystical creature parts *before* they get to star shards, but I think this lesson is best in reverse."

Nasbit nervously chuckled. "Why, Professor?"

"Because we already know what we want from these trinkets and artifacts—we want to be able to explore the abyssal hells without dying. Since abyssal dragons and their arcanists can do that just fine, their magic is *obviously* perfect."

"Are these really from a Death Lord's eldrin?" Rosella asked, eyeing the scales.

"They're from Deimos's eldrin," I whispered to her.

Her eyes grew big as she stared. I feared she might grab a scale and dash out of the room with it, but Rosella kept her hands together. Her little kappa eldrin pulled himself up to the edge of the table, peeking over like only a child could.

Professor Lolian grabbed a scale and then opened the box.

The contents of the container shimmered so brightly, they almost hurt my eyes. But then the dazzle wore off, and inside I gazed upon two dozen star shards. I had seen them many times before—I may have even been the one to collect a few of these shards specifically—but they were still glorious.

Star shards were basically clear crystals with luminescent glitter inside.

Beautiful.

"First lesson," Professor Lolian said as she plucked a star

shard from the box, "is that a trinket is any magical item made with less than ten star shards. Anything made with *more* than ten is an artifact."

Nasbit wiped away some of his sweat. "The more star shards used, the more magic is permanently infused into the item. That's what all the books say."

Lolian snapped her fingers, fixed her thick glasses, and then frowned. "Don't interrupt. I have a flow." She placed the star shard against the abyssal dragon scale. "So, star shards act as an adhesive. They will glue magic to the abyssal dragon magic, and thus create something permanent. Trinkets and artifacts can be passed from person to person, or even attuned to fit just a single person or their bloodline. They're extremely useful. *Extremely.*"

Professor Lolian glared at the scale and then removed a star shard from the box.

"But behemoth magic isn't about living or surviving—it's about procreation. So we don't want to mix *my* magic with the abyssal dragon, do you understand? If I imbued behemoth magic into an abyssal dragon piece, we'd get an item that likely prevented births altogether, or caused stillborn children, or perhaps resulted in perfect births with no chance of death. Do you understand?"

"It's a beautiful equation," Nasbit whispered to Phila. "Mixing together magics—that's why *artificer* is its own course of study."

"It's so intricate that we don't have time to discuss all the myriad of possibilities. All we need to ask ourselves is: Who here thinks their magic would be a synergistic fit with abyssal dragon magic? We want armor. We want protection."

There was a long moment of silence.

This was a tall order.

Sorin rubbed his chin. "What about my knightmare

magic? I mean, knightmares are rather defensive, right? Perfect for armor?"

"That's some good logic," Raaza muttered.

Nasbit nodded once. "Yes. You have good instincts, Sorin." Then he turned his attention to me. "But I was actually wondering... What if we combined the abyssal dragon magic with a mimic's? What does that do?"

Another round of silence as everyone turned their gaze to me. I just offered a shrug. I wasn't an expert on magical items.

"I've never heard of a mimic item before," Exie mused aloud.

Ashlyn shifted down the table until she stood only an inch away. "Well, what about typhoon dragon magic? I can breathe underwater, and my eldrin is another dragon, after all. Won't my magic be the strongest?"

Professor Lolian waggled her finger. Then she grabbed one of the tools on the table—the mysterious scalpel with a misty blade. "This is made from blue phoenix magic." She grabbed a handful of scales and then applied the tip of the scalpel to the edges of mystical creature parts.

And right before our eyes, Professor Lolian fused them together. With expert skill, she basically fitted scales together until she made an armor-like fabric.

"Knightmare magic is perfect for armor and weapons," she said. "Knightmares are rather adept at hardening shadows, and using their magic we could make protective gear for the abyssal hells." She motioned my brother closer.

Sorin stepped forward with a hesitant smile. The shadow around his feet fluttered. Was Thurin also excited?

"If I make armor, can I put symbols on it?" Sorin asked.

Professor Lolian frowned. "Whatever for?"

"I'd like to make them personalized. Like with a signature? Or a mark of some sort? I like the idea of crafting unique magical items."

The professor subtly rolled her eyes as she handed Sorin the scales and a star shard from the wooden box. "Yes. You can make it as unique and special as you desire. But first you must make it—so that we know whether your theory is correct."

My brother was handed the patchwork of scales and the star shard. He glanced from one and then the other. "And you want me to fuse my knightmare magic to this?"

"Push your magic into the scales. Since they're from an abyssal dragon, you might find it a little different, but it should work. Once you're done, press the star shard close and allow it to melt into your handiwork." Professor Lolian watched with intense eyes, never blinking.

The others in class leaned forward, all of them rapt by what was happening.

I already knew Sorin would succeed. He would make an amazing item, because for whatever reason, he had always been remarkably talented with knightmare magic. He learned faster than everyone, and got things on the first try most of the time...

This would be no different.

So I turned my attention to Professor Helmith and Headmaster Venrover. While everyone was focused on my brother, I moved away from the table and walked behind most of the other students.

Professor Helmith and the headmaster were whispering to themselves, but they quickly stopped when I approached.

"I'm glad to see you're okay," I said to Helmith, keeping my voice low. "I had thought... you might never recover."

Her purple eyes went wide for a moment, but then she calmed as she smiled. "Oh. Thank you for your concern, Gray, but it'll take a lot more than the fragment of a Death Lord to stop me."

I chuckled, but it reminded me of our dreams together.

She always had fun turns of phrases, and was rather confident, but in a quiet way.

"I'm married now," I said. "Gray Kross is the name, just in case you hadn't heard."

She grinned. And then motioned to the table where everyone else was. "I'm aware—but shouldn't you be paying attention to the lesson? This will all be important soon, I fear."

"Actually, I wanted to speak to you both about that." I gestured to the headmaster, though he made no effort to speak or interrupt me. "I think something is wrong with Death Lord Deimos, and if you're feeling better... I was wondering if you could release his piece of his soul? You know, the one still trapped in me?"

Deimos's anger was immediate and thorough. Speaking through me, he growled, "*I told you and my brother that I don't want that.*"

"You're ill—or something," I snapped back, arguing with myself.

"I can handle it."

"But..."

It was Professor Helmith's true form ethereal whelk magic that kept his soul fragment bound. She could release it—and then perhaps the Death Lord would recover.

My bizarre conversation with myself seemed to surprise her. She was quiet for a long moment before exchanging a silent glance with the headmaster. When she turned back to me, it was with understanding. If anyone had the empathy to understand what I was going through, it was Professor Helmith.

"Gray, I believe the only way we're going to enter the abyssal hells is through your connection to the Death Lord," she said.

"What?" I asked. "Really?"

Deimos's anger subsided. Perhaps he knew this all along.

"Yes. That was how you got there in the first place, wasn't it? Being pulled through the magical connection you shared with Deimos. If I release his soul fragment, we might not have a way to get into the abyssal hells. You... understand, don't you?"

Of course I understood. I was just worried about Deimos. I figured, if Helmith was okay, and her magic working properly, she could somehow help him, but if his soul was the only link we had, I supposed we couldn't.

"We have spoken to Deimos's brother," Headmaster Venrover finally cut in. "And he has another plan to enter the abyssal hells."

"You spoke to Zahn?" I asked.

Professor Helmith motioned with her hand for me to keep my volume down. The other students were cheering and patting Sorin on the shoulders, which meant he successfully did whatever was asked of him—which I knew would happen.

"Yes, Zahn has agreed to help us," Headmaster Venrover said. "In exchange, he has agreed that once this is over—once the abyssal hells are open—he will face punishment for his many crimes. However, we can't really trust him, since he put so many students in danger when he was last here, so Zahn continues his work away from Astra Academy."

"He agreed to face punishment?" I asked.

"He did. So long as his brother is allowed to leave the abyssal hells, it seems Zahn will do anything. But that's why he shouldn't be trusted completely."

I exhaled. "I actually need to see him."

Well, I didn't need to see *him*. I needed to see the soul catcher arcanist. But Zahn would be with him, I just knew it.

"You sound as though this is urgent," Professor Helmith said.

She always knew how I was feeling.

I nodded. "It *is* urgent."

"Then, we can make arrangements for you to see him tomorrow?" Helmith glanced over to Venrover. "What do you think, Adelgis?"

I rarely heard the headmaster's first name, but whenever I did, it amused me. Headmaster Venrover always grinned in a small way.

"I think that can be arranged," the headmaster stated. "I will make a summons for Zahn, and you can see him here at the Academy, but only under the protection of Captain Leon. Do you understand?"

"If you make a summons for him, can you please ask that he brings the soul catcher and its arcanist?"

Professor Helmith's eyebrows lifted at the same time. "The soul catcher arcanist? Why must you speak with her?"

"I think... it's important for my magic," was all I managed to say.

The headmaster and Professor Helmith mulled over my statement but then eventually nodded their heads. It seemed I'd get to have my chance at a true form myself—tomorrow. I had to be prepared.

"Gray!" my brother called out. "Look at this!"

I turned on my heel. Sorin held up the fused scales. They had a tint of black to them, as though a shadow were permanently being cast over them and them alone.

"It worked," Sorin said. "I imbued this item, and apparently it'll prevent people from dying in the abyssal hells."

CHAPTER 36

ONLY THE BEST

I walked over to the lab table. Professor Lolian held up a piece of parchment for everyone to see.

"This paper can identify the purpose of magical items," she said matter-of-factly. "And as you can see here, our little knightmare arcanist has done it. He's created just the very item we were looking for."

The paper read:

Abyssal dragon magic
Knightmare magic
One star shard
Shields against instantaneous death, draining
death, and damage to the soul

I moved closer to Sorin. He gave me a great big hug as soon as I was near, his large arms practically crushing me. I wheezed.

"Do you see this?" he asked, still holding me. "We need to make tons of these!"

I patted him on the back. "It's great." When he finally released me, I took a deep breath.

"We don't have *unlimited* abyssal dragon magic," Professor Lolian stated. "We have a whole dragon arm's worth of scales, and that should make us enough armor... Well, as long as they're small pieces."

Professor Helmith stepped close, her face beaming with delight. "Oh, we should make them into pauldrons. That way they're easy to wear—everyone in the abyssal sentinel class should keep them on at all times."

All times? That seemed a little drastic. Then again, I was randomly spirited away to the abyssal hells at a party, so perhaps this was a great idea.

"It can be a symbol of your status in this major," Professor Helmith concluded.

"What is a pauldron?" Phila asked. She wasn't asking the group; her attention was squarely on Nasbit.

And Nasbit happily replied, "A pauldron is a piece of armor worn on the shoulder. Heavier pieces of armor limit the motion of the arm, but pauldrons offer protection *and* the ability to fully move. S-So it's really useful."

"Oh, I see!"

"Do I get to make them all?" Sorin asked, eagerness in his voice.

Professor Helmith nodded, her demeanor bright. "As long as Professor Lolian is satisfied with this result. Are there no better combinations or trinkets we could use?"

"I'll do a bit of research," Professor Lolian stated. "But I do believe this will be the most useful for the cost. One star shard for full protection against the wrath of the hells? Ha! That's a bargain."

It was good to return to a familiar setting. I had forgotten how pleasant it was to just have a standard routine, and Astra Academy's classroom schedule felt like putting on comfortable boots after wearing something two sizes too small for a month.

Each day focused on one subject, split into two-hour classes with breaks and lunch in between. We studied six days a week, leaving one day for rest or clubs. Today's class was apparently called *Abyssal Hells Preparation*, and tomorrow we'd be taking *Intermediate Combat Arts*. I wondered if Professor Jijo would be there...

However, it was lunch that I really looked forward to. The moment we were allowed to leave the magic lab, I traveled with Ashlyn and Sorin down the long hallways and straight to the dining hall.

The room was massive, and it was bustling with laughter and chatter that echoed off its oval walls. Every student, no matter their year, had lunch in the same space, which meant larger eldrin were mixed in with the smaller ones. Ashlyn's typhoon dragon, Ecrib, was already here, his bright blue scales easy to spot in the pandemonium.

I stayed near the edges, avoiding the larger eldrin, and went straight for the table that Ecrib had reserved for us. Twain leapt off my shoulder and landed on the tabletop. Then he stretched and yawned, his eyes blinking out of sync.

"That class was taxing on my mental health," he said.

"Let's go grab some food, love," Ashlyn said to me.

Love?

I almost stuttered over my next words, but I recovered quickly. "Wait a minute. I wanted to tell you both something. The headmaster is going to let me see Zahn tomorrow—and he's going to bring the soul catcher arcanist with him."

Sorin caught his breath. The shadows in our corner of the dining hall shifted a bit, but quickly settled down. "You mean you're going to fight him?"

"Yes," I replied. "That's the plan. I want Twain to be a true form mimic, after all."

Twain nodded along with my words. "Sounds good to me."

I turned to my brother. "Do you think you can keep helping me? Maybe tonight, after the last of our classes, you can evoke your terrors on me again? I think we were getting somewhere with that."

My brother rubbed at his robes. Then he hardened his expression into something determined. "You can count on me. I'll be there for you, and I'll even accompany you to see the soul catcher."

Ashlyn placed a hand on my shoulder. "I'll be there with you, too. You're my husband. We're a team."

"Yeah." I hesitantly touched her hand. My brother wouldn't even look at us, which told me everything I needed to know.

This pained him. He wanted to be happy for me, but our affection clearly reminded him of Nini. I could imagine no worse torture, so I gently removed Ashlyn's hand and silently gestured to my brother.

The second Ashlyn glanced over, she seemed to understand what I was trying to indicate. She nodded and then took a step away from me.

"Let's eat," she said. Then she placed a hand on Sorin's shoulder. He flinched as he turned to face her. "C'mon. Let's keep our spirits high."

"Ah, yes," Sorin muttered.

The central table overflowed with today's lunch: grilled meats on skewers with fragrant rice as a side. The rich aroma made my stomach growl as I made my way over, weaving through the crowd with a surprising amount of grace.

Fortunately, some of the grilled meats were fish. Twain would love that.

And once we ate until it hurt, we could go back to class and create more trinkets.

"I really liked creating magical items," Sorin said as he stepped up to my side. He took a few skewers, but it wasn't even half of what he usually took. "I feel like I'm making progress toward saving Nini."

"You should eat more than that," I said.

Sorin took one more skewer. Barely anything. "Do you think Nini is getting enough to eat?" he whispered.

My chest twisted into a knot. Thankfully, Deimos took over for me. "She doesn't need to eat," Deimos stated. "The magic of the abyssal hells sustains her. It isn't pleasant, but as a Duke of Demise, she is capable of living there for all time. You needn't fret."

Sorin took a few seconds to absorb that. Then he muttered, "But she's all alone. And with nothing. I just... don't feel like eating when I think about that, you know?"

Before I could argue, Sorin turned away. He headed back to our table, his steps confident, but slow. I hated that he worried so much, but I didn't know what to tell him. What could I do to ease his anxiety? Was there anything outside of heading straight into the abyssal hells?

I'd have to give it more thought.

For the rest of class, Sorin imbued more of the abyssal dragon scales. Professor Lolian fused the scales together, fashioning pauldrons out of them, and Professor Helmith led the rest of the class.

Headmaster Venrover had left, which was a shame. I wanted to speak to him more, but perhaps it would have to wait.

Since the magical lab was so big, Sorin and Professor

Lolian could be at their own table while the rest of us stood around another. Professor Helmith brought jars of abyssal dragon blood, mucus, and bits of bone. We were all allowed to observe and theorize about the best use for the items.

"It is theorized that the abyssal hells are filled with water," she said to the class.

"Not *all* the hells have water," I muttered. Everyone turned to me, curious. "There's a desert," I continued. "It's called the *Graveyard of Empires*. But there's also water, yeah."

Helmith's eyes twinkled as she stared at me. She gestured me to come around the table to be on the side with her. I sheepishly made my way over.

"Why don't you tell everyone about the abyssal hells?" she asked. "Or perhaps... Deimos would like to run this part of the class?"

Rosella practically started clapping right then and there. She softly patted her hands together, a smile spreading across her face. "Yes! Yes. Please. Death Lord Deimos should teach us. All hail the Death Lord!"

The room went dead silent after that. Everyone stared at Rosella, but that didn't dissuade her. She continued her quiet clap as though the rest of us weren't even here.

She stared right at me like I was a deity mingling among men. It made me a little uncomfortable, to be frank.

Ashlyn stepped between me and Rosella. She smoothed her blonde hair and then smiled. "Well, Gray? What do you think? Could Deimos give us a few words of wisdom?"

I half shrugged my shoulder. "Uh, sure. I guess."

"It would be amazing if a Death Lord told us everything about the abyssal hells," Nasbit stated. "I don't want to be swearing allegiance to him or anything, though."

Rosella narrowed her eyes into a glower but said nothing. Even Rooks offered Nasbit a harsh glare.

"I agree," Raaza said, stepping forward. "Deimos would be

the best teacher. Might as well learn everything we can from him."

"And whatever he tells us, we can use that information to make the trinkets," Phila happily chimed in.

"Well, I think Ashlyn's instincts about making water-breathing trinkets is useful." I gave her a quick smile. "I mean, she was there with me in the abyssal hells. She knows the first abyss has a lot of water. At least, in certain parts."

Exie frowned. "So we'll have to be swimming? Gross."

"It's not too late to change your mind and join a different class," Raaza snapped. "*Swimming* will be the least of our problems."

Professor Helmith held up her hands. "Please. Let us focus. We'll hear about the abyssal hells, and then we'll brainstorm possible magical items—or enchantments—we would need to overcome such challenges."

She stepped aside, giving me center stage. Some people got nervous when all eyes were on them, but I wasn't *some people*. This was my time to shine.

I cleared my throat. "The first abyss is actually made of four different biomes. There's the *Silkshade Grove*, which is a forest. There's the *Specter Sands*, another desert. There's the *Wraithborne Orchard*, a swamp or mire. And lastly, there's the *Lament Valley*, a place of mountains with flatlands between."

"Why?" Exie asked, completely interrupting me.

Rosella held a finger to her lips. "*Shh*. This is highly valuable information."

"It's a place where you get reincarnated," I said. "And depending on the location, you get reincarnated into different things. The forest reincarnates you into plants, trees—you know. Magical things that fit a forest. But none of that really matters."

"Why not?" Phila asked, quieter, her brow furrowed.

"Because we need to get down to the third abyss as quickly

as possible." I leaned on the table and exhaled. "That's where Deimos is waiting. It's where he's been fighting the other Death Lords off and on for some time. The first abyss is just a place—a sacred place—but it's like the front door. We need to get through it as quickly as possible."

"Remember, I found that book on the many layers of the abyss," Nasbit said. He nervously laughed as he added, "I committed most of it to memory. The second abyss is a labyrinth. A gigantic maze meant to confuse anyone trying to get to the lower depths."

"First off, Deimos knows how to get through that, so we'll be fine. Second, the third abyss has the Requiem Throne." While I had never been there, Deimos's memories filled my own. "It's a sanctuary. No one can do anything violent there. Deimos uses it as a place to rest and recuperate. So, all we really need to do is make it there."

"What about the fourth abyss?" Raaza asked. "We don't have to prepare to go through there?"

"Well..." Deimos took over, confident and mildly irritated. "It's run by elder creatures," Deimos said through me. "If you want to get through there, you'll need to fight your way through those beasts—all of whom will want to consume your soul."

"No pressure," Nasbit sarcastically murmured.

"And the fifth abyss is some sort of oblivion," Professor Helmith said, startling me. She stepped closer, smiling gently. "Correct? It's a place of void?"

"It's a place of nothingness," Deimos said. "It's the vast void before the *Oblivion Gate*. Death Lord Umbriel believes she can cross the fifth abyss and reach this mystical gate, thus gaining the power of all destruction. But she hasn't yet."

Phila stood straight, her body stiff. "Oh, no. That means we'll definitely need to cross the fourth abyss."

The class went silent.

It was a lot to take in. What kind of magical items and enchantments would give us the best chance at surviving? Obviously, the pauldrons would. But what else? Ashlyn's water breathing, sure, but we needed better things than that.

"Astra Academy has these new magical barriers," I said. "Can we get armor that has that? And weapons that can kill elder creatures faster?"

The others nodded.

"I'll speak with the headmaster," Professor Helmith said. "At the end of the week, you'll be meeting with some of the strongest arcanists around. They'll be joining the abyssal sentinels as your professors and guiding you through your magical development."

"The strongest?" Nasbit asked. "Like who? Will the Warlord of Magic be returning to the Academy?"

"Him, along with a few others." Helmith brushed back her inky black hair. "I think some of them might have the magic we need to make the best possible items."

CHAPTER 37

SOUL CATCHER CONFRONTATION

Once class was over, and we had dinner, I went to the bathing rooms and cleaned myself off. Only after I was finished, and dressed in loose-fitting trousers and a tunic, did I meet my brother and Ashlyn in the second-year dormitory hallway. Twain stayed on my shoulder, perched happily and content to follow me no matter what.

We were supposed to go to bed, but I wanted to face my fears again.

I wanted to prepare myself for the confrontation with the soul catcher tomorrow.

Sorin and Ashlyn both wore more comfortable clothing. Sorin had the same outfit as me, but Ashlyn wore a white silk shirt and flowing black pants. It was in that moment I got to remind myself that she was my wife, and I was the luckiest man in the world.

Sorin always had his knightmare eldrin with him, even if he wasn't wearing him. Thurin shifted with him in the shadows, stalking Sorin's every step.

As a group, we snuck over to a window and climbed out onto the massive branch walkway. It was a path to the

Treehouse, where all the eldrin of the students slept, but tonight, it would be our training area.

"This will be perfect," I said as we walked along the wooden path. There weren't any handrails or guards, just minor bumps to keep mystical creatures from falling.

"Why is this perfect?" Ashlyn asked as she walked along behind me. "It doesn't seem safe."

"Gray is afraid of heights," Sorin replied. He walked in front, and turned around to face me only when he came to a three-way intersection in the branch. It was wider here, and the walkway thicker. "Okay, we can train here, I think."

Ashlyn stood off to the side, her arms crossed. "Are you sure this is a good idea? For real? Do you see how high up we are?"

I forced myself to look over the edge. The instant I did, my heartrate shot upward. We were at least a few hundred feet above the ground. If we fell, we'd land on jagged rocks outside of the Academy. There was no way the doc could put us back together again after *that* fall.

"Yeah, this is good."

Twain shuddered on my shoulder and then leapt off. He hurried over to Ashlyn and actually jumped to *her* shoulder. "I'm going to stay over here with the sane person."

"Hey," I barked.

Twain just shrugged.

When the wind picked up, I shielded my eyes. The evening sky was filled with stars and the largest moon that had ever hung over the Academy. It graced us with an abundance of light.

With my heart still beating fast, I turned to my brother. He was so tall and bulky—he looked imposing in the middle of the night. A real knightmare arcanist.

"Okay, Sorin—use your terrors. And even if I'm scared, and tell you to stop, just keep up your evocation."

Sorin furrowed his brow. "A-Are you certain? We can take this one step at a time. Maybe just a short amount first, and then—"

"No. We were doing that last time." Sure, we spent *hours* doing it, but we got nowhere. "Plus, I think Deimos's thoughts were mixing with my own, and I really need to focus on just my fears. I can't overcome both of our mental hangups."

My brother shifted his feet outward, taking a firm stance. I moved to the center of the three-way intersection; that way, if I fell down from fright, I wouldn't go over any edges. Once I was prepared, I took a deep breath and nodded.

Sorin lifted his hand. For a long moment, he did nothing. "Are you sure, Gray? I don't want to feel like I'm torturing you..."

"It's not torture if I ask for it."

"Really? I don't think that's how it's defined."

I ran a hand down my face. "Sorin, I swear, if –"

But he was just using the conversation as a distraction. As soon as I started speaking, he evoked his nightmarish terrors. They were an invisible force that muddled the mind, making me see things that weren't really there, even when I closed my eyes.

They already reminded me of the dreams Helmith had given me—just a hundred times more frightening.

At first, the images flashing before me were disjointed and confusing. It was like before, when Sorin had used his terrors. I saw snippets of Deimos's past, and I pushed past that. I needed to focus on what scared me—everything else needed to fall away.

Then the ground beneath me shifted, and I realized I was no longer in a place I recognized. Instead, I stood at the edge of a sheer cliff, the drop so steep and endless it seemed to swallow the night sky. My breath caught as I peered down.

There was no bottom, only a yawning abyss that devoured light and sound. My feet teetered on the very lip of the precipice, a single step away from plunging into nothingness.

"Oh, why did I do this?" I sardonically asked myself.

The air around me grew colder, thinner, until each breath felt like drawing shards of glass into my lungs.

I tried to step back, but my legs refused to move, as if Sorin's magic had seized control of my body. Panic clawed at my chest as the wind rose, fierce and howling, tugging at my clothes, my hair, my balance.

It whispered to me in cruel tones, daring me to fall, daring me to give in.

"Sorin!" I shouted, the terrors too real. "*Stop!*"

But he didn't.

Then the ground shifted again.

The cliff edge crumbled beneath my feet, the rocks tumbling away in slow motion. I lurched backward, my arms flailing, but there was no safety to be found. The world around me was in motion now, the ground fracturing and sliding, tilting me toward the void.

My stomach lurched.

What if, in my flailing, I actually went over the side of the branch? What if I was plummeting to my doom—toward the stone rocks around Astra Academy?

And then I was falling.

The sensation was immediate and visceral.

The wind tore at me, deafening in its fury, my body tumbling wildly through the air. The night sky horizon spun in dizzying loops, stars and moon trading places until I couldn't tell which was which.

My screams were swallowed by the roar of the wind, and I felt my heart pounding against my ribs, desperate and wild.

I reached out, grasping for anything to stop my descent, but there was nothing. My hands clawed at empty air, my body twisting as though sheer will alone could defy gravity. The more I struggled, the faster I seemed to fall, spinning out of control in a chaos of motion that made me feel weightless and helpless all at once.

"*Sorin!*"

In the distance, I saw the ground rushing up to meet me, impossibly fast. The jagged edges of cliffs and crags reached for me like grasping claws, and for a fleeting moment, I thought I could brace for the impact. But my body betrayed me again, and I remained limp, spinning, nothing more than a leaf caught in a storm.

I was going to die.

Just as the ground surged to swallow me, Sorin's terrors ended.

I stumbled forward, back to reality. There I was, still in the middle of the three-way intersection on the branch, my tunic soaked in an unbelievable amount of sweat. My heart had never felt so forceful.

I grabbed my shirt, my mouth dry.

"Are you okay?" I heard my brother ask. "I... I didn't want to do it that long. I'm so sorry."

I shook my head. My black hair was wet and sticking to the side of my face. All sweat. What a crazy trip.

What a feeling.

Somehow, through this all, the euphoria of *not* dying actually kind of felt pretty good.

I started laughing. Honestly, truly, laughing.

"Gray? Are you okay?"

I didn't know who had asked because my laughing grew a little louder. I honestly felt pretty good.

"Sorin," I said through my chuckles. "It is so *awesome* that I'm not dead right now." I glanced up, my senses coming back to me. "Have you been practicing your terrors? Those were *extreme*."

My brother stared at me, almost in disbelief. "You're not mad at me?" he whispered.

I shook my head. "No." I grabbed my shirt again and fidgeted with it. "No. You did exactly what I asked you to." But I still couldn't rid myself of the joy.

I *wasn't* dead. I hadn't fallen.

"Damn," I said. "It is so good to be alive."

"I think you've broken him," Twain quipped. "He's lost it."

Ashlyn rushed over to my side. When I turned to face her, it was with a smile.

"I'm fine," I said.

She eyed me up and down, her blue eyes piercing. "Well... You look okay. But you don't sound well."

I shrugged. "It happens."

The sensation of falling lingered, a phantom weightlessness that I couldn't shake. Even as I stood on the branch, my feet firmly on something solid, I still felt the cold pull of the wind, reminding me that control is an illusion, and gravity waits for us all.

It was a little exhilarating.

How odd.

"Do you want me to do it again?" Sorin asked.

I shook my head. "No. I think I've got this." I stood straight and brushed myself off. "It's time to face the soul catcher and put an end to all my terrors."

When I woke in the morning, I took a moment to wake Ashlyn with a kiss on the cheek. When she blushed, and fluttered her eyes open, I realized again, I was truly lucky.

Too lucky.

If my father was here, he'd tell me not to think this,

because it would welcome in ironic bad luck. But I couldn't help it. I felt blessed every time I looked at my wife. I was going to enjoy being with her as long as I could.

So, once we dressed, and woke Twain, the three of us headed out. My brother was already in the hallway, his knightmare a shadow on the floor that shifted back and forth beneath his feet. He stood straight and smiled. Then, as a group, we headed to Headmaster Venrover's office.

It wasn't difficult to find—we had lived at Astra Academy for a year now. Everyone knew where the headmaster's office was, and while Venrover was a little bit odd, all the students felt comfortable enough to tell him whenever they had problems.

The sun rose, shining into the long hallways of the Academy, sometimes through colored glass. It painted the walls with rainbows, and made everything seem more magical than it already was.

The shields around the Academy shimmered in the morning as well. Sparkles danced in the distance.

When we reached the headmaster's office, I was surprised to see him standing outside the door. When he spotted us, he smoothed his long black hair and then smiled.

"Ah, there you are, Gray Kross." He turned his keen eyes on my brother and Ashlyn. "I wasn't aware the two of you would be accompanying us today."

Ashlyn took my hand. "I'm going to stay by my husband's side."

"He might have a different last name, but he's still my twin brother," Sorin stated.

The headmaster let out a long sigh. "I suppose being late to your second class isn't the worst thing in the world." He gestured with a wave of his hand. "Come. Let us see Zahn and his soul catcher friend. They're in the entrance hall with Leon."

I held my breath as we traveled with the headmaster at our side. I glanced around, hoping to see his eldrin, but I didn't spot her. Was the sphinx just left in his office? Or was she doing something else?

What was I doing? I was a mimic arcanist! I could sense her, if I wanted.

After a few moments of concentration, I felt the sphinx was, in fact, in his office...

But I also felt a wendigo and a wendigo arcanist walking *alongside us* right at this very moment. When I wildly turned my head, expecting to see them, I saw nothing.

They were invisible.

I smiled to myself as I returned my attention to the hallway. The wendigo arcanist was *Fain*—the headmaster's assassin—but he was easy to forget about, considering how hidden and mysterious he was.

"Are you okay, Gray?" Sorin asked, one eyebrow lifted.

"Oh, yeah," I said. "Totally."

Fain wasn't going to hurt us. He had actively protected me on a couple occasions, and I knew he was loyal to Headmaster Venrover. It was still creepy to think an arcanist and his eldrin was here, and no one was acknowledging him, though. The headmaster never even indicated he was around.

We made our way through a good portion of the Academy before finally arriving at the entrance hall. Guardian Captain Leon was there with his cerberus eldrin, Styx.

I loved Styx. He was a good boy with three heads, a black and rust-colored coat, and a muscled frame that made it seem like he was secretly a bodybuilder. The cerberus was just as large as a horse, and had fangs that would impress a tiger, but he still had a friendly aura whenever he glanced my way.

Leon wore his silver armor, carried a sword *and* pistol on his belt, and kept his arms crossed at all times. He exuded irritation with the situation, and only offered the headmaster a reverse nod, with the jut of his chin, the moment we neared.

Zahn and a woman were also here.

Deimos's presence in my mind sharpened when I laid eyes on his brother. Had Deimos missed him? It seemed like it.

Zahn was a tall and wiry man with dark muddy hair neatly tied back in a tail. His small glasses were positioned on the very tip of his nose, and he glared daggers at anyone who drew near. He wore clean robes of black with gold edges, and he seemed almost regal.

His arcanist mark was the same as mine. A blank seven-pointed star.

His mimic, Twice, sat perched on his shoulder. She was a lithe cat, but with pink fur. It practically shimmered whenever she moved, and her eyes were two colors, just like Twain's—only hers was gray and tan. Unlike Twain, she had normal-sized ears and a longer tail. It swished back and forth, betraying her irritation.

The woman next to Zahn...

I had seen her before.

And her arcanist mark gave the rest away.

She had a seven-pointed star with a spider woven throughout the points. A spider with a human face. It was as disturbing as her thin body and sunken face. She didn't look... right. The woman even had dark rings under her eyes, as though she hadn't slept in years.

Her clothing consisted of a long dark coat, a black tunic, dark pants, and boots that went to her knees. Her hair, scraggily and matted, hung to her shoulders, but just barely.

Most arcanists looked young—in their prime—no matter their real age, but this woman looked as though she had been hit by a train and left on the tracks for a few days before someone finally peeled her off and gave her the bare minimum medical attention.

Her eldrin stood behind her and Zahn, in the darkest corner of the entrance hall, looming with all the dread of a nightmare given flesh.

It was a soul catcher. A wooden puppet-looking mystical creature in the shape of a spider. It had a human mask over its "face" and at the end of its eight legs were hands. The fingers were nothing more than knives, and when it flexed its fingers, it sounded like rusted metal scraping against itself.

The soul catcher was large, too. The same size as the cerberus, and ten times more frightening.

"Adelgis," Zahn said, turning to the headmaster. "I've come as you requested."

Headmaster Venrover went over to Leon. He forced a smile. "Thank you for arriving, Zahn. Gray wishes to speak with you. He also wants to speak to your, uh, friend." The headmaster gestured to the woman.

She snorted and said nothing, her eyes glazed over with disinterest.

"This is Cordelia," Zahn stated. "The soul catcher arcanist you requested."

CHAPTER 38

TRUE FORM FIGHT

I took a deep breath and stepped forward. Leon, Headmaster Venrover, Zahn, and even Cordelia, all glanced over with lifted eyebrows, as though no one understood why I was making my presence known.

Sorin and Ashlyn knew, though, and they gave me silent, but encouraging, gestures. Twain, perched neatly on my shoulder, purred a bit.

"I want to challenge your soul catcher arcanist to a duel," I said.

That shocked most people. Cordelia widened her buggy eyes, her confusion apparent and rapidly worsening.

"You wish to engage in a Magi Cross?" Zahn asked.

"No," I quickly stated. Then I shook my head. "No, no. That's when you fight to the death, right? No. I don't need that. I just need to beat her in combat. To overcome a fear, really."

"What fear?" Leon asked.

Styx stared at me with all three heads. "I'm curious, too," one head stated.

"Well, she *did* try to kill me several times." I gestured to her. "For years she stalked my dreams with her weird eldrin, and she got close a few times. That creates traumas, everyone can agree on that, right? Professor Helmith had to protect me with her ethereal whelk magic. I think I'm owed a little fight."

Cordelia held up a skeletal finger. "First off, it wasn't just me. Zahn and his creepy mimic also hunted people in their dreams—we both went after you in your dreams."

It was my turn to hold up a finger. "*First off,*" I said, copying her raspy voice, "mimics aren't creepy."

"I second that notion," Twain said.

Twice swished her tail. "I third that notion."

"Have you seen what you're bonded to?" I sarcastically asked. "You're the creepiest arcanist here by a wide margin."

Cordelia rolled her eyes, and they were bloodshot at the edges. It only added to her creepiness.

Ignoring everything everyone had said, she continued, "Secondly, I'm not a fighter. I'm just a woman."

"You look like a corpse," Leon muttered under his breath. The headmaster gave him a scolding glance.

"Finally," Cordelia said, her voice rising, "even if I wanted to fight, it would be in the dreamscape, and not in the world of the waking. I manipulate *dreams*. Fighting in a weird school would be my last choice."

"Well, how about I just fight your eldrin," I said. "It's the soul catcher I'm really afraid of—not some vagabond."

Cordelia turned to Zahn. She tugged on the sleeve of his robe, and he leaned over to speak with her. They had a whispered conversation for quite some time before Zahn leaned away.

"All right," Cordelia said. "Fine. You can fight my eldrin, Skitter. But it's not to the death, right? You'll give your word?"

"It won't be to the death," I replied.

Twain tilted his head and then poked my ear with his wet nose. "Am I fighting with you?"

"No, you stay off to the side. It'll just be me and the, uh, *Skitter*."

"But you'll use your mimic magic at least?"

I nodded. "That's all I got."

Satisfied with my answer, Twain leapt off my shoulder and then ran over to Ashlyn. Once he was secure on *her* shoulder, I walked into the middle of the entrance hall. The vaulted ceiling was at least twenty feet above us, and we had thirty feet on all sides of basically empty walkway.

I hadn't imagined fighting in the middle of Astra Academy, but here we were...

Cordelia motioned for Skitter to step forward. The massive wooden puppet eldrin click-clacked across the floor, its knife-fingers practically scraping across the tile.

The face mask didn't move. It was white, like some sort of theater prop, with black lines for eyes, and a curved black line for a smile. Nothing else. No other emotion. No indication it was intelligent—it was just pure night terror.

"Okay, let's do this," I said.

The soul catcher said nothing. Instead, it lifted its two front legs, its fingers fanned out, the knives glittering from the daylight that streamed in from the tall windows. In all regards, it was scary. It was the monster from my longest nightmares— the creature I thought would surely bring about my death.

Defeating *this* would surely equate to overcoming fear itself.

I grabbed at Vivigöl and it *click-click-clicked* into the shape of a sword. The golden blade was the length of a longsword, but lightweight. The guard was made of six flared blades pointing toward the enemy, three on one side, three on the other.

The soul catcher hesitated for a moment. Then it glanced back at its arcanist.

Cordelia just shrugged.

Clearly neither thought I had been carrying a weapon.

When the beast returned its attention to me, I lifted the sword and spread my feet, getting into a combat stance for the best balance. What kind of magic was best? Of all the people here, I had plenty of options.

Sorin's knightmare magic.

Ashlyn's typhoon dragon magic.

A sphinx. A cerberus. A wendigo.

Even the soul catcher in front of me.

Not to mention I always had access to Deimos's abyssal dragon magic... And when I thought about it like that, I almost felt bad for the monster in front of me. Did the soul catcher even stand a chance?

The beast lunged forward, two of its bladed hands outstretched. I leapt to the side, ducking under a swipe, my footing sure, my confidence high. I slashed my blade at one of its legs, but the soul catcher was fast. It lifted all the legs on the side closest to me, removing them from the arc of my swing.

I tugged on the thread of magic that led back to Styx. Twain bubbled and shifted, and before he turned into a cerberus on Ashlyn's shoulder, he leapt to the floor. Midfall, he transformed into a three-headed dog with black and rust coloring, the fur short, the heads massive.

My arcanist mark burned as the symbol of a cerberus appeared interwoven between the seven points.

Once the cerberus magic flowed through my body, I held out my hand and evoked flames. The scarlet heat burst from the wrinkles of my palms and washed over the wooden puppet. I almost laughed manically—nothing felt better than watching that monster burn under the power of my own magic.

The soul catcher actually screamed as it scurried out of the flames. Scorched and blackened at points, it hurried into the corner of the entrance hall, trying to get away from me as much as possible.

I gave chase, rushing forward with my sword in hand. Once trapped in the corner, the soul catcher turned around, lifting four of its eight arms, its knives pointed at me.

I slashed with Vivigöl, managing to catch one of the monster's hands. I lopped it off, and it clattered to the floor. Again, the soul catcher screamed. When it backed away, its wooden, half burned body, slammed into the wall. Its face was the same as it was before—unmoving, unchanging—but the creature was trembling now.

And...

It didn't scare me at all.

I had my sword in hand, embers glowing in my other palm, and this soul catcher was so frightened that I felt *bad* for hurting it so much. It didn't make me feel mighty, or secure, or in charge of my destiny. It just reminded me that this was a fear I had in my childhood.

It wasn't a fear I had anymore.

Cordelia actually leapt between me and the soul catcher. "S-Stop," she said, holding up a hand. "Please. Leave Skitter alone. This isn't a fair fight and everyone here knows it."

"I don't think a murderer has any right to complain about a *fair fight*," Leon darkly stated.

Headmaster Venrover stepped forward. "Please, calm down, Leon. We both know that Zahn and this woman will stand trial for their crimes once we've dealt with the abyssal hells. She's right—we don't need to torture them."

Zahn huffed. "*You* brought me and Cordelia *here*. Was it simply to abuse a soul catcher? Was that really the only reason?"

I released the cerberus magic and stepped away from

Cordelia. After a deep breath, I turned around and faced Twain. He was still a cute little orange cat with big lynx-style ears. He wasn't true form, and I hadn't defeated my fears.

What was I missing? Did I just need to practice with Sorin more?

Maybe that was the solution. Perhaps this was just silly.

Cordelia approached her eldrin and gently stroked one of its long legs. "There, there," she whispered to it. "Everything will be okay. I'm here. Let's get you somewhere safe, and I'll bandage you up."

The soul catcher relaxed and actually wrapped two of its arms around her in an awkward embrace. It was almost sickening.

"I think it's time for the three of you to get to class," the headmaster said. He motioned to me, Sorin, and Ashlyn. "Hurry along, now. I'll speak to Zahn and Cordelia. Leave the rest to me."

Intermediate Combat Arts was a little different than I thought it would be. We were out on the training field, just like before, but this time we were forced to wear padded leathers as armor over our vital spots and told we'd be using more of our magic while learning how to wield various weapons.

And for some reason, there were several pots of paint and paint brushes sticking out of them. I wasn't entirely sure why, but it amused me to think that while some students were sparring, others would paint what they saw.

The grass around the track was green, and the inner field was darker than the surrounding, but everything was neatly trimmed.

Fortunately, Knovak had returned to class.

Unfortunately, his eldrin was also here.

Starling the elder unicorn was definitely not looking well. Or maybe he was? It was hard to say. He was large, bulky, and his mane and tail were now a faint blue. His eyes had pupils that were slits and his mouth had fangs, which didn't seem natural for any horse-like creature.

His horn, which had once been beautiful, was now like a gold shard of abyssal coral sticking out of his forehead. It looked ominous, or like it was jabbed into his skull and somehow impaling him straight in the brain.

It was difficult not to stare at him, and I wasn't the only one struggling. Everyone else in class—Nasbit, Ashlyn, Sorin, Exie, Phila, Rosella, Raaza—they all snuck quick glances whenever they thought Starling wasn't staring in their direction.

Everyone else's eldrin was here, but none got attention like Starling.

Professor Jijo stood before us, his little nimbus dragon darting through the sky like an expert. Jijo's bald head reflected the afternoon light a little *too* much.

"Real combat does not follow rules," he said. "Sometimes, you must do whatever it takes to succeed. In those moments, outwitting your opponent is more valuable than a lifetime of footwork techniques."

I stood near the back of the class. Ashlyn and my brother were never far—it seemed they wanted to stay close to me no matter what. I appreciated them both, but my self-loathing was hitting an all-time high.

"What's wrong?" Twain whispered. He hunkered down on my shoulder and nuzzled the side of my neck.

I scratched his back. "Why can't I achieve your true form?" I asked under my breath. "What's wrong with me? I should've been able to do this by now. *But nothing I do makes any difference.*"

"Maybe you're working your way there."

"So, today, for our warmup practice, I want everyone to partner up." Professor Jijo motioned to the class. "You will have a sparring match. Each of you will hold a paint brush, and the first to paint their opponent with a streak of color wins."

Sorin perked up. "Oh, really? Just... hit them with the paint brush? Are there any rules?"

"No rules." Jijo glowered. "I just told you—real combat has no rules. Use whatever magic you have at your disposal."

Interesting.

Ashlyn immediately turned to me, her eyebrows raised. I knew what she wanted—she wanted us to spar together. I liked that, so I nodded.

Phila and Nasbit stood together as a pair, both coyly smiling. Exie walked over to my brother and batted her eyelashes. Sorin nodded and the two of them were a sparring team.

I almost barfed.

Then Raaza approached Knovak, and the two of them whispered something to each other before they were a pair.

Rosella was the last one. We were a class of nine, after all, so the odd number wasn't beneficial. Plus, no one in class seemed to care for her much. I never saw anyone speaking to her, and her little kappa—still dressed like a child—obviously bothered the others.

I felt bad for her.

When I glanced back over at Ashlyn, she was staring at Rosella as well. Then she sighed, turned to me, and lifted a shoulder. She was silently suggesting I go over and spar with her. I waved my hand, gesturing for her to go instead.

"*You're both girls*," I mouthed.

Ashlyn rolled her eyes as she walked over to Rosella. Once there, Rosella seemed to perk up, a smile blossoming across her face.

"You'll partner with me?" she asked.

Ashlyn nodded. "As long as that's okay."

"You're one of Death Lord Deimos's mistresses—it would be an honor to spar you."

Ashlyn's expression went from neutral to angrily disgusted faster than a song bird in a hurricane.

"Death Lord Deimos's *mistress*?" Ashlyn hissed.

Before that conversation spiraled out of control, Professor Jijo went from person to person, handing out paint brushes. Some had red paint, others had green, and a few had white.

"You all decided you wanted to become abyssal sentinels," Jijo said as he walked around the class. "What does that even mean? It means you'll have to face monsters and horrors the likes of which no one has ever seen before."

When he walked by Knovak and Starling, he slowed his pace, his smile curving down into a frown.

"Or perhaps you *have* seen them," he muttered, "but you don't truly know what they're capable of until you're in a death match. If an elder creature kills you, the beast *will* consume your soul." Jijo handed the paint brush to Knovak, his eyes narrowing.

Knovak said nothing. He held his paintbrush like a weapon.

When Professor Jijo handed one to me, he continued his monologue. "You must be prepared to defend yourself. You must think quick and act faster. Every blow to the opponent, no matter how small, is one step closer to victory. Do not hold back, looking for a finishing blow. Attack with everything you have."

"Uh, professor," I said as Jijo began to walk away. "I don't have a partner."

Jijo smiled as he turned back around to face me. "It seems the two of us are destined to face off against one another. I'll be your partner, Arcanist Kross. I can't wait to see what skill you have in *this* competition."

I hated the way that man loved to fight against me.

"Everyone has a paint brush?" Jijo asked. "If you do, go ahead and begin. Remember—any amount of magic is okay, but actual physical harm isn't the purpose of this experience. Just touch your opponent *once* with the wet end of your brush."

CHAPTER 39

PAINT BRUSH TRAINING

"Wait," Nasbit shouted. "Are our eldrin allowed to fight with us?"

"Not this time," Jijo quickly replied.

"Oh. What a shame."

While the others squared off against their opponents, I stood and waited for Jijo. He made certain everyone was complying with his instructions before making his way over to me. The man walked with the confidence and strength of a warrior—I knew he was handy with a lot of weapons—and for some reason, when he picked up a paint brush of his own, he held it as though he had wielded it many times before.

"Are you ready?" he asked as he approached me.

His brush had red paint on the bristles and mine had blue. Twain puffed up his orange fur and leapt away from me, cringing the whole way. He definitely didn't want any of this paint in his fur.

"I'm ready," I stated.

The moment I finished speaking the word *ready*, Jijo lunged for me. That was what I had been hoping for. I held my paint brush up, and smirked. He swished his brush, paint splattering outward from the force of his swing.

As I sidestepped, and he moved past me, I threw my brush.

I only had to touch him once, right? I didn't need magic— I just needed to outwit him.

In the half second it took the brush to leave my fingertips, Jijo manipulated the wind around us. As a nimbus dragon arcanist, he was rather adept at such techniques, and I had been hoping he wouldn't be able to react quickly.

He whipped the wind into a frenzy, and my brush flew halfway across the training field, leaving me with nothing.

"Reckless," Professor Jijo scolded as he turned to fully face me. His paint brush was held tightly in his grip. "You honestly thought you could surprise me?"

"I was hoping," I said with a chuckle.

Then I pulled on the thread of magic that led back to my brother's knightmare. My arcanist mark burned as it shifted, but Jijo didn't let me finish gaining the new magic. He leapt for me, smirking. Then Jijo threw *his* brush, using his wind manipulation to carry the brush like an arrow shot from a bow.

With exact precision, I tightly turned on my heel, barely dodging the attack. The brush flew a mere *inch* from my arm, yet somehow, I had gracefully moved.

No, it wasn't "somehow"—this was Deimos. I recognized the move from when he used it against the elder thunderbirds. I had used his artful dodging, but I couldn't relax. Jijo was still in control of the wind, so as soon as I could, I stepped into the darkness, dipping into the shadows like it was water.

Moving across the ground as a shadow without an object casting it, I slithered at a freakishly fast pace across the field. The moment I neared my paint brush, I jumped from the darkness and stepped back onto the field, my veins icy with knightmare magic.

I grabbed my brush, but Jijo had anticipated my move. He whipped the wind around, his brush carried along, and the howl of his power washed over me. I dipped back into the shadows half a second before his brush touched me.

Damn.

I wouldn't win this unless I outplayed him.

Where could I emerge from the darkness that he wouldn't anticipate?

Deimos's thoughts flooded mine. He wanted me to use a magical aura. I remembered his *inevitable aura,* and for a moment, I was confused. Deimos's memories then filled with a darkened sky. Knightmare arcanists had an *eclipse aura*—they blotted out the sun with their magic to cast the nearby area into utter darkness.

I hadn't ever created an aura before...

But I had experienced Deimos's aura, and his confidence pumped through my veins. Could I make an aura with his help?

Unfortunately, I couldn't breathe in the realm of shadows. I shifted through the darkness and stepped out of the void behind Ashlyn, hoping to hide from Professor Jijo. I gasped for breath as I came up next to my wife, and she flinched upon seeing me.

"G-Gray?" she shouted, which drew Jijo's attention.

I took in a deep breath, waved to her, and then dove back into the shadows.

Okay. I needed to make an aura. If I used the eclipse aura, I would shroud the training field in darkness, and I'd be able to stand and hit Jijo with my paint brush.

But first I needed to do this aura. How did Deimos do it? He flooded his body with magic until it spilled out of him. His very presence washed out into his surroundings, affecting everything nearby.

I could do that. I hoped.

Focusing my new knightmare magic into my body, I concentrated. Unfortunately, it was much too difficult to hold my breath and focus on filling my being with magic. I had to emerge, but if I did so anywhere near Jijo, he would surely see.

So I slid as a shadow off the field entirely. I moved away from the class, slithering fast, until I reached the edge of the barrier that surrounded the Academy. Only then did I step out of the darkness. The training field was in the distance—about one hundred and fifty feet away—and no one seemed to know where I was. Even Jijo was glancing around wildly, his brow furrowed.

"Okay, I can do this," I muttered.

I closed my eyes and concentrated. I knew how this worked—I had been with Deimos when he made his aura—so I tried to replicate those feelings.

"You shouldn't let your guard down," Deimos said through me.

"I'm focusing," I sardonically replied.

"When you close your eyes on the battlefield, you invite your inevitable defeat."

"This helps me sense my magic."

And after I stated that, I pushed Deimos's thoughts from my own. Sorin's knightmare magic was cold and powerful, and I enjoyed the sensation of it rushing through my extremities. More and more, I felt my magic rising, my chest tight, my head pounding.

"You're doing it incorrectly," Deimos said in a tone that bordered on bored.

I opened my eyes, annoyed he would be critiquing me in the middle of my first attempt. Then I caught my breath, my shock overtaking everything.

The sky...

There was a black sphere in front of the sun. It didn't completely mask the daylight, but it was substantial.

Everything looked like dusk—all the students in class had their attention on the sky, some of them shouting and pointing.

Professor Jijo glared at the black splotch. His nimbus dragon darted around, flying at super speeds. He was searching for something—likely me—and I realized that even though I hadn't fully made an aura, it didn't matter. I now had my chance.

I dove into the darkness, slithered over to Jijo, and then lunged out of the shadows. While his eyes were on my half-formed eclipse, I managed to whap him with my paint brush. Blue paint splattered across his tunic.

The fake eclipse faded from the sky, and sunlight flooded the training field once again.

"*What was that*?" Raaza barked.

Professor Jijo frowned down at his outfit. With a sigh, he turned to the class. "Well, I suppose I invited this when I said you could use any magic." After he cleared his throat, he raised both his hands over his head. "Students, attention please. Pause your bouts if you're still in the middle of them."

The rest of the class turned to face Jijo. Everyone had wide eyes and shocked expressions. The epic-ness of the faux eclipse still lingered.

"That was a magical aura," Professor Jijo stated. "Every arcanist can create one, but they're rather difficult to fully form. A knightmare arcanist can create an eclipse aura—which is when their darkness magic covers the sun. While under the shadows of an eclipse aura, knightmare magic is strengthened."

"Oh, that's awesome," Raaza muttered.

Exie raised her hand. "Do we all have combat-oriented auras? I *really* don't like fighting."

She was already coated with paint. She grimaced and motioned to the red splatter on her robes. It obviously disgusted her more than anything else, and Sorin stood nearby, sheepish.

"Erlking arcanists create the *grand contentment aura*," Professor Jijo said matter-of-factly. "This is an illusion-based aura that makes the nearby area serene and delightful. They say it increases happiness, and that major cities employ erlking arcanists to help their citizens feel relaxed."

Exie actually perked up a bit, a smile spreading across her face. "Oh, really? I love that. Delightful."

Raaza jerked his hand into the air. "What about kitsune arcanists? What kind of aura can they create?"

While most people likely would've been annoyed by constant pummeling of questions, Professor Jijo seemed delighted. With a smile, he replied, "Kitsune arcanists create the *mystic moon aura*. It increases the strength of illusions and negates all mind-controlling magic, like knightmare's ability to make terrors."

"Oh, wow. It sounds like some of these auras would be amazing if used together." Raaza actually turned to Exie. "Can you imagine *my* aura and *your* aura working together? That city would be *super relaxed*."

Exie mulled that over for a moment. After a lifting a perfect eyebrow, she slowly nodded. "Hm. That would be quite interesting."

I allowed Sorin's knightmare magic to leave me. "Can eldrin create auras?" I asked as my arcanist mark shifted back into a blank star.

"No," Jijo quickly stated. "Only arcanists."

"*Elder creatures* can create auras," Deimos said through me, his tone angry. "With the many human souls in their body, they create powerful auras. It's another reason they believe they don't ever need arcanists—because they can become *whole* without them."

Oh.

Gross.

"I wasn't aware of that," Jijo whispered. "The headmaster will need to know..."

Everyone silently and slowly glanced over at Knovak. He stood next to Raaza, his paint brush firmly gripped in his hand. He wasn't covered in paint—Raaza was.

Knovak's unicorn stood on the side of the field, his frightening appearance casting a pall over our learning. My father definitely would've called this a "bad omen."

I hoped it wasn't.

"Okay." Jijo clapped his hands together once. "Everyone who won their match, partner up with another winner."

Ashlyn stepped forward. She didn't have paint on her—of course—but she seemed concerned. "How do we make our auras? Can we use them in these sparring matches?"

"Well, others may attempt it, but I doubt yours will help," Jijo replied.

"Why? Are you saying typhoon dragons are weak? Because I'll have you know that—"

Professor Jijo held up a hand, cutting her off. "Typhoon dragon arcanists create an *ocean heart aura*. Everything submerged in water has its energy drained away, sometimes even causing people and mystical creatures to succumb to unconsciousness."

"But we're not in water," Ashlyn muttered, finishing Jijo's rationale.

Jijo nodded. "Very good. I'm glad you caught on quickly."

Even though I hadn't asked, Nasbit leapt forward. He was covered in paint, from his neck down to his knees. "Mimic arcanists create *chimera auras*." His excitement was palpable. "That's when the mimic takes on characteristics of all nearby mystical creatures and the arcanist gains access to *all* the magics at once!"

"Correct," Jijo said, pointing to Nasbit. "It is extremely

powerful, but a lot of mimic arcanists struggle to control it. All that magic coursing through their body... It's too much. Sometimes maddening. You have to have willpower as strong as steel to even use it for a few minutes."

"I guess Gray will have to train for a long time." Nasbit rubbed his chin. "Or just master using everyone else's aura, since he *is* a mimic arcanist."

The chimera aura...

It would be rather powerful, for sure. Did I have willpower as strong as steel? Well, I liked to imagine I did.

But I hadn't even created an eclipse aura properly... So perhaps Nasbit was right. Perhaps I did need to train more.

"Next time, listen to my advice," Deimos murmured.

I rolled my eyes as I walked over to the class. "Okay, who wants to face me, the brave arcanist who attempted an aura before I was even instructed on how to do it?"

It looked as though Ashlyn was about to take me up on my offer—and that was who I *wanted* to face off against—but it was actually Knovak who stomped close.

"Me," he stated. "I'll fight you, Gray."

CHAPTER 40

ELDER PROBLEMS

Knovak...

His eyes were hard and his expression dour. He wanted to fight me? Fine. He wouldn't be much of a threat. I nodded once and then smirked.

"Sounds good," I said.

Knovak clicked his tongue. "Tsk. You're just cocky because you think I'm too weak to beat you. But you'll see."

We squared off against each other in the middle of the training field. With my paint brush in hand, I rotated my shoulders, loosening up.

"What kind of aura do unicorn arcanists create?" Raaza asked, drawing the class's attention.

Professor Jijo ran a hand over his bald head. "They create a *ferocity aura*. The unicorn arcanist—along with all his allies— become determined and focused. They can't fall asleep, their concentration is rock steady, and they move at blinding speeds. It's quite useful."

"For combat," Exie said, rolling her eyes.

That was when I realized that everyone in class was just watching us. I glanced around, indignant. "What's going on? I thought everyone else was supposed to pair up and finish their matches?"

"I'd like to see this fight first," Sorin said, shrugging. "If you don't mind an audience."

The others nodded along with his words. Everyone wanted to see this, apparently.

I shook my head. "Whatever." Then I returned my focus to Knovak. "You ready?"

"Of course," he said. Then he brandished his paint brush.

"Begin," Jijo announced.

Knovak threw up his hand and evoked raw force. It was like an invisible punch straight to my chest. I was slammed backward, all the wind knocked out of me. When I hit the grass I slid a few feet, my vision spinning.

Damn. That hurt.

I gritted my teeth as I rolled to my side. My insides felt like jelly, and I was pretty sure I had forgotten everything I had learned in my first year of school, that was how rattled my brain was.

With what little concentration I could muster, I tugged on the exact same magical thread I had before—Sorin's knightmare. But instead of diving into the darkness and running, I stayed on the ground, trying to catch my breath.

Knovak ran over, anger in his breaths. He went to hit me with his paint brush when I lifted my hand and evoked terrors.

"Agh!" Knovak grabbed the sides of his head and screamed. He had been a mere foot from me when I caught him by surprise.

Thankfully, my brush wasn't far from me. I had dropped it when hit, but while Knovak squirmed, I grabbed it and then threw it at him.

Throwing my weapon—it was a technique Deimos always used. Now it was somehow part of my go-to skillset. He really was rubbing off on me.

Unlike Professor Jijo, who was a combat master and always on his toes, Knovak didn't dodge. My blue brush hit him square in the chest, leaving a mark of paint. That was it—match over.

I stood, ended my terrors, and brushed the grass off my clothing. "Well, that was fun," I sarcastically said.

Knovak held out his hand again and blasted me with his force evocation. Once again, I was winded and thrown to the ground. My solar plexus felt as though it was shattered this time—my vision actually went black for several seconds. With my stomach twisting as though I might vomit, I rolled on the grass.

Everyone in class was yelling now. I was too busy trying to breathe to pay attention.

Sorin, Twain, and Ashlyn were on either side of me when I finally managed to regain my sight. Twain nuzzled my cheek while Sorin and Ashlyn placed their hands gently on my upper arms, urging me to stand.

"What happened?" I asked as I got to shaky feet.

Knovak was storming off the field, his shoulders bunched at the base of his neck. Starling snorted when he neared, as though he were disgusted. The professor jogged after him, shouting for him to wait.

"I think Knovak needs a time out," Ashlyn quipped.

Sorin sighed. "Is treating him like a child really the answer? It's clear he's not well..."

"He can't be allowed to do whatever he wants because he's sick in the head. That's not helping anyone."

I rubbed my chest. My body felt like uncooked dough. Since when did unicorn evocation feel so terrible?

"I'll speak to him," I said through gritted teeth. "I saw what happened to him in the abyssal hells—and Deimos is with me. Maybe we can talk some sense into him."

Ashlyn pursed her lips. I knew she didn't like this idea, but since she didn't have another idea, she didn't feel comfortable telling me no. My brother seemed less skeptical, but still deeply concerned.

Knovak...

What could I possibly say to ease his troubles?

Astra Academy had amazing food, and after our physically demanding combat arts class, I ate so much meat I felt bloated when I returned to my dorm room with Ashlyn. However, before it was technically curfew, I left to go speak with Knovak.

Twain accompanied me on my shoulder as usual. He clung tighter than before and felt tense the entire walk down the hallway.

"You okay?" I asked.

Twain nodded. "I'm just worried. Knovak is acting too weird."

"I suppose. Maybe we'll have to take Ashlyn's advice and knock him around."

Deimos's thoughts bubbled into my own. He liked this idea.

"Maybe we should invite Sorin to go with us," Twain muttered. "At least then we'd have at least one reasonable voice when we go to talk to him."

That wasn't a bad idea. I almost went back for Ashlyn as well, but it probably wasn't a great idea to approach Knovak as a group of people opposed to him. If we spoke one-on-one, it would be a little less aggressive and confrontational. I wanted this to go smoothly—I didn't want it to be a fight.

So, I went to the boy's dorm room and tapped on the door.

Raaza answered in just a tunic and shorts. His kitsune was

hopping up and down on his bed in the room, her flaming feet bright but not actually catching anything on fire.

"What's wrong?" Raaza asked.

I shook my head. "Where's Knovak?"

"He left. Said he wanted to get in some more training. I think he's down on the field."

I sighed. Why did Knovak make everything difficult? It was somehow a personality disorder with him.

"Thank you." I turned away from Raaza and jogged down the hall.

The smell of hot cocoa wafted through the air, and I knew my fellow arcanists were getting cozy for the night. I envied them, but this was something I had to do. Knovak had been with me in the abyssal hells, and at some level I felt responsible for him. He never would've had the opportunity for his eldrin to eat those souls if I hadn't dragged him down into the depths.

"It wasn't you," Deimos curtly said. "It was Death Lord Naiad. Remember that."

I nodded once as I flew down the stairs. "That's true. If Naiad hadn't tried to kill you…"

"Are you talking about whose fault it is?" Twain asked. He chuckled. "Because it's really *Deimos's* fault. If he hadn't tried to kill you, then his soul fragment wouldn't have been trapped in you!"

"He has a point, Dee," I said.

Deimos scoffed. I could practically hear his eyes roll through his thoughts. But he didn't deny it. Which meant I was still responsible for Knovak, because I was now friends with Deimos. I had to make this right.

I had to.

I flew out the entrance hall and into the night air. It was chilly since Astra Academy was perched up on a mountain, but the barriers around the school seemed to stop the worst of the wind. A gentle breeze carried with it the scents of pine needles. It was pleasant.

I dashed down the walkway and around the side of the Academy. The training field wasn't far.

That was when I heard half a scream. It was like someone tried to shout, but was cut off half a second later.

"Did you hear that?" Twain asked, his large ears twitching.

I nodded. "Where?"

"Over there! Quickly, Gray. I think someone is in trouble."

With my mimic magic, I reached out and tugged on the thread of magic that led to my brother's knightmare. Twain leapt off my shoulder and then transformed into a hollow suit of shadow armor. My arcanist mark burned, and I slipped into the shadows to move faster and stealthier.

When I emerged at the edge of the training field, I spotted Knovak and Starling. Knovak's back was to me—he was still dressed in his Academy robes, and he was shouting at his eldrin. Starling had his head down, eating grass.

The field was lit with a few clusters of glowstones built into chest-high stone pillars. During the day, I thought they had just been markers for the edge of the field, but now I saw they had many purposes.

My borrowed knightmare magic allowed me to see in the dark, however, so the glowstones were more of a hindrance than anything.

"*Starling*, you're not listening to me," Knovak shouted.

Had I heard his yell a moment ago?

The unicorn didn't respond. He continued to eat, his teeth gnashing so intense, I heard it from the other side of the field.

"*You shouldn't be doing this*," Knovak continued, his hands balled into fists. "I can train or master my magic or—"

Starling lifted his head and whirled around. As a large horse, it was rather impressive, and his muscles rippled underneath his white coat. He was somehow bulkier than before.

And his muzzle was stained with crimson.

"*You're weak*," Starling said with a growl. "You always lose. You're always pathetic. Why would I listen to what *you* have to say?"

Knovak rubbed his eyes. "It won't... It won't always be that way."

"Oh, I know it won't. Because I'll make sure of it!"

When Starling turned again, that was when I saw it. That unicorn hadn't been eating grass—he was consuming a *person*. There was a groundskeeper on the field, completely unmoving, his clothing torn, his gut opened up for stars to gaze upon his insides.

"*Knovak!*" I shouted, unable to contain my rage. "*What have you done?*"

Knovak spun on his heel. He stared at me with wide and frightened eyes. Then he threw his arms up, putting himself between me and Starling. "Wait! Please, I can explain!"

"Look who's here," Starling said with a chuckle. He lifted his head, blood dripping from the edge of his mouth. His mane was bluer than before, his eyes a sickly yellow. "You're that disgusting vessel for the Death Lord."

"I like to think I'm an acting Death Lord in the mortal realm," I stated.

Knovak's lip quavered. "I'll fix this! Gray, just get out of here."

I grabbed Vivigöl from my body, yanking the weapon from the collar of my shirt as it transformed. The clicking noise it made as the abyssal coral rearranged itself into a new shape was a signal that things were about to get real, and I felt my heartbeat quicken just from listening to it.

"I'm not going anywhere." Vivigöl transformed into a

sword, and I held it firm. "You two are going straight to the headmaster."

Starling snorted. Then he bashed Knovak out of the way with a swing of his neck. He was practically the size of a full-grown draft horse, with the muscles of two more, and when he hit Knovak the man went flying. With his horn pointed at me, Starling growled.

"You arcanists are pathetic. You wouldn't even have magic if you weren't bonded to your eldrin!"

Twain, in his knightmare form, rose up from the shadows, his feather cape fluttering behind him. Although his helmet was empty, he still spoke, his voice practically echoing in the armor.

"When a mystical creature and a human are bonded, both grow and improve—when you eat the souls of humans, you're nothing but a force of destruction. Nothing about what you're doing is right."

Starling stomped his front hoof, digging a deep furrow in the ground. "Once I'm stronger than any unicorn you've ever seen, you won't be so mouthy, *cat*."

Knovak got to his feet and stepped between me and Starling once again.

"*Stop this*!" Knovak held up his arms. "I'm your arcanist! We're supposed to be a team, Twain is right. We need to—"

The air turned icy.

Starling crunched his fangs on the side of Knovak's neck and then pulled backward, taking a chunk of muscle, arteries, and trachea straight from Knovak's body.

Although I was stunned, I wasn't frozen. I dove into the shadows, rushed across the field, and jumped from the shadows in one fluid motion. I swung Vivigöl, the golden blade flashing from the light of the glowstones.

Starling dodged with impossible speed. He moved out of

the way, his mouth dripping blood, flesh caught between his fangs like green bits of broccoli.

"*You're weak*," he shouted. Then he lowered his head and evoked force.

This was ten times worse than Knovak's blast from earlier in the day. I was hit hard and thrown to my back. My head pounded, and for a second, I couldn't breathe.

Twain leapt to my side and manipulated the darkness around the field. Tendrils of shadows rose from the grass and attempted to tether Starling in place. The unicorn danced away—unicorns were naturally fast, but this was bordering on ridiculous.

I couldn't allow this to continue.

As soon as I could focus, I tugged on the magical thread that led to Deimos's abyssal dragon. My arcanist mark burned and Twain transformed into the fearsome beast of the abyssal hells. Wings made of souls, scales rotting, and six eyes of malevolent force. He towered over Starling, and then roared the moment he was fully transformed.

"You're the weakest one of all," Starling said, undaunted. "You're *nothing* when you can't steal the magic of others around you."

Chapter 41

Soul Manipulation

Deimos's magic coursed through me like wildfire, intoxicating and wonderful. It was power without boundaries, strength that whispered promises I knew I shouldn't rely on but couldn't resist. When I used up a soul fused on the dragon, I completely regained my breath. All damage was removed from my body. When I used another, I was faster, stronger.

The instant I stood, my heart pounded.

"You're a monster," I said, my voice trembling more with adrenaline than fear. "I should've left you to rot in the abyssal hells the moment you started devouring souls."

The elder unicorn, Starling, snorted, his brilliant white coat gleaming like polished marble. He stood poised, regal and deadly, his horn glinting with latent power. Before he could retort, I lunged.

Starling's smirk faltered as I moved faster than he anticipated, my blade slicing through the air with enough force to cleave a tree in two. Yet, even with my enhanced speed, the unicorn twisted, pulling back with inhuman grace. The tip of my sword grazed his side, drawing a thin line of crimson against his pristine coat.

Starling's laugh was cold, echoing across the field. "You humans were always meant to be food. Souls exist to feed the powerful. *Die, little arcanist.*"

The air thickened, charged with heat and malice. A haze settled over the field, suffocatingly humid. Sweat trickled down my spine as I scanned my surroundings, the oppressive weather clouding my thoughts.

What was this? I knew it was magic, but what exactly was happening?

"The unicorn's ferocity aura," Deimos said through me.

Starling charged, his horn gleaming like a spear. He moved *fast*, almost to the point I couldn't keep my eyes on him. I barely sidestepped, relying on Deimos's instincts to guide my body. Starling's horn grazed my arm, searing through muscle and leaving a burning pain in its wake. The unicorn's momentum slammed me to the ground, his weight crushing the breath from my lungs.

Starling reared, hooves glinting, ready to bring them down in a death blow.

Before I could react, Twain's tail whipped through the air, slamming into Starling with enough force to send him sprawling. The unicorn rolled, his movements seamless as he sprang back to his hooves, eyes blazing with fury.

Twain, massive and steadfast, let loose a beam of raw magic, the bluish energy slicing through the air. Starling dodged, leaping skyward, his movements fluid and impossible to track.

But in the air, Starling was vulnerable. He couldn't run or change direction.

I held up my hand and evoked the same bluish beam of magic.

And caught Starling through the chest. His body convulsed midair before crashing to the ground, lifeless.

His one mistake had cost him the whole fight.

Victory should've tasted sweet, but my attention was wrenched to the side where Knovak and the groundskeeper lay bleeding. I sprinted to their sides, my breath shallow, and fell to my knees beside them. Knovak's arcanist mark was fading. My chest tightened as I realized what that meant—he was no longer an arcanist. His body couldn't heal itself anymore.

"Curse the abyssal hells," I muttered as I set Vivigöl down on the grass.

My hands trembled as I pressed them to Knovak's wounds. The groundskeeper wasn't faring any better. Blood pooled beneath them both, and their lives slipped away with each labored breath.

Twain stomped over, his huge dragon form intimidating.

"What shall we do, Gray?" he asked, his voice haunting and deep.

I tried to sense the threads of magic—to find the golden stag of the Academy's doctor—but I was having trouble. Was he just too far away?

And then it started to happen. Somehow, in some way, I sensed that Knovak and the groundskeeper were dying. Their souls were slipping from their flesh. Was this an abyssal dragon ability? Sensing death?

"You feel it now," Deimos said, his voice cool and unyielding. "Death Lords know when a soul is about to slip free. You are their keeper. Do your duty."

I swallowed hard. "What do I do?"

"Keep their souls tethered. Prevent their escape. You said you were the acting Death Lord of the mortal realm—prove it."

I shook my head, frustrated. How? *How?* What should I do?

"Control their souls—use your manipulation like you would with any other magic. Knightmares manipulate shadows, don't they? Take the souls here and force them to stay with the body."

The weight of his words pressed against me, but I had no time to question. Placing my hands on both bodies, I closed my eyes and reached inward. Their souls were delicate, faint motes of blue light slipping through my grasp like water. I focused, imagining the way shadows cling to forms, and willed their essence to stay.

Abyssal dragons and their arcanists were the lords of souls, and in that moment, I knew why.

I felt the life of both Knovak and this other man. They were still here. Delicate. Fragile. I gently applied pressure and kept them from leaving—preventing their death.

But the strain was immediate, like trying to hold back a tide with bare hands. My magic surged, wrapping around their souls, binding them to their bodies.

"I can't do this forever," I whispered, my voice cracking under the effort.

"You must heal their bodies," Deimos said.

"Twain! Help me. Let's carry them to the infirmary. We have to find Doc Tomas, no matter what."

Twain lowered his massive head and angled it so we could collect the bodies. "Of course. I'm here to help."

Once we were close to the main courtyard in Astra Academy, I felt the thread of magic that led back to Doc Tomas. However, I didn't dare switch away from the abyssal dragon, for fear that Knovak and this other man would die faster than I could heal them with golden stag magic.

So, we went straight to the infirmary and woke Doc Tomas.

He healed Knovak, then the groundskeeper, and then me. I hadn't even thought about my own injuries until that moment, but the doctor seemed to care about my wellbeing and even asked that I stay the night in the infirmary. The other two also got beds. Both were unconscious, and I didn't blame them. If my soul had been trying to escape my body for several minutes, I'd probably be pretty tired, too.

When I woke a few hours later, I sat up and rubbed my arm. No injuries. No scars. I was fine, the unicorn attack no more.

Twain was curled into a tight ball and purring. He slept on the bed between my calves, his ears twitching. As soon as the bed groaned with my movement, his head shot up, his eyes wide.

"Gray?" he asked.

I nodded. "Still me."

"Oh, thank the good stars." He smiled wide, his whiskers high. "I was so worried."

"I've been through worse," I quipped.

Twain snickered. "I feel like we can't even get a month's worth of rest before you get us into more trouble. I thought having an arcanist would mean I would lead an easy life, but look at us now."

I swung my legs off the bed and stretched. My clothing was on the chair next to my bed, so I quickly dressed and then stood. The infirmary was quiet.

Three dozen individual beds were positioned along the length of the two longest walls, with windows at the far end of the room—windows that stretched from the floor to the ceiling. The curtains were tied back, and I realized it was midnight. The moon beyond the large window was bright with life.

There were two other people in the infirmary with me. Knovak and the groundskeeper. They both appeared to be under their blankets and sleeping, their even breaths causing their chests to rise and fall in slow motions.

I tiptoed toward the door, desperate to see my wife again.

As I walked by the foot of Knovak's bed, I glanced over. He wasn't asleep. He stared at me with sunken eyes, dark rings marking his face like he was a raccoon.

Knovak didn't look well.

His faded arcanist mark—the melted seven-pointed star—haunted his forehead.

For a long moment, neither of us said anything. His eyes were glassy with water.

Perhaps it would be best if I spoke to him...

After a short sigh, I walked over to the side of his infirmary bed. He watched me, silent as the dead. I sat next to him, careful not to disturb his sheets much. Twain leapt up and sat on the end bedpost, his ears twitching.

"Are you okay?" I asked.

It was such a terrible question. Of course he wasn't okay! But what else was there to ask?

"I'm sorry," Knovak whispered, his voice rusty. It sounded like it pained him both physically and emotionally to voice those words.

"You know what they say," I said with a shrug, "the best apology is changed behavior."

Knovak turned his head until one cheek was on the pillow. He looked ready to die. It bothered me, even though he had almost gotten me killed several times now.

I tapped my fingers on the top of my leg. I supposed honesty was the best policy.

"Normally, I bluster my way through life," I said, half

laughing at my own admission. "I say whatever I think will help me the most in any situation, sometimes doling out advice that I don't even believe, just to further my own goals. But... in this instance... I'm not even entirely sure what I should say to make you feel better. I don't think words alone can do that."

Knovak said nothing.

"Sorin would know what to say," I whispered.

Still, silence.

Twain stared at me with a frown. He wanted me to be better at this.

Then Knovak finally spoke up. "This is all my fault. If I hadn't pushed Starling in the abyssal hells, this wouldn't have happened. I just wanted... to be stronger."

I had heard this before—from Raaza.

"Why?" I asked.

Knovak turned his half-dead gaze to me. "Hmm?"

"Why? Why get stronger?"

He didn't answer. That was fine. I think I understood. He wanted respect—but not for deeds, just being *amazing*.

"If Sorin said he wanted power, it would be because he needed it to help others. He would fight for the weak, save those in danger, and defend people from the wicked. And Raaza, when he told me he needed to be better, it was because he wanted to save his sister and mother from a bad situation."

Knovak still didn't reply. He probably had no idea where I was going with this.

"My point is," I said, "they all had a purpose. Something to *do* with their strength. Knovak, what did you want to do with your newfound power?"

"Nothing," he whispered as he closed his eyes.

"I think you should probably mull that over." I stood from his bed and brushed myself off. "I'll tell the headmaster this wasn't entirely your fault. I mean, you wouldn't have been in the abyssal hells if it weren't for me, so this is somewhat my doing. I think Headmaster Venrover will go easy on you."

Knovak exhaled as he turned his head away from me. "What does it matter? Let him punish me. I deserve it."

"Maybe you can bond with another mystical creature and start over at Astra Academy." I shrugged. "We just brought creatures to the Menagerie, including a gabbro dragon hatching. That's something, right?"

No response.

Twain motioned with a jerk of his head. He wanted to go. I agreed, perhaps this was a discussion best had another day, when Knovak wasn't feeling so down on himself.

"I'll see you around," I said as I headed for the infirmary door.

Hopefully.

CHAPTER 42

THE LOTUS DIAMOND RUNESTONE

--Nini's Perspective--

The air was damp, the kind that clings to your skin and seeps into your bones. My footsteps echoed faintly off the stone walls, the sound quickly swallowed by the oppressive silence.

I felt one with death when Waste and I were merged. The abyssal hells didn't frighten me—but the fear I may never see my home, or Sorin, ever again did.

The hidden labyrinth under the main one was strange and seemed more alive. At several points, I thought I heard the beating of a heart, but whenever I focused on the noise, it mysteriously disappeared. How much did the labyrinth want to mess with my thoughts?

Despite that, I pressed on, Waste's magic coursing through me.

"Help me," a voice echoed from down one of the many corridors.

I stopped in my tracks, my eyes wide behind Waste's mask.

His scythe flew into my hands, and a tingle ran down my spine.

"Is someone there?" Waste and I said as one.

"Help," the voice came again.

Was someone actually in trouble? I had thought no one could enter the abyssal hells, but I supposed there was the occasional mistake—like me. Perhaps someone *was* in danger. I had to do something.

"*Be careful, my arcanist,*" Waste telepathically warned.

I nodded once before rushing down the long tunnel of the underground labyrinth. The ceiling glowed with an eerie blue, illuminating the path, but only barely. As I continued, it grew foggier, and the chill of the water on my skin caused me to slow.

"Hello?" Waste and I called out.

"*Something approaches.*"

Waste's reaper magic swelled within me. My veins filled with ice as I turned to the subtle noises hidden in the mist.

The click of claws put me on edge. A monster was here. Something horrid.

I held my scythe high, and the golden chains lifted like tentacle arms. The four lanterns blazed brightly.

"Hello?" a younger male voice asked, the words floating through the mist.

The voice sounded familiar...

"*Be wary,*" Waste telepathically said.

I nodded, prepared to fight whatever came out of the mist. But then...

A man appeared.

He stepped through the mists with a stumbling gait. His blood-red hair and freckled face were striking. His eyes, dark green, were deep and haunting. At first, I thought it was Father. He had the same hair color and eyes... But this was different.

I almost dropped my scythe as I lost my breath.

"Nini?" the man asked.

My brother.

He wore a long tunic and carpenter's pants, just like the night when he had died. The edge of his clothing was singed, and the smell of ash lingered in the air around him.

I couldn't speak. I couldn't breathe. Was this real? Was my brother here? Right now? In front of me?

"Avery," I whispered.

My concentration was so rattled, Waste and I almost unmerged. Somehow, through the strength of Waste's conviction, we remained together.

Avery walked forward, his boots falling hard on the dirt floor. Why was he here? Or was this his soul? Had he been lost in this labyrinth, suffering?

"Have you come to save me, Nini?" My brother brought a hand up to brush his red hair back. "After all this time? You've finally come to my rescue?"

"*You don't need to answer.*" Waste's anger was merging with my own. "*This is a trick. As a reaper arcanist, you can sense souls. Do you sense one now?*"

I...

I didn't.

So what was this?

My brother continued forward, until he was just a breath from me. Shaken, I stared into his familiar green eyes.

"I'm sorry," was all I could bring myself to say.

Avery was just as I remembered. His face was marred with angry lines. His fists were always balled. He had hurt me so many times that I always felt like a helpless child in his presence. Even now, as a true form reaper arcanist, my strength seemed far away.

"You set the house on fire," my brother whispered, his expression turning cold. "You *killed* me. And you got away with it, too. No punishment. No consequences. You're a regular villain."

"*Cut this beast down*," Waste commanded.

I didn't know if I could.

My brother reached out a hand, his fingers outstretched and inches from my cloak and chains.

I didn't move. I felt too overwhelmed with guilt to do anything.

"*My arcanist!*"

Avery touched my shoulder.

A sharp, lancing pain shot through my body.

Something had struck me from behind.

When I glanced down, I saw the spine of something had pierced through my cloak, but only halfway. The spine was in my side, and all my hesitation faded.

I used my chains to help pull my body free. Then I dove into the blood on the floor and emerged from the splatter on the nearby wall.

While the fog was thick, and hindered some of my sight, I spotted Avery *and* my attacker easily—mostly because the monster that had attacked me was quite large.

It was a house here in the tunnels of the maze?

No.

It was the shattered remains of a building, animated through magic, much like a relickeeper was a dragon held together by threads.

This creature was once an iron and wood building. It was shattered, and the wood and iron were now held together with visible hate. The furniture once inside was torn to shreds and acted as a sort of guts for the fractured interior. It had a single arm made of splintered wood from the front door, and glass shards it used as "claws" at the end of the eight fingers.

The thing was squeezed in tight to the labyrinth, its walls pushed up against all four sides of the tunnel.

"*It's a haunt,*" Waste telepathically said. "*A dreadful mystical creature who plays with people's memories and conjures images of familiar ghosts to lure people into their house-like body. Like a flytrap plant, a haunt will collapse on the unsuspecting person and kill them.*"

I had never seen something like this—but I believed Waste. Had it used illusions to keep itself hidden? That was the only explanation. No doubt the haunt couldn't keep those illusions intact after attacking me.

"Nini?" my brother asked.

No. This wasn't my brother. It was some horrible joke made by yet *another* creature who thought they were strong enough to face a *Duke of Demise*. How dare this miserable pile of lies try to harm me!

I rushed forward, ignoring the illusion of my brother, even when it pretended to lunge for me. I slashed with my scythe, stabbing straight into the wooden body of the haunt. The beast cackled and then slashed with its hand. I sidestepped, but the pieces of glass tore through my cloak.

The rattle of my chains drew my attention.

My heart quickened.

Through sheer spite, I lashed out with two lanterns and struck the body of the haunt. The doors of the lanterns flew open, and fire spilled out onto the wood.

Then I waved my hand and manipulated the blood on the floor and wall. Creating axes from the crimson, I hurled them at the haunt. They slammed into the creature's body. It was too stuck to move.

With the embers taking their toll, I leapt away. The haunt attempted to pat away the fire, but I used the bloody axes to hack away at its arm.

"*Foolish arcanist,*" the haunt hissed. "You will die down here! You will die!"

What a pathetic lump. I moved further away, bothered by

the flames, but not frightened. They were growing—spreading across the haunt's body.

"I have better places to be," Waste and I said as one.

Then I turned and limped away, the injury to my side still bleeding. I needed to find a way out of here...

My footsteps echoed faintly off the walls, the sound quickly swallowed by the oppressive silence. How long had I been traveling? Too long... The injury in my side wasn't aching anymore. No more blood spilled on the ground. But I felt weak. Tired.

I rounded a corner and stopped short. There, at the end of the narrow passageway, stood a door. Not a simple wooden thing to be pushed open, but a towering structure of black iron, its surface worked with strange, twisting words. It went from the ceiling to the floor, impressive and imposing.

I hadn't seen any doors in the labyrinth until this point.

"What is this?" Waste and I said as one.

The words on the surface of the iron door writhed when I lifted my lanterns to get a better look. At the center of the door was a circular emblem, divided perfectly in half. One side was bright, polished gold. The other was tarnished silver, dull and lifeless.

The words...

They formed into something I could read.

I am born of silence yet bring no peace.
I touch all things, yet leave no trace.
In my grasp, kings fall and empires cease.
Speak my name, and you shall pass.

I stepped closer, the uneven stone beneath my feet shifting slightly, and traced the words with my fingertips. The door was cold.

"What is this?" Waste and I asked.

"*A riddle.*"

I nodded once. The door seemed to be waiting for my response. It felt wrong to rush, as though the labyrinth itself would punish haste.

"Born of silence..." I closed my eyes. "Brings no peace? Kings fall... Empires cease..."

The answer seemed obvious to me. Was this meant to be difficult?

I was a Duke of Demise now. Such a riddle couldn't stop me from moving forward.

"Death," Waste and I said to the door. "Your name is *death*."

For a heartbeat, nothing happened. Then the words flared to life, and the emblem spun in its place. The grinding of gears rumbled through the labyrinth, and the iron door began to shift, opening inward with agonizing slowness.

I stepped back, my breath catching as a new wave of air rushed out from the opening—a cold, dry breeze, like the exhalation of something ancient and long dormant. The light of my lanterns flickered in the strange current.

The door stood open now, revealing a small closet-sized room. Inside, there was a pedestal, and on top of it was a diamond.

Well...

Maybe a diamond? It was in the shape of a rectangle and about as thick as my pointer finger. I stepped in close and examined the diamond with my eyes. Runes were etched into one side, one of which appeared to be a lotus flower. Did I dare flip it over to see the other?

"*Take it,*" Waste telepathically said. "*That is the lotus diamond runestone, meant for the god-arcanists. At some level, it is a prize.*"

"But this is the abyssal hells," we said together. "Should I really remove something so precious? The lotus diamond runestone sounds important."

"*Perhaps Death Lord Deimos will know what to do with it.*"

That was a good point. With a shaky hand, I reached out and took the diamond. When I flipped it over, there was an etching of a tower. How strange. What was this?

The labyrinth rumbled, and stones fell from the ceiling.

"*Do you feel that? This presence... A Death Lord is nearby.*"

My blood ran icy. Waste was right. Something was nearby, and it felt like the twist of a hundred souls that were crying out in pain. It *was* a Death Lord, but it wasn't Deimos. He never felt like this.

It was...

Death Lord Naiad.

Somehow, in the pit of my stomach, I knew she had come for me.

CHAPTER 43

INSURGENCY

The most interesting class we had to attend took place at the end of every week. It was *Advanced Knowledge of the Abyssal Hells*. That surprised me, considering how little everyone seemed to know about it, but it seemed the headmaster had planned for me to speak from the very beginning.

We gathered in the lecture hall and the chalkboard was silent. Instead of everyone sitting around the room in separate seats, everyone congregated in the center, sitting next to one another. It was wholesome, but somehow made the whole lecture hall feel smaller.

Our eldrin all stayed at the back of the room—even Twain. He was taking a nap on top of Ecrib's head. The mighty typhoon dragon seemed to like him there. Occasionally I saw him petting Twain on the head, though Twain was completely unaware.

Phila's coatl, Nasbit's golem, and Raaza's kitsune seemed to be playing a game of cards. Kitsunes could apparently make illusions with a tangible feeling, so Miko was creating dice, cards, and other things to play with.

My brother's knightmare, Exie's erlking, and Rosella's kappa were having a whispered conversation. Nothing seemed wrong, but it was intense. It made me curious.

Before I could ask them what was going on, six individuals entered the room. I recognized four of the individuals. One was Headmaster Venrover. He wore a striking outfit of blue and silver robes, tailored to his slender body. His black hair was pulled back in a loose tail and he had a sort of sophisticated grace about him.

The next one was Professor Helmith's father—Volke Savan, the Warlord of Magic. He strode into the room with such confidence and purpose that it was obvious he was an arcanist who had seen plenty of fighting. He was also the tallest one here, which was saying something.

His inky black hair was short and windswept, revealing his arcanist mark for all to see. He had a true form knightmare—his seven-pointed star glowed with an inner light. So did the cape and sword laced throughout. It was brilliant.

A sword in an ebony sheath was tied at his side, and a kite shield as dark as midnight hung on his back. I had seen these before, when last he had come to the Academy. He had taught us about true forms, after all.

The most impressive part of Volke was the many tattoo runes that sparkled across his skin. He had a black mark on one forearm, a red one on the other, and a blue swirl along the side of his neck. When he turned to face me, I noticed one of his eyes was also marked with a rune—it shone with a gentle gold. His other eye was plain, which was fine, but exciting, like the rest of him.

I needed my runes...

And I was lucky, because the next person to enter after Volke was none other than his brother, Ryker, the Mother of Shapeshifters arcanist. I wanted that man to give me a rune, mostly because I wanted to have all the mimic powers imaginable. If I gained a true form mimic, *and* had the runes of the Mother of Shapeshifters, I would be the very best—like no one ever was.

Ryker was tall—wiry and lean—with black hair slicked tight to his head. His arcanist mark was a star with nine points, and the creature woven throughout was some sort of blob. He wore an outfit of white, and walked without much confidence at all, really. A rat sat on his shoulders, and I knew it to be a piece of the Mother of Shapeshifters. She could make herself into many tinier creatures, which was pretty amusing.

Sorin elbowed me. "I told you," he whispered. "There he is! He's going to help you with that rune."

"Excellent," I replied.

The fourth individual entered the room, and I knew him, too. Lynus Dodger, a man in black leathers that barely covered his muscles. While Volke was tall, and Ryker thin, this man was burly. His coppery hair also made quite the statement, as it was practically metallic in sheen—which was perfect because it matched his eldrin.

Lynus's arcanist mark was the seven-pointed star with a lion wrapped around it. And sure enough, Lynus's nemean lion strode in behind him.

The lion's immense frame moved with a deadly grace. Its fur was not fur at all, but a gleaming coat of metal strands, each one glinting in the faint light like tempered steel. The silvery fur shimmered with an almost liquid quality, yet there was no mistaking the clanking sound that echoed with each step, like armor plates shifting against one another.

Nasbit smiled and then waved. Lynus acknowledged him with a jut of his chin, a little reverse nod.

So did his nemean lion.

I knew Nasbit was a member of the Dodger family, but sometimes it was hard to wrap my head around. Everyone I had met in that family seemed to be some sort of unmitigated badass. Physically, I should add, because Nasbit was quite talented academically, but never seemed the same as the others with the Dodger name.

"I didn't know Uncle Lynus would be joining this class," he said with a smile.

"Joining the class?" I repeated.

The nemean lion's mane was a crown of razor-sharp filaments, while his claws curved like polished scythes. His fangs, long and serrated, gleamed like honed daggers when he opened his powerful maw.

"Naz," the lion said. "I hadn't expected to see you here."

"I had to join, Vaysil. I've already learned so much about the abyssal hells, and helped Gray with much of his problems —why wouldn't I?"

Vaysil, the nemean lion, lifted a metal eyebrow. "You aren't the... adventuring type."

Which was the kindest way to put that.

"He's part of a team," Phila interjected. She placed a delicate hand on Nasbit's shoulder. "And not every member of the team needs to be the same. We need different strengths. Isn't that right, Nasbit?"

He half chuckled and nodded.

Vaysil and Lynus exchanged knowing glances before returning their attention to the rest of the classroom.

There were two other arcanists who entered—a man with wild red hair, plenty of muscles, and a long black coat, and a woman of slender stature with a hat on that dipped down in front, covering half her face, including one of her eyes. Which was odd. Didn't she need her depth perception?

The woman was a phoenix arcanist, and the man had some sort of dog in his arcanist mark.

His dog eldrin entered the room after him. At first glance, it resembled a husky—a strong, muscular frame with the sharp lines and regal stance of a working dog. But where a husky might wear a coat of fur as white as snow or patterned with grays and blacks, this beast seemed cloaked in shadow itself. Its pitch-black pelt absorbed the light, the edges of its form blurring as wisps of darkness trailed from its body like smoke rising from a dying ember.

A rougarou.

They were shadowy dogs meant to quell rage—noble beasts, or so Professor Helmith had taught us. And they were somewhat rare, as rougarou were only born when a wolf died under the light of a blood moon.

The rougarou turned to me, its pale blue eyes unblinking.

My brother leaned over. "I like that one."

"They can merge with their arcanists," I whispered back. "So, kinda like a knightmare when you think about it."

"I like it even more."

Technically, when a rougarou and its arcanist merged, they became more a werewolf than a knight, but I didn't bother explaining that. Now wasn't the time for mystical creature studies.

Headmaster Venrover went to the podium at the front of the class, directly in front of the chalkboard. He forced a smile and then motioned for these new arcanists to take some seats.

"Hello, abyssal sentinels," the headmaster said. "As you can see, our numbers are growing. I've enlisted the help of the best arcanists around. Volke Savan, once the world serpent god-arcanist; Lynus Dodger, once the typhon beast god-arcanist; Zaxis Ren, once the fenris wolf god-arcanist; Biyu—"

"Wait." I threw my hand up in the air, my heart hammering.

Headmaster Venrover, as well as all the new arcanists, turned to face me. "Yes, Gray?"

"I'm so sorry—are you intending for these arcanists to join us in the abyssal hells?" I nervously chortled as I searched for the correct words. "Because that might not be the best idea."

"Why is that? They're already battle tested, and there's no one I'd rather trust with such an important task."

I shook my head. "I'm certain they're powerful and trustworthy. That's not the problem. You see, I just learned that the god-arcanists have special souls."

"Souls?" Volke asked, his dark eyes narrowing.

"Yeah. Because they were once bonded to god-creatures. If one of the Death Lords gets them and binds them to their abyssal dragon, it could be bad. At least, that's what Death Lord Deimos thinks."

After I made that statement, the room was quiet. The rest of my class all had silent conversations conducted through looks and glances.

"What're you suggesting?" the headmaster asked.

"Uh, that they not follow us into the abyssal hells." I shrugged. "Maybe they can, I dunno, watch the gates or something when they're opened. Ya know, fight elder creatures. Just not the Death Lords themselves."

That was when Lynus stood. He radiated *anger*, and I suspected everyone felt it. His lion's metallic fur stood on end, and when he walked over to the podium, it was with barely contained rage.

"*Adelgis*," he hissed through gritted teeth. "I *will* go to the abyssal hells, do you understand me? No one is going to stop me from rescuing Everett."

Headmaster Venrover shook his head. "These are all new developments. What do you want me to do? Ignore a warning from one of the few people who has actually gone to the abyssal hells?"

Lynus grabbed the headmaster by the collar of his robes. "Either I go to the abyssal hells with you, or I'm going to join one of those lunatic cults and go there with them. The choice is yours."

Volke stood and all the shadows in the room trembled. His

glowing white arcanist mark sparked a bit of red as he said, "*Lynus, control yourself.*"

And just like that, the man released the headmaster. Then Lynus turned on his heel, his face neutral. "You heard me. I'm not going to be stopped. I don't care if the Death Lords want my soul. *Let them come for me.* We need to kill them all anyway, right? This might make it easier."

"And they call *me* cocky," the redhead said. He glanced around, as though waiting for someone to laugh, and when no one did, he grew visibly grumpy. With a scoff, he leaned back in his seat and stared at the ceiling.

Volke faced me with a serious expression. "Gray—I fear there will be no dissuading Lynus. His husband is in the abyssal hells, and Lynus would watch the world burn if it meant saving Everett."

No one in the room disagreed with that statement.

I shrugged. "I don't know what to tell you. Deimos thinks it's a bad idea to allow any of the Death Lords to get your souls."

"Then perhaps only a few of us will go with you." Volke motioned to himself, and then to Lynus. "And the rest of us will use whatever power and knowledge we have to prep for the eventual insurgency."

Nasbit sat up straighter. "Insurgency?"

"Yes. That's what the headmaster called our operation to infiltrate the abyssal hells. We're going to go in, attempt to solve the problems, and hopefully set things right. *Without* involving the whole world."

Oof.

An insurgency?

On the other hand, it was probably the best bet. We didn't want those other Death Lords getting out, after all.

CHAPTER 44

ENCHANTMENTS AND ARTIFACTS

The abyssal hells were made up of five layers.

Speaking with Deimos, we went over the layers, and over the purpose of each one. The first abyss was for reincarnation. The second abyss was a massive labyrinth where lost souls lingered. The third abyss was where the Death Lords lived, and held major locations, such as the Spire of the Gods. The fourth abyss was where most of the elder creatures roamed.

And the fifth abyss was the edge of oblivion.

Apparently, Death Lord Kallikore dwelled mostly in the fourth abyss. He was amassing an elder creature army, since now he was mostly mystical creature himself—after fusing parts of his own dragon to his body.

Death Lord Umbriel was in the fifth abyss, looking for a way to open the Oblivion Gate. She thought it would give her unlimited power, but Deimos was much more skeptical.

And lastly, Death Lord Naiad—the crazy loon who tried to kill me once already—was hunting the other Death Lords down. She wanted to bind all their souls to her dragon in the hopes of achieving some sort of apotheosis. Or maybe she thought it would cause her abyssal dragon to achieve true form...

There were also mysterious places in the abyssal hells that Deimos had mentioned to me in passing. Like a place that housed all knowledge from life or even places where empires went when they were dead.

There was a lot, and by the time I was done telling everyone about it, the sun had set and it was time for dinner.

However, after this special session of lecture was dismissed, Sorin urged me to stay behind. Twain ran from the back of the room and landed on my shoulder, clearly ready for food. The Mother of Shapeshifters arcanist, Ryker, also stayed, and I greeted the man with a quick nod.

"It's good to see you again," I said.

Ryker chuckled and half smiled. "We've met?"

"Yeah, during my first year." I held back all my sarcastic commentary. "I'm certain your eldrin remembers."

The little brown rat on his shoulder had glowing red eyes, and they pierced straight through me, as though seeing into my soul. Then the rat glanced over to Twain.

"My precious baby," the Mother of Shapeshifters whispered. "Are you well?"

Twain nodded. "I couldn't be better. Gray is going to make sure I achieve my true form. He's been working on it day and night."

"Oh? I've only ever known one other arcanist to achieve their true form with a mimic."

"R-Really?" Twain wiggled his whiskers.

The red-eyed rat rubbed her ears. "Yes. But I have faith in you. Fear can be defeated."

"Thank you."

The rat once again stared, somehow with more intensity than before. Again, I nodded, this time awkwardly.

"I've almost done it," I said, though I wasn't entirely certain if that was accurate.

"Can I take you to the magic lab?" Sorin asked Ryker. "I was hoping you could enchant Gray, but also, I was wondering if you would look at some of the items in there and see if we could make any equipment with your unique magic."

"Unique?" Ryker asked.

"Oh, yes. We learned in class that arcanists with nine-pointed stars for their mark meant their creature was one of a kind. Like the Source of the Storm. So, your magic is unique, right? We should have equipment made with it. And I need to show you the armor I've been making for the rest of the class."

"Uh..." Ryker eventually shrugged. "Sure. We can do that. My wife said she wanted to pal around with all her old friends who had arrived at the Academy, so she won't get too bored."

"Perfect!" Sorin slapped my upper arm. "Let's go get your occult ore! This is our chance, Gray."

I went to my room to gather my occult ore before joining Sorin and Ryker in the lab. Twain hung on my shoulder, as always, purring the entire time as we traveled down the hall.

"The Mother of Shapeshifters thinks you're going to triumph over your fears, Gray. Doesn't that make you excited?" He was practically vibrating with the force of his adorable purrs.

I petted him as I pushed open the door to my room. "Yeah, I know we'll do it, Sorin's evocation has been helping me."

That last session... It was eye-opening. I was close. That rush of joy I felt after the fear had gone was *something* in the right direction. Soon, I would have this under control.

Ashlyn was already in our room, dressed in her white

tunic and sleeping pants. She sat on the bed, reading one of our class books. Without glancing up, she said, "Have you thanked your brother?"

"I've told him." I went to my belongings and rummaged through them in order to find the tiny vial that held my occult ore. It had been a gift from Phila. She was much too kind.

"Me and my brother have never gotten along," Ashlyn intoned as she turned a page in her book. "You're lucky to have a brother like Sorin."

I nodded once, my thoughts drifting. I was lucky.

Then my hand grazed the wooden box that held Ashlyn's gift to me—the blood of the corona phoenix. These god-creatures were so powerful that even a small drop of their blood radiated energy. Even within the box, I felt the magic within.

No wonder the god-arcanist souls were altered.

After a long sigh, I picked up the box. What had Lucian said? The corona phoenix was a creature of fire *and* shadows...

"Would you be angry if I gave this away?" I asked, holding up the box.

Ashlyn put her book down, her eyes narrowed. For a short moment, I thought she was going to give me a long rant. But then her brow softened, and her eyes widened with realization. She shook her head.

"No, I won't be mad."

I tucked the box under my arm and smiled. "Thank you. I'll be back later tonight, okay? This shouldn't take too long."

"Fine. But if it's more than a couple hours, I'm going to come find you." Ashlyn pointed at me. "No adventures without your awesome wife."

"It's a deal."

I stepped into the magic lab, happy to see the glowstones kept the place illuminated with a warm yellow hue. Shelves loomed high above me, crammed with jars that gleamed faintly as though they held their own light.

Sorin and Ryker were already here.

Along with a hundred rats. I almost jumped when a dozen of them came scurrying over to my feet. Although I knew each was a tiny part of the Mother of Shapeshifters, it was still weird to see her in so many pieces.

"Hey," I awkwardly said with a wave. I carefully stepped around the rodents as I made my way over to my brother. "Sorry that took so long. I brought the stuff."

"Stuff?" Sorin lifted an eyebrow. "I thought you just needed one thing."

I pulled the wooden box out from under my arm and handed it over to him. "Here. I think you should have this. For, uh, your armor or your weapons."

"What is it?"

Sorin smiled as he held the box close. His shadow whipped around his feet and then lifted up, becoming a hollow of suit of armor right next to him. Thurin was quite intimidating, but I actually enjoyed him taking shape to spend time with us. He rarely did it.

"This is quite powerful," Thurin muttered, his voice echoing in his helmet.

Even *he* could sense it.

Sorin opened the box, the drop of blood from the corona phoenix glittering within. My brother hesitated for a long moment, his brow furrowed.

"This is for me? But wasn't this... a gift from Ashlyn?" Sorin closed the box, the light of the blood sealed within. Then he handed it back. "I can't take this."

"But you probably should," Ryker cut in.

Sorin and I both jumped.

Ryker stood at the opposite side of the largest crafting table. His arms were crossed, and he stared at us with the kind of impatience that only manifests when you've been waiting in silence for too long.

"That's a piece of a god-creature." Ryker gestured to the box. "It's rare, and the magic of the corona phoenix would be perfect for a knightmare arcanist. Nothing controlled the void quite like that divine beast."

He almost made me regret handing it over. But then I shook the feeling away. Sorin had always been there for me. This was the least I could do for him.

"That is what Lucian said, too." I pushed the box deeper into Sorin's grasp. "You take it. Or, better yet, let's use this lab and have you craft something with it."

"I don't know." Sorin fidgeted with the box. "I mean, I'm not the best at making trinkets yet. Shouldn't I wait until I'm better before using this?"

"You can make repairs to items later." Ryker shrugged. Then he rolled his hand, trying to hurry us up. "Didn't you say you wanted me to enchant one of you? I do want to go to bed at some point."

I walked around the large table and handed over the glass vial to Ryker. Inside was a powdery dust—it was the occult ore ground up and made into something that could be tattooed on me. Well, "tattooed" wasn't the right word, but it would eventually look like a tattoo when he was done.

Ryker's eldrin scurried around the room, some of the rats on the shelves, moving things around, and some of them gathering tools and dragging them to the table.

"Enchanting a human body is similar to crafting a magical item," Ryker said. He stepped close and then pointed to my body. "However, your body only has so much room. Once you've enchanted every last inch of your skin, you won't be able to carry more. Does that make sense? The more powerful the enhancement, the larger it'll be."

I held up my left arm. "Can you enchant my shoulder? And work down my arm?"

"What kind of my magic do you want?"

"I want whatever shapeshifting powers I can get," I said. With a grin, I added, "I want to be the best mimic arcanist."

Twain leapt off me and sat on the table. "I'll supervise everything from right here."

Ryker stepped close to me. Then he pulled off the stopper on the vial. "Very well. The Mother of Shapeshifters can change her physical body—and so can I. With a little work, I can give you some of that, but it might hurt during the application process." He held up a hand. "Not too much! Just a little."

I pulled up my sleeve. "Don't worry. I'm not afraid."

CHAPTER 45

RUNES ON THE SKIN

I sat on the side of the table, the cold air brushing against my bare shoulder. Ryker worked on his enchantment right next to me, his focus perfect. He rarely blinked, and even when I turned to him, he didn't stop what he was doing.

I had never seen an enchantment before...

Ryker wielded a strange tool with a needle at one end. The needle wasn't ordinary—nothing about this was ordinary. It gleamed faintly with an inner light, and the ink poured from the tip like droplets of rain water. The ink was just the occult ore powder mixed with some water and then augmented with Ryker's magic.

The color...

It was gray.

Which delighted me, to be honest. I smiled most of the time, even though the needle stung whenever it pierced my skin, even if it only did so for a moment.

At first, I thought Ryker would be drawing an image on my skin, but that wasn't what happened. Whenever he poked me, the ink coursed through my skin. It spread out on its own, forming shapes as though it was alive and already knew the image it wanted to be crafted in.

Ryker moved with precision, poking me a few inches down, and then further toward my elbow. He worked in silence, pausing only to mutter under his breath.

And then I felt it—the magic reaching for me, probing, testing. It wasn't just an image being etched onto my skin; it was a doorway being carved open. The power thrummed beneath the surface, coiling and uncoiling like a living thing. My shoulder burned, the fire spreading down my arm and into my chest, and for a moment, I thought I couldn't endure it. I gritted my teeth, wondering if this was how enchantment always went.

Didn't Volke have a rune on his eye? How had he handled *that*?

But then the pain shifted, softening into a dull, aching hum, and I realized it wasn't trying to harm me—it was becoming one with me.

"Breathe," Ryker murmured. "You're quite tense."

I obeyed, inhaling deeply, and the magic surged in response. "This is my first time," I quipped.

Ryker chortled.

While he worked, my brother was at another table. He had pulled out his trident from the darkness—the weapon he had crafted himself with knightmare magic. Out of the corner of my eye, I watched as he fitted the phoenix blood into the base of the tines. Was he improving his Woldräm, Voice of the Departed? That was a fantastic choice.

When Ryker jabbed my elbow, I almost yowled. I snapped my attention to him, glaring.

"Sorry," he sheepishly whispered. "I'm not the best at enchanting others."

"Don't tell me that," I said.

He shrugged. But then he only poked twice more, having

the rune curve down to my wrist. Once finished, he took a step back and motioned to my arm.

The image across my skin looked like an amalgamation of feathers, scales, and fur. It was just lines, almost tribal in nature, and the markings went around my whole arm, like a sleeve. The gray was silvery when the light hit it correctly, glimmering beautifully.

The pain subsided relatively quickly.

"Thank you," I said.

Ryker half shrugged and half nodded. "Everyone is talking about this abyssal sentinel plan as though it is very serious. I told your headmaster I would donate what I could to the cause."

"So, uh, how do these work?" I rubbed my new enchantment. "Do I shout an attack name and *poof*, magic?"

I was joking, obviously, but Ryker frowned as though I was a midwit who had been shaken as a baby for far too long. "Uh, you are a second-year student, aren't you? Surely, you're familiar with how to use your powers by now."

I rolled my eyes. "But I've never used one of these before."

"Ah. Well, you need to focus on your arm—you'll feel the magic there. Then you imagine using your abilities as before. This is an augmentation, so you'll want this new magic to infuse your body. When it does, you will transform. The new shapes are temporary."

Ryker held up his hand. Before my eyes, the skin on his fingers rippled. Within half a second, he went from having normal fingers to having five octopus tentacles for a hand. I leaned away, my stomach twisting in disgust.

"Ew," I said on instinct.

"Well..." Ryker ended his augmentation magic, and his hand snapped back to normal. With a red face, he crossed his arms. "Listen, this is an extremely useful ability. I understand it's gross, but in a pinch, you'll find it invaluable."

"Uh-huh."

I held out my arm. Then I stared at the sparkling gray rune on my body. As a mimic arcanist, it was easy to feel how the magic in my skin was different than my mimic magic. After just a moment of concentration, I tapped into the Mother of Shapeshifter's abilities and held my breath.

What did I want to change about my body?

I didn't want octopus fingers. Gross.

What else? Perhaps...

I imagined a bird, hoping I would somehow manifest wings. Wouldn't it be amazing to fly? But instead of having wings sprout from my back, like I was picturing, the skin of my arm and shoulder rippled, and out sprouted white feathers.

Soft, down feathers.

I held up my arm, my eyes wide.

"Wow," Twain said. "You're like part chicken."

I shot him a glower. "What a great eldrin you are."

He pawed his face, smoothing his fur. "I know. I'm excellent. Want me to tell you a chicken joke? I've got several."

"What happened?" I asked, turning to Ryker. "You're the Mother of Shapeshifters arcanist—tell me what I'm doing wrong."

Ryker ran a hand over my feathered arm. "You're likely just getting used to this. I would recommend practicing until you get better. When I first shapeshifted, it was difficult rearranging my, uh..." He leaned in closer and whispered, "I hated rearranging my bones. So it was difficult for me to change those."

Bones?

I hadn't thought about that.

I examined my feathered arm and allowed the augmentation to relax. The feathers receded into my body.

"Well, we're more alike now." I glanced over at Twain. "You can change shape—and now I can, too."

Twain puffed out his chest. "That's true—but I'm better at it."

When I glanced back down at my regular arm, I smiled. Then I wondered what Deimos thought about this. When he was an arcanist who roamed the mortal realm, they didn't have enchantments. This was a recent development—a magical breakthrough, if you will.

"Hey, Dee," I muttered. "This is amazing, right?"

Nothing.

Deimos was distracted again.

I sighed. Hopefully he wasn't in any danger. Then I remembered how I saw through his eyes before, and wondered if I could do it again—will it to take place—by simply concentrating.

Ryker walked over to my brother and the rats of the Mother of Shapeshifters continued to frolic around the room, investigating and gathering. Twain stayed by my side, one ear down, one ear perked up.

"Are you ready to go to bed?" he asked.

I shook my head. "I need to check up on Deimos first." I closed my eyes. "Just watch over my body for a bit, okay? I have a bad feeling... like Deimos might be in trouble."

Most of the time, when he was absent from my consciousness, it was because something important was happening in the abyssal hells. Was that the case this time? I hoped not, but I was about to find out.

CHAPTER 46

SAVING NINI

I closed my eyes and focused. My connection with Deimos was different than before. I used to have dreams about seeing him, but lately they didn't happen. Instead, I had found myself seeing what he saw almost accidentally.

Now, without much effort, I found myself drifting away from my actual body, and finding myself within Deimos's.

Sure enough, when I managed to open my eyes again, I was with Deimos.

And we were in the middle of a battle.

Death Lord Deimos was in the middle of the second abyss, deep in the labyrinth. The sky was black with stars, the walls were pristine white, and the floor mirror-polished. Deimos and his abyssal dragon eldrin, Hektor, stood in a wide-open section of the maze.

A tower was here, surrounded by a deep moat of pristine water. From Deimos's thoughts, I knew we were in the very center of the labyrinth in the second abyss—a place known as *The Eternal Rest*. Apparently, if a person found this spot and rested too long, their energy would be sapped and they'd never be able to leave.

The huge moat did look inviting—the cool waters practically sparkled.

Standing in the same open area around the tower was Death Lord Naiad. I knew it was her because we had met once before, when I was accidentally pulled down into the abyssal hells.

Her scalp was stripped bare of hair, revealing the lattice of deep scars that carved their way from her brow to the base of her neck, as if blades had taken their time leaving their stories upon her. Her arcanist mark was similar to Deimos's—a seven-pointed star etched with a dragon at its heart. Yet Naiad had altered it, cutting two crossed swords into the star's edge with precision. The scar tissue there was grotesque and deliberate.

"Your little reaper arcanist is here, isn't she?" Naiad asked, her voice rusty.

Naiad's armor was sparse, almost like she didn't care about her own safety. A small chest piece shielded her torso, but the skirt she wore was more macabre—crafted from bone, stretched skin, and twisted metal. It hung with eerie grace, rattling softly as she moved.

Her body itself was her weapon, honed to perfection, but she was also wearing clawed gauntlets, the metal a sick golden hue that told me they were fashioned from abyssal coral. From her lithe frame and the scars upon her skin, it was clear she relied on speed and ferocity in combat. Deimos's knowledge whispered to me: her style was one of relentless, blistering strikes—slashes that overwhelmed before her opponent could think to counter.

I remembered.

Blood-red paint also adorned her body. Handprints ran up her legs, her arms, her torso, painted as though countless souls had clawed at her, trying to drag her back into some dark abyss.

Her eyes were dark, endless wells of intensity. Her tan complexion was vibrant, a contrast to the grim adornments she wore. Death Lord Naiad was just savage, and her abyssal dragon stood behind her, its six eyes turning with ferocity.

The dragon's body was a rotting pile of sickly scales, skin, and muscles. Mucus covered the dragon, dripping off every portion of its body. The beast's wings were a cobweb of transparent faces...

They were grafted souls—some of which were other Death Lords, and they were the souls that sparkled, their magic still contained within.

Would the god-arcanists' souls look like that? I shook my head, trying to dispel random thoughts. Now wasn't the time for that!

"*She is, isn't she?*" Naiad barked, her lips curving upward in a twisted smile. "I don't know how you keep making new friends, Deimos, but your pathetic attempt to resist me ends here. You, your reaper arcanist, your deformed minion—*you'll all be souls on my dragon soon enough.*"

"You came here looking for Nini?" I asked through Deimos.

He gritted his teeth and held back a growl. He was right—now wasn't the time for talking, either.

"Last time I tried to take your soul, there were complications." Death Lord Naiad motioned to her eldrin. Several of the souls *popped* out of existence and then Naiad twitched slightly, her muscles quivering as strength, agility, and raw power clearly flooded her.

Naiad ran forward.

She was so fast, she reminded me of Knovak's elder unicorn and his ferocity aura.

Within half a second, she was on top of Deimos.

Deimos had no weapon. I should've insisted on returning Vivigöl when I had the chance! But Deimos must've been planning on her getting close, because he was ready with his evocation. He blasted raw magic from his palm, striking Naiad through the gut. The blast of energy was brilliant, and it reflected off the mirror floors of the labyrinth.

Naiad had twisted her body slightly, so that the beam went through most of her side—and her soft organs. A blow like that would've downed an average person, but Naiad was far from average. She continued her strike, the rest of her innards threatening to spill from her as she clawed Deimos's face.

Hot blood splattered across the pristine labyrinth.

Hektor lunged for Naiad. He crunched his massive jaws around one of her arms and flung her from his arcanist.

That was when Naiad's dragon got involved. The beast still had all four of his legs, and leapt over, his soul wings half flapping. When he crashed down onto Hektor, the two massive dragons were at each other's throats. Rotted scales sloughed off to the ground, splattering everywhere like Deimos's blood.

Naiad stood, and more souls *whished* off her dragon. Her gut was healed, and then her arm. Within a matter of seconds, she was rotating her shoulders and loosening up for another round.

Deimos also healed himself, but it was slower for some reason.

He just... wasn't himself.

"You lost to Naiad once before," I whispered through Deimos.

"I refuse to lose this time," he replied, breathless.

Something *was* deeply wrong. But he wouldn't tell me.

"Well, you're *not* going to lose," I said. "Because you've got me."

Deimos's half a chuckle was almost insulting, but I didn't care. He had been lending me so much of his skill and magic, and now it was time to return the favor.

I sensed around for threads of magic. Clearly, there were abyssal dragons nearby, but that wasn't what I was looking for. My body—part of my presence—was still in the living realm, and the strings of magic were more diverse there.

I immediately tugged on Sorin's knightmare. I had come to rely on his the most, and within a few seconds, the cold power of his shadow magic filled me... and also gave it to Deimos.

When Naiad turned to face us, she offered a cruel smile. Then she rushed forward, her golden claws flashing.

Deimos stepped into the darkness, slipping into the shadows as though they were a deep pool of water and his body was made of rocks. He slipped right out of Naiad's attack and then shifted through the darkness until he was behind her. When Deimos stepped out into the labyrinth, Naiad was clearly confused.

She stood there, glancing left and right, baffled.

"What?" she asked.

Because she wasn't aware of *my* capacities. She had no idea that Deimos and I had become so merged. She wasn't familiar with mimic magic, and I seriously doubted she understood how Deimos could pull off such a feat.

Deimos lifted his hand and blasted her with his raw magic. Again, she was blasted, the magic cutting straight through her chest, exactly where her heart should be. Deimos was also so good with his aim that the raw magic pierced through Naiad and then kept going until it also struck her eldrin. The abyssal dragon cried out as the magic sliced through one of his legs.

Hektor took this opportunity to slam his fangs on the other dragon's neck. They spun and slammed to the floor of the labyrinth, cracking some of the mirrored tiles.

Unfortunately, Death Lords weren't easy to kill.

Several more souls *popped* off Naiad's eldrin. Her chest knitted itself back together in an instant, heart and all. Then she stood, her bones cracking as though her whole body were being reinforced with more and more magic.

When she faced us this time, her eyes screamed *deranged*. Death Lord Naiad wasn't having a good time.

"I don't know what you've done," she whispered, her voice heated, her body shaking, "but I know all your weaknesses. *You'll never defeat me.*"

Naiad flew at us. And she was faster than anything I had ever faced.

Deimos managed to plunge into the shadows before she got her claws around his neck, but it was damn close. When he emerged, he did so far from Naiad, practically on the other side of the massive labyrinth room. The tower in the center of this "clearing" was rather thin, and Deimos stayed far from it.

His thoughts told me that the tower lured people into it, promising them safety and comfort. Deimos didn't want to get tempted. His fatigue was weighed heavy, and the mind-altering powers of the tower would muddle him.

Souls popped off Hektor, but not as many as Naiad had used. Deimos became stronger and faster, his breaths easier.

"You said you wanted to help me," Deimos muttered. "I could use a weapon."

"I can give you access to my magic, but not too many creatures evoke *swords*," I equipped. "What do you want me to do?"

"I told you what I need, boy. It's your job to come up with a solution."

It didn't take Naiad long to find us this time. She whirled on her heel and shot straight for Deimos.

He lifted his hand and the shadows in the corners of the labyrinth answered his summons. They hardened into tendrils and grabbed Naiad's arms and legs, attempting to stop her. Unfortunately, they couldn't seem to hold her down—they only slowed her as she slashed with her claws.

When she finally was free, she growled as she slashed a claw at Deimos. He managed to side-step, and then he evoked terrors. For a split second, Naiad shouted, and that was when Deimos evoked more raw magic. Naiad managed to roll out of the way, avoiding the beam completely. The invisible terrors tormented her thoughts, but it wasn't enough to keep her from being battle ready.

Deimos's blast of magic slammed into one of the labyrinth walls and then dissipated. Poof. Gone.

In a flurry of lightning-fast attacks, Naiad slashed at Deimos, and then again, cutting through the arm on his shoulder. The bone and metal that made up Deimos's outfit was quite sturdy, and I was shocked her abyssal coral claws could cleave through it.

Deimos took one step into the shadows and Naiad managed to get him a third time. Her claws cut so deep into his chest, she managed to cut through Deimos's ribs.

Despite that, Deimos didn't flinch. I felt the pain—the sear of the abyssal coral—but he didn't gasp, hesitate, or even breathe differently. He moved slightly, to lessen the blow of her strikes, but that was all. Cold. Calculated. The man didn't even take his eyes off his opponent.

Once Deimos dove fully into the darkness, he was free of her relentless attacks, but I knew he needed something else—something to really give him the edge. Knightmare magic was amazing for battles, but since abyssal dragons could continue to heal so long as they had souls to use, that meant Deimos had to work faster.

We had to kill Naiad so many times that she ran out of souls.

But how?

I felt around the threads of magic in Astra Academy while Deimos moved through the darkness. Deimos couldn't remain in the shadows forever—while in the darkness, he couldn't breathe. Once he emerged, he would need to do something.

If I could find the right magic, perhaps I could give us the edge.

Ashlyn's typhoon dragon.

Raaza's kitsune.

Exie's erlking.

Sorin's knightmare.

Phila's coatl.

Nasbit's stone golem.

Rosella's kappa.

Professor Jijo's nimbus dragon.

The headmaster's assassin's wendigo.

Doc Tomas's golden stag.

Captain Leon's cerberus.

And even... Nini's reaper. She was nearby!

Which one? *Which one?*

Oh. Then it hit me. I needed *all* of them.

CHAPTER 47

THE ULTIMATE CHIMERA AURA

Deimos stepped out of the darkness on the other side of the tower.

His dragon and Naiad's dragon splashed through the moat, their roars echoing throughout the labyrinth. I ignored them, even though it was clear that Hektor was losing. Missing a claw was too much of a handicap.

"Deimos," I said through him. "Help me form my aura! The mimic aura, it can—"

"I was there in class when you learned," Deimos growled.

"*Then help me.* You're the only one I know who has willpower as steel as the bars of the Academy gate."

"Feh."

Despite Deimos's initial hesitation, he quickly relaxed and then exhaled. Was he focusing? How was this going to work? Could he actually form my chimera aura? He could access my other magics, so he *had* to be able to do this.

Right?

Death Lord Naiad dashed around the tower. She, too, avoided getting too close and ran a wide circle around the area.

417

The second abyss labyrinth was circular in nature, so this whole place was one giant open circle space with the tower at the dead center. Despite that, Naiad was so fast that she was quickly coming up on our position.

"Dee?" I whispered.

The air thickened with magic.

Despite the fact that my consciousness was with Deimos in the abyssal hells, I felt my body back in the land of the living. My arcanist mark was burning more than it ever had before, the flames of the magic spreading to all of my limbs.

That agony spread to Deimos. He shared my magic, so he shared the sting.

And while it was causing me to lose some of my focus, I had been right about Deimos's willpower. He didn't flinch.

Naiad turned and darted straight for us.

The area grew heavy with fog.

When Death Lord Naiad was close, she reared back her hand to slash. In that split second, with the magic growing more intense, it felt like the enchantment on my arm was more *part of me.* I tapped into it, and the magic of my rune *also* went to Deimos. He gained my shapeshifting powers.

His skin rippled, and a claw of his own formed, his fingers growing talons, his skin hardening with scales. Naiad struck him in the chest, her abyssal coral weapons sinking into his flesh, but that was when Deimos struck.

He slashed at her neck, clawing out half her throat.

Naiad evoked raw magic from the claw buried in Deimos's body. The *blast* ripped through his chest. His vision darkened at the edges. The pain was more intense than my chimera aura.

I feared... Deimos's willpower wouldn't be enough.

Pop. Pop. Pop.

Both Naiad and Deimos used souls that they had grafted onto their abyssal dragons. They only had a limited number of them—each dragon must have a hundred or so in the wings and down the spine, but they were vanishing at a fast rate.

And Deimos had visibly less than Naiad's.

However, when the souls were used, Deimos's chest was healed, Naiad's throat repaired itself, and the blood all over the floor looked as though it had come from nowhere.

Death Lord Deimos *never* lost his concentration. Through the beam, through the agony, through everything. The beat of his heart had picked up, but this man was still going! Even witnessing all that had me pumped.

"You've lost," Deimos growled.

The color drained from the nearby area. The bluish scales of the abyssal dragon became a pale gray. Naiad's red paint marks became nearly black. All colors were gone, leaving us in a realm of black and white—which was the sign Deimos had activated his inevitable aura.

Why?

The inevitable aura couldn't kill other Death Lords...

Deimos held up his hand. I thought he was going to evoke raw magic again, but instead, he blasted the whole area with hurricane-level winds. Naiad's eyes grew huge as she tumbled away, completely caught off guard by Deimos's sudden use of strange magic.

Then Deimos waved his hand. He manipulated the water out of the moat. Like a giant snake made of liquid, the moat rose up, maintaining its form, and even carried Hektor and Naiad's dragon. They were panicking, clearly also taken aback by the power on display. They attempted to swim out of the moving moat, but that proved too difficult.

My body in the living realm hurt. More and more. The magic I had stolen was *vast*.

All creatures near my body, including Jijo's nimbus dragon and Ashlyn's typhoon dragon, were pouring into me.

That was how Deimos had evoked wind and controlled the moat—he was also tapping into all their magic.

Then the fog in the area thickened.

Deimos's frantic thoughts filtered into my own.

He was attempting to use the aura of *all* the creatures we had mimicked. He wanted to use the eclipse aura, the ocean heart aura, the mystic moon aura, the grand contentment aura —and all the others! I could barely remember them all!

And that was when the world started getting crazier. It was already black and white, but...

A crescent moon appeared in the sky above us. Then the blackness parted and a sun emerged, only for a disk of black to move in front of it. The sun and moon in the sky—it reminded me of when the abyssal hells were opened.

Clouds also began to gather, even though it appeared as though they came from nowhere.

The water of the moat became restless. Waves and ripples formed all of its surface.

And then everything was more beautiful! Illusions were sprouting up, hiding the blood, giving the labyrinth a beautiful charm.

"What is happening?" Death Lord Naiad screamed. Her eyes were huge as she wildly glanced around. "*Where is all this magic coming from?*"

More strange phenomena... The area stank of blood and offal, and Deimos began to feel hungry. What kind of magic was this?

"*I won't allow you to do this!*" Naiad screeched as she flew toward Deimos.

The pain...

It was becoming too much, even for Deimos. He didn't move his legs, for his knees were threatening to buckle. Instead, he flicked his wrist. The moat came crashing down. It hit Naiad, and she was swept up in the waters.

The typhoon dragon's aura was the *ocean heart...* Everyone in the water had their lifeforce drained.

Then Deimos held out his hand and evoked ice. It hit the water, chilling it. The winds in the labyrinth picked up, and the strength of the ice also increased. The water was rapidly becoming slushy and almost impossible to swim through.

That was the wendigo evocation.

But Deimos was panting now.

He curled his hand and the water balled itself. Despite all that, Naiad got ahold of herself, used up even more souls, and then jetted out of the moat. She slammed onto the floor of the labyrinth and went straight for Deimos. In one lightning-fast attack, she grabbed him and threw him at the tower.

The Eternal Rest...

Deimos collided with the wall. The air was knocked out of his lungs, and his head was rattled, but he, too, used souls to quickly remedy all problems.

"Rest, you dog," Naiad shouted.

But she didn't know...

The kitsune mystic moon aura meant that mind-controlling magic no longer had any effect. Deimos was next to the tower, but the ominous building wasn't attempting to get him to lie down.

Deimos controlled the shadows, made them tentacles, and grabbed Naiad by the ankles. She hadn't been expecting it. Deimos flung her into the floating sphere of water, and at the same time, he managed to get his own eldrin out of the swirling moat.

Once again evoking ice, and controlling the wind, and being empowered by the false eclipse, and having the typhoon dragon magic...

Deimos had trapped Death Lord Naiad in the water—and then he started striking her again and again. He shot raw magic beams, used the shadows to form swords and slice, and then even occasionally evoked lightning to electrify the moat.

Blast, blast, blast.

He was doing everything quickly, pushing his body and mind to the edge.

Pop. Pop. Pop.

Naiad was running through souls! However, unlike last time, it didn't look like she was healing. Was there some aura here that made healing difficult? Her dragon attempted to escape the waters, but it just couldn't. Its wings shrank. Its flails became more desperate.

As soon as Naiad had *no* souls on her dragon, she would have no way to avoid death. The next strike after zero souls would be the final one.

But the pain...

It was becoming difficult to stay with Deimos. I was slipping back to the realm of the living. Images from the magic lab were slipping into my thoughts. Twain was there, but he was a chimera. He had the head of three different dragons, and the body of a cerberus, and wings of the erlking, chains of a reaper, armor of a knightmare, things I couldn't even describe, and the feet of the kitsune...

He was a merge of all of them.

"*Deimos!*" I forced myself to say through him.

He must've sensed it. I was about to return to the realm of the living.

So he stopped all the auras. All of them. No more chimera aura. No more eclipse aura.

Everything snapped back to reality as though slapped. The clouds, moon, and sun all vanished. The winds calmed down. The water crashed to the floor of the labyrinth. The fog was gone. The color switched back on, bright and vibrant, all in a matter of a half second.

Deimos quickly leapt over the empty moat, desperate to

get away from The Eternal Rest before the mind-altering abilities snagged him.

Without the pain of the chimera aura, I didn't feel like I was slipping anymore. But...

"I can't," Deimos forced himself to say. "It was too much. *You finish this.*"

"Me?" I asked.

"*Do it.*"

His soul...

It was fragmented and hurting. The amount of magic that was just channeled through it damaged him. I felt it, like cracks spreading across a broken mirror. They were getting worse and worse, and this *definitely* didn't help.

Deimos surrendered control of his body over to me, so he could rest.

I stared down at my new self—at the ruined bone and steel armor. He was physically whole, but now I needed to make sure Naiad didn't get up.

After a deep breath, I ran over to her. Water was everywhere, rushing across the tile floor of the labyrinth. It was a few feet deep, and I had to slosh through the worst of it, but it didn't take much of my strength.

Death Lord Naiad was trying to stand. Her dragon had just two glittering souls left. Death Lord souls. I held out my hand and *blasted* raw magic through her chest.

Pop.

One more.

Naiad, bloodthirsty and enraged, whirled around, went down on all fours like a damn animal, and then leapt at me. We were twenty feet apart, but she somehow shot across that distance with the ferocity of a drugged-up toad. She slammed her whole body into me. We crashed to the floor.

"Get off me," I shouted.

I dug my clawed hand into her upper arm.

"*Look what you've done,*" she hissed through clenched teeth. "I almost had them *all*! Every Death Lord! I was almost perfect!" Naiad held me with both her hands and yanked. "I don't care if more of your friends are pulled here! I'll have your soul for my own!"

She wasn't yanking me physically, but spiritually. As an abyssal dragon arcanist, she could manipulate souls, and she was attempting to pull Deimos's soul from his body—but she was manipulating mine.

I evoked more raw magic. Another beam cut through her body.

Pop.

When she yanked again, I felt sick. I couldn't be separated from Deimos! I didn't know if he could handle it...

So, with the last of my willpower, I evoked the magic again.

And then I heard her abyssal dragon scream.

Hektor, who had been patiently waiting, finally leapt at the wingless abyssal dragon. He slammed down on it, pinning it to the floor, and then went for the back of the neck, snapping its spine.

All this...

Was too much.

Deimos had been right.

Now it was time to rest...

And that was when I lost consciousness.

CHAPTER 48

DEFEATING FEAR

When I finally managed to open my eyes, I thought I'd be back at Astra Academy, but that wasn't the case. I was still in the labyrinth...

I rolled to my side, surprised how different I felt. When I got to my feet, I took note of how strong I was, how heavy the armor was, how limber—which meant I was definitely still Deimos. Chuckling to myself, I stood.

"Dee?" I asked.

But there was no response.

For half a second, I feared the worst. Thankfully, after a prolonged moment, his thoughts filtered to me. He was resting. Channeling so much magic had drained him.

His abyssal dragon loomed over me, his body sturdy, and his front leg healed completely. He had all four clawed feet, and the injuries he sustained from the fight were no more. When he lowered his head, his six golden eyes swiveled in their sockets until all pupils landed on me.

"My Death Lord," Hektor said before he...

Nuzzled me.

He pressed his long dragon snout up against my chest

and pulled me close with a claw. It was both the most adorable and disgusting thing that had happened to me. His rotted scales reeked, and the souls on his body moaned in agony.

Despite all that, I gently patted him. "There, there."

"Not even Naiad could kill you." Hektor stopped his affections and lifted his head. "Kallikore and Umbriel already know of her demise, which means they'll come for you harder than ever."

"First off, I'm not Deimos," I said. "Secondly, those chumps don't know what's going to hit them. Deimos and I make a great team."

Hektor snorted. His breath stank of blood.

And then that reminded me. "Where's Nini?" I asked.

"Death Lord Deimos and I came here because she was in danger," Hektor replied. The souls across his body sobbed and moaned, their incessant noise agitating. How did Deimos tolerate this?

"You didn't answer my question," I said. "Where is she?"

"In the labyrinth beneath us. The tunnels below are home to forgotten treasures. If ever an object is lost in the abyssal hells, it somehow ends up in the tunnels, behind locked doors."

That sounded intriguing. But why were the abyssal hells so bizarre? It felt like this place was alive.

"Why hasn't she made it out of the labyrinth?" I asked.

Hektor shook his head. Then he flashed his fangs. "I know not the reason. She may still be blind. She may not have used one of the bells. The labyrinth tries to steer you in the wrong direction by showing you things you fear most."

Excitement flooded me—which was a strange reaction, I knew, but that was my honest reaction. I ran a hand over my busted armor. Well, it was Deimos's busted armor, but it was mine for the time being.

"I'll get Nini," I said. "I owe it to my brother—and I want to see if this labyrinth can frighten me."

"You *want* to see if it can frighten you?" Hektor's skepticism was thick.

I laughed once and shrugged. "It's a long story. But yes. I can't wait."

Last time Sorin used his terrors on me, it was such a rush to make it through them. I was certain the abyssal hells would have something even *more* terrifying than knightmare magic, which just offered yet another chance for me to defeat fear itself.

I was so pumped.

"I cannot join you," Hektor stated. "The tunnels are small. Abyssal dragons are not." He spread his soul wings and slammed his tail on the mirror floor. He was rather huge. And that was fine. I didn't need a dragon escort.

"I'll save Nini and stay in Deimos's body until he's recovered," I said. "Then I'm returning to the realm of the living. You, uh, do whatever Deimos told you to do before you both got mixed up in this."

Hektor snorted. "I will wait for you at the exit of the labyrinth."

"Oh, right. How do I get out of this place?"

The massive dragon placed a clawed hand on his chest. With his fingers, he ripped something from his rotted scales and then handed it to me. It was a silver bell—one without a clapper inside.

He just... had that inside of his body?

Gross.

Holding back a sneer, I took the bell. "This looks useless," I quipped.

"Ring the bell. If it makes noise, you're in the correct corridor leading to the exit. If it makes no noise, you're in the wrong location. It's a simple trick."

"It'll ring, even though it has no clapper?"

"Indeed," Hektor stated, his tone rather regal. "But in order to get to the underground tunnels, you need to look out for tiles in the floor that are capable of moving. Once you're down below, it should be easy to find the reaper arcanist."

I took the bell. "All right. I'll meet you at the exit, but don't get too comfortable, because it won't take long."

Starting from the center was an odd way to solve a labyrinth, but that didn't matter. I had a magical bell, after all, and it worked just like Hektor said. Whenever I stepped into a new corridor, I gave the bell a shake. If it chimed, I continued forward, and if it didn't, I picked a new way.

However, three turns into my trek, I started seeing things in the peripheral of my vision. At first, I thought they were shadows, but the more frequent the images came, the more I was convinced they were illusions of some kind.

Was the labyrinth toying with me?

"Can you believe this, Twain?" I asked.

No one replied.

Because Twain wasn't here.

I stopped in the middle of the labyrinth passageway. The walls were fifteen feet high, and the sky above was just pitch black. The mirrors below me seemed ominous, and half the time I saw movement it was in the reflection, and not in the area around me.

"Deimos?" I whispered.

But he was still too tired to reply.

Sorin... Ashlyn... Professor Helmith...

All the people I would call on in a time of need weren't here. For the first time in a *long* time, I was truly alone.

I took in a deep breath. Technically, *I* wasn't even with me, considering I was inhabiting someone else's body. That thought got me chuckling, but the sound bounced off the stark walls, the echo reminding me I was completely alone.

There wasn't time for me to dwell on that. I continued forward, my heart pounding.

"Well?" I shouted to the labyrinth. "Aren't you going to try and scare me? *Huh*?"

There was no response, obviously, but I somehow knew this strange place was alive. It heard me. It knew what I wanted.

Instead of walking this infernal maze, I decided to sprint. This labyrinth wanted to toy with me, it wanted to subtly and quietly play tricks with my mind.

"What's the matter? You think I'm scared of you?" I darkly chuckled as I picked up my pace. "Think I'll back down just because the stakes are high? No. I like this—this feeling that one wrong move sends me tumbling. That's the thrill, isn't it? The edge of it all!"

My voice carried with me, a haunting echo. I ran now, and when I turned, I didn't bother with the bell. The images at the edge of my vision grew darker and more frequent.

I was going the right way—because the closer I got, the more the labyrinth tried to spook me. There was no need for the bell. This labyrinth's own tricks were working against it.

"You know what else I like? *Heights*. The kind you look down at and say, *no one in their right mind would leap from here*."

I was laughing now.

The mirrored floor started to change. Cracks formed in the mirror, some even broke. I stumbled over one—because it was real. The labyrinth was threatening to collapse, to send me sailing down to the next layer of the abyssal hells.

"I don't care," I shouted, holding my arms up. "I'd jump just to see if I could stick the landing."

But apparently my taunting had angered the labyrinth. The inky sky melted down, like chocolate put on heat. It poured into the labyrinth, splashing like thick water, coating the walls in darkness. It was coming for me, making everything slippery as the floor continued to break.

The bits of mirror that cracked away fell into an empty void below me. There was nothing to land on.

"I don't care how much you throw at me," I shouted my heart hammering. "I don't care how deep the shadows stretch —I go hard, no matter what!"

Was I talking to the labyrinth? Or just myself?

Both.

The more the ink flowed and coated the floor, the faster I went. I turned down a hall, and there were no cracks on the floor, no darkness on the walls, and I knew it was the wrong direction. So I turned back around, happy to get back into the fray.

This feeling...

Was I cracked in the head? Probably. But I was sharp enough to keep my wits. I dashed forward, avoiding the holes in the ground. What was this feeling? This thrill? This excitement?

I *wanted* the labyrinth to try to stop me. I wanted to make it through *the worst* the labyrinth had to offer, because in the end, it was just another obstacle I would overcome.

Nothing would stop me.

"You think I'm crazy?" I asked as I leapt over the crumbling floor, sailing over the void the labyrinth threatened to send me down. When I landed, my feet almost slipped off the edge. I gritted my teeth, leaned forward, and smiled once I realized I had made it. "I don't care what you think."

Then I spotted it—a tile panel, one that led to the tunnels below.

Cracks in the floor stretched outward, webbing their

way toward the panel. I ran, my footfalls causing more and more of the floor to crumble. This excitement was exhilarating. Would I make it in time? Would the labyrinth fall apart?

The fear...

It just made it so I had the willpower, energy, and drive to make it through anything. I loved it. This feeling. This moment.

Maybe Ashlyn was right. Maybe *fear* was more my friend than my enemy.

And right as the cracks reached the panel, so did I. Through the thrill of it all, I opened up the tile and flung myself into the tunnels, laughing like a loon the entire time.

I slammed down into a stone and dirt passageway. When I glanced up, thinking the ink and the shattering labyrinth would follow, I found nothing. The walls of the labyrinth above were white and pristine. The floor was no longer crumbling.

It had been an illusion.

With a dark laugh, I shook my head. "Not even the labyrinth of the abyssal hells could stop me."

"Death Lord Deimos?"

I whirled on my heel. The tunnels of the underground labyrinth were long and rough, but the ceiling glowed with a dim blue, and floating motes of light kept the corners illuminated. Not far from my location was a girl swaddled in a blood-red cloak, her face covered by a white mask, golden chains flowing around her like specters.

Four lanterns hung at the end of the chains, each lantern ablaze with fire.

Nini and Waste.

They looked like they had been through a lot together—but they were still alive.

I held out my hand. "Nini. It's me, Gray. I'm, uh, helping

Death Lord Deimos. Come with me. We need to get out of here."

"Death Lord Naiad..." Nini and Waste spoke with a double voice that was rather spooky, but awesome.

I smiled. "She's no more."

"You defeated her?"

"Deimos and I handled it. Now c'mon. My brother would never forgive me if I left you a second time."

CHAPTER 49

MIMIC AND ME

As a team, Nini, Waste, and I made it out of the labyrinth. With the bell, it was easy, even though Nini seemed irritated I knew how to use it.

However, as we neared the exit, Deimos was finally rested enough to take control.

We stopped halfway down a long corridor, and his consciousness returned. After a deep breath, he was the one operating his body once again.

"Thank you, mimic arcanist," he said as he closed and opened his own hands, balling his fists so tight he almost dug his nails into his palms. "You are more useful than I thought you would be."

"You're such a flatterer," I said through him.

Nini waited. She never unmerged from her reaper, nor did she interrupt.

"Sorin is worried about you," I said.

She perked up at the mention of my brother. "Tell him I'll be home soon. And that... I love him so much."

"I will."

"You should be getting back to your own world," Deimos

433

stated. "And you should tell my brother we haven't much time. You and your... sentinels... need to get down here."

He was probably right. Now that Naiad was dead, the other two remaining Death Lords would grow restless. They'd likely attempt their crazy plans soon, even if they weren't fully prepared.

"Should I insist the god-arcanists wait in the realm of the living?" I asked.

"God-arcanists?" Nini tilted her head. "I have something related to them." She pulled out the largest diamond I had ever seen from the folds of her red cloak. It was rectangular, and flowers had been carved into both sides.

Was this the lotus diamond runestone that Deimos had been searching for? It was impressive.

Deimos took the diamond and turned it over in his hands. "I've searched for hundreds of years and never found this. Perhaps the labyrinth gave it to you for a reason."

"You talk about it like its alive," I said.

"It is," Deimos whispered, gaze focused intensely on the runestone. "And I won't ignore this blatant sign. Let the god-arcanists come. Perhaps they are needed in the Spire of the Gods."

I hoped Deimos was correct.

Plus, we needed all the power we could get. We couldn't deny allies in our time of need, even if their souls were special and could fuel our enemies. Although, now that Naiad was defeated, that fear was greatly diminished. The other Death Lords weren't hording special souls—they had other plans.

"All right, well, I should probably get going, then," I said. "Next time you get into a fight with a Death Lord, you need to call on me immediately though, Dee."

Deimos snorted back a laugh. "I'll consider it."

Slipping my consciousness from the abyssal hells back to my body in the realm of the living was near instantaneous. Like teleporting. How and why was this possible? It was definitely because of my soul link with Deimos. Somehow, he was seeping into me, and now vice versa. Probably a bad sign, but we'd have to deal with that *after* this problem was solved.

I opened my eyes—my *real* eyes—and found I was back in the Academy's infirmary.

Wait... the *infirmary*?

I sat up, irritated. "I wasn't sick," I said aloud.

It was night, and the stars twinkled through the nearby window. I would've said they were my only companions, but I was clearly wrong. Twain was on my bed, curled into a larger than normal loaf. So adorable.

It was dark, but somehow my bed was slightly illuminated, as though cradled in the gentle glow of moonlight. However, there was no moon to be seen. I touched my blankets, surprised by the glow of soft white light.

When I turned my head, the light followed.

Strange.

I glanced over to the side of the bed and found a pitcher of water and a glass. Confused, I grabbed the pitcher—it was made of polished brass. I held it up to catch a glimpse of my own reflection.

Air caught in my throat and I almost dropped the pitcher.

My arcanist mark...

It was glowing a soft white. The light was from *me*.

"Twain," I said, breathless. I placed the pitcher down, my hands shaking. "*Twain*. It happened. Twain. Get up!"

I shook my mimic, frantic to tell *someone* what had happened.

My little eldrin lifted his head, his eyes frosted with groggy crust. His ears twitched as he stood and arched his back. And then...

A second cat stood up. It was the same color as Twain, orange and adorable, with equally large lynx ears, its whiskers long. And this cat also had two-colored eyes, one bluish-gray, one pink.

It was identical.

"What's going on?" I managed to ask.

Twain and the other cat smiled at the exact same time.

"I'm glad you're finally awake, Gray." Twain motioned to the other cat. "When your arcanist mark started glowing, I, uh, *mimicked myself* and grew a double me."

The other cat nodded. "That's right. I'm Twain Number Two."

"No," Twain snapped. "I told you, we need a better name than that."

Twain 2.0 shrugged. "Okay, we'll keep workshoppin' it."

Twain returned his attention to me. "This is my true form! I'm a twin. Again. I suppose. A real twin! I've mimicked myself, and now your eldrin is *us two together*."

"I have *two* eldrin?" I asked, unable to stop myself from smiling. "And you're both mimics? And you both... transform into things?"

The two cats nodded together. It was a little creepy, but also pretty awesome.

"Maybe my name can be *Two?*" the second Twain asked. "Or *Two-placate?* Like *duplicate?* Get it?"

Twain rubbed his paw to his chin. "Hm. We need to keep thinking. Something more clever than that, I think."

I scooped up both mimics into my arms, so happy I felt like my chest would explode. "What happened while I was away? Why am I in the infirmary? Where's Ashlyn? Where's Sorin?"

"I transformed into a chimera," Twain said.

"Your brother forged himself an artifact weapon with the blood you gave him," the other Twain added.

"Ashlyn was here until it was time to go to bed. She said I should scold you when you woke because she doesn't like it when you go on adventures without her."

The other Twain nodded. "And Doc Tomas said you're the only student he's ever had that has been to the infirmary this many times in such a short time span. He said you should just focus on your studies and maybe you wouldn't almost die so frequently."

I hugged both my eldrin, laughing like I was insane. "Oh, this is amazing. One of the best days of my life."

"How did you do it?" Twain asked, his breath being squeezed out of him from my hug. He wheezed a little as he continued, "How did you defeat fear?"

I loosened my grip and smiled. "I made it my ally," I sarcastically replied. Then I shook my head. "But seriously—I just think about fear differently now. I like it. I like the sensations it gives me. It pushes me to my extreme, makes me better, makes me feel alive. I *want* things to try to scare me. I want the rush. The adrenaline. The feeling that I might not make it."

Both my eldrin stared at me, their eyes unblinking.

Then the two-placate snorted. "Oh, we're going to have a *great* time. You're definitely the arcanist for me."

"Well, you sound a little off your rocker," Twain said. But then he purred. "But I wouldn't have you any other way."

I kicked off my blankets and stood. "C'mon. Let's go. I have a lot to do—and so much gloating—before I'm ready to head into the final battle in the abyssal hells."

Twain and his new twin purred in unison.

THE END

Blooper Scene

What if Astra Academy Was Written with Gen-Z Slang?

I stepped off the wooden gangplanks, which were rather basic. Then I glanced up at the Kross compound, with its towering walls and major *villain energy*. I was shook.

Unfortunately, this was supposed to be my new home, no cap. That thought hit me harder than a rogue wave. The typhoon dragon statues were based, but that was about it.

Twain remained perched on my shoulders, vibin' like he owned the place. Sorin walked down the gangplank, his eldrin lurkin' like a cryptid in the shadows near his feet. Real casual.

"This place inspires me," Sorin said, already slipping into his poetic nonsense. He cleared his throat like he was about to drop some bars. *"Beneath the waves, where silence reigns... Typhoon dragons swim watery plains..."*

I had a savage quip locked and loaded for that last line, but before I could fire it off, the Archduke himself stormed down the gangplank like he thought he was the main character. He was an absolute unit if he didn't speak, but the moment he opened his mouth it was nothing but red flags.

"Was that *poetry*?" the Archduke asked, cutting through

Sorin's soul with his tone alone. "That's what they're teaching at the Academy?"

"Don't be salty," I said. My bro's poetry slapped—why did the Archduke have to harsh Sorin's buzz?

Twain rolled his eyes and whispered, "This guy needs to get out and touch grass."

The Archduke's death-ray gaze locked onto me. "*You*," he barked. "Come."

Daddy Archduke wasn't really one of my crew, but I had to gaslight him into thinking that he was, so I followed.

Archduke Kross power-walked down the dock, straight for his dragon-themed lair. I shot Sorin a quick look, and he gave me the universal sibling head-tilt: *Bruh, you're on your own*. With a sigh, I followed the Archduke into the belly of the beast.

The compound? Yeah, it was bougee. Massive fish tanks. Schools of neon-colored fish. Servants fillin' the halls, carrying lilies and decorating like this was the set of a rom-com wedding montage.

"You've got a nice setup here," I said, trying to keep it upbeat so that the Archduke didn't unalive me.

"Consider it your home, too," the Archduke replied, but the way he spat the words made it clear he wanted to yeet me out the window.

Twain leaned closer. "I love this place. That's my bedroom right there." He pointed a paw at a tank full of bright orange fish, his eyes gleaming with unhinged delight.

"Don't even think about it," I muttered. "This boomer doesn't want us gettin' comfortable."

"He thinks you and Ashlyn are just gonna Netflix and Chill, and then you'll run out of here."

That hit different, because I hadn't thought about things from Daddy Archduke's viewpoint.

"I decorated this whole compound like a castle,"

Archduke Kross said, glazing himself more than a donut. "That door leads to the kitchen, this one to the main dining room. And here's our library."

This place was lit. There were floor-to-ceiling bookshelves, and a fire couch for reading.

"You seem pleased," Archduke Kross said.

"Nothin' but green flags here, bestie," I replied.

"Good, because you'll be here whenever you're not at the Academy. So I can keep an eye on you and my daughter."

"Don't worry, boss. This isn't a situationship. Ashlyn is a queen and I'm here to watch her slay."

"My arcanist is no simp," Twain interjected. "He's got rizz *and* chivalry. I won't let him be goonin'."

Archduke Kross stared at me like I was an ick. Finally, he sighed and said, "I seriously have no idea what any of you kids are saying these days."

I felt that.

IYKYK.

THANK YOU SO MUCH FOR READING!

Please consider leaving a review!

Gray's story concludes in *Elder Arcanist*!

To find out more about Shami Stovall and Astra Academy, take a look at her website:
https://sastovallauthor.com/newsletter/

To help Shami Stovall (and see advanced chapters ahead of time) take a look at her Patreon:

https://www.patreon.com/shamistovall

Want more arcanist novels? Good news! The Frith Chronicles is where is all started! Join Volke and the Frith Guild as they travel the world.

ABOUT THE AUTHOR

Shami Stovall is a multi-award-winning author of fantasy and science fiction. Before that, she taught history and criminal law at the college level and loved every second. When she's not reading fascinating articles and books about ancient China or the Byzantine Empire, Stovall can be found playing way too many video games, especially RPGs and tactics simulators.

Shami loves John, reading, video games, and writing about herself in the third person.

If you want to contact her, you can do so at the following locations:

Website: https://sastovallauthor.com
Email: s.adelle.s@gmail.com

 facebook.com/SAStovall
X x.com/GameOverStation